Divine
Intervention

Also by Lutishia Lovely

Sex in the Sanctuary

Love Like Hallelujah

A Preacher's Passion

Heaven Right Here

Reverend Feelgood

Heaven Forbid

All Up in My Business

Mind Your Own Business

Taking Care of Business

Divine
Intervention

LUTISHIA LOVELY

Kensington Publishing Corp.
http://www.kensingtonbooks.com

DAFINA BOOKS are published by

Kensington Publishing Corp.
119 West 40th Street
New York, NY 10018

All Kensington Titles, Imprints, and Distributed Lines are available at special quantity discounts for bulk purchases for sales promotions, premiums, fund-raising, and educational or institutional use. Special book excerpts or cus-tomized printings can also be created to fit specific needs. For details, write or phone the office of the Kensington special sales manager: Kensington Publishing Corp., 119 West 40th Street, New York, NY 10018, attn: Special Sales Department, Phone: 1-800-221-2647.

Dafina and the Dafina logo Reg. U.S. Pat. & TM Off.

ISBN-13: 978-0-7582-6581-4
ISBN-10: 0-7582-6581-6

First trade paperback printing: October 2012

10 9 8 7 6 5 4 3 2 1

Printed in the United States of America

For all of those who've experienced interventions . . .
of the divine kind.

ACKNOWLEDGMENTS

Even though it was more than twenty years ago, I vividly remember my first conscious experience with divine intervention. It was also my first experience with an angel. Now, whether or not this angel was already human or became so on my behalf I'm not sure. But what I do know is that Kassoum Kamagate was an angel, *my* angel, in mideighties Paris, France. He was the instrument that Spirit used for an intervention of the divine kind.

I was traveling with an edutainment group, Up with People, and we were performing in Denmark. We had a rare few days off and I and a cast mate, Andre Pruitt, got the bright idea of traveling to Paris during this break. After all, France was only eight hours away by car. When would we ever be so close again? I spoke with my host family, whose friend was a truck driver. As it happened, he'd be traveling through France in a couple days. I could ride with him for free! After getting a release from my parents and making plans to meet Andre's train in Paris, I climbed into the cab of a semi and headed south. (This journey, where the driver spoke no English and I spoke no Danish or German, is a whole other story, but I won't digress.)

I arrived in Paris, armed with my luggage and the phone number of Andre's friend who was studying abroad. Being dumped on the corner of a busy intersection in a foreign country was a bit daunting, but I swallowed my fear and headed to a pay phone to dial Andre's friend. My first uh-oh. The number Andre had given me was a WRONG NUMBER! *Seriously?* "Don't panic, Tish. You can do this." Even though I had no francs, no friends, and now no idea what the heck I was doing in Paris, I kept up the pep talk. Especially when I saw a brother decked out in dashiki and knit cap, looking like he was from the South Side of Philly or downtown New Jersey. *Thank you, Jesus!!!* I walked over to him and asked for directions to the Gare du Nord train station. Uh-oh number two. Brothah man is not American, but African. *No parlez-vous Anglais!*

Two hours later, I arrived at the train station. YAY! Less than two hours before 8 p.m., when Andre's train was scheduled to arrive. I hunkered down on my suitcase and waited. Right on schedule, the trains pulled in and people piled out. Searching, searching, searching. No Andre. The trains depart. The people leave. No Andre. What do I do now? *Wait for him.* Yes, you read correctly. That was my bright idea at 9 p.m. at night in a strange train station in a foreign city where I knew no one. Hurry up and wait. But in my defense, options were limited. I'd arrived too late to have my Danish kroner changed into francs, which meant I had no money. No credit cards either, and by now, only an apple left of the nice little sack lunch my host family had lovingly provided. In other words, I was up you-know-what creek without a paddle! So yes, "just chillin'" sounded like a good idea at the time.

An hour later, the once bustling station was almost empty. That's probably why I instantly noticed this young, black man walk by, looking at me intently while trying to act as though he wasn't looking. When he walked by the second time, I looked him directly in the eye, as I'd been taught: on full alert, showing no fear. *Uh-huh. I see you.* By the third time he passed, I was in full self-protective bluff mode. Frown set. Eyes narrowed. *Nucka, what?* Finally, he walked over. The following conversation, abbreviated for the sake of this note, was conducted entirely with Kassoum speaking French and me speaking English. Yes, really.

Kassoum: Hi. Who are you waiting for?
Me: I'm waiting for my *ami*. (*friend* was one of five French words I knew. *Merci beaucoup, pomme frites,* and *qui* rounded out my stellar vocabulary).
Kassoum (with worried look): There are no more trains tonight.
Me (shrugging): Doesn't matter. *Mon ami* is coming here, eight o'clock.

I emphasized *friend* and pointed to the eight on my watch, so he wouldn't get it twisted. I had back-up coming and was sooo *not* the one!

We "conversed" for several minutes, during which time Kassoum showed me his ID and work permit (a mechanic) to convey that he was an honest man who meant me no harm. Then he pointed to a group of young tough-looking jokers at the end of the platform.

Kassoum: See those men down there? They hang around here to prey on people like you. This place will be closing soon. You've got to come with me!
Me: No. Effing. Way.

After all, the number I'd given both to the group and my parents was wrong. If anything happened, no one would ever find my body! More debating, more denying, and then I hear the voice of Spirit: *It's okay. Go with him.*
So I did.
The trepidation in my spirit and the lump of fear in my throat fled as soon as Kassoum opened his apartment door. It was clean and neat, with pictures of his family on the table and a beautiful one of his native West Africa on the wall. He brought out covers and a pillow for me to sleep on the couch. I vowed to myself that I wouldn't close my eyes for a second!
When I woke up, it was six-thirty. Kassoum and I went back to the train station. Shortly after 8 a.m., the tall, lanky body of my friend Andre appeared among the crowd. *He's here! Hallelujah!* I introduced the two men, informed Andre about the wrong number, and learned that he'd incorrectly read his ticket as p.m. instead of a.m.! We all hugged and then Andre and I left the station to embark on five fun-filled days in Paris. I felt like Josephine Baker. *Bonjour, Paris!* This was pre-Internet, so without a correct number,

we never found Andre's friend. Instead, we stayed in a hotel that Kassoum suggested, right across the street from the train station. We saw him often and would wave like old friends. I swore to myself that I'd learn a little conversational French and keep in touch. Sadly, I did neither. But with today's technology, hope springs eternal that I'll again run across this angel whom God used that night to keep me safe.

So now, more than twenty years later and wherever he is, I have just two words for Kassoum Kamagate: Thank. You.

To this day, divine intervention continues. From the bottom of my heart, I thank the angels who help my literary career soar, and whose love and support are why you're now holding this book in your hands: my editor, Selena James; art director Kristine Mills-Noble (the cover is divine!); and all the rest of "Team Lutishia" at Kensington Publishing. You guys are amazing. Big hug! My agent, Natasha Kern; promotions guru Ella Curry; book clubs, book stores, and radio shows across the country; every avid reader who's ever picked up a book in the Hallelujah Love Series or the Business Trilogy and, of course, my family. I love you all. *Merci beaucoup*!

1

Here Comes the Bride

Princess Brook stood with her father at the back of his church, and today Mount Zion Progressive Baptist was SRO—standing room only. She was a vision in white. Her princess cut wedding dress (with a name like that, what other style could she wear?) was a stunning combination of silk and chiffon, with Swarovski crystals creating an intricate design on the bodice before continuing—as though sprinkled by Glenda the Good Witch herself—along the skirt and twelve-foot train. The cut accented her perfectly sized breasts and small waist, while giving just a hint of the bootylicious that completed the brick house that one of her mother's old-school favorites sang about in their hit song. The dress was strapless, revealing smooth, blemish-free caramel skin, but a tiara-held veil provided appropriate modesty, and her "something borrowed," a teardrop diamond necklace that her father had given her mother years ago, was the perfect accessory around her gracefully slender neck. The purposely messy upswept do fashioned from her straight, shoulder-length hair further highlighted the borrowed gift . . . and Princess's heart-shaped face.

"Are you ready, baby girl?" King Brook asked.

She nodded. "Are you?"

Princess's mega-minister father looked liked glory hallelujah and Jesus, have mercy combined, decked out in a black tuxedo complete with tails and waistcoat. The silver cummerbund and bow tie were perfect accents for his deep chocolate skin, his closely cropped hair, and expertly trimmed goatee—all working in his favor. Many women were already breaking their necks to look back and take multiple peeks. The feigned fainting would come later . . . when he smiled.

"I'm ready to walk you down the aisle," he said, after gazing at the daughter who seemed to have grown up overnight. "And I guess I have to give you away. But you'll always be my baby girl."

"Stop it, Daddy," Princess admonished, fanning her eyes to dry unshed tears. "You'll ruin my makeup by making me cry!"

The Musical Messengers, a group who'd performed many times at Mount Zion Progressive, broke out into a jazzy, gospel-tinged version of the traditional wedding march and within minutes, Princess stood at the altar. King kissed her cheek, shook hands with her soon-to-be husband, and walked behind the Plexiglas podium.

"Dearly beloved," he began, his voice a sexy baritone that over the years had caused many a lustful thought, "we've gathered here today to join my daughter, Princess Nicole Brook . . ." He faltered, his voice growing raspy with emotion. More lusting occurred. After clearing his throat, he continued. "My daughter, Princess Nicole Brook, and Rafael Scott Stevens together in holy matrimony."

The words continued, but it was as if Princess was in a fog. She couldn't hear a thing. She stood there smiling at a man whose love for her could fill an ocean . . . and she was thinking about someone else. *Kel . . . No! I dare not even think his name! He's a part of my yesterday. This man, Rafael, is the man I want in my life. I love you, Rafael! I do! Rafael . . . Rafael . . . Rafael . . .*

As Rafael began speaking, Princess forced her mind back to the very important matter at hand. "I give you this ring," he said, sliding a beautifully cut diamond onto her French-manicured finger, "as a symbol of my love and faithfulness. I commit myself to you: mind, body, and soul. Let this ring forever be a reminder of the words I've spoken this day." There were tears in his large, chocolate brown eyes, which peered from a handsome, clean-shaven face. Rafael was the color of toffee, and just as sweet... all five feet ten inches of him were filled with integrity and devotion.

Princess continued to stare at him, knowing that it was her turn to recite vows, and willing the words to come out.

"Princess, is there anything you'd like to say?" King asked, gently encouraging his disconcerted daughter and bringing a bit of levity to the solemn affair.

Princess managed a slight chuckle as she took a deep breath and repeated what Rafael had said, sliding a simple, platinum band onto his thick, manicured finger.

"If there is anyone present who knows of any reason that this couple should not be joined in holy matrimony, speak now or forever hold your peace."

Was it Princess's imagination or was her heart precariously close to thumping out of her chest? She looked at her mother, Tai Brook, who stared back at her with an unreadable expression. Princess's mind went back to a conversation they'd had just days ago.

"Mama, were you in love with Daddy when y'all got married?"

"I thought I was, but honestly, I didn't even know what true love meant when your father and I said 'I do.' "

"So when did you know that you were in love with him—not only that you loved him, but that you were *in* love?"

Tai had looked up from the reality TV show she'd been watching, and muted the sound. "Why are you asking me this, Princess? Are you questioning whether or not you're in love with Rafael?"

"No," Princess had answered, a bit too quickly. "Rafael and I grew up together. I love him very much."

Tai pressed the issue. "But are you *in* love with him?"

Princess shrugged.

"Let me ask you this. Do you feel the same way about Rafael that you did about Kelvin?"

"Of course not, Mama. They're two different people."

"Exactly. You're always going to have a certain feeling about the first one, your first love, Princess. There is an excitement there, the thrill of experiencing something you've never felt before, which never happens twice. But don't confuse that feeling with true love. Anybody can see why you'd be attracted to Kelvin. He's tall, dark, handsome, and now successful and rich. But when it comes to relationships and being there for the long haul, traits such as faithfulness, loyalty, devotion, honesty . . . those are the ones that matter. As you think about the man you're about to marry, and whether or not you should, think about those things. Rafael is a good man, baby," Tai finished, reaching out to place her hand on Princess's arm. "He comes from a good, Christian family. And he absolutely adores you. I believe that he will do everything in his power to give you a great life."

After a very brief pause, King continued. "Then by the power invested in me, and in the name of the Father, Son, and Holy Spirit, I now pronounce you man and—"

"No!"

A collective gasp went up from the crowd.

"No!" Six feet and five inches of delectable determination made his way down the aisle that King and Princess had walked just moments before. The murmuring that had begun as soon as the handsome young man had uttered those two letters followed him down the aisle, pew by disbelieving pew, turning into a slight cacophony as he reached the front.

Tai stood, a look of horror plastered on her face. Rafael's parents were looking between her and the stranger who now stood between their son and his soon-to-be wife. Princess's grandparents were as wide eyed as hooting owls. Camera phones were being snapped and flying fingers were sending texts.

His next words silenced the crowd as much as his first one had sent tongues wagging. "You can't marry him, Princess."

The eyes of a deer caught in headlights could not have been wider. She opened her mouth, but words were frozen along with her body.

"Don't do this to us, baby. You're my girl. I love you!"

Rafael was the first one to come out of the surprise-induced shock and react. "She's not your baby," he growled, taking a step toward Kelvin, a balled fist at his side.

"Oh, and she's yours?" Tense seconds passed as the two men glared at each other. "She'll never love you, dog," Kelvin continued. "She can't give you her heart. *I've* got that." He turned to look at Princess . . . which is why he didn't see the fist that connected with his jaw.

Kelvin stumbled back, but quickly recovered. He pushed Rafael with enough force to send the slighter man stumbling into King, who'd moved from behind the podium with the thought to step between them. King had been a second too late, and was now on the bottom of a wrestling pile as Kelvin, who'd jumped on top of Rafael, who was still halfway on top of King, was now pummeling Rafael with his fists. Rafael was pummeling back. Words that shouldn't be used in church were flying between them.

"Stop! Both of you!" Princess cried, kneeling down into the fray. But it was as though she hadn't spoken, almost like she wasn't there. They kept swinging and swinging, each punch landing harder than the one before. King finally wrestled himself from beneath the two fighting men, but this move caused Princess to fall over.

"She's mine!" she heard Rafael cry before hearing the sound of knuckles hitting flesh.

A similar sound preceded Kelvin's response: "In your dreams, you punk-ass mutha—!"

Pow! Another moment of fist and flesh connecting.

Where are the ushers? Where's security? Why doesn't someone stop this fight? Princess tried to right herself, but her dress was twisted around her legs, effectively imprisoning them better than a mummy wrap ever could. She kicked and she kicked, but to no avail. She couldn't get up and she felt that unless she did the man she was in love with and the one she was about to marry would kill each other. *God, please help me.* And as had always been the case, God came through. He helped her. How, you may be wondering? The answer is simple.

Princess woke up.

2

Mr. Wrong

"It was awful, Sarah, just awful." Mere hours had passed since Princess Brook's dream wedding had turned into a nightmare, one that had caused her to fight the sheets wrapped around her legs and break out in a sweat. She was now wide awake, sitting in the middle of the scene of the crime—otherwise known as her bed—and talking to Sarah Kirtz. She'd thought about calling her best friend, Joni, but considering how her heart still pounded, she figured she needed prayer more than camaraderie, hence the phone call to her prayer partner. "They just kept fighting and fighting, and I couldn't stop them!"

"Thank God what you experienced was a dream and not real life," Sarah said, with a sigh for punctuation.

"It might as well have been, as crazy as I feel right now."

"What do you think this means?"

Princess heaved an audible sigh herself. "I don't know."

"Are you having second thoughts?"

Her answer was interrupted by a knock on the door. "Princess, you awake?"

"Yes," Princess answered loudly, before talking back into the phone. "Sarah, it's my mom. Let's pray later."

Tai Brook entered her daughter's room, filled with a mama's

wit and a mother's love. She'd been worried about Princess for months, a year actually...ever since Princess had said yes to Rafael's proposal. Having lived more than half her life with the man of her dreams, yet experiencing some marital nightmares in the process, Tai felt she had viable cause for concern. "Getting your beauty sleep, I see," she said upon entering.

"No, I've been awake for a while."

Tai walked to where her daughter lounged in her canopied bed, the one they'd purchased together when Princess was thirteen years old. It never failed to warm Tai's heart every time Princess returned to the bedroom that remained largely unchanged from how it had looked five years ago, when Princess left home for UCLA. Tai and King had discussed various uses for the unoccupied space: an exercise, theater or storage room, or an office for Tai. But these ideas somehow never went beyond the thinking phase. In everyone's mind, this was still Princess's room. *But not for long,* Tai thought as she sat down on the bed. Her baby was getting ready to take a pivotal step. She was getting ready to become someone's wife, and this was the last night Princess would spend in this room as a single woman. A Stylistics classic song popped into her mind. Yes, she was a big girl now, and after looking into her daughter's strained expression and tired eyes it appeared as if grown folks pleasure was equaling grown folks pain. "How are you doing, baby?"

"Fine."

Tai gave Princess a look. "Girl, have you forgotten who you're talking to? You're two days away from taking the biggest step of your life. There's no way you're *fine.*"

Princess laughed, hoping that the sound covered the pit of fear that had gripped her stomach ever since she'd had the dream. "You're right, but I'm trying to stay calm and not freak out. I was just on the phone with Sarah, giving her the details about the rehearsal dinner and...everything."

And those details included something being awful, followed by an ex-

asperated sounding "I don't know." Of course Tai didn't voice these thoughts. It wouldn't help for her daughter to know that she'd been standing at the door a few seconds before knocking, and had heard snippets of a conversation that confirmed the discomforting feelings concerning the upcoming marriage that she too had felt. "Did you feel better after talking to Sarah?"

"I always feel good after talking to her." An unlikely pair, the years older Princess had befriended Sarah Kirtz during Sarah's first year of college at UCLA. Like King, Sarah's father, Jack Kirtz, was also a well-known minister, and her stepmother, Millicent Sims Kirtz, who'd once been an integral part of her Uncle Derrick's church, was now very active in her husband's ministry. The two women had instantly related on what it meant to be a preacher's daughter.

Tai nodded her understanding, but decided it was time to get to the point of her visit. "Princess, I know we've talked about this but our last conversation about your upcoming nuptials left me feeling uncomfortable. I know you love Rafael. But I want to make sure you're totally at peace with this decision to marry him."

"Dang, Mama. I wish I'd never even asked about you and Daddy."

"I know, but I'm glad you did. And I don't mean to be a nagging mother or a broken record, but if you have any reservations, Princess, any doubts at all about your being able to stay in this marriage for the long term . . . then you'd be doing Rafael a disservice by saying 'I do.' "

"Don't worry, Mama. I don't want to back out." She tried to lighten the mood. "And even if I did, it's too late now. I'm not even trying to return five hundred gifts and refund people for money spent on plane tickets and hotel rooms!" Tai didn't get the joke. "Really, Mama, you need to chill."

"And you need to listen. At the end of the day, the gifts, flowers, dress, guests . . . none of that matters as much as this vow you're getting ready to take for the rest of your life. I know that nowadays divorce is as common as the cold, but I've tried to live my life as an example that marriage is an institution to be honored, and that those vows are not to be said or taken lightly." Tai paused, remembering the words that her own mother had told a then nineteen-year-old, six-months pregnant Tai, who was getting ready to walk down the makeshift aisle in her grandmother's flower-filled backyard. "It ain't too late, baby," her mother had whispered, filled with doubt as to whether her soon-to-be son-in-law, King Wesley Brook, could curb his whorish ways and be satisfied with and faithful to her daughter. But Tai—blinded by love and encouraged by the foot of her oldest son, Michael, kicking her in the side—had taken her father's arm and walked into the holy matrimony that at times had been a holy mess.

"I trust Rafael, Mama."

Rafael isn't the one I'm worried about, is what Tai thought. "I know," is what she said.

Tai remembered not too long ago when Princess, then a freshman in college, had defied her parents to remain at her boyfriend's side—and in his bed. Tai had seen herself in her daughter's defiance, and in the unbridled love she'd seen in Princess's eyes. And she'd recognized some of the same traits in Kelvin Petersen that had attracted Tai to King: charm, good looks, swagger, and endless testosterone. Princess was a lot like her mother, but she was also her father's daughter. Tai worried that in time it might be Princess, not Rafael, who'd sleep outside the marriage bed. But Princess and Rafael had been counseled to within an inch of their lives, so even though she couldn't shake the ominous feeling that had plagued her for days, she figured there was no more to be said.

Standing, Tai turned and faced Princess. "Derrick and Viv are arriving in a little bit and I'm going to spend some sistah-girl time with her at their hotel. Do you need anything before I go?"

"No," Princess said, reaching for her ever-present iPad and scrolling the task bar. "My dress will be delivered in about an hour, and then Erin and I are meeting for lunch before I go to the airport to pick up Joni."

"Erin has been an absolute godsend."

Princess nodded. One of Kansas City's premiere wedding co-ordinators, Erin Flynn had been written up in the *Kansas City Star* at the precise time Princess was searching for help in planning her big day. She'd been thankful to snag one of two remaining openings in Erin's very full schedule. "She should be. We're paying enough."

"Correction, darling. Your Daddy is paying enough."

"Ha! Okay, Mama. Point well taken."

And to his credit, Tai gratefully thought, *he hasn't complained a bit.* "When is Sarah flying in?"

"She gets in late tonight and will take the shuttle straight to the hotel."

"All right, baby." Tai kissed Princess's forehead. "I'll see you tonight."

Princess stared at the door her mother exited and couldn't stop the tears that welled up in her eyes. Her mind was telling her to marry Rafael, but her heart—and her dreams—were being invaded by another man. And no one besides the prayer partner whose number she now dialed would know that the woman getting ready to marry Mr. Right was thinking about Mr. Wrong.

3

Like a Good Neighbor...

"How do, Maxie." Henry Logan's long, sure strides quickly ate up the distance between his yard and Maxine Brook's driveway. "Here, let me get those groceries for you."

Mama Max chuckled at the name that only Henry called her. Besides her husband, Obadiah, who called her Maxine, everybody—including those who were older—called her Mama Max. "Now, Henry, don't strain yourself. I might be old, but I think the Lord's done left me a muscle or two."

"It's no trouble," Henry replied, easily hoisting the two grocery-filled sacks into his arms and following Maxine through the garage and into the kitchen. "Besides, you might think you're getting older, but I say you're getting better."

"Ha! Man, you'd better get on way from here with that foolishness." Maxine's face was fixed with a frown, but her dark brown, still-bright eyes twinkled. Truth of the matter was, she'd come to appreciate Henry's company since her longtime neighbor's son had moved back home to care for his mother. Just after he'd arrived, Beatrice Logan had had a stroke and Henry was forced to put her into an assisted-care facility. Maxine appreciated that he hadn't wanted to be more than a phone call and a ten-minute ride from the woman who'd raised him single-handedly after her husband died. He said he was keeping the place ready for his mama's return but neither one of them really thought that eighty-five-year-old Beatrice would ever come back to the block. There was somebody else who Maxine thought would never again live on the block or, more specifically, in her house, which again made her all the more thankful for this kind man's company. Henry was a man, but harmless, with Maxine having known his mama nigh unto thirty years, and him being so much younger than her. Maxine wasn't sure how old he was, but she had a pretty good idea that she'd beat him into glory.

"What do you think about this unseasonably warm June weather?" Henry asked, removing groceries and setting them on the table as if it were the most natural thing for him to do. It was. He'd been Beatrice's only child and not only had she been an overprotective disciplinarian, but she'd also taught him everything that the daughter-she-never-had would have needed to know. Henry could cook, clean, wash, and iron. And what Beatrice hadn't taught him, the army had.

"This Kansas weather can't be any crazier than last year," Maxine replied as she placed flour, sugar, and other baking goods into the pantry. "Over a hundred degrees one day, and under fifty the next? Whoever heard of such? I think those old folk were on to something. Weather ain't been quite the same since we started sending men to the moon."

Henry smiled but said nothing.

"Beatrice would agree with me, son. In fact, if she was here she'd tell you that if God wanted us all up in the air, he would have given us wings."

"Ha! She would indeed. But I don't think it has anything to do with our space travel." Having handed Maxine the two-liter bottle of cola, Henry leaned against the doorjamb. "I think it's all about global warming."

"Well, God said no more water but fire next time. I thought he was talking about a few fields, or cities, though. Not frying up the whole earth!"

Knowing it would be pointless to go into a diatribe about climate systems, greenhouse gases, and fossil fuels, information gleaned from his addiction to the Discovery Channel, Henry looked at his watch instead. "I've got a couple more yards to cut before the sun goes down, so I'd best be getting a move on. I'll get to yours tomorrow, Maxie."

"I sure appreciate it. You plan on seeing your mama tomorrow?"

"Of course."

"Well, give her a how-do for me. And tell her that I'll see her on Monday. My grandbaby is getting married on Saturday, so it's going to be real busy these next couple days."

"I remember your telling me that. Princess, correct?"

Maxine nodded.

"Well, Maxie, I wish her every happiness. Marriage isn't easy but a good one is worth the sacrifice."

Maxine didn't dare touch that sentence with a ten-foot pole. "Thanks for helping with the groceries," she said by way of dismissal. "And don't forget to drink a bunch of water while you're cutting those yards. They was talking on the news about keeping hydraulic."

"Uh, you mean hydrated, Maxie?" Henry countered, hiding a smile.

"That too. Whatever word keeps you from passing out and crushing my lilac bush."

"I'll be sure to put a gallon jug on the back of my lawn mower." With a wave of his hand, Henry was gone.

Maxine hummed a verse as she decided on whether to bake a lemon, red velvet, or buttermilk cake. "*What a friend we have in Jesus, all our sins and grieves to bear. What a privilege to carry, everything to God in prayer.*" "I haven't made a buttermilk cake in a while," she muttered to herself, opening the fridge to reassure herself she had all the right ingredients. *But then Obadiah loves my red velvet.* "Who gives a good hallelujah what that rascal likes?" she asked aloud, reaching for the lemons and the buttermilk and pointedly ignoring the semisweet chocolate. Thinking of her soon-to-be ex-husband almost took away the joy of cooking. Obadiah Brook had lost his mind and spurned his marriage almost a year ago, and that she was thinking about the cakes *he* favored made Mama Max want to slap her own face.

"'Jesus, keep me near the cross,'" Maxine sang loudly, chasing unwanted thoughts away with every word, "'there a precious fountain, free to all a healing stream, flows from Calvary's mountain.'"

The phone rang.

Maxine heard it but she sang on, even louder than before. "'Near the cross, near the cross. Be my Glory ever.'"

The phone rang again.

"'Till my raptured soul shall find... rest beyond the river.' Hello?"

"Hey, Mama," King Brook said. "Sounds like I interrupted your church service!"

"Hello, son. Just praising the Lord is all."

"He's worthy."

"That He is."

A brief pause and then, "Mama, I was just wondering if you'd heard from Daddy."

And with one sentence, the rest her raptured soul had found flew straight out the window, replaced by indignation. "Why would I be hearing from that man?"

Because "that man"—as trifling as he is—is still your husband. She heard King sigh into the phone. "I'm not trying to start nothing, Mama. I just called his house and his cell. When I didn't get an answer, I tried to reach Tai and got her voice mail, too. He's supposed to get in sometime today. I just thought that maybe you'd heard from him."

"Hmph. Ain't a reason on this earth that that rascal would be calling me."

"Really? You have no plans to speak to Daddy this weekend?

During this special time when your first grandchild is getting married . . . this is how it's going down? Listen, Mama, I don't want to take sides here—"

"Only one side to take and that's the Lord's—"

"And I know you're still upset—"

"And with your father trampling all over his marriage vows, I shouldn't be the only one—"

"But for Princess's sake, do you think that we can be civil for just a few hours, maybe even all of Saturday? If we can just get through the ceremony and the reception, then you and Daddy can go on"—*acting like old fools*—"not talking to each other."

This wasn't a new plea to Maxine's ears. Tai had spouted a similar one for the last two months. She'd promised her daughter-in-law not to cuss him out on the church grounds (Maxine was a Christian after all) but that was as far as her word could travel. "If he comes to the house," she'd finished, "then he just might get real acquainted with my cast iron skillet. *Real* acquainted."

"I guess we don't need y'all side by side at the rehearsal dinner, but it would be nice if you could sit together on Saturday. Do you think that could happen?"

Maxine almost smiled. King Brook was a grown man, almost fifty years old, but in this moment he sounded like he did when he was fourteen and wanted to go to the high school dance where the devil's music was being played. "Even though you're asking me to take the chance on lightning striking me, son, you know how much I love Princess. Come Saturday, I'll behave."

4

Friends...How Many of Us Have Them?

"Sistah!" Tai opened her arms as her best friend, Vivian Montgomery, entered the restaurant lobby. "Girl," she whispered as they hugged, "you get on my nerves!"

Vivian gave her best friend of more than twenty-five years a firm embrace. She stepped back, still holding Tai's shoulders but looking into her eyes. "What'd I do?"

"It's what you haven't done. You never change, sis." Tai's look, or more specifically her weight, went up and down more than a yo-yo, and while she hadn't put back all of the fifty pounds she'd lost the past eighteen months, there was more jiggle to her wiggle and more bounce to the ounce than she'd like.

"Girl, please, if you saw how hard my personal trainer worked me, you'd know what I pay to maintain this size six."

"Hmm, sounds like a story there. Does Derrick have some competition?" Tai signaled to the hostess that her guest had arrived.

"Not unless I've switched lanes," Vivian answered, nonplussed. "My PT is female, and her workout is a beast."

"Well, you look good as always," Tai said honestly. "I'm glad you're here."

Tai and Vivian had been friends for almost as long as either could remember, having met at a Baptist convention in Florida when Vivian was thirteen and Tai was one year older. They'd spent the entire week together sharing teenage secrets, and even a hundred-mile distance during their high school years hadn't diminished their friendship. In an age before the Internet, Tai and Vivian had written countless letters and made hundreds of phone calls, giving themselves front row access into each other's lives. From the beginning, Tai had imagined herself the housewife, Vivian the professional. In a way, both women got their wishes. After a few years at Sprint during the early part of her and King's marriage, Tai had settled in to life as the mother of his four children and a preacher's wife. For Vivian, her well-planned path from college to career woman took an unexpected turn. She'd graduated with a degree in broadcast journalism and when she met her husband, Derrick, was already on her way to becoming the pre-Oprah, black Barbara Walters. Even when love came knocking, along with Derrick's call to the ministry, she'd imagined herself a Superwoman who could successfully juggle marriage and career. An old church member affectionately called Mother Moseley—who'd observed the single sistahs circling around the hardworking, handsome, passionate young preacher—had pulled Vivian's coattail and suggested that if she wanted to keep her husband she'd need to lose her job. It was some of the best advice that Vivian had ever received. Every day she thanked God that she'd listened, and she still mourned the fact that the woman who'd been like a second mother for almost two decades had recently gone home to be with the Lord.

After being seated near a window and having their water poured, the two women quickly scanned the menus and then dove right in to catching up. "So . . . how are you holding up?" Vivian asked Tai.

"Girl, I don't even know."

"Ha!"

"Where the ceremony itself is concerned, things are going surprisingly smooth. That's due in no small part to Erin Flynn."

"She's the wedding coordinator, right?"

"Along with her team she's a wedding maestro! Besides the consultations, I've hardly had to do a thing. The women of the church have been willing mother hens, more than happy to stay all up in my daughter's wedding business, and Joni, her maid of honor, has flown out twice in the last four months to help keep Princess's blood pressure down. So as far as the ceremony goes . . . I'd say we're doing pretty good."

Vivian took a drink of her water, eyeing the friend she could read like a book. "Why do I feel there's a *but* at the end of that sentence?"

"There's nothing I want more for my daughter than a happily ever after," Tai said, pausing as the waiter set down their ice-cold teas. "But Rafael is only Princess's second boyfriend."

"Uh, and just how many did you have?"

"That's true. King has been the only man in my life and honestly, I don't know if that's a good thing. I mean, when I married King, I had no one to compare him to."

"But Princess does. She has obviously compared Rafael to Kelvin, and has made her choice." Living in Los Angeles, Derrick and Vivian had been in unwittingly close proximity as Kelvin and Princess's love affair unfolded.

"That's what she says, but I've had a funny feeling about this wedding for months now and I can't seem to shake it. I've prayed about it, talked to Princess about it, but it doesn't go away." Tai looked at Vivian. "She's still in love with Kelvin, Viv. She says she isn't, but Mama knows."

"I wouldn't make too much of these emotions, Tai. Princess is your oldest daughter, and the first of your children to marry. It's normal that you'd feel discomfort and have reservations. But at the end of the day, you're going to have to put your trust in the Lord."

"I trust in the Lord, Vivian. I just don't totally trust Princess . . . or Derrick's son."

Derrick's son. Vivian pondered this irony after the waiter had taken her order and while Tai decided on what she'd eat. It had been six years since Vivian and Derrick had received the shock of their lives—that instead of two children, Derrick had three. Part one of the who-woulda-thunk-it was that had it not been for Tai and the suspicions that her own husband, King, was hiding something, the secret may have remained Tootie's alone. Tootie was the oh-no-she-didn't irony part two. Never in a million years would Vivian have guessed that the woman who'd been a thorn in Tai's side since high school would play such a significant role in her own life.

King and Derrick were both from Kansas City and had both gone to school with Janeé Smith. They were the high school's basketball stars, and Tootie's cheering for them hadn't stopped when they walked off the court. Derrick only hit it a couple times but King had had an on-again off-again relationship with her for years, one that unfortunately didn't stop after King's "I do." Shortly before Princess was born, Tai found out it was still going on and moved out of the house. King ended the affair, which devastated Tootie. King had been her one true love. Derrick went over to make her feel better. Nine months later came the proof of how good a job he'd done. But by then, Tootie had moved to Germany, got married, and began using her middle name. Tootie Smith became Janeé Petersen and life went on.

Fast forward fifteen years. Tootie returned to Kansas City to care for her ailing mother. That's when Tai found out that Tootie had a son who was fifteen years old—just a few months younger than Princess. This meant Tootie was pregnant while still in Kansas City, which, in Tai's mind, meant that the baby belonged to King. She was determined to find out the truth and enlisted Vivian's help to do it. They found the young man all right, but when they saw his face it wasn't Tai's mouth that fell open. It was Vivian's. Kelvin was the spitting image of Derrick Montgomery, and that's how the woman who'd comforted Tai regarding all things Tootie had then needed Tai to comfort her. Even now, Vivian deduced, life couldn't get any more ironic than that.

"Wow, sis, you've gone all quiet on me."

Vivian shook her head slightly. "Sorry, just thinking."

"I didn't mean to offend you," Tai said, misreading the slight frown on Vivian's face. "You know it isn't so much that Kelvin is Derrick's son, but that he's Tootie's, too."

"I didn't take that personally. I was just thinking about how crazy life is, and how unpredictable. No matter how much we'd like to, we can't live our children's lives. Princess is an intelligent and spiritually grounded young woman. I have a feeling that King will walk her up the aisle"—Vivian winked at Tai—"and Rafael will walk her back down it."

The waiter brought out their salads and Vivian filled Tai in on the next big SOS conference that would take place in Chicago. An idea inspired by Vivian and molded and shaped by Ladies First, a pastors' wives group based in Los Angeles, the Sanctity of Sisterhood meetings had grown to epic proportions, bringing thousands of women together annually for networking, fellowship, learning, and support. By the time their entrées arrived, the topic had changed once again.

"Is Doctor O in town yet?" Vivian asked, as she placed a liberal amount of butter on a warm honey-wheat roll.

"King will pick him up later this evening." An eye roll accompanied Tai's answer.

"Uh-oh. What's wrong?"

"I'm just hoping for Princess's sake that for one day he and Mama Max can put on their grown folks britches and get along."

"Of course they can," Vivian said, with more confidence than she actually felt. "Their separation has flown under the radar all this time, and with a national spotlight shining on Princess's nuptials, I doubt either would do anything to shake that facade."

Tai thoughtfully chewed a perfectly medium-rare rib eye. Vivian was right. Most of the public had bought the story about Obadiah mentoring a new, young pastor in Palestine, Texas, as his reason for being away from home. There was some truth to the story. Obadiah had come out of retirement and pastored the

Gospel Truth Church for a year before admitting that at the age of seventy-two he no longer had the stamina for full-time ministry in a church of this size. But there was no keeping a true man of God out of the pulpit, so when Obadiah returned to Texas, albeit Dallas, he still made his way to Palestine two Sundays a month to help the young man who was enjoying his first position as senior pastor. Only a handful of saints knew that on his other days Obadiah was busy enjoying something himself—adultery. Something with which Tai doubted the Lord was pleased. "You know the saying that there is no fool like an old fool?"

Vivian nodded.

"Well, you know I love Daddy O and Mama Max like my own flesh and blood, but that's what I'd call both my in-laws right about now—fools."

"You still think there's no chance for reconciliation?"

"You know what the scripture says. . . . All things are possible to him who believes."

"But you don't believe it."

"I want to, but pride and pussy has Daddy O standing his ground, and a stubborn streak the size of the Grand Canyon has Mama Max holding hers. God knows that if he has the audacity to bring that home wrecker Dorothea to the wedding, as he recently suggested to King that he might, then shortly after witnessing Princess's wedding . . . we may finally be seeing him and Mama Max divorce."

5

It's So Hard to Say Good-bye to Yesterday

The Reverend Doctor Pastor Bishop Overseer Mister Stanley Obadiah Meshach Brook Jr. placed one last tie in his bag and zipped it up. During the time it had taken him to pack two suits, three shirts, an extra pair of slacks, and plenty of underwear along with his accessories, he'd almost been able to drown out Dorothea Noble Bates Jenkins's whining. Almost, but not quite.

"It's not right, Obadiah," Dorothea snapped, pacing the length of the modest master bedroom that was a part of Obadiah's two-bed, two-bath condo. "I'm supposed to be your woman, yet you're leaving me behind on such an important occasion? The very first wedding of one of your grandchildren? I love you more than life itself, but I swear I don't know how much more you think I'm supposed to take. It's been almost a year since you moved down here and we're no closer to our own nuptials than when you arrived. We're living in the same complex but not the same house. This relationship isn't progressing at all!"

"I'm a married man, Dorothea."

"Oh, really? Why don't you tell that to your peter while it's poking my kitty."

Obadiah's mouth became a straight line as he determined not to beat an already dead horse into its final resting place. They'd had this conversation before. More than once. But Obadiah's heart was fixed and his mind was made up. He might be a low-down dirty dog in some people's eyes, but he was still a man of God with a heaven to gain and a hell to shun. Which is why he'd not be bringing his mistress to the same town where his wife lived. Sure, he'd thought about it, but his mind was as far as that madness had traveled. *Lord,* Obadiah wondered as he brushed by a still ranting Dorothea on the way to his car, throwing a "see you when I get back" over his departing shoulder. *How in the world did I get to this place?* And on his way to the Dallas/Fort Worth International Airport, he pondered the answer.

His interest in sex began when he was around seven or eight years old, when the thirteen-year-old daughter of a neighboring farmer showed him her privates. More than showed him, truth be told. She actually let him touch her "pocketbook," as the female genitalia was referred to in 1930s rural Texas. That moment in the hen house, amid the scratch of the hay and the stench of the poop, was a defining one for young Stanley Obadiah. He'd experienced his first hard-on brought about through outside forces, and a few years after that his first wet dream. At the ripe old age of fourteen he became a man, when sixteen-year-old Sadie Mitchell, the daughter of the farmer on the other side of the Brooks' twenty-acre spread, decided to make him her birthday present. He became obsessed with women as soon as his pole slipped into her hole, bedding women up and down the roads of Clay County. But it wasn't until 1961 that he met his match. He was twenty-two at the time, already a father, a pastor, and a fairly well-known revival preacher around various parts of the Lone Star and surrounding states. He'd heard about the beautiful Noble sisters and had been almost certain he'd spotted one mere moments after, along with ten other preachers, he'd walked onto a Texas pulpit.

He'd been right. Her name was Dorothea. And from the moment he laid eyes on her, he knew one thing for sure: he had to have her.

Obadiah recalled this initial meeting, which had happened in the hosting minister's home. They were sitting around the dinner table and, whether by fate, luck, or the devil's wishes, Dorothea had been seated on his left-hand side.

"Enjoyed your sermon," she'd said, as she ate fried chicken with a knife and fork.

"Uh-huh." Rarely had the Reverend been at a loss for words, but now was one of those times. She was without a doubt the most beautiful woman he'd ever seen up close, reminding him of Lena Horne or Dorothy Dandridge. All uppity and whatnot with fingers too cultured to touch fowl and Crisco, smelling like vanilla and flowers and all types of goodness, and sounding like a lark. It had taken all of dinner and two rounds of dessert before mustering up the courage to try and have what he wanted.

"Sister Noble, correct?"

"Yes, Reverend."

"Would you be so kind as to give me a ride home?" It was then that he'd learned that Dorothea had ridden to the house with her sister. His eyes had always been almost as expressive as his conversation, and he'd let them do the talking. Dorothea's answer was that she'd call a cab. They'd gone to her house and screwed up one side of her modest yet chicly furnished Dallas home and down the other. There were very few affairs that lasted half a century. Obadiah Brook's and Dorothea Noble Bates Jenkins's had been the exception.

After parking in long-term, catching a shuttle to the Delta terminal and being freed from the long security line by an airline employee who was also a fan, Obadiah plopped down in a chair at the gate, waiting for the boarding process that would began in less than an hour. As he mindlessly stared at the television monitor locked on CNN, another set of memories came to mind. They were of a young, holy-rolling country girl with the big four: lips, hips, booty, and thighs. The Johnson family farm was located on the other side of the fork in the road, a couple of miles and a large catfish pond away from the Brooks' country spread. Like most of the boys in those parts, Obadiah had eyed Maxine's ample assets for quite some time and, after being taunted by some of his peers, became determined to approach her.

"Miss Maxine," Obadiah drawled, in as manly a voice as sixteen could muster at the time. "You sho' looking good today, girl."

"Well, you ain't," Maxine retorted, quickening her pace at the same time.

"Is that so? Then why you trying to run away before you kiss me?"

"Ain't nothing wrong with running away from trouble. And you're trouble with a capital *T*."

"Ain't nothing about me for you to be scared of, Maxine. You not like those other girls."

She kept walking, fast enough to keep him chasing but slow enough so that she could hear every word he spoke. "That's right, I'm not."

"I know you're not. You're special. That's why I'm gonna marry you."

Maxine's heart skipped a beat as she stopped and turned around. "To how many girls have you told that lie?" she asked all nonchalantly.

"Aw, girl, why you got to act like that? I'm serious. I'm gonna be a big-time preacher, and you'll make a good preacher's wife."

"What makes you think I'll marry you?" Maxine asked, even as she worked hard to keep the smile off her face and out her voice.

"Maxine, get on up to this house!" Maxine's mother's yell cut through the flirty atmosphere surrounding her and Obadiah.

"Yes, ma'am."

Maxine gave Obadiah a slight smile before turning to walk toward her mother's hard stare.

"I'ma marry you," Obadiah whispered confidently, before walking in the opposite direction.

Barely a year later, Obadiah had gone and done just that, and within a year of their union Maxine was pregnant. This one ended in a miscarriage but after a couple more years of trying, Maxine became pregnant again and nine months later, King Brook was born. Obadiah pulled out his Bible as he remembered the joy he felt at holding his first child and then, as though pushing a fast-forward button in his mind, he remembered the mixed emotions that accompanied the announcement that King was getting married. It was even harder for Obadiah to relinquish his daughter's hand, so he was well aware of the turmoil that King must now be experiencing.

It's good to be going home, Obadiah thought, when the boarding process began and he made his way down the Jetway. He had friends throughout Texas but Kansas had been his home for more than thirty years. He missed those things he'd grown used to over the years: LaMar's Donuts, Gates Bar-B-Q, his barber, Glover, and the Mount Zion Progressive congregation. And truth be told if one dared tell it, he missed something—correction, someone— even more.

6

Fathers Be Good to Your Daughters

King Brook and Derrick Montgomery strolled off the basketball court. For the past hour, these two best friends had talked trash and shot hoops in Mount Zion's recreation center—a twenty-first century jewel in the church's building expansion. Along with the basketball court (complete with bleachers and an electronic scoreboard) was a tennis court, a jogging track, Olympic-size swimming pool, and rooms to handle exercise classes from aerobics to Pilates to step to yoga.

"Man, I can tell you're about to turn fifty," Derrick teased, after taking a long drink of water. "I had to ease up on you those last ten minutes just so you could keep up!"

King swatted Derrick with his sweaty towel. "It's a shame to lie on church property," he said in a somber tone. "Hadn't been for those lucky three pointers at the end, that last game would have been mine. And let us not forget that you're only a hop, skip, and a jump younger than me. You're coming down the same road I'm headed, junior."

"God willing."

"And the creek don't rise."

"Ha! You're sounding more like your old man every day."

"Yeah, don't remind me. I spent the first fifty years of my life running away from any similarities, but as I get older, I'm beginning to embrace some of the very things he holds dear."

The men reached King's brand new champagne-colored, customized Lincoln MKS, which sat glittering like a jewel in mid-June's midday sun. He popped the trunk, they dumped their bags, and soon after were heading back to the InterContinental Hotel in the Plaza, a swank combination of stores, eateries, and landmarks that had been fashioned after its sister city, Seville, Spain.

Derrick fastened his seat belt and settled in for the ride. "Ah, man, that workout felt good! I haven't been getting it in like I need to."

King cast a glance at Derrick. "Still burning the candle at both ends?"

"I'm trying not to but, man, my schedule is insane."

"Tell me about it. On Monday morning, I leave for Barbados and will be gone for two weeks."

"Tai going with you?"

"No. The twins have a full summer schedule. Her hands are full just managing that."

"That's a long time to be away from your good thing, my brothah."

"Believe me, I'm not thrilled about it. But somebody is." Derrick shot King a questioning look. "My assistant pastor is practically pushing me out the door."

"Ha!" Derrick had met Mount Zion's prolific number-two man, Solomon Cole, on several occasions and knew he'd enjoy delivering the Sunday message. He was chomping at the bit to get his own church.

King smoothly turned the car onto the highway. "I'm surprised Wesley didn't invite you down to this year's conference." Wesley Freeman was the senior pastor of His Holy Word Cathedral in Barbados.

"He did but I declined. I've already been to South Africa three times this year, have a slew of revivals and conferences on my plate, and the Sunday crowds are now out of control. I've put it off as long as I can. We're going to have to expand."

"Many preachers would consider that a good problem to have."

"I'm thankful, King. Truly I am. But to whom much is given much is required. Many of the ministers out there see the numbers, but they don't see the hard work and sacrifice that comes with these large crowds. I'm fortunate to have Cy Taylor in my corner." Cy was an associate minister at Kingdom Citizens Christian Center, and also one of its wealthiest members. "He's heading up the fund-raising for our new building and is also participating in our needs and feasibility study. But no matter the direction in location, construction, and design, we're looking at a good ten to twenty mil. My head hurts just thinking about it."

"Been there, done that, bro, and expanding is definitely no joke. I'll be glad to share with you everything that I know, and should you desire, I'll also make those who led up our building project available to speak with you."

"I appreciate that, man." A few moments of silence passed as King's new car fairly glided down I-35. It was a beautiful summer day—bright, blue sky, fluffy cumulous clouds, and thick greenery courtesy of the spring's heavy rains. "So are you ready for this next big step in your life? Ready to give your daughter away?"

King let out a whistle. "As ready as I'll ever be."

"I can't even imagine how that feels. Elisia isn't even a teenager and I'm already sweating."

"Enjoy her now, while she still thinks the sun rises and sets on your head and before some young nucka convinces her otherwise."

"Oh, I already told her how it was going down in my house. She can't date until she graduates!"

"Ha! Good luck with that."

"Wishful thinking, I know."

"What is she now . . . ten, eleven?"

"Lis is twelve going on twenty-one and D2 is fourteen going on forty!"

King shook his head, remembering the last time he saw Derrick's namesake a year ago, a teenager wearing a double-breasted suit, wide tie, wing tips and a bowler hat. "He still want to be a preacher?"

"Yep." Derrick took in the flat Kansas landscape, whizzing by him at a cool seventy miles per hour. "I keep waiting for the pretty young thang who's going to make him open his nose and close his Bible."

"Hmm, as I recall, those PYTs from back in the day didn't interfere with your scripture reading."

Derrick chuckled. "See, that's what happens with a friend who's known me as long as you have. You know where all of the skeletons are buried."

"Heck, man. I helped dig half the graves!"

"Ha!"

When King spoke again, his focus had gone back to Derrick's most provocative question. "It seems like only yesterday I was changing that girl's diapers."

"You wiped doo-doo?"

"You didn't?"

"Naw, I could handle a pee diaper but when it came to number two..." Derrick made a face. "I don't know nothing 'bout 'dat 'dere."

King laughed at both Derrick's squeamishness and his attempt at youthful slang before the smile scampered away from his face. "Well, I did. And before I knew it she was crawling away from me into preschool, then kindergarten and grade school. I remember her first rite of passage—when we let her go with a group of girls to the junior high dance. I was waiting in the parking lot when it was over, and I can still remember her shiny eyes when she got into the car. 'It was so much fun, Daddy,' " King mimicked, in an impressive falsetto. "She was all smiles and bubbles then," King said, his misting eyes a total surprise. "But growing up . . . they change."

"Yeah, man. I hear you." Derrick knew the exact moment that King was talking about: when he and Tai had come to Los Angeles and found out more about their eighteen-year-old daughter than they ever wanted to know. It was the moment that they were forced to realize that Princess was no longer their little girl but a grown-ass woman with a mind of her own. "But I'll be there to help you get through it, dog. Complete with Kleenex and everything."

"I wish I could tell you to store your hankie, dude. But a brothah might break down for real."

"Naw, you can't do that. You're not only the father giving away the bride, but the officiating minister. Responsibility trumps emotion. You'll hold it together."

"I'd better, otherwise I'll have to answer to Rafael. I must admit I've never seen a man want to get married more than my soon-to-be son-in-law."

"From what I've seen and what you've told me, he's a solid young man. Congrats again, King."

The two fist bumped. "Thanks, Derrick. It's good to have you here."

7

Girls Just Wanna Have Fun

"Princess!" Joni swatted her friend's bootie-clad foot off the ottoman. "It's your big day tomorrow. Go to your room and go to bed!"

It was near midnight on the night before the biggest day of Princess's life. It had been a full Friday. Last minute fittings, mani/pedi/massage marathons, the fairly flawless rehearsal dinner, and now this: the final day of singlehood before Princess became a married woman. Instead of a bachelorette party, nine of Princess's friends had joined her in Hawaii last month where in her words they'd "done everything I can't do once I get pregnant." On this topic both she and Rafael were in agreement: they wanted to be young parents. So the women had snorkeled and parasailed, flown over volcanoes in helicopters and flown over the beautiful Hawaiian expanse attached to parachutes. Everyone had agreed that skydiving had been one of the most beautiful freedoms they'd ever experienced, and an absolutely perfect way to see the world. Well, since Princess's best friend, Joni, had kept her eyes tightly shut until feeling terra firma, she couldn't quite cosign on this last claim.

Princess grabbed a pillow and crushed it to her chest. "I know that I should leave y'all, but I'm too wired to sleep! This moment is so surreal. I can't believe it. I'm getting married!"

"It's no big deal," Joni said, in an attempt to calm her frazzled friend. "All it means is that you get to start washing dirty drawers and, in your case, cooking very bad meals."

"Forget you, heifah!"

"As your maid of honor, I'm just doing my job. Urging you to get your beauty rest and wiping that rose color off your glasses."

The women laughed.

"Princess," Sarah said, her light, melodic voice wafting across the room from the king-size bed on which she sat Indian style. "Don't mind, Joni. In a few short years you'll become the next Oprah and, like her, you'll be able to hire all of the help you need to do the dirty work."

"Hey, speaking of Oprah types, are you sure you want to share your nuptials with the world?" This question came from Brittany Williams, the bridesmaid who'd known Princess since they were both four years old. Brittany's family had moved from Kansas City to Chicago when Brittany was thirteen, but the two women had kept in touch.

"Yes," Princess said. "But it's only because of how much I trust Carla. I know that she will do a story that uplifts and inspires. Plus, it will be a ratings bonanza and I'd be lying to not admit how much I feel I owe her. She and Lavon are why I'm so successful, plus they're friends of the family. They'll be arriving tomorrow, and staying at the same hotel as Uncle Derrick and Aunt Viv."

Carla Chapman was the host of the hugely successful talk show, *Conversations with Carla*. For the past several months, Princess had served as a once-a-month cohost and off-site correspondent for stories involving the twenty-something crowd. She refused the title "celebrity," but more often than not when she went out in public her chances of being recognized were quite high. A two-man camera crew from the show had been filming Princess at various wedding-oriented activities since arriving earlier in the week.

"I personally think it's great that you're getting ready to be a reality TV star." Princess rolled her eyes. "And why didn't you put us up in the Plaza?" Joni teased. "You know your parents have the paper."

"Because...I wasn't going to take a chance on an accident, mechanical malfunction, act of God, or anything else getting in the way of y'all being at the church on time. From here, we can take the highway or if it's backed up, we can hit the streets. Besides, which one of y'all is too good for the Marriott?" No one answered. "Uh-huh. I thought so."

Chandra Willis, who'd known Princess since the Willis family joined Mount Zion in the late nineties, chimed in. "I have no problem staying here. I'm just wondering what room your fine brother is in."

Princess rolled her eyes. "Girl, please. You don't want to hook up with that ho." Princess loved her older brother, Michael, but swore he had a different woman for every week of the year.

"Girl, everybody can't keep a lock on it until a brothah puts a ring on it." Chandra slapped five with another member of the party. "So help a sistah out, Princess. I know the entire wedding party is being picked up from here. So what's his room number?"

Princess shrugged. "I honestly don't know it and wouldn't give it to you if I did. Embarrassing things can happen when a woman shows up to a man's hotel room unannounced."

"And uninvited," Joni added, with an arched brow.

"Spoken like two married women. Y'all both get on my nerves."

Brittany looked at her watch. "It's about time for me to crash but before I go, let's play 'final curtain.' "

An instant frown formed on Chandra's face. "What the heck is that?"

"It's where each of us asks the bride-to-be the final question of her single life. The questions can be funny or serious, off-the-wall or heartfelt. But the bride must promise to answer each question truthfully." Brittany cast big, brown, twinkling eyes on a wary Princess. "You game, sistah?"

Princess groaned. "Maybe I should just go to bed."

The rebuttal was immediate.

"Chicken!"

"C'mon, Princess!"

"Where's your big girl panties?"

Similar monikers and entreaties spewed from the seven brides-maids and one maid of honor in the room.

"Okay, fine." Princess said, tossing the pillow at Chandra, the instigator. "But let's make it quick. All of a sudden I'm *really* tired."

"More like really scared," Joni said with a laugh.

And so it began.

"Okay, I'll go first," Brittany offered. "Princess . . . my girl. At the risk of being accused of getting all up in your biz-ness . . ." Princess rolled her eyes. "How long after the 'I do's' do you think it will be before you and Rafael get your freak on?"

Sarah gasped, tossing blond curls out of a face that had turned a rosy shade of pink. "Brittany!"

"Listen, Miss Virginity, this is grown folks business happening up in here." Brittany tossed her own black, shoulder-length curls over her shoulder. "So pay attention. And take notes."

Princess studied her French-manicured fingers as she gave an answer. "Well, as y'all know, Rafael and I have been engaged for al-most a year, and he has been very patient." Princess glanced at those around the room, her eyes a mix of shyness and devil-may-care. "Let's just say there's a reason why we're heading to a hotel in-stead of the airport tomorrow night. I'd say we'll be trying to make babies before they clean up the last grain of rice."

"Ha!" Brittany slapped five with her childhood friend, even though she knew that Princess had opted for bubbles instead of the traditional rice shower. "That's what I'm talking about!"

Bolstered by Brittany's personal question, Chandra went next. "I still can't believe you haven't even seen what the man is work-ing with. That's like buying a dress without trying it on!"

"Not quite," was Princess's dry reply.

"Seriously, girl. What are you going to do if the man has an earthworm instead of a cobra? The worse question that you could ask on your wedding night is 'is it in?'"

The ladies howled. Princess stood. "Okay, now that I see what's behind the final curtain I'm going to make this my final curtain call."

"Wait, Princess," Joni asked, crossing the room to where Princess stood. "Don't mind the horny singles. I have a question for you." Princess shifted her weight from one leg to the other and crossed her arms. "It's legit, I promise. We know he's special since he took you off the market, but for you, what makes Rafael Stevens stand head and shoulders above all the other men in the world?"

Princess plopped back on the bed, pulled her knees to her chest, and rested her chin upon them as she pondered her answer. "So many things," she said softly. "But simply put, Rafael is a good man, a nice guy. I know they say that nice guys finish last, but that's only because women are too stupid to recognize a good thing when they see it. We often go for the bad boys, the brave men, the instant spark instead of the steady flame."

"Speak the truth, sistah!"

"Shut up, Chandra."

"Girl, that sounded like it could go on a Mahogany greeting card."

"Whatever," Princess said, laughing.

"She is a best-selling published author," Joni said, reminding a group that didn't need to be reminded. Princess Brook's memoir, *Jesus Is My Boo*, became a *NYT* bestseller. "So everybody knows she has a way with words."

"I'm going to *go* away in about sixty seconds. Y'all done?"

"We don't want our girl looking tore up from the floor up tomorrow, y'all," Chandra said with exaggerated seriousness. "Let a sistah answer the questions and be done."

The questions from the remaining six ladies rained in, encased in plenty of jokes and laughter.

"If Jesus is your boo, who is Rafael?"

"My husband."

"Are you going to live in LA or KC?"

"Ugh! I've already told y'all this. I'm going to move into Rafael's downtown condo and schedule periodic trips to the West Coast."

"What's the thing you'll most miss about being single?"

"That would be my sleeping attire of choice, oversized T-shirts and cotton pj's, in favor of sexy negligees."

"Do you think you'll ever learn to cook?"

"Not as long as there are restaurants and takeout."

Laughter and zingers aimed at the bride-to-be abounded.

Finally, as the clock on the wall neared 1 a.m., Sarah asked the last question. "If there was one collective prayer you'd have us say tonight, a prayer for you and Rafael . . . what would it be?"

The atmosphere shifted as the room got quiet. Suddenly, the mood was all serious and reflective. "I'd have y'all pray that God will bless my marriage," she answered, eyeing each woman. "And that His will be done."

8

Here Comes the Bride...Again

An expectant energy pulsed through the seven hundred and fifty well-wishers that packed the Mount Zion Progressive Baptist Church for the 3 p.m. nuptials. After personally inviting almost five hundred guests, a lottery had been held for the remaining seats and every single one was taken. The marriage of the church's first daughter was in and of itself enough to garner such attention but the promise of both Christian and secular celebrities in the mix no doubt added to the hype.

For a moment, King stood at the back of the church and took it all in. It was a vantage point that he rarely experienced, and one that he found interesting indeed. Had Tai been the one standing there, she would have noticed how the fuchsia and lilac color scheme had been meticulously carried out throughout the room, would have appreciated the lilac silk liner that covered the aisle and the intricately woven archways of various fuchsia plants paired with fragrant white stock through which the wedding party would make their entrance. She would have considered the perfection in having the white stone walls covered with sheer, billowy fabrics of purple, fuchsia, and iridescent silver. And she would have teared up at seeing how the entire pulpit area had been turned into a fairy-land of iridescent fabrics and Swarovski crystals that kissed the strategically placed chandeliers casting rainbows on the ceiling.

That's what Tai would have noticed. But King's focus was on the crowd. He watched the women with wry amusement as Darius Crenshaw made his way into the sanctuary from a private side entrance and joined the Musical Messengers already sitting on stage. Once a gospel standout who was now a secular star, Darius and Company—also called D & C—had put out hit after hit since their first one, "Possible," soared to number one several years ago. That was also about the time that Darius Crenshaw came out and announced that he was gay. For a time the backlash shook Darius's faith in the church, but it didn't shake his pastor's faith in him. In a move rarely seen in Christian churches, Derrick Montgomery accepted the news of Darius's homosexuality and allowed him to continue on as Kingdom Citizens Christian Center's minister of music. The talented singer and musician's popularity had waned in religious circles, but his crossover success kept him in high demand. *And it's obviously kept him attractive to the ladies,* King mused, as he witnessed the side profiles of women who were obviously celebrity smitten. A similar reaction happened moments later when Cy Taylor came out of that same private door. No matter that his gorgeous wife, Hope, was beside him. Some of the women still ogled him like he was a barbequed rib. Then King caught himself eyeing Hope like she was a thick, sauce-slathered fry and figured he'd better judge not. Hope used to be a member of Mount Zion Progressive, and had been one of the many who'd drawn Tai's suspicions. Nothing had ever happened between King and Hope. But that didn't mean that the pastor hadn't lusted in his heart a time or two. King continued to look around, noting that Lavon had taken a seat next to Carla, turning this part of the taping over to the capable hands of Mount Zion's media ministry. They were sitting next to another gospel heartthrob, Nathaniel Thicke. He couldn't see her face, but King was sure that Nate's tenderoni wife, Destiny, looked as stunning as ever. He made a mental note to give his ministerial brother a call, tell him about a church in Las Vegas that would soon be looking for a pastor. Next to Nate and Destiny sat Derrick and Vivian Montgomery. King's heart warmed at the sight of his best friend in the world.

His eyes continued sweeping up the aisle, stopping on the second row where his extended family sat. Building the ministry had called for sacrifice, and he wasn't as close to his siblings as he'd like to be. Geography had also separated them. Queen, the sister eighteen months younger than him, had married a military man. She and her family of three had lived in four different countries and several states. Currently, they called Hawaii home and King had promised a visit before the year was out. After more failed relationships than a Baptist church had fans with pictures of Jesus, King's baby sister, Ester, had fled to Alaska where there was little sun but lots of money. King was still trying to figure out who the red-headed, red-bearded lumberjack-looking joker was sitting by her side, looking as out of place in his black big and tall suit as a Ku Klux Klansman at the MLK Memorial, but with an arm tightly squeezing his sister's satin-clad shoulder. King was closest to Daniel, his baby brother. Perpetual bachelor Dan lived in Las Vegas and attended the church King intended to discuss with Nathaniel. *I need to hook those two up, make sure Dan is in Nate's inner circle.* Without even realizing it and on his daughter's wedding day no less, the workaholic King had automatically reverted back into business mode.

King felt a tap on his shoulder, and turned to find Erin talking into her earpiece. "Yes, get the bridesmaids ready to line up. And have Jennifer get the groomsmen. Things will get underway very shortly. Sorry about that, Pastor Brook," she said, punching a button on her phone. "We'd like to clear this space and line everyone up in order. So if you could please join your wife and daughter in your office, I'll come get you in a few minutes, just before the procession begins."

"Thanks, Erin. Will do." King entered his office and was taken aback at the sight. He'd never seen Princess look more beautiful than she did in this instance. She turned large, doe-brown eyes on him and his eyes misted over. He looked at Tai, noticing how the fuchsia-colored gown she'd had designed especially for the occasion highlighted the red tones in her skin as well as her naturally reddish brown hair's highlights. The long, wide-belted jacket flared at the hips and effectively camouflaged the extra chips that had settled on her hips as well as gave the illusion of a smaller waist. Her hair was done in big curls that teased her shoulders and framed her face. The makeup artist's work was perfect: not too much, not too little. King and Tai's eyes met and held. It was their baby's wedding day. And after twenty-five years together as husband and wife, so many words were translated in that look that none needed to be spoken aloud.

"You look good, baby," he said to Tai, giving her a kiss on the cheek. "And you," he said turning to his daughter. "I've never seen a more beautiful bride. I love you, baby girl." He hugged her.

"Stop it, Daddy. You're going to make me cry!"

A light tap on the door interrupted the moment. "It's about that time," Erin gaily announced as she walked briskly into the room. "If you will please come with me, everyone is in place and we're ready to begin."

As the guests waited for the ceremony to begin, the Musical Messengers played jazzy versions of a variety of well-known love songs. Now, as Erin gave the signal for the processional to begin, they seamlessly slid into a more classical sounding wedding march, with the synthesizer evoking the sounds of harps and violins. After candles were lit, both sets of grandparents entered, followed by the groom's parents, Mr. and Mrs. Stevens. Next came the seven bridesmaids and groomsmen followed by the maid of honor and best man. Finally, it was time for Princess to enter along with her parents, both of whom were walking her down the aisle.

Princess had a vague sense of the crowd, who turned toward her with smiles and whispered compliments, comments, and reactions. But as soon as she looked up and saw Rafael staring at her, it was as though she entered a tunnel, was moving through murky water where there was no sound. She admired how handsome he looked. The single-breasted, deep silver tuxedo he wore was tailored to perfection, emphasizing his well-proportioned, five-foot-ten frame and creamy brown skin. His close-cropped hair was a barber's masterpiece, accenting deep-set brown eyes and a determined square jaw. His slightly full lips were unsmiling, but his eyes drank her in as though she were ambrosia. As she got closer, she noticed those eyes were extra bright. *Oh, my goodness. Is he getting ready to—*. Before she could finish the thought, one lone tear slowly slid down the side of his face.

Princess's mouth went dry. Her heart beat so rapidly that she thought she might faint, and was sure that everyone around her could hear its sound. She swallowed and tightened the grasp she had on her parents' arms. Her hands became clammy, her legs began to tremble, and for a moment she had serious doubts whether she could stand for thirty more seconds on those high Louboutin heels, let alone the thirty or so minutes that the ceremony would last. Just when she thought she really just might pass out, she felt the calming pressure of her mother's hand. Tai, who was walking on Princess's left side, had taken her left hand and gently, yet firmly, placed it on Princess's arm, giving it a pat and then a squeeze. A mother's strength flowed through her fingers and the moment of panic passed. Her heart was still beating wildly but by the time they reached the front of the church, Princess had regained a modicum of control.

As Tai hugged Princess and went to her seat, King took his place behind a Plexiglas podium.

And the ceremony began.

First, a very popular, A-list actress stood to recite a poem she'd written. Kiki Minor had become a star through the hit TV One show, *Love Rectangle*. Hollywood came calling shortly thereafter and fortune smiled when Jerry Seinfeld tapped her to play his long-lost daughter (who just happened to be African-American) in last year's breakout comedy, *The Birthday Switch*. A year older than Princess, Kiki had been impressed while watching Princess's interview on *Conversations with Carla* and following a Twitter introduction, text messages, phone calls, and a couple of meetings, a friendship was born. She'd personally asked to be a part of Princess's special day, and had created a poem just for the occasion, inspired by the biblical love chapter: 1 Corinthians, Chapter 13, and more specifically, verses four through eight:

> *"Love is patient; love is kind; and special when shared by*
> *   two like minds.*
> *It does not envy, it is not proud; its actions are better than*
> *   words spoken aloud.*
> *It does not dishonor, or seek for self; but rather puts the*
> *   one it loves above all else.*
> *Not easily angered, nor keeps track of wrong,*
> *Love is the endless heartbeat in true marriage songs.*
> *Love doesn't like evil, but rejoices in truth,*
> *With compassion, forgiveness, and God at its root.*
> *It protects, trusts, hopes, perseveres; believes in all goodness,*
> *   eliminates fears.*
> *The Light of Love will always prevail.*
> *Love is pure Spirit . . . that's why Love never fails."*

The audience applauded as Kiki took her seat and Darius joined the band. His latest hit song, "Forever You," was not only a number-one R & B Billboard sensation, but it was also the perfect message for this special day. The wedding atmosphere took on that of a concert as Darius encouraged the audience to wave their hands in the air. With anyone else, this may have seemed inappropriate, but for Darius Crenshaw . . . unconventional was expected. Following this somewhat exuberant beginning, a sense of tradition was restored as the Lord's Prayer was recited and King prepared Princess and Rafael to recite their wedding vows.

"These two children of God have come here today out of respect for God and in obedience to his command that has been from the very beginning. For of three institutions ordained by God, the home is the oldest. Since its origin is of God, it is honorable and is to be held in the highest esteem of all mankind." A cough interrupted King's speech. He looked up to see Derrick lightly touch his fist to his mouth and slightly loosen his tie. *Brother is looking as nervous as I feel,* he thought with a smile. That was simply a testament to their closeness. They weren't blood relatives but Derrick and Vivian had often been more of an aunt and uncle to his children than his own siblings.

After a quick sweep of the crowd, King continued. "So while this ceremony is the legal blending of two hearts that have already been beating in unison, a home is also being formed, and a relationship established that has not only been approved by the state but has been ordained by God and sanctioned by His Holy Spirit."

At this time, Reverend Doctor O stood and spoke into a cordless microphone. Anyone listening to his booming, authoritative voice would know he was a preacher. "Who gives this woman to be married to this man?"

Tai stood, and she and King said in unison, "We do."

Bam!

Princess froze as her heart dropped. Without even looking (because her eyes were squeezed shut) she knew what was happening. Kelvin had entered the church and was now heading toward the stage. Her dream was coming true! She stole a look at Rafael, and was surprised to see a look of concern instead of shock and anger on his face. All of this was processed in the matter of seconds it took Princess to turn around. When she did, she discovered that the commotion was not in the center aisle, as she'd envisioned, but rather at the front of the church.

"Oh my God!" Without even thinking, Princess scooped up her train and clumsily followed her father, whose long strides had quickly eaten up the distance between him and the ceremony's interruption. "Oh my God," she whispered, as she looked down at the man she loved almost as much as she did her father.

But it wasn't Kelvin Petersen.

It was Derrick Montgomery, sprawled out on the sanctuary floor. And he was not moving.

9

Ball Of Confusion

"Somebody call nine-one-one!"

The soft murmur that began after Princess's outcry quickly built to a low-grade roar. Necks craned, bodies leaned forward, and people stood to try and see what was going on at the front of the church. But Mount Zion's well-trained security team was already on it. They formed a tight circle around the felled pastor, disallowing would-be gawkers the chance to pull out their phones and shoot a YouTube moment. The media director instructed the camera crew to point all cameras away from the mayhem, and upon seeing his son otherwise occupied, Reverend Doctor O quickly stepped up to the microphone that King had recently abandoned.

"Saints of God, we're in the house of the Lord," he said, in a tone that immediately caused the talking to lessen but not totally cease. "And one of our brothers is in trouble. If you are a child of God who knows how to call upon the name of Jesus, I beseech you to pray right now. Pray to a just and merciful God. Saints, you don't need to know what happened or who it is. God sits high and looks low. He sees all, and knows all!"

Some old habits died hard and others didn't die at all, and within the span of thirty seconds the atmosphere had gone from wedding to panic to a Sunday-go-to-meeting church service.

"Amen, Pastor!" Elsie Wanthers, one of Mount Zion's oldest members—heck, one of the county's oldest citizens—stood and waved her bright pink handkerchief. "Have mercy, Lord!" she cried, before turning toward the pew to get on her eighty-something-year-old knees.

Not to be outdone, her good friend of more than fifty years jumped up next. "We serve a mighty God," Margie Stokes screeched. But few people heard. Her tinny high-pitched voice was no match for either Sister Wanthers' robust announcement or Reverend Doctor Obadiah's rich baritone, which filled the building, telling the guests-turned-parishioners what time it was.

" 'Sweet hour of prayer! Sweet hour of prayer! That calls me from a world of care. . . .' "

The Musical Messengers fell right into line, forgoing their signature jazzy sound and playing straight-up gospel.

" 'And bids me at my Father's throne, make all my wants and wishes known.' "

Those who knew the song chimed in (which was a small number considering the hymn was penned around 1810). Those who didn't know the words either hummed . . . or prayed.

" 'In seasons of distress and grief, my soul has often found relief, And oft escaped the tempter's snare, by thy return, sweet hour of prayer!' "

Darius stepped to the microphone with tears in his eyes. Having been raised by a religious grandmother who had him in church five days a week, he not only knew the song's first stanza, but all the others as well. The melodic, emotion-laden sound of his voice caused hands to raise and tears to fall.

" 'Sweet hour of prayer! Sweet hour of prayer! Thy wings shall my petition bear. To Him whose truth and faithfulness, engage the waiting soul to bless.' "

Paramedics rushed in. The Spirit of the Lord was so thick in the building that some did not even notice them.

" 'And since He bids me seek His face . . .' "

The EMTs hurriedly checked Derrick before loading him onto the gurney.

"Believe His word, and trust His grace..."

Security created a moving human shield as the gurney was wheeled through the private side door.

"I'll cast on Him my every care, and wait for Thee, sweet hour of prayer."

Erin had rounded up most of the bridesmaids and groomsmen but a few of them followed Rafael and Princess through the private side door. Michael, Joni, Sarah, and Rafael's best friend, Greg, looked bewildered and concerned as they watched the senior pastor of Kingdom Citizens Christian Center, arguably the most popular mega-church on the country's West Coast, being wheeled out of the building and into an ambulance. Vivian scrambled into the back as well, oblivious to her now snagged designer suit and scruffed up Jimmy Choos. King turned to his assistant, Joseph, who hurried away to take care of business, and then rushed into his office. Upon seeing Princess's fear-filled face, and for the first time since seeing his best friend on the floor, he remembered that a wedding was being conducted. He walked over to where the group stood in various poses of disarray.

"Daddy, what happened?" Princess rushed into her father's arms. "Is Uncle Derrick going to be okay?"

"I don't know, baby," King said, forcing the raspiness of emotion from his voice. "Your mama and I are headed to the hospital now."

"Where are they taking him?"

King shook his head. "We're finding that out now. I'll tell you more as soon as I know it, baby, but right now...I've got to go."

Rafael, who'd been standing next to Princess, reached out and grabbed King's arm as he passed. "But, Pastor...what about our wedding?" He knew it sounded insensitive, but as bad as Derrick's situation was, Rafael had other priorities right now. He felt Princess's incredulous eyes on him, but he kept his eyes trained on

King, waiting for an answer. At this exact moment, Joseph came up to King and whispered in his ear.

"I'm sorry, son, but I've got to go." King turned and started walking with Joseph to the outside door. He looked over his shoulder and said to Princess, "They're taking him to Shawnee Mission." Then he, Tai, and a couple of associate ministers headed out the door.

Princess started for the room where she'd gotten ready.

Rafael stopped her. "Baby, where are you going?"

Princess jerked out of his grasp. "Where do you think, Rafael. To the hospital!"

She started away again, and again, Rafael grabbed her arm. "Princess, this is our wedding day! Does that suddenly not mean anything to you?"

Princess's brow creased. "My uncle just got rushed to the hospital and my dad, the man who was marrying us, is on his way there. Does that mean anything to you?"

Greg stepped up to calm his friend. "Man, I'm sorry this happened, but there's nothing we can do right now. Maybe after they make sure the pastor is all right, y'all can go ahead and get married tonight."

This reasonable statement snapped Rafael out of his unreasonable state. He took a deep breath and visibly calmed. "I'm sorry, baby," he said, taking Princess in his arms. "I didn't mean to sound insensitive."

Well, you did.

"But I've waited so long to make you my wife that I just . . . I'm just . . ." At a loss for words, Rafael rested his forehead against that of the woman he loved. "I love you, Princess."

Princess felt bad that her focus was elsewhere, that her priorities were different than the man earlier described as her beloved. But she couldn't do anything about that right now. Now, she had to get to her uncle.

"I have to change," she said, pulling away from Rafael and heading down the hall. "And get to the hospital as soon as I can."

Joni and Sarah ran into the room with Princess. Erin entered just seconds behind them and she and Sarah began working on the thirty pearl-styled buttons on the back of the wedding gown. Joni found her purse. Her hands trembled as she reached for her phone and sent a quick text. She didn't know Pastor Montgomery all that well, but Joni's husband was best friends with his son. She couldn't even imagine how Brandon would feel if he found out that Derrick had died.

In less than ten minutes, Princess was out of her wedding dress and putting on the summer dress she'd worn to the church. Sarah and Joni had also changed into their street clothes. "Where's my purse?" Princess asked.

"I've got it," Sarah answered. "Let's go."

They headed for the door.

"Wait," Joni said, stopping midstride. "We all came together in the limo. How are we going to get to the hospital?"

A knock interrupted the conversation. Princess opened the door.

"You ready?" Rafael had changed from his tux to a pair of jeans. Greg stood next to him.

"Yes, but we don't know how we'll get there. Should we take the limo?"

"Of course." Rafael reached for her hand and led her down the hallway. "I've got you, baby. Come on."

10

Pray

Mama Max thanked the church member who'd given her a ride home, and then hurried up the sidewalk to her front door. She was still reeling from what had happened before her very eyes: a strong, fine, healthy looking man keeling over, appearing for all the world as if he was dead. "Lord have mercy," she said, fumbling in her oversized bag for the keys to her home. She found them, but in the rush to get the key in the lock, dropped the keys and then her purse. Contents spilled out everywhere. "Jesus!"

Next door, Henry was exiting his house and walking toward his Toyota Camry parked in the driveway. When he saw his neighbor in an apparent panic, he bypassed his automobile and crossed the yard. "Maxie, you okay?" He reached the porch, took the steps two at a time, and began helping Mama Max gather her things.

Maxie looked up as he kneeled down. "Oh . . . hi, Henry."

"Is everything all right?"

Having retrieved all of her items, Mama Max attempted to stand. Henry helped her up. "I've been better, to tell you the truth."

"You just came from the wedding, right?"

Mama Max nodded, placing her key inside the lock and giving it a quick turn. She walked into her home and threw her purse on the table.

Henry followed her inside. "Well, for what is generally thought of as a celebratory occasion, you sure don't seem too happy."

"Princess didn't get married, Henry." Mama Max continued into the living room and, after retrieving the cordless phone, took a seat on the couch. "Something happened to one of the pastors who was attending, a close family friend. He passed out right in the middle of the ceremony. They rushed him to the hospital in an ambulance."

"Oh, Lord, Maxie. I'm sorry to hear that."

"Me too." Mama Max began dialing a number, and then looked up at Henry. "I don't mean to be rude, neighbor, but I need to make some phone calls right now."

"Oh, sure, of course," Henry said, backing away before turning and heading to the door. "I sure am sorry to hear about your friend. Let me know of any way I can help."

"You can pray," Mama Max answered without hesitation.

Henry's pause was almost imperceptible before he responded, "All right."

The door had barely closed before Mama Max completed dialing the number. "Nettie," she said once her call had been answered. Located in Palestine, Texas, Nettie Thicke Johnson was a mighty prayer warrior and one of Mama Max's closest friends. "We need to circle the prayer wagons, sister. The devil is trying to steal one of our own."

The waiting room at Shawnee Mission Medical Center was filled with folk from the almost-wedding. King stood in one corner, along with his father, Obadiah; his assistant, Joseph; his son, Michael; Cy Taylor and Nate Thicke. Concerned friends surrounded Princess and Rafael in another corner, with Joni providing a play-by-play to her husband, Brandon, by cell. Mount Zion's prayer circle lined the chairs along one wall. They included the two oldest mothers of the church, Elsie Wanthers and Margie Stokes (or Sistah Alrighty and Sistah Almighty as they were referred to in the inner circle), along with a few deacons, trustees, and—truth be told—a couple lookie-loos who couldn't wait to telephone, telegraph, telegram, or tell-a-fellow-church-member the latest scoop. Down the hall, just a short distance from the waiting room, was a seldom used office. The doctor had graciously allowed Vivian to wait in there, with an anxious-yet-trying-to-be-calm Tai sitting right by her side.

"It's going to be all right, sis," Tai said, rubbing her hand across Vivian's tight neck and shoulders. "We know that with God, all things are possible. He never fails."

Vivian said nothing, just continued to rock back and forth, whispering a barely audible prayer in tongues.

"Was there any indication that something was wrong?" Tai queried, after a time. "Has he been sick, tired, complaining of headaches . . . anything?"

Vivian rocked a few more times before rising from her chair and pacing the office. "I've been asking myself that since he collapsed. I went over the last few weeks, months even, in my head. He's been so busy, Tai," she continued, reclaiming her seat next to Tai. "Back and forth to South Africa, revivals everywhere. And there's been so much stress with the expansion. . . . I guess it was just too much. I should have seen it," she declared, again rising and pacing. "I'm his wife! I should have sensed that something was wrong!"

Tai walked over to where Vivian leaned heavily against the wall. "Don't do this to yourself, Viv. Sometimes these things just happen. There's nothing you could have known, and nothing you could have done. The only thing we can do now is pray and have faith in God's healing powers. Do you believe?"

"I want to," Vivian whispered. "But he looked so pale, Tai. My cocoa brown baby had a gray sheen on his skin." Fresh tears cascaded down Vivian's face and although the room was quite warm, she shuddered against the power of her thoughts. "I kept talking to him, telling him, *begging* him to wake up. My God! If something happens to him, Tai, I don't know what I'll do."

★ ★ ★

Back inside the waiting room, Rafael sat next to Princess. Her head was on his shoulder as he mindlessly ran a soothing hand through her now tousled, errant curls. His mind was racing a mile a minute, a plethora of thoughts vying for space. He was still trying to process what had just happened. Why instead of eating grapes and sipping champagne in the junior suite of Kansas City's downtown Hotel Phillips, he was comforting his would-be wife in an anesthetic-feeling and smelling hospital waiting room. Why after waiting for what felt like half his life, the woman by his side *still* wasn't Mrs. Rafael Stevens. He felt bad for Pastor Montgomery, he really did. Hopefully the prolific and charismatic man of God would be just fine. *But dammit! This was my day! This was my moment with the woman I love!* Suddenly, Rafael eased Princess's head off his shoulders and stood.

"Where are you going?" Princess asked, noting the determined glint in Rafael's eyes.

"Not far, baby. I just need to take care of something." He paused, as if wanting to say something, and then changed his mind. "I'll be right back."

A little over twelve hundred miles away, just outside Phoenix, Arizona, Kelvin Petersen sat brooding in his ten-thousand-square-foot mansion. Like the question of where one was when JFK got shot, or the Twin Towers had fallen, or Michael Jackson had died, Kelvin was bookmarking where he was when the love of his life got married and his world collapsed—sitting in a darkened theater room, with a muted ESPN channel serving as the only light... trying to get as fucked up as necessary to take away the pain. He was normally a Bud man, but in the spirit of trying to break one habit today, he'd simply traded it for another and even now precariously poured himself another shot, spilling some of the two-hundred-dollar a bottle liquid on his calfskin sofa in this process. "Damn, man, you make a sloppy drunk," he said to the empty room. He picked up the remote and flipped to ESPN2. When his phone rang, he didn't answer it. Within seconds, his text message indicator beeped and then immediately his phone rang again.

"Damn, can't you see when a brothah don't want to be bothered?" No doubt it was one of his WIR—women in rotation. Truth be told, he was ready to dump the whole present lot of ten or so and start a new cycle. Sleep with a woman more than a couple times and she started looking for bills to be paid, floor tickets for the next game, or some Benjamins in her wallet. The real fools would even hint at babies, bling, rings, and things. But when it came to Suns star Kelvin Petersen, those babes obviously got things twisted. After finally getting his baby-who-was-not-his-baby's-mama out of his life, Kelvin swore he'd never get caught up again. *Unless it was Princess. If given the chance, I could have gotten caught up with her.*

Kelvin's phone rang again. This time he sighed, flung back what remained of the Johnnie Walker shot, and reached for his cell. Seeing that the call came from one of his best friends did nothing to lighten his mood.

"Whatever you're selling I ain't buying, a'ight?" he said without hostility but with a cadence that sounded like it was spoken in slow motion.

"Kelvin, man, are you all right?"

"In a few hours, I'll let you know. Other than that, Brandon, I'm just chillin' . . . wanting to be alone with my thoughts, so if you don't mind, I'm going to end this situation. I mean, conversation." Kelvin started laughing at his mistake-turned-joke.

"Kelvin, pull yourself together, man. I'm calling about your father. It's serious."

Brandon's words were like a pitcher of ice cubes dumped on Kelvin's face. His head momentarily cleared. He sat up. The room began to spin. He plopped back against the couch. "You're talking about Derrick, right?"

Brandon understood the question. He was one of the few in

Kelvin's circle who'd met both his stepfather, Hans Petersen, and his biological. "Yeah, man, Derrick Montgomery. Joni called me and said that in the middle of the wedding ceremony your dad passed out and was rushed to the hospital . . . by ambulance."

This revelation brought Kelvin to his feet. "Damn!" *Why'd I have to pour that last shot?* "What's wrong with him, Brandon?"

"They don't know. Joni and everybody are at the hospital now, waiting to speak with the doctor . . . hoping that he'll bring them good news."

"But he's going to be all right—right?"

"Joni said he hasn't come to yet, so they don't know."

"Which hospital is he in?" When Brandon told him, he said, "Okay, man, thanks for the info. Let me get off this phone and make some things happen."

"You're going there, right?"

"It's my father, dog. Of course I am."

"You want me to come with?"

Kelvin pondered the question as he walked from the theater room to his master suite. "Naw, just chill for right now. I'm going to call my boy and have him hook me up on a charter. Once I get there and see what's up, I'll give you a call."

"Okay, dog," Brandon said. "Keep your head up. Keep thinking the positive and everything will work out the way it should."

Kelvin barely responded before ending the call and dialing his agent. "Hey, man," he said as soon as the call was answered. "I need you to get me on a charter flight to Kansas City."

"When?"

"Five minutes ago. I'm going to have my driver drop me off at the airport."

"If you don't mind me asking, what's in Kansas City?"

"My father. He's in the hospital and no one knows what's going on or whether or not he'll make it. I've got to get there, man. As soon as possible."

11

What's Going On?

It had been more than two hours since Derrick had been wheeled beyond the DO NOT ENTER sign and Vivian's life had begun to hang in limbo. After her initial panic and near breakdown with Tai, she'd managed to pull herself together and now sat sipping a cup of chamomile tea, trying to remain calm. King had joined her and Tai in the office and Princess split her time between there and the waiting room. Many of the people who'd joined them initially had left, but King's assistant, Joseph, co-pastor Solomon Cole, the associate ministers, Reverend Doctor O, Cy and Hope Taylor, and a few from Mount Zion's prayer circle still remained.

One of the deacons walked over to where Obadiah sat, reading his Bible. "What do you say, Doc?" he asked, as he sat down beside him.

"God is able," Obadiah replied.

"Sure is taking them a long time to find anything."

"No news is good news, I reckon."

The deacon nodded. "I reckon so."

At this moment, "news" walked into the office where Vivian, King, and Tai were seated. "Hello," the short, deeply tanned man with kind eyes said as he entered. "I'm Dr. Bhatti."

Vivian was up on her feet in an instant, meeting the doctor at the door. "How is he, Doctor?"

Dr. Bhatti closed the door behind him and stepped farther into the room. "His vital signs have stabilized. This is encouraging."

"Where is he? I need to see my husband!"

King walked up and put a comforting arm around Vivian. "We're very anxious, Dr. Bhatti, as you can imagine."

The Indian doctor's brown eyes were full of compassion as he nodded. "I totally understand."

Vivian took a deep breath and tried to calm down . . . again. "Do you know what happened?"

The doctor took off his wire-rimmed glasses and slowly cleaned them with the hem of his white jacket. "That is what we're hoping the tests will prove. But we're only able to perform a limited amount at this time."

"Why's that?" Tai asked.

"Because Mr. Montgomery has not yet regained consciousness."

Vivian's heart sank and her eyes fluttered closed as she leaned against King for support.

"This is not in and of itself a bad sign," the doctor continued, his voice professional and devoid of emotion. "Often the body shuts itself down as a defense mechanism, thus preventing further damage from occurring. Once your husband has regained consciousness, we can perform another series of tests. At that time we'll determine whether he should remain here or whether you'd prefer he be transferred to a location that specializes in whatever diagnosis he's given."

"But I don't understand, Doctor. My husband seemed fine up until this happened."

The doctor reached into his breast pocket for a pen, and began writing on a chart that no one even noticed he carried. "So then, there were no complaints from him in say, the past three weeks or so? No mention of headaches, vomiting, difficulty breathing, or limited blood flow in his extremities?"

"Limited blood flow?"

"Has he complained of his arms or legs falling asleep, or of any tingling sensations?"

Vivian slowly shook her head. "No, nothing like that." Her brow creased in thought, however, because Derrick was from the old school and "took pain like a man." He probably wouldn't have told her if any of what the doctor asked had occurred. She hadn't noticed anything unusual but with their busy schedules and the limited time they'd spent together, that didn't necessarily rule anything out.

Dr. Bhatti jotted several things down on his pad. "What about his sleep patterns lately? Any fluctuations there, like sleeping more or less, or complaining of insomnia?"

"He's been getting little sleep but that's due in large part to a major expansion happening at our church. Plus, he's been in and out of the country frequently, spending a lot of time in South Africa." Vivian's eyes widened as a thought occurred. "Do you think this could have anything to do with his overseas travel, Doctor? He received the required inoculations, but could he have possibly contracted some type of disease while traveling?"

"At this point, we won't rule anything out," Dr. Bhatti answered. "But until we can conduct further tests, anything I say will be simple speculation."

King ran a weary hand over his face. "Can we see him?"

"Because of the precariousness of his situation, I want to limit the amount of extraneous stimulation he receives. It will be okay for him to receive one visitor at a time, but only for a few minutes or so." When Vivian would have protested, the doctor held up his hand. "At least for now. Let's continue to monitor him, and if his vitals remain stable over the next few hours, then we'll see about longer visits."

An inner strength arose in Vivian, her back straightening and chin lifting as a result. "I'd like to see my husband, Dr. Bhatti." The look in her eye told him she meant business, and she meant it right now.

"Very well," he nodded, opening the door. "Come with me."

While Vivian followed Dr. Bhatti down the hall, King and Tai walked into the other room to update those waiting. At least a dozen sets of eyes locked onto them as soon as they turned the corner.

King held up his hands, staving off the slew of questions he knew were heading his way. "We still don't know anything specific about why Pastor Montgomery passed out," he said, "but his vital signs have stabilized, which the doctor said was good news. They have to run more tests before anything more concrete can be established. Right now, the doctor said he just needs to rest. His wife is in with him now."

"Thank you, Jesus!" one of the members of the prayer circle exclaimed.

"Thank the Lord," a deacon added.

"What a mighty God we serve," said yet another member.

Obadiah closed his Bible and stood. "I think that we should go to his room and have prayer, set a hedge of protection around him and invoke the Spirit of the Lord."

"That's not possible, Daddy," King answered. "At least not right now."

"Why not?" Obadiah asked, with a touch of indignation.

King had purposely chosen not to disclose that Derrick had not regained consciousness. For the most part he trusted everyone in the room, but he was a big believer in the right hand not having all of the information that the left hand possessed. "Because even though his vitals have stabilized, the doctor wants him to remain in as calm and undisturbed an environment as possible, at least for the next twenty-four hours."

This answer seemed to satisfy Obadiah, and everyone else.

"So with that said, I think that y'all should keep him lifted up in prayer as you return to your homes. You all know that to me Pastor Montgomery is less like a friend and more like a brother. So I appreciate your concern for him, and your support of me."

"Will you be at church tomorrow?" one of the members asked.

King doubted it, but since he wasn't sure, he chose not to answer directly. "I'm not certain, but regardless of whether I am there or not, I'll make sure the church gets an update on Derrick's progress."

With that said, everyone from the church gave their hugs, said their good-byes, and began filing out of the waiting room. The only ones who remained behind were Joseph, Obadiah, Princess, Sarah, Joni, and Greg.

While King pulled Obadiah aside to speak with him privately, Princess turned to her friends. "Thank you, guys, so much for being here. It has made this incredibly easier for me to handle."

Joni gave Princess a hug. "We wouldn't be anywhere else, girlfriend."

Sarah looked around. "Where's Rafael?"

Princess had been so absorbed in worrying about and praying for her uncle that she'd not even been aware that her fiancé hadn't returned. "He left earlier, said that he had something to do."

"We'd better call him," Greg said. "Let him know that your uncle is resting and tell him where to meet us."

Joni turned to Princess. "Are we going back to the hotel? Or to your house?"

"I think you and Sarah should go back to the hotel," Princess answered. "Greg, I think you should find out where Rafael is and make sure he's okay. I think I'm going to stay here for a while, with Mama, Daddy, and Aunt Viv."

"Are you sure, Princess?" Joni looked at her friend with concern-filled eyes. "This has been a very trying day for all of us. And as early as you got up this morning, you must be exhausted."

"I couldn't sleep right now if I tried," Princess said. "I love you guys and appreciate your caring about me, but really, I'll be fine. Take the limo back to the hotel or if you want, have him drive you guys around Kansas City. You saw the Plaza, but maybe you'd like to check out our other tourist areas. Eighteenth and Vine is a historic jazz district and downtown has some nice spots, too. It's unfortunate what happened to Uncle Derrick, but I don't want that to stop you two from having fun."

Sarah looked at Princess with comprehending eyes. "Are you sure you don't want us to wait with you?"

"I'm positive. And if anything changes I have your cell numbers. So get on out of here," Princess admonished, wrapping her arms around her friends' shoulders and guiding them to the door. "And remember you're married," she said to Joni. "Don't do anything I wouldn't do!"

"How can anything like that happen when I'm partying with Mother Teresa?" Joni asked, with a nod in Sarah's direction.

"Ha! True that. Then go to a nice restaurant, enjoy some live music or something."

"Call us if you need us," Sarah demanded. "No matter what."

"I'll have Rafael call you, too," Greg said. He hugged Princess and left.

Princess watched her friends walk out of the building and then turned toward the office where she assumed her mother waited. When it came to her uncle's condition and what her father had told the group, she felt certain there were some pertinent details that he'd purposely omitted. She wasn't leaving until she had the answers she needed, and knew beyond a shadow of a doubt that her uncle would be okay.

12

Power of Love

Rafael reached for his phone as he left his parents' home. He'd returned their call as soon as he'd finished handling some business with one of his good friends who worked at City Hall. Cleavon Jackson was not only a mentor of sorts to the ambitious mayoral assistant, but he was also one of Rafael's staunchest supporters. Barely a week went by when he didn't ask when "Mr. Stevens" would become "Mayor Stevens." Next to his own father, when it came to people Rafael knew personally, Cleavon was the man he most admired. He'd been standing just outside the hospital talking to Cleavon on his cell phone when his mother had beeped in and demanded he come over. The visit hadn't gone as well as he'd liked, but he understood his parents' frustration. He couldn't really blame them. Knowing how she felt about her uncle, Rafael was trying to be patient with Princess. But he felt frustration as well.

"Yeah, man, what's up?" he said, as soon as he'd reached his Lexus and started the car.

"That's what I'm trying to find out from you," Greg replied. "Where you at?"

"Just left my parents."

"You don't sound too happy."

Rafael snapped. "Would you be happy if at the end of your wedding day you still weren't married?"

"My bad, man. I'm sorry about putting it to you like that. This shit is messed up, dog, for real."

Rafael sighed. "Tell me about it. But if all goes well, I'll be a married man by this time tomorrow."

"Word? You talk to the pastor?"

"No, my man Cleavon is going to hook us up." Along with being Rafael's mentor and staunch supporter, Cleavon Jackson was also a justice of the peace.

"I'm happy for you, dog. I know how long you've been waiting for this to happen." Greg had not only known Rafael a long time, he was more than a little familiar with the Stevens household and their family dynamics. "So are your parents going to be there for the final 'I do'?"

"Man, my parents aren't feeling any love for Princess or her family right about now."

"For real?"

"Mom can't understand why Pastor Brook couldn't take ten minutes and finish our ceremony, and they are upset that their calls to both his and Miss Tai's cell phones have gone unanswered."

Incredulity was more than evident in Greg's voice. "Your wedding was interrupted slash basically cancelled, and the bride's parents have not talked to the groom's?"

"Exactly."

"Damn." Greg held the word for at least three seconds.

"Dad knows Pastor Montgomery and understands how upset King is that his best friend is lying in a hospital, and for all we know clinging to life." Mr. Stevens, a certified public accountant with a subdued personality, was usually the voice of reason and peace in Rafael's household. "Mom, on the other hand, says there is no excuse for how the Brooks are behaving. She feels how they've acted is disrespectful and rude. My parents spent a grip for our honeymoon. If we're not on that plane tomorrow at noon, I think Mom is going to go gangster and whup some serious butt."

"Ha! As bougie as your mom is, dude, I can actually see that happening."

"Mom hasn't always been a deacon's wife," Rafael said, with one of the few smiles he'd managed since Princess left him at the altar and ran to her uncle's side. "She took no prisoners when she lived in the Lou." Rafael heard a beep and looked at his caller ID. "Let me bounce, man. This is Princess." He switched over. "Baby, perfect timing. I'm on my way back now."

"Oh, okay."

Rafael would have preferred a response such as "thank God," "can't wait," or "that's great, baby, I need you," but . . . okay. "How is your uncle?" He asked this question strictly out of obligation.

Princess told him what the doctor had said. "We won't really be able to know anything until he's conscious," she finished. "Until then . . . we'll just keep praying."

"But you did say he is stabilized, right? He's out of the woods for right now?"

"The doctor is cautiously optimistic."

"But . . . for right now . . . he's okay."

Princess's answer was low and soft. "Yes, I guess."

"Good," Rafael said with authority. "I'm coming to get you and then we're going to our hotel."

"Rafael—"

"No, Princess. That was a statement, not a question." He took a deep breath and softened his tone. "Baby, I understand that you're conflicted, that part of your heart is there with your uncle, and your family. I know that Derrick Montgomery is your father's best friend. But, Princess . . . we were ten minutes away from getting *married* today. If what happened hadn't happened, you'd be my wife right now. We'd be beginning our life together. Right now. You and me. And we still can. . . ."

"I hear you, Rafael. I really do. But—"

"But what?"

Princess paused before answering. "But we didn't get married. And I'm not your wife."

An even longer pause before Rafael responded. "So what are you saying? That you don't want to marry me?"

"Of course not!"

"Really, Princess? Because I can't tell."

"So much has happened today, baby. . . ."

"All the more reason I come get you, we go to the room, chill, have some dinner . . . and then I have some news for you."

"Really? What?"

"Good things come to those who wait, my love. And it's good news, I promise. I'm just about fifteen minutes away, so you won't have to wait long. Oh, and can you ask your mom to please call my mother? She's about to blow a gasket for real!"

"Oh my God, Rafael. I'm so sorry. Your parents are probably furious with me."

That's an understatement. "No one could control what happened today. They just need to hear from someone, that's all."

"Okay, I'll call her. And, Rafael?"

"Yes."

"I love you."

Rafael's smile could have lit up the sky.

13

Working My Way Back to You

Kelvin sat in the back of the Town Car that was speeding down I-35 on the way to the hospital. He stared straight ahead, barely aware of the scenery around him. A myriad of thoughts and emotions fought for dominance inside his head. Hands down, the one that won was of Princess. Married. Out of reach. The irony wasn't lost on him that on this, his first trip to where the love of his life had grown up, he wouldn't get a chance to see her. He looked at his watch. Seven o'clock. *She's with him right now,* he thought, his heart dropping with each passing mile. He tried to shut down his mind against the images that assailed him. The wedding night was one of the most romantic ever experienced. He imagined Jacuzzis and rose petals, bubbles and champagne. Princess naked, her smooth flawless skin being touched by—*Damn, man! Give it a rest! You were such a fool. Here you are the rich, talented pro baller with women falling at your feet. But the one you wanted the most . . . has just married another man.* He sighed heavily, reached for the bottle of water beside him, and swallowed half its contents. He'd had his driver stop at one of his favorite restaurants, and had eaten a large burger and fries before boarding the plane. That had helped to soak up the alcohol. Then he'd slept the entire two and a half hours from Phoenix to Kansas City. So even though he'd become great friends with Johnnie Walker earlier in the day, he'd landed at Kansas City International Airport feeling sober and relatively refreshed.

"We're here, Mr. Petersen."

Kelvin looked up and realized they'd pulled into the Shawnee Mission Medical Center. "All right, then, man. I'm not sure how long I'll be so . . ."

"No worries, Mr. Petersen. I'll be right here. And you have my number, so if there is anything else that you need, please don't hesitate to let me know."

"You know how to pray?" Kelvin asked.

The driver smiled. "Yes, sir."

"Well . . . do that."

"I feel bad," Tai said to Princess, having just checked her phone and confirmed the missed calls from Rafael's mother. "She has every right to be furious."

King was less understanding. "I don't give a damn about their hurt feelings. My boy is in there fighting for his life and I am not going to apologize for being by his side. I'll make sure and give Ralph a call in the morning, but it's probably best that I don't talk to them tonight."

"I'll call them," Tai said quickly. "And, baby, don't worry at all about leaving with Rafael. By his side is exactly where you should be."

"Thanks for everything," Princess said, hugging her mom. "I should go out to the waiting room so that Rafael doesn't have to look for me." She hugged her father. "Give Aunt Viv a hug for me and tell her I'm praying."

"Will do, baby," King said, hugging her back. "Please tell Rafael how sorry I am. It's possible that I can finish your ceremony sometime tomorrow so . . . let him know that everything is going to be all right."

"I will, Daddy." Princess walked to the door. "Call me if there's any change."

"We will, baby," Tai said, with a little wave. "Go with Rafael and get some rest."

Princess carefully shut the door behind her, took a deep breath, and walked down the hallway toward the waiting room. She turned the corner, and the first person she saw was . . . Kelvin Petersen.

He was standing at the front desk and, before she could gather her thoughts or get her composure, he turned and looked at her. His eyes reflected several different emotions in an instant: surprise, disbelief, confusion . . . and a deeper, more intense one that caused a shiver that shook Princess to the core of her being.

She could barely reflect on that, however, because of the deep swell of emotions going through her body: surprise, disbelief, confusion . . . and a deeper, more intense one that caused a twitch or two in one of Kelvin's lower extremities.

"Princess?" He took several steps until he was standing directly in front of her.

"Kelvin," Princess said, shocked that with all that had happened she hadn't once considered that he would race to his father's side. "Of course you'd come."

Kelvin's eyes narrowed as he drank her in. "Of course."

Princess swallowed, her entire body warming with a feeling that she could neither define nor deny. Tears came to her eyes and suddenly everything felt perfectly right and totally wrong.

"Baby, don't cry." Acting on pure instinct, Kelvin took one more step and enveloped Princess in his arms. He noticed several things at once: the softness of her body, the feel of her hair, the scent wafting from her neck and temples . . . and how right she felt in his arms.

Princess knew that she should pull away but for the life of her, she could not move. Of their own volition, her arms wrapped themselves around Kelvin's hard, lean body. Her hand swept across the broad expanse of his back as she nestled her head into the middle of his chest.

"Baby..." Kelvin wrapped his arms more tightly around her. "I didn't think I'd see you. But I'm so glad you're here."

The two UCLA graduates, ex-roommates, and ex-lovers stood stock still, caught up in the moment of the embrace. The entire world had melted away. Each was only aware of each other. Which is why when Rafael entered the lobby, talking on his phone to Cleavon, who was calling with last minute details of tomorrow's ceremony, the nurse was the only one who noticed him stop in midstride, hang up his phone without ending the conversation, and stand in livid disbelief as he took in the scene before him.

After several seconds that seemed like hours, he slowly yet resolutely made his way to where Princess and Kelvin stood embraced, oblivious of the storm that swirled around them. "Baller," Rafael began, his voice deceptively low and calm, "if you want to keep shooting three-pointers with those arms, you'd better take them out from around my wife."

14

I Will Always Love You

Princess's reaction was immediate. "Rafael," she said, quickly stepping away from Kelvin. "I was waiting on you."

Rafael's eyes stayed on Kelvin as he answered. "I'm here. Let's go."

He reached out his hand to Princess. She took it and stepped forward. Kelvin placed his hand on Princess's arm, stopping her in her tracks. "Princess, can I talk to you for a quick minute?"

Rafael immediately pulled Princess out of Kelvin's grasp. "Man, didn't you hear what I told you?"

"Rafael, please. Let's just go."

Rafael looked hard and long at Kelvin before turning with Princess in tow and heading for the door.

As he watched her walk away, something snapped in Kelvin. Suddenly, he wasn't the strong, successful professional basketball player with a multimillion-dollar contract, fancy homes, cars, and more women than he could count. He was that ten-year-old boy living in Germany, trying to fit in with a bunch of blond-haired, blue-eyed classmates who didn't look like him. He was that boy who liked Martina, the brunette neighbor who often looked as lost as he did, and whom he wouldn't approach because he was afraid of rejection. *But why am I afraid of it now? It's too late for any of this. She's already married.* Yet, in spite of himself, he called her name. "Princess!"

"Don't turn around," Rafael encouraged, tightening his grip on Princess's hand.

And even though her head told her that Rafael was her future, there was no way her heart would allow her to walk away from her past. Not now, not like this. "Wait, Rafael," she said, even though they'd reached the door and Rafael was holding it open for her to pass through. "I need to talk to him." Rafael opened his mouth to protest but before he could do so, Princess hurried on. "Just for a minute, baby, no longer, I promise." Rafael's body was as stiff as a board. He couldn't even look at Princess. "He and I were close once, Rafael. It's his father lying back there, and we don't know whether he will live or die. I know you won't believe this, but I saw Kelvin mere seconds before you came in. We were hugging because we'd just seen each other."

Rafael cut a glance at Princess. "Does it matter what I think, Princess? Will you walk away from him right now, come with me without looking back if I ask?"

"Just one minute," Princess pleaded, ignoring Rafael's question because really . . . what could she say? "Wait right here. Don't leave me. I'm just going to tell him what I know about Uncle Derrick. And then we can go."

Watching Princess walk over to where Kelvin stood waiting, Rafael's wide-legged stance showed determination; his crossed arms evidence of his displeasure. *Keep your cool, dog,* he told himself. *She's leaving with you.*

Princess stopped about two feet away from Kelvin. "I'm sorry about your father, Kelvin, but I think he's going to be okay."

"What happened?"

Princess shrugged. "We still don't know. We were in the middle of our ceremony and he just collapsed."

Kelvin's eyes were drawn to Princess's hands, which were nervously clasped to her chest. One thing stood out immediately. Engagement ring—check. Wedding band—MIA. His heartbeat increased as Princess's words sank in and an unthinkable scenario seeped into his head. "This happened before you and Rafael got married?"

Princess looked into Kelvin's eyes and read into his soul. "Your father is still in intensive care. Aunt Viv is in there with him." She pointed Kelvin in the right direction.

Rafael looked at his watch. "Princess."

Princess looked over her shoulder. "Okay." She turned back to Kelvin. "I've got to go."

"Don't do it, baby."

She knew what he was talking about, but asked anyway. "Do what?"

"Marry him. Don't throw away something that comes only once in a lifetime. I still love you, Princess. I never stopped. I always will."

Princess dropped her head and turned away. She walked to Rafael, who quickly put his arm around her and ushered her out the door. He looked back at Kelvin, a don't-eff-with-this message written all over his face. But Kelvin didn't read the memo. His eyes were on Princess, his thoughts on the fact that she was walking out the door and taking a part of his heart with her—and that she did so without looking back.

15

It Ain't Over Till It's Over

Kelvin was beside himself. He hadn't felt this helpless since he was thirteen years old. At the time he entered his teen years he'd been a shy, unsure, and out-of-place student at one of Germany's elite private schools—one of the few people of color who walked the large, picturesque campus. Then, in a matter of months, he grew several inches and his thin, lanky frame filled out to one of muscle-chiseled perfection. And something else happened. His uncle sent him a basketball, signed by Kobe Bryant and Shaquille O'Neal. Having always been a baller fan, he found out that he was also gifted at hoops. Instantly, he had a focus, a dream, and fans. His new physique and impressive b-ball skills took him from being a student on the fringe to the big man on campus. Girls wanted to be *with* him and boys wanted to *be* him. A heady time for a boy who'd spent a lot of his early years alone.

He vividly remembered the moment that he looked in a mirror and wondered just who it was staring back at him. It certainly wasn't his stepfather, a serious yet compassionate German with salt and pepper hair and ruddy fair skin. And the more time passed, it really wasn't his mother either, an attractive woman with toffee-brown skin, a round face, and average height. When he first asked about his biological father, Janeé Petersen was evasive. When he was sixteen years old, however, he traveled to California to spend the summer with his Uncle Geoff, the one who'd recognized his athletic potential early on. That summer not only did Kelvin find his scholastic niche, but he also met his father.

Kelvin's phone rang and he snatched if off the marble table in the elegantly appointed Ritz-Carlton room where he sat. "Yo, dog. Took you long enough."

"Slow your anger roll, KP. I was at the gym. Just got your message." Kelvin could hear his best friend, Brandon, gulping water from a bottle. "How's your dad?"

Kelvin relayed what he knew and then added, "I saw Princess."

"For real?"

"Yeah, she was at the hospital."

"On her wedding day? I mean, I know your dad is like her uncle and everything, but that's crazy!"

"You haven't even heard crazy yet."

"Talk to me."

"She's not married yet."

"Stop bullshittin'."

"Real talk."

"What do you mean she's not married?"

"Dad passed out in the middle of their ceremony. You can about imagine the chaos, especially from Princess's father, King, who views Dad like a brother. Folk followed the ambulance from the church to the hospital. Miss Tai said that King never left Dad's side. He's probably still at the hospital right now."

A low whistle came over the line. "Did y'all get a chance to talk?"

"Not much. When I saw her, man, it was like . . . I can't even explain it, but this feeling came over me like I've never felt before. I was sad and happy at the same time. We were like magnets, in each other's arms as soon as we saw each other. Then Rafael had to walk in and break up the moment."

"Oh, shit! That couldn't have gone well."

"If it had gone the way it should have, I wouldn't be on the phone with you right now. I'd be with her." Silence, and then, "I need to see her, man."

"Kelvin..."

"It's still there. I could feel it. I could see it in her eyes. If I could just talk to her for a few minutes, get her to see reason, she wouldn't marry that clown!"

"Man, I think it's a little late for that. For all you know, she could be married by now."

"Didn't you hear me? King is still with my dad."

"He's not the only preacher in Kansas. They may have found someone else and tied the knot." Brandon sighed. "I know you don't want to hear this, dog, but maybe it's time to concede that it's over... and Rafael won."

"What? Are you crazy? I will never concede that shit, man, never!"

"You know I'm feeling you, KP. I was there when you and Princess jumped off. I was there last year, when you took your son to LA and had Princess pray for him, and you told me all about when she spent that weekend with you and then left because of all the females blowing up your phone. There are hundreds, maybe even thousands of women throwing themselves at you, dude," Brandon concluded. "There's probably somebody out there who will make you forget all about homegirl."

"Hey, man, I need you to call Joni," Kelvin said, as if he hadn't heard a word Brandon had spoken. "Get her on three-way. I need her to tell me where Princess is at."

"No."

"What?"

"You heard me. I love you like a brother, but I'm not putting my wife in the middle of this again. It took Princess a long time to get over Joni's indirect involvement in helping you contact her the last time. If she helps interrupt what could be her wedding night... that would probably be the end of their friendship." The silence spoke loudly before Brandon continued, his voice soft and full of compassion. "Let it go, Kelvin. Let her go. I know you're used to getting what you want in life, but when it comes to this situation, you need to face facts. It's over."

"It's not over until it's over," Kelvin replied, his voice calm, resolute. "And it's not over until I say it is."

A different kind of pleading was happening on the other side of town. Rafael stood behind Princess, massaging her tight shoulders. "I've waited a year, Princess. I think I've been more than patient. All I'm asking is for us to take a shower together, and then let us go to sleep with you wrapped in my arms."

Princess dropped her head as Rafael's strong fingers moved from her shoulders to the nape of her neck. "That's what you say now, but I think once we're butt naked in the shower you'll be asking for a little bit more."

Something in Rafael snapped. He ended the massage abruptly and came from behind the chair to confront Princess face to face. "Would that be asking too much? We had about five minutes of the ceremony left, Princess. Five minutes! And then we would have been husband and wife. What's left is a mere formality and I've already told you that by noon tomorrow, even that will be taken care of."

Princess was in turmoil. How could she counter what Rafael said? It made perfect sense. True, at this time in her life she was the poster child for virtuousness and had vowed to be married the next time she made love. But she felt that even Jesus would admit that these were some pretty extraneous circumstances. How could she deny this man who'd been so patient with her? And then, an even more disturbing thought. How could she deny the feelings for the man who'd caused fireworks in her body with one simple glance?

"I know this isn't how we imagined tonight," she finally said, reaching out to grab the hand of the patient, understanding, worthy man whose pleading eyes now bore into hers. "I've been antic-ipating it as much as you. I can't imagine many men who would have honored me the way that you have. But if we give in to our passion tonight, before our marriage becomes official, then the last twelve months would have been in vain." Princess stood, placed her arms around Rafael's neck. "Just a few more hours," she mur-mured, kissing him on the cheek. "And then . . . I'm all yours."

16

Forget You

Everyone survived the night. Derrick had still not awakened, but his vitals remained stable and his heartbeat was strong. After trying without success to talk Vivian into coming with them, King and Tai had left the hospital shortly after one in the morning. Vivian had refused to leave her husband's side, but had accepted the hospital's offer to have a small cot wheeled into Derrick's room. After talking with Brandon and making a few more calls, Kelvin had gone down to the bar in his hotel. He'd drunk Johnnie Walker Blue over ice, entertained the small crowd gathered at that late hour, signed a few autographs, and finally, around three in the morning, was sufficiently inebriated to get some sleep. Rafael had wished for alcohol, but when it came to his partaking in peaceful slumber, he'd chosen prayer instead. Princess had suggested that they could spend the night cuddling, but knowing the permanent hard-on that would cause, Rafael had opted for the pull-out sofa in the suite's living room. The last time he looked at the clock it was 4:45.

Princess's night had been harrowing at best. Sleep was elusive. Dreams were not. In one of them, she and Kelvin were back on the campus of UCLA, walking from one of the buildings to his car. They were holding hands and kissing, in between waving at people they knew. Suddenly, this woman named Fawn, a real-life nemesis who for three years convinced Kelvin that he was the father of her son until a DNA test proved otherwise, roared up in a candy red convertible.

"Get in!" she'd said, as Kelvin and Princess neared her vehicle.

"Forget you, girl," Kelvin huffed, reaching for Princess's hand and turning them to walk behind the car.

"You can never forget me!" Fawn screamed, holding up a newborn baby girl. "You won't be able to deny this one! I gave him the daughter you aborted, bitch!"

Princess had sat straight up out of that nightmare, her heart beating faster than it had at the church. She'd shaken her head to try and clear the cobwebs of that horrible subconscious state. She realized that the content of this dream was the result of the subconscious guilt she continued to carry, remorse about the pregnancy she'd terminated even though she felt forgiven. "It was a boy," she'd whispered into the darkness, although the dream caused her to speculate that she and Kelvin's child could have indeed been a girl. That's when the tears had come, and she'd tiptoed into the bathroom and turned on the water so that Rafael couldn't hear her cry.

"Baby, are you awake?" Rafael sauntered to the doorway of the bedroom and now leaned against the doorjamb, looking fondly at the lump in the bed that was his soon-to-be wife.

Princess nestled deeper into the covers. "Barely. What time is it?"

"Time for us to get up and get moving. Cleavon is expecting us at the courthouse at eleven and our flight leaves at three, so we can't be late." He walked into the room and sat on the bed. "Did you sleep okay?"

"It took me a while to fall asleep, but once I did, it was okay. I probably got around five hours of sleep."

Rafael smiled. He felt good knowing that Princess's night had been similar to his, physically wanting something that was so close, yet so far away. "Well, you get around ten minutes more sleep while I take a shower. Or better yet, why don't you order us some room service so we can have a quick bite before we leave?"

"Okay." Princess threw back the covers and sat up on the side of the bed. Because he was behind her, she didn't see the raw desire that blazed in Rafael's eyes as he looked at the satin-clad woman who made his blood boil and his bone hard. "But let me use the bathroom real quick."

The ride to the courthouse was a quiet one, as had been the breakfast that they'd shared in the room. Rafael had been amorous, barely able to keep his hands off Princess, wanting to continually bury his tongue deep inside her mouth. Princess had complied a time or two, but the more he pressed for physical affection, the tighter the knot in her stomach had become. She'd already resigned herself to the fact that there was nothing she could do. Rafael had been more than patient; she had to see this through. The proverbial horse was well out of the barn and there was no bringing it back. *If you have any reservations, Princess, any doubts at all about your being able to stay in this marriage for the long term . . . then you'd be doing Rafael a disservice by saying "I do."* For the past twenty-four hours, the words of the conversations with her mother had been on a continuous loop inside her head. In her alone time, she could see the sensibility of what her mother had spoken. But now, in this moment, she felt that to not go through with these plans to become Mrs. Stevens would be the worse disservice to Rafael. *That's it. I've got to do it.* Princess reached over and grabbed Rafael's hand. He glanced over, gave her hand a gentle squeeze. In just a few short moments, she'd take his last name.

Because today was Sunday, parking downtown was easy. Rafael found a spot near the entrance to City Hall, then walked around to the passenger side to open the door for Princess. As beautiful as she'd looked yesterday, he almost preferred the understated elegance of what she wore today: a floral dress made of material silky soft to the touch, and sandals that added three inches to her height. Today, she wore her hair down, the way he liked it. Her jewelry was understated, makeup minimal. He felt his attire equally casual: tan slacks, a striped button-down shirt, and loafers. He planned to change into jeans for their flight to Montego Bay.

"You ready?" he asked Princess, as he pointed his key chain toward the car and locked it.

"Yes," she answered, not daring to look Rafael in the eye, lest he see her true feelings. "Oh, wait. I forgot my phone. Unlock the door, baby."

"Leave it in there. We won't be long."

"You know I've been waiting on word about Uncle Derrick. Just let me get it, okay?"

Rafael acquiesced and unlocked the door. Princess had just retrieved the phone when it rang in her hand. She gave Rafael a look. "Told you." Linking her arm through his, she answered the phone. "Hello?"

"Princess, it's your mom. I've got good news."

Princess stopped. "What is it?"

"Derrick woke up."

"Praise God!" She told Rafael what her mom said.

"Yes, we are thankful and the doctors are cautiously optimistic."

"Why cautiously?"

"Because, baby, he's awake and seems to be lucid enough but the doctors have still not been able to pinpoint what happened. They're running additional tests, but Viv wants him transferred to Cedars-Sinai. They'll likely be moving him in the next few hours."

"I want to see him."

"The doctor is allowing only a few minutes per visit, but he's letting all of us go in. Your father is with him now." Tai's conversation was interrupted by the drone of a low-flying plane. "What's that sound? Where are you?"

"At the courthouse. A friend of Rafael's, who is also a justice of the peace, is going to complete our ceremony."

"Oh, baby, that's wonderful! Your father and I are so sorry about what happened yesterday. If it had been anyone other than Derrick—"

"It's okay, Mama." The droning sound got louder. "Geez, where is that plane?" As if to answer her specific question, the noisy biplane came into view. "Look, Mom, I'll call you later. Rafael and I will stop by real quick on our way to the airport." Princess hung up the phone and looked up, shading her eyes against the bright sun. "Can you see what the banner says?" she asked Rafael.

"I couldn't care less," Rafael said, reaching for Princess's arm and pulling her toward the concrete steps. "If we're going to stop by and see your uncle, we need to do this."

"Wait!" Princess said, having caught part of the message on the widely circling plane. "Is that my name?" She linked her arm with Rafael's, sure that this was his doing.

It was not. He looked up with as much curiosity as Princess. Ironically, they ended up reading the message at practically the exact same time:

PRINCESS, IT'S YOU AND ME FOREVER, BABY. LOVE, KP

For a moment, both Rafael and Princess were stunned into immobility. Rafael recovered first. "Come on." Again, he reached for Princess and headed toward the steps.

But Princess couldn't move, only stare.

"Baby, come on!"

Baby, I'm so glad you're here.

"Rafael, wait."

Don't do it, Princess.

Rafael snapped. "Don't you think I've waited long enough?"

The tears came of their own accord. Princess didn't try and wipe them away.

"That asshole is doing this on purpose! It's just a game to him,

Princess, and your boy wants to win. He's trying to mess with your head long enough to get you back and then watch. He'll go back to doing the same things that made you leave him all those other times!"

Are you questioning whether or not you're in love with Rafael?

"I don't know what to say except this doesn't feel right." The biplane, which had been making large, lazy circles around all of downtown, now headed south, toward the suburbs. Princess read the banner one last time before it flew away. She felt her heart breaking as tears fell in earnest. "I'm sorry, Rafael."

Rafael sighed as if he'd been punched. "About what, Princess?"

"I can't do this."

Rafael crossed his arms and glared at her. "Do what?"

"Marry you." Princess dropped her head. "Not right now. Not like this. I'm so sorry."

A string of expletives flew out of Rafael's mouth. "I'm sick of this shit, Princess!" he finished, exasperation evident in between every word.

Princess turned and began walking away.

"If you leave now, it's over!" Rafael yelled. "I mean it, Princess. If we don't do this now . . . I'm done."

Princess stopped and turned around. "The last thing I want to do is hurt you, Rafael. But this just doesn't feel right."

"Yeah, whatever. I see how you treat the man you supposedly love." Princess bowed her head. "I'm going to go in here and talk with Cleavon. Maybe it would be best if you call a taxi."

"I do love you. It's just that—"

"Save the swan song. I've heard enough." Rafael stared at Princess a long moment, a myriad of thoughts furiously swirling inside his head. Then, with one final sweeping head-to-toe perusal of his almost-but-not-quite wife, he turned and walked toward the building's entrance.

Through a curtain of tears, Princess watched Rafael walk up

the steps and out of her life. More of her mother's words wafted across her mind. *He absolutely adores you. I believe that he will do everything in his power to give you a great life.*

A wave of panic rolled over her. *Father God, please help me! What have I done?*

17

Time To Make A Change

Mama Max was all smiles as she pulled her CTS into one of Mount Zion's reserved parking spots. James Cleveland blasted "Give Me My Flowers" from her stereo. She turned off the engine, waving and greeting people as she opened the door. "How do, sister. Good morning! Praise the Lord!" She nodded and greeted and hugged her way down to the third seat, right side, first row—the spot she'd occupied for three decades at least. Her guest sat down beside her.

Shortly thereafter, the usher led another member to the seat next to Mama Max. "Morning, Elsie," Mama Max said, with a wink and a pat.

"Morning, Mama Max. How you doing this morning?"

"Tolerable well. Elsie, this here is Henry Logan, my neighbor Beatrice Logan's son. He came back to help take care of her following the stroke."

Elsie leaned over and shook Henry's hand. "Lord have mercy, and looking just like her. I'd plum forgot she had a child. How is your mama, Henry?"

"Some days are better than others, but overall she's doing well."

"Tell her that Elsie Wanthers said hello and that I'm praying for her."

"Will do, ma'am."

"How's Pastor Montgomery?" Elsie asked Maxine.

"Last call I got, he's doing okay. They're still performing tests, but God is able."

"A doctor in the sickroom and a lawyer in the courtroom."

"Hallelujah!"

"What about your granddaughter? Poor child has got to be beside herself. On the day that was supposed to be the best of her life, she had the worst thing happen . . . her uncle pass out like that. We were all so worried! He could have died!"

"Well, thank the good Lord he is yet among us." Mama Max nodded as Elsie's best friend, Margie Stokes, took her place beside Elsie. "How do."

"Duty bound, praise the Lord," Margie replied. After Maxine had introduced her to Henry, Margie continued. "How's your grandbaby?"

"Worried about her uncle, but all things considered, she's doing all right."

"She's probably married and on her honeymoon by now," Elsie said.

Margie's face scrunched into a frown. "How you figure?"

"Everything was over but the shouting. . . . King could have finished that ceremony in the parking lot."

"I don't think that happened," Mama Max said, a chuckle accompanying her twinkling eyes. "But I know how determined that young man looked. I don't think he has it in him to wait too long."

"Speaking of waiting," Elsie said, her voice dropping as she shifted the conversation, "how are you doing, Maxine? With Obadiah mentoring that young man in Texas and all? Ain't it been almost a year since you left him down there all by his lonesome? Lord knows I would never have left my man like that."

Mama Max bit her tongue so hard she almost drew blood. It was either that or say what she was thinking: that Elsie hadn't had a man in so long that she wouldn't have a clue on what to do with one.

"Although I understand your having to come back here and look after the house and affairs and all. And I can sure understand you missing the grandkids. Still, you've got to be missing that man around the house, having been with him all these years."

Mama Max nodded, plastering on a smile as fake as a cat's bark or a dog's meow. So far, the "official" story had held: that a homesick Mama Max had voluntarily returned to Kansas and given her blessing on Obadiah remaining in Texas to help with the transition at Gospel Truth Church. Located in the small town of Palestine, Texas, Gospel Truth was the church for which Obadiah had come out of retirement and tried to bring this once heralded ministry back from a scandal involving their pastor, Nathaniel Thicke. But Mama Max wasn't stupid. Elsie might be flirting with what she called Old Timer's (and the rest of the world called Alzheimer's) but Maxine Brook was still very much clothed and in her right mind. She saw straight through Elsie's "concern" and inwardly called it what it was—a great big case of nosy-itis—a disease that had plagued her good friend since last year. That's when she'd invited both Elsie and Margie down to Texas for Thanksgiving dinner. The women were lonely and getting up in age so it had seemed like a good idea. At the time she hadn't known that Palestine's other colored preacher, eighty-plus-year-old Reverend Jenkins, would choose this particular Sunday of their visit to conduct a "do drop in" while proudly squiring his new bride on his feeble left arm. Said wife, Dorothea Noble Bates Jenkins, had been Mama Max's nemesis for more than forty years. Knowing that Dorothea had little respect for wedding rings or marriage vows, Mama Max had always believed her moving to Palestine and tying the knot shortly after Obadiah had relocated to head up Gospel Truth in Palestine was a little too convenient. She'd thought correctly. Dorothea and Obadiah revived their decades old affair, one that few in the Christian community knew about—except Elsie

Wanthers. Octogenarian Wanthers had been there in the beginning when a young Maxine Brook, juggling the roles of preacher's wife and motherhood, had first learned of Dorothea Bates. That fateful Sunday, Old Timer's had abated just enough for Elsie to remember where she'd seen the uninvited visitor's face before. A ruckus ensued and Elsie had been digging for information ever since. *Hmph, keep on trying there, Miss Alrighty.* There was no way she would allow for these messy mamas getting all up in her business. Elsie was trying to fish without a pond or a pole. Mama Max had no plans to take the bait.

She looked past Elsie and spoke to Miss Almighty. "Margie, girl, your face is the perfect shape to wear a hat like that. It looks really nice, and that gray color complements your skin." In actuality the color made her skin look ashen, but Mama Max knew that giving Margie a compliment and not throwing one in Elsie's direction would be enough to get Miss Alrighty out of her business and back into her own.

"Thank you, Mama Max," Margie said, with a smile. "I right like that hat you're wearing, too."

"My niece sent mine from a fancy shop in Dee-troit," Elsie offered, moving her head in a way that caused the foot-long feather to bob and weave like a fencer's sword.

"It looks nice," Mama Max offered, thinking that it looked even better when Elsie's mouth was shut.

Small talk continued until devotion began. After the reading of scriptures, prayers, and church news from the bulletin, it was time for the worship service. This was Mama Max's favorite part; she loved singing praises unto her God. Following worship service was the lifting of offering and giving of tithes, another part of the service she enjoyed. "If God can give me a hundred percent, then I sho'nuff can give Him ten." She was filling out her offering envelope when a rumbling began in her stomach. *Uh-oh.* Mama Max closed her eyes and pressed her hand against her midsection. For her an upset stomach was not only uncomfortable, but was also usually an indicator of something out of order. *What is it, Lord?*

Her answer came by way of Elsie nudging Margie in the side and exclaiming in a whisper loud enough to wake the dead, "Well, praise the Lord if it isn't the good old Reverend Doctor!" She turned to Mama Max and continued, "Why didn't you tell us that we'd be getting a treat today? Course, with what happened to Pastor Derrick and all, I'm sure King has his hands full. Having your husband in the pulpit is a sight for these feeble eyes, yes sirree. Hallelujah!"

Margie joined in with similar comments. Both women babbled on, so caught up in the surprise of today's "treat" that they didn't notice Mama Max's nonparticipation, or how after completing the information on her offering envelope, she kept her head bowed and opened her Bible. Turning to Psalms 30 served two purposes: it helped keep Mama Max's mind on the Master instead of murder, and it kept her from taking her oversized, giant print, King James Bible and beating today's "treat" upside the head!

As soon as the ushers had collected the offering, a spattering of clapping began. Mama Max looked up. *I should have known.* There her husband stood, looking quite refined and dignified, and reaching for the microphone that the praise leader offered. She'd always loved a chocolate man in a dark brown suit and even at almost seventy-five years of age his broad shoulders and upright carriage did a suit quite proud. People often said that if Obadiah dyed his salt and pepper hair, he'd look ten to fifteen years younger. In this moment, Mama Max agreed. Yesterday, with the flurry of wedding activity going on, it was easy to ignore Obadiah. But not now, not as he stood there looking good and sounding nice—with his rich, pitch-perfect baritone floating across the masses.

" 'Father, I stretch my hand to Thee,' " Obadiah began, acknowledging the applause with a nod of his head. Congregants immediately joined in with this age-old hymn's call and response model. " 'No other help I know . . .' "

Mama Max bowed her head and began to read the scriptures before her. *"I will extol Thee, O Lord; for Thou hast lifted me up, and hast not made my foes to rejoice over me."* Emotions were now roiling along with her stomach: anger, sadness, confusion, guilt. She was angry to see the length and breadth of Obadiah's nerve—that he could be down there in Texas cavorting in adultery yet walk with head high into the pulpit, looking like he'd been born to be there and acting just as righteous as you please. This is what also brought the sadness, that right now the elder Brooks were living a lie. Confusion came from the fact that while Mama Max knew she had very good reason to hate this man, a modicum of love still seeped through, and guilt for this same reason: how could you love someone who treated you badly? She focused her eyes on the words she read, hoping to drown out Obadiah's singing with the word of the Lord.

" 'If Thy withdraw Thyself from me . . . oh wither will I go?' "

"O Lord my God, I cried unto Thee, and Thou hast healed me." Memories flooded in: their first meetings in the Texas countryside; the birth of their four children: King, Queen, Daniel, and Ester; countless revivals and Sunday dinners . . . and Dorothea. Mama Max began to rock with the effort it took to hold her peace. *"Sing unto the Lord, O ye saints of His, and give thanks at the remembrance of His holiness."*

The pianist began a soulful solo, the congregation hummed along, and Obadiah encouraged the worshippers to give God praise. Mama Max worked to keep her thoughts on God and all things holy, but snippets of memory—particularly those from the past year—intruded upon her joy.

It's them Noble bitches, stirring up my blood again! I passed by the bedroom and heard the Reverend Doctor talking all lowlike. So I tiptoed into the guest room and picked up the receiver. Now, you know I'm not one to the nosy, but when the Spirit nudges me to do a thing, I try and be obedient. So I picked up that phone, yes, I did. And I heard her.

Mama Max shook her head and continued to read the calming Psalm. *For His anger endureth but a moment; in His favor is life. Weeping may endure for a night, but joy cometh in the morning.*

Obadiah began his sermon. "Giving honor to God who is the

head of my life, to the ministers on the pulpit, the fabulous choir, faithful church workers, all of you who make up this wonderful congregation, and most importantly, to my stalwart helpmeet, my companion for nigh unto fifty-five years"—Mama Max couldn't help her shocked reaction—"Maxine Brook. Woman of God, can you please stand and greet the people?"

If there were any mind readers in the midst, they would have gasped and sputtered at the thoughts running through the head of Maxine Brook. But calling upon her professional decorum, Mama Max once again put on a fake smile, stood as asked, nodded at the crowd, took her seat, and made a decision: it was time to put an end to her sham of a marriage.

18

You Dropped A Bomb On Me

King, Tai, and Vivian stood in Derrick's hospital room, quietly conversing at the foot of his bed. The doctor had ordered them to spend only a few minutes with his recently awakened patient, and to not bother him if he fell asleep. Derrick seemed to be sleeping peacefully. His visitors appeared calm on the outside, but worry and fear ran through all of their veins.

"He looks well," King observed, though his brow was creased with abject concern.

"His mental faculty seems sound, too. No loss of memory, speech impediments, or anything like that," Tai added, clasping Vivian's hand in her own. "He's going to be all right, sister."

Vivian nodded, unable to speak. There'd been a hole in her heart and a lump in her throat ever since she watched her husband fall to the floor at Mount Zion Progressive Baptist Church. That she'd barely slept last night had nothing to do with the less than comfortable roll-away bed the hospital had provided and everything to do with the thought that Vivian had never before considered: life without Derrick.

Her phone rang, and Vivian excused herself from the room. Shortly afterward, she opened the door to Derrick's room and motioned King and Tai to join her in the hallway. "That was Cedars-

Sinai," she whispered. "They'll be transporting Derrick within the hour, and he'll be met at the hospital by Dr. Black."

Tai breathed a sigh of relief. "I know that's what you wanted, Viv, and I'm glad they were able to make it happen so quickly. You'll feel much better once the doctor you've chosen has had a chance to check Derrick out."

The doctor Vivian had chosen was Keith Black, the world-renowned African-American physician whose knowledge of and success rate with brain-related illnesses had set him apart in the medical field. Ironically, she'd just recently learned of him through a church member who'd given her a copy of his autobiography, *Brain Surgeon*. She'd skimmed the pages and was impressed by the doctor's background, tenacity, and focus. However, before she could fully immerse herself between the book's pages, her attention was diverted by the pressing needs of an upcoming Sanctity of Sisterhood conference. Her already busy schedule became even more so and all thoughts of medical miracles were forgotten. Later, Vivian would acknowledge that what seemed to be a casual exchange of information from church member to first lady was actually part of God's divine intervention that would help save her husband's life.

"I need to speak with Dr. Bhatti," Vivian said, even as she punched numbers on her cell phone. "And also let our parents know that we're on our way back to LA. I'm sure they'll want to meet us at the hospital."

Tai nodded, shooing away Vivian with a wave of her hand. "Go on and handle your business, Viv. We'll be right here." Tai sought and found comfort in King's arms. She leaned her head against his shoulder and because of this proximity, felt his body the minute that he tensed up.

"It's Princess," he murmured, as if just remembering the matter of yesterday that remained unfinished.

Tai's head jerked up. *Princess, here?*

"I need to finish the business with her and Rafael."

Tai turned around just as Princess approached them. Tai immediately noticed her troubled countenance—the red-rimmed eyes and tightly drawn mouth. She also noted that Joni and Sarah were standing beside her instead of her fiancé. "Baby, what's the matter? Where's Rafael?"

"How's Uncle Derrick?" Princess answered Tai's question with one of her own, an act that didn't go unnoticed. "Can I see him?"

"He's asleep right now, Princess," King responded. "Vivian has gone to find the doctor. They're getting ready to transport him to Los Angeles where he can get more specialized care."

"But he's okay, right?" The deep concern in her heart was mirrored in her eyes.

"He's not out of the woods, but we're believing in God," Tai responded, taking a step toward Princess and seeing a troubled soul through her expressive eyes. "But right now, I'm more concerned about you."

"Baby, I'm so sorry about all this," King interjected. "When Derrick collapsed, I forgot about everything else that was going on around me. But I can make that right in about five minutes. Where's Rafael? We can finish the ceremony right away, even right here in the hospital if you'd like."

Tai looked at her watch. "Yes, and that way you guys will still be able to make your flight." She knew that Princess and Rafael were planning to spend the night in New York before continuing on to Montego Bay. But her daughter's glistening eyes—unshed tears that threatened to fall at any moment—told her something else. "Baby, what is it?"

Tears fell as Princess answered. "Rafael and I broke up."

King and Tai's one-word response was spoken in unison: "What?"

Princess haltingly relayed what had taken place near City Hall. "When I saw the banner," she finished, "all of these feelings just welled up inside me. I couldn't think, could barely breathe. I knew that was no way to go into a marriage, with all of these conflicting thoughts inside my head. So I hesitated and Rafael went off. I don't blame him. I understand it. Had the situation been reversed I'm sure I'd feel the same way."

Tai pushed aside the déjà vu numbness she felt and focused on her main aim: salvaging her daughter's marriage. "I can understand why Rafael was so upset. But don't give up yet, Princess. I'm sure he'll be more reasonable after he calms down."

"He told me that if I walked away right then, that if I didn't go with him into Cleavon Jackson's office, then it was over. And I believe him!"

King pushed aside a grudging admiration for anyone who would go to the lengths that Kelvin did to prove his point, and presented a united front with his wife. "Your mother is right, Princess. It had to be hard on a man's ego to see you being affected by Kelvin's message. But Rafael loves you. Have you tried calling him since y'all parted?" When Princess shook her head, he said, "Well, give him a call and let him know that I want to talk with him."

"That's a good idea, baby," Tai added. "In fact, we'd love you two to come by the house if you have time." Tai had planned a large Sunday dinner for everyone who'd come into town and even though it was still going to happen, the food would come courtesy of Gates Barb-B-Q. "Even if you can't stay, it would be nice to be able to officially send you on your way."

Princess wasn't exactly feeling what her parents were saying but was too emotionally drained to argue. She stepped away and placed a call to Rafael. At the same time, Tai's phone rang. It was a loyal Mount Zion member and SOS participant, calling to see if there was anything she could do to help the family through this tumultuous time. Tai breathed a sigh of relief as she rolled off a list of items to get at her favorite barbeque joint: ribs, chicken, sausage, sliced beef, barbeque beans, slaw, potato salad, and several orders of the restaurant's tasty thick fries.

Just as she was ending the call, she looked up to see Vivian coming back around the corner. She wasn't alone. Tai wasn't pleased. And she couldn't have cared less that the boy's father was flat on his back in a hospital bed. Tai wasn't the least bit happy to see Kelvin Petersen.

And she got the distinct feeling that this wouldn't be the last time that Derrick Montgomery's son caused her some chagrin.

19

Dilemma

King and Tai looked back and forth between Kelvin and Princess, but for the two ex-lovers, it was as if no one else was in the room.

Kelvin stopped at the group huddled near Derrick's hospital door. "Hey, Princess."

"Hey."

"Can I speak with you for a minute?"

King stepped into Kelvin's line of sight. "I'd think the first person you'd want to see is your father, the man who's lying on his back on the other side of this wall, maybe fighting for his life."

Kelvin glanced at King, but instead of commenting, simply looked back at Princess. "Just two minutes and I won't bother you again."

Tai snorted.

Princess tried to control the fluttering of feelings now swirling around her. "It was crazy what you did, Kelvin." Her tone wasn't as stern as she'd hoped.

"That's just it, baby," Kelvin responded with a crooked smile. "You got me looking so crazy right now."

Tai stepped in between the silent love fest happening before her eyes. "What you're really looking like is a disrespectful home wrecker who's full of himself. How dare you hire a plane and send out a message all over Kansas City, just so you can interrupt my daughter's happiness!"

"I hired eight planes, Miss Tai," Kelvin replied with a nonplussed attitude. "And instructed them to fly five hours nonstop, to cover every inch of the metropolitan area in the hopes that Princess would read my message and follow her heart."

Tai rolled her eyes. "Spoken like someone with an ego the size of the sun."

King looked at the tall, confident man before him through narrowed eyes, remembering a past confrontation with a then eighteen-year-old Kelvin, who, when King had threatened an ass-kicking, had stood his ground. He understood where Tai was coming from, but decided on a different approach. "It's clear that you didn't want Princess to marry Rafael. But let me ask you this, Kelvin. What are *your* plans regarding my daughter?"

There was no hint of nervousness or doubt as Kelvin answered King's question. "That's a very good question, sir. And I do have an answer. But it's one I'd like to first share with your daughter." He looked at Princess. "Baby, can I please speak with you? *Alone?*"

Vivian, who'd been watching this exchange dispassionately, looked beyond King and Tai's shoulder and saw the doctor entering Derrick's room. She excused herself, followed the doctor into where her husband lay and seconds later announced to the group huddled just beyond her, "he's awake!"

Everyone heard this and, for the moment, put aside their differences and entered Derrick's room.

"Dad." Kelvin's voice broke as he stepped up to the bed and grasped Derrick's hand.

From the opposite side of the bed, Vivian reached for Derrick's other hand. "How are you feeling, baby?"

Derrick looked at his wife. Although no words were spoken, a tome of conversation was transmitted with their eyes. He continued to look around the room, smiling at King and Tai, and then his eyes stopped on Kelvin. "Good to see you, son," he said.

The years fell away, and Kelvin felt like the seven-year-old boy living near Hamburg, Germany, who'd just found out that his pet bird would live. "I'm here for you, Daddy." His voice was hoarse, his eyes glassy. "You're going to be all right."

Tai observed Kelvin's obvious love for his father. It didn't change her thoughts about this young man not being the right choice for her daughter. Before the end of the day, however, she'd discover that Kelvin's opinion wasn't the only one that she'd want to change.

A little over an hour later, Mama Max sat in Tai's dining room, unaware that her daughter-in-law had just traded one minefield for another one. At the time Tai had mentioned having all of the family and a few close friends over the day after the wedding, it sounded like a good idea. Now, faced with the reality of this decision . . . not so much.

The dinner itself had been drama-free. Between all of their children and extended members of their church family, there had been enough people in King and Tai's dining room to keep Obadiah and Mama Max out of each other's space. But now, two hours later and with most of the company leaving or already gone, the frosty elephant in the middle of the room could no longer be ignored.

"It was good to see you again, Pastor," Elsie Wanthers said, pulling Obadiah into a big bear hug. "We sure hope that you're able to settle that church in Texas real soon, and get back to your church home here in Kansas"—Elsie snuck a look at Mama Max—"where you belong."

Mama Max acted as though she didn't hear Nosy Elsie's comment, even as she made a note to suggest that Sistah Alrighty mind her own business in the not too distant future. She further disrupted her murderous chain of thought by rising to clean off the table, balancing plates and cups and saucers and silverware as if she'd waitressed half her life. A part of her wanted to take the ivory china and bounce it against the walls, to take a glass or two and throw it up against Obadiah's head, but for all her posturing and strong-willed talk, Mama Max had never been a violent person. So instead of doing either of these things, she asked her teen twin grandchildren, Timothy and Tabitha, to help her clear the dining room table and warm up the cobblers she'd baked last night. She'd almost successfully ignored the living room goings-on until she heard Obadiah speaking to one of the deacons.

"Nobody said the road to heaven would be easy. It's absolutely hard being away from everything here—the city, the church, the wife. It is a burden to bear. . . ."

The rest of his statement was drowned out by the waves of anger beating against her consciousness. *Not easy? Being away from his wife a burden? You low-down, lying hypocrite!*

"Grandma, you're going to break that dish!"

Mama Max heard Tabitha's words at the same time she looked down and realized she was precariously close to snapping in half the casserole dish she was rinsing. She covered her anger by taking great pains in placing it and other dishes into the dishwasher, while having Timothy take out the apple, peach, and three-berry cobblers and place them in the oven. "Make sure the temperature is set to three-fifty—no higher. I don't want my pies to get burnt."

The oven temperature could have been set to six thousand degrees and it wouldn't have been hotter than Mama Max. After putting the kitchen in order, she couldn't hold on to the facade any longer. She told Tabitha to get her mother and have her meet Mama Max in Princess's old room.

Tai was there within minutes. "Mama, you've been tense all afternoon. Are you worried about Princess?"

Princess's announcement that she'd broken up with Rafael, and the fact that she had stayed with Kelvin at the hospital and then was a no-show at this family function had been a concern for all of them, but right now Mama Max was more focused on making her own exit from this family affair.

"Why didn't you tell me that Obadiah would be preaching today? If I'd known that, I never would have set foot in the building!"

"Mama, I didn't know until this morning myself. Last night, when King left the hospital, I assumed he'd gone home to go over his sermon for today. I got home late, and then left early to meet Vivian for breakfast. But honestly, when I later saw King at the hospital, I didn't give it a second thought. I'm sorry, Mama."

"What's happening isn't your fault, daughter. I just need to leave, that's all."

"Why? Did Daddy O say something to you? I've heard him saying good things—how he misses home, misses you, and wants to come back here."

"Yeah, well, his actions are speaking so loud they're drowning out those lying words. Every day that Obadiah stays with that floozy is a slap in my face. But I don't even blame him anymore. It's me who's putting up with the foolishness." Mama Max leaned forward until she was just inches from Tai's face. "But no more, darlin'. I've listened to you and King talk about the ruckus my divorce from Obadiah will cause, but I'm ready to face whatever happens. The property, insurance stuff—I'm ready to settle all of it. I don't intend on spending another year living in limbo. I want to straighten out my life and live however much of it that's left in some sort of peace."

Tai and her mother-in-law chatted a few more moments. After getting Mama Max's promise that she wouldn't do anything before first talking to King, she led her beloved mother-in-law out a side door and made her apologies to the remaining guests. "Mama Max felt a pounding headache coming on and decided to go and take a nap. But she sends her love."

Later, it was King's turn to be the voice of reason to a hard audience—his dad. "Try and see this from her point of view," he told a man who felt he'd been disrespected all day. "Mama was blind-

sided when you walked into the pulpit. It's understandable that
she'd be . . . at a loss for words."

Obadiah scowled at his son while mixing vanilla ice cream
with Mama Max's apple cobbler and spooning it into his mouth.
"I'm surprised you didn't choke on that lie you just told. More
than once, I've tried to talk to Maxine since being here—at the rehearsal dinner, just before the wedding, and right before I left for
the hospital. She's got her behind sitting up on her shoulders, acting like she hung the stars and the moon."

*Perhaps that's because you're shacking up with your mistress and act-
ing like your feces doesn't have an odor,* is what King thought. "I can
understand her being upset," is what he said.

Obadiah wasn't as understanding. "How you figure? I admit
my sins before the Lord, but Maxine ain't blameless in all that's
gone on. At least I'm acting civil. I did what she wanted by not
bringing Dorothea with me. I actually thought this might be a
time for me and Maxine to talk a bit, find out if there was any way
we could . . ." Obadiah's words trailed off as he looked beyond the
den's large picture window and tried to see a calm tomorrow.

King tried to still his now rapidly beating heart, in the moment
totally empathizing with his children when they felt he and Tai
might not stay together. "Dad, can I get personal for a minute?
How are things with you and Dorothea?"

Obadiah took another bite of apple cobbler à la mode. "Some
things aren't to be discussed between father and son."

King remembered a conversation where Obadiah was questioning him about *his* marriage, but felt now was not the time to
make this point. Instead he waited . . . patiently . . . quietly.

Finally Obadiah spoke, looking out the large picture window
as he did so. "Sometimes the icing on a cake might be as sweet as
sugar, but taking a bite reveals that there are some ingredients gone
missing in the batter." His statement was cryptic, but well understood. And in time King would come to appreciate it even more
than he did now.

20

The Power Of Love

Princess wandered amid a profusion of flowers, listening yet again to Rafael's instruction to leave a message at the end of the tone. She'd done that already, several times, and her ex-fiancé's silence was so loud that it was deafening. Pushing the button to end the call, she sat on a bench that offered an unobstructed view of the glistening lake water rippling several yards behind the floral land- scape. In another place and time, Princess would have appreciated the tranquil atmosphere, warm summer breeze, and clear blue sky. Right now, however, all she kept seeing was Rafael's face, and how crushed he looked when she stopped on the sidewalk and admit- ted that marrying him did not feel right. *If only I could talk to him,* she thought, reaching for the phone, hitting redial and feeling an- guish at hearing his voice mail again. She even thought about call- ing his parents again, but quickly rejected that idea. The first call had been bad enough, with Mrs. Stevens not only refusing to come to the phone but loudly telling Mr. Stevens that she didn't want to talk to that "selfish, coldhearted *female dog.*" Except the word she used to describe this canine began with a *B* and ended with what happens when one gets poison ivy. It wasn't a word that Princess could have imagined coming out of Mrs. Holy's mouth, but then again, having broken their son's heart only hours ago, she could understand the Stevenses' feelings toward her being less than Christian.

Her phone buzzed. She hurriedly looked down, hoping it was Rafael. No. It was Kelvin calling. Again. She almost regretted that she'd given him her number. He'd called three times since she'd left him at the hospital. After he'd poured out his heart to her, after he'd said things that she'd never thought would come out of his mouth. He'd asked her questions. She had no answers. Too much had happened, she'd explained. The whole weekend was crazy! He pressed. She balked. Finally told him that she needed time alone, to think and clear her head. That's how she'd ended up here, at Shawnee Mission Park. Being in nature always made her feel closer to God, and Lord knew she needed to feel Him right now.

Father God, please help. What should I do? What is going on?

Upon hearing God's answer, she stopped short. They were the same words that had come to her this morning, while she was taking a shower. They were the same words that she'd forgotten... until now. And they were the same words that Kelvin had offered, when Princess had told him how his father's unfortunate episode had affected her life. Wow, had this conversation actually happened just over an hour ago? Princess stood and began to meander along one of the park's trails, remembering what was said.

"Princess." Kelvin stood near her at the foot of his father's bed, watching the exchange between him and King. "I need to talk to you."

"Not now," she'd answered between gritted teeth. "Everything isn't always all about you."

"But right now is all about us," he hissed back, pasting a smile on his face when his father glanced his way. "Just give me two minutes. What I have to say can't wait."

Princess bit back a sigh and a huff and all but stomped out of Derrick's hospital room. "Uh, we'll be back," Kelvin mumbled before he too hurried out of the room. "Princess, wait!" She wasn't listening, so it was up to Kelvin to follow Princess out the hospital door and into the parking lot. "Princess!"

She whirled around. "What?!"

"Baby, can we just calm down enough to talk for a minute?"

"Hmm, let me take a look at the last twenty-four hours: my wedding was interrupted, my favorite uncle knocked on death's door, and my ex-boyfriend flew a message-bearing plane over the courthouse where I was headed with my fiancé. You tell me just how damn calm you think I should be right about now!"

Princess observed the surprise in Kelvin's eyes before he quickly recovered his calm demeanor. "I'm sorry about everything that's happened to you, Princess."

"Really? You're sorry that I didn't get married?"

Kelvin's countenance was serious, his eyes unblinking as he answered, "Everything except that." Princess hung her head. Kelvin dared to reach out and touch her arm. His confidence was bolstered a bit when she didn't snatch it away from him. "I know that you're dealing with a lot right now, baby, and that your emotions are all over the place. I know how crazy you are about my father and that you believe that you truly do love Rafael." Princess looked up, her eyes wide and questioning. Kelvin took a deep breath and moved a step closer to Princess. "But I don't think you were in love with him." Before she could protest, he hurried on. "I know you're hurting, Princess, but I've got to say this. And I've got to say it right now. I know how it was between us, and I don't think what we feel for each other can be experienced with someone else."

Princess turned away from his probing eyes. "Kelvin, now is not the time to—"

"Now is the perfect time." Kelvin stepped around until he was again facing Princess. He caressed her chin, raising it until their eyes met. "Have you given that any thought, Princess? The timing? How you've told me that God's timing is perfect and He doesn't make mistakes? I know you think that all of your religious mumbo jumbo goes in one of my ears and out the other, but I hear you when you're talking. Now, I need you to hear me." His voice dropped, his tone warm and earnest. "As bad as the situation is with my father, maybe everything happened exactly as it was supposed to. Maybe it was the only way for God to stop what was happening, get your attention and give me another chance. Baby, maybe what happened was divine intervention."

Princess brushed away the tears and looked at the caller ID of her ringing phone. In the last thirty minutes her phone had rung no less than five times, courtesy of Kelvin and Tai. *Don't be so insensitive, Princess. She's just worried about you.* Clearing the tears out of her throat, she answered her phone. "Hey, Mom."

"Princess, where are you? Kelvin said you left the hospital. I've been worried sick!"

"Sorry, Mom. I saw that you'd called. I just needed some time away from everyone . . . and everything."

"Where are you?" Princess told her. "Where is Kelvin?"

Princess shrugged. "At the hospital, I guess."

"I doubt it. Vivian left the hospital with Derrick a little while ago. A chartered plane is transporting him to Cedars-Sinai." A pause and then, "Maybe he went with them."

Princess tried to ignore how her heart clenched at this news. She wasn't ready to examine how Kelvin potentially being away from her made her feel. Her mother's next sentence insured that she didn't have to, at least not right now. "Ralph called."

At the mention of her would-be father-in-law's name, Princess's thoughts went straight to Rafael. "They're so mad at me."

"Phyllis is furious, and I can't say I blame her. But I think Ralph is more disappointed than angry. He already viewed you as his daughter-in-law."

"Mama, I'm so sorry for everything that's happened. A part of me really wanted to marry Rafael. And I can't really explain why I didn't because I don't even fully understand it. I just know it wasn't right to enter a marriage while feeling this conflicted."

A brief pause and then, "So are you finally ready to admit what your daddy and I have known all along?"

"What's that?"

"That you're still in love with Kelvin Petersen, and he's the reason you're not Mrs. Stevens right now."

Princess's answer was so long in coming that for a while Tai felt that either she wouldn't answer or they'd been disconnected. "Princess? You there?"

"I'm here," came the quiet, hesitant response. A muffled sniffle and then, "Yes, Mama, I'm still in love with Kelvin. I thought if I focused on someone else long enough, prayed hard enough, or got busy enough . . . the feelings for him would go away. But they're still here. Stronger than ever."

21

Got Me Looking So Crazy Right Now

A few hours later, Princess walked—as if in a dream—to the private plane located on an isolated section of Kansas City International Airport's runways. The entire weekend had been a whirlwind and this felt like the eye of the storm—strangely peaceful and totally surreal. After another thirty minutes on the phone with her mother, Princess had placed calls to Kelvin, Rafael, Joni, Sarah, Michael, and Erin . . . in that order. She'd learned of Kelvin's whereabouts and agreed to meet him, left a final message on Rafael's voice mail, cried with a still shocked Joni, prayed with Sarah, asked her older brother, Michael, to retrieve her car from the airport, and coordinated with Erin a letter of apology to accompany the return of over five hundred wedding gifts.

Now, as she sat buckling her seat belt, dispassionately taking in the buttery leather seats and gleaming cherrywood of the private plane, she again asked the question that played like a loop in her head: *What are you doing?* Even as she wondered this, however, she marveled even more at how right it felt to be taking actions that signaled she'd lost her mind. *You got me looking so crazy right now.* A brief smile scampered across her face. *Yeah, Kelvin. Me, too.*

"Is that a smile I see?" Kelvin asked, stretching out his long legs in front of him. When she didn't answer immediately, he reached over and clasped her hand. "I'm glad you're here with me, Princess. I don't know if I could handle what all is happening with my dad if you weren't around."

"Mom and Joni think I'm crazy to be leaving with you like this."

"Your mom never liked me and Joni knows you're crazy." Princess chuckled. Kelvin began making light circles on Princess's palm with his strong, thick thumb. Princess pulled her hand away. "I've missed you, Princess."

"Kelvin—"

"Have you missed me?"

Princess took a calming breath. "Kelvin, I'm as concerned about Uncle Derrick as you are and am here to help a friend through a rough time."

"Just helping a friend, huh," Kelvin drawled, reaching again for Princess's hand. Again, Princess jerked it away. Kelvin hid a smile. *Uh-huh.* "When are you going to admit that I'm more than a friend to you, baby?" he asked, air quotes underlying the emphasized word. "I've always been more, I'll always *be* more, and if you'll let me, I'll prove to you that is exactly how things should be." The flight attendant came over to take their drink orders, and to let them know there would be a brief delay in their departure. As soon as she'd left them, Kelvin continued. "It's been what, a year since we've seen each other? Tell me you didn't feel something the minute you saw me."

Princess looked out the window. She could not tell a lie.

"Exactly. You shut a brothah, your *friend,* completely out of your life; changed your phone number, wouldn't even let me get at you through a three-way with Brandon or Joni. They finally convinced me to back off, leave you alone, respect your relationship with old boy and what not. And I did. But I've never stopped thinking about you, Princess. Never stopped loving you . . . never."

Princess turned to look into Kelvin's eyes. "Did you ever stop sleeping with every woman who threw herself at you?" she asked.

"Or do you still have a girl in every nightclub and a woman in every town?"

"I'm a single, healthy young man," Kelvin responded. "I have needs and I'm not going to lie. They get met. I'm not like you, Princess, believing that you have to be celibate. Heck, God made pussy. Don't you think He knew what He was doing when he hooked up that shit?"

"Look, I don't want to fight about our different beliefs. I only bring it up because these differences are the very things that stand between us."

"They don't have to."

"How do you figure?"

"Because..." Kelvin reached for her hand again and wouldn't let go. "I know about some pussy that would shut down all the others."

"Really, Kelvin, you need to watch how you're talking to me and let go of my hand."

"Why? We're both grown! What's wrong with being real? Oh, would you prefer I call it cootchie, or vagina? Hell, both of those words sound nastier than *pussy* to me." They were silent as the attendant brought Princess a soda and Kelvin a beer. "Baby, I know we had our share of rough spots. But when we were in the groove, nobody could touch us!" Kelvin leaned more comfortably into the seat, released her hand, and looked straight ahead. "I remember the first time I saw you, over at Dad and Mom Vee's house. You walked in with your peeps, looking all good in those tight-ass jeans. You had on this oversized pink top that exposed your shoulder with a black tank underneath, coordinated with hot pink tennis shoes with black laces. Your hair looked as soft as silk and you were wearing very little makeup. You almost pulled off being city cool, but then I peeped that whack-looking purse you were carrying and saw small town."

"Ha! Whatever." Princess took a sip of her drink. "With your remembering all the details, I must have made an impression."

"Yeah, I made an impression on you, too. Even though you tried to act like I didn't, tried to act all preoccupied by spending that whole afternoon with the phone glued to your ear."

"You weren't all that."

"Girl, please. You couldn't keep your eyes off me."

"Yeah, especially since you kept parading back and forth in front of me like God's gift to humanity." Princess smiled, remember the seventeen-year-old girl who'd spotted the months younger boy and experienced love at first sight.

Kelvin smiled, too. "You must have liked what you saw since you dropped those digits before a brothah could even ask you."

Princess swatted his arm. "Liar! I did not!"

Kelvin laughed. "You hinted hard enough." He adopted Princess's higher-pitched voice. "I'm thinking about going to college out here. Maybe we can stay in touch."

"I *was* thinking about going to school in Los Angeles, and did."

"True that, but you liked me, too."

Princess's smile widened. "I did."

The plane took off, and so did the wind beneath Princess and Kelvin's rekindling love affair. They talked about those early months of clandestine phone calls and Kelvin teased Princess about her novella-length e-mails. Even though those first several calls were innocent—mainly about school, sports, music, and life in LA—they kept this interaction on the down low because of how Princess's mom felt about Kelvin's mom. Tai had forgiven Janeé "Tootie" Smith Petersen for the on-again off-again affair with King that had lasted for years, but she would never forget it. Then there was the fact that though not by blood, his being Derrick's biological son made Kelvin almost family. "*Almost* ain't is," he had informed her during Princess's next visit to Los Angeles, shortly before their first kiss.

Not long after Princess arrived in Los Angeles the following year, they'd shared something much deeper.

Kelvin nodded as the attendant placed down a simple yet scrumptious-looking meal of baked chicken, steamed vegetables, and rice. He reached for the pumpernickel roll he'd chosen, broke it in half, and slathered butter on both sides. "Remember how we used to sneak around after church; using our friends as shields to try and see each other?"

"Aunt Viv could read my face like a newspaper," Princess said, laughing as she recalled their undercover antics during her first year away from home. "I couldn't even look at you when you came to church."

They both ate in silence for a moment, and then Kelvin broke the silence. "Oh, man!"

"What?"

"You know what I just thought about?" Princess raised her brow in question, while taking a bite of veggies and rice. "That time when we were in Dad's Jaguar and that crazy woman tried to run us off the road!"

"Oh my God, Kelvin, that was a trip! She was weaving in and out of the cars and later we found out that she had a gun and had actually been shooting it—at us!"

"Yeah, that fool thought it was Dad she was chasing. When she saw that her stalker style wasn't working to break up him and Mom Vee, she went to some gangster shit!"

"For real! And then remember how her car clipped a truck or something and she flipped over like three times. I'd never seen anything like that before in my life. I thought for sure she was dead."

"Yeah, well, one thing's for sure. She's dead now." For a moment, silverware against china was the only sound heard as both Kelvin and Princess remembered Robin Cook, the crazy woman who for a time invaded the Montgomerys' lives.

Throughout dinner, the easy flow of conversation continued, largely about their shared past: attending UCLA, especially their time in the condo with Joni and Brandon; their Christmas holiday spent with the Petersens in Hintereck, Germany; and Princess being Kelvin's biggest cheerleader as he became a Bruins basketball star. Unpleasant memories were interwoven with all of these moments, but the conversationalists chose to ignore these—for now.

Shortly after the captain had come out and chatted with Kelvin about basketball, the attendant approached them. "Is there anything else I can get you? An after dinner drink or coffee, perhaps?" Both Kelvin and Princess declined. "Well, then, just sit back, relax, and enjoy the rest of your flight. We'll be landing in Las Vegas in about twenty minutes."

Princess frowned as the attendant walked away. "Las Vegas?" she said to Kelvin. "Doesn't she mean Los Angeles?"

"No, she meant Vegas. We've got to make a stop there first."

"Why? What's in Vegas?"

"Our future." Kelvin shifted so that he was facing Princess more directly. His look was at once smoldering, determined, and pensive all at the same time.

Princess's heart pounded. "Kelvin, what are you talking about? I don't understand."

"It's quite simple, really. I want us to get married, Princess. I want you to be my wife."

22

Meet Me at the Altar in Your White Dress

Princess was stunned, sure that she'd heard incorrectly. One thing was for sure: she was out of the eye of the hurricane and back into the straight-up storm! "Kelvin, you can't be serious."

"I've never been more serious in my life. I don't want us in separate rooms when we get to LA. I not only want you, but I *need* you, Princess, by my side, in every way. If there's one thing that's come out of what happened to the rev, it's that life is short. We can't take it for granted that we'll be here another day, another year. And I can't take it for granted that you'll be here either. I came this close to losing you, baby." Kelvin placed his thumb and forefinger less than an inch apart to emphasize his point. "I don't want to take that chance again."

An unexpected tear slid down Princess's cheek, almost before she realized she was crying. "I can't believe this is happening. Did you forget that barely twenty-four hours ago I was standing at the altar with another man? That if it hadn't been for"—*divine intervention*—"your father's illness I would be married to Rafael right now?"

"I'm remembering it all too well," Kelvin responded, his rapidly blinking eyes suspiciously moist. "It's how I know that I don't want to spend another day without you being my wife."

When Princess turned to stare out the window, he continued. "Baby, please hear me out. I know that this feels sudden and crazy and unexpected. But is it really? When you look deep down in your heart, is there a place where this feels right and perfect and a long time in coming? Is there a part of you that knows that even as unorthodox as this all looks, it's exactly what should be happening right now?"

Princess spoke barely above a whisper, still not looking away from the darkening sky with Sin City beckoning just beyond them. "Is this what you had in mind when you asked me to come with you? When you whisked me away without even a change of panties, telling me that you'd take care of everything?" She finally turned to look at him. "Is this the everything"—she used air quotes—"that you had in mind?"

Kelvin shook his head. "No. When I asked you to come with me to be with my dad, it was because I honestly wanted you beside me during this time. Then, when I was on my way to the airport, it hit me: why not take a little side trip that would keep you by my side forever? I know we love each other and even more than that, we have a special bond that can't be denied. You've already done the whole big hoopla church thing, worn the gown, had the party."

"Are you serious? You think what happened this weekend counts?"

Kelvin shrugged. "Doesn't it?"

A heavy sigh was Princess's answer.

"I thought we could do something nice and quiet, simple, no fuss. Then later, we can have a party and invite the world if you want. I'll do whatever it takes, Princess. I just want you with me."

Princess railed against her feelings, worked to stay connected with her head, not her heart. "What about our different beliefs?"

"I know what you're trying to say...that we'd be unequally yoked." Princess could not help but show her surprise. Kelvin chuckled. "Uh-huh, you didn't believe me when I said I was listening to some of the religious yakety-yak. I know you think I'm a straight-up heathen, but I'm not. I believe in God, Princess. I just don't believe that you have to go to church every Sunday and wear your Christianity on your sleeve or your face. Believe it or not, the rev has been schooling me about the Bible and whatnot." Kelvin looked a bit sheepish as he added, "And whether or not you should become my wife."

Princess crossed her arms, her face one of indignation. "So you didn't have this planned but yet you've talked to your father about me."

"Months ago, when I kept trying to reach you, kept hoping you would call. I told Dad how I felt about you, and that I wanted to marry you. That's when he hipped me to the whole unequally yoked concept."

"And you're still here, popping the question? He must not have hipped you very well."

"Ha! That's just it, baby. He said that phrase don't have anything to do with superficial qualities—liking the same food, or watching the same TV shows, or even attending the same church. He said the definition goes deeper, to a soul level. We both believe in God and at the end of the day, I believe we both want the same things: to be good people, raise a healthy, happy family, make a difference in the world."

The wall around Princess's heart began to descend, along with the plane. "What about your lifestyle, Kelvin? All of the women?"

"That comes with the life of a sports star, love. But we'll deal with them together. Look, when I say 'I do' to you, it will be 'I don't' for all them other clowns. I swear to God."

"These words are coming from the single, healthy young man who earlier spoke of needs that are regularly getting met?" Princess's face could have been in the dictionary, next to the word *skeptical*.

"That's just it. Even though I'm young, I've been in this game a minute. The novelty of pussy on a platter gets old after a while;

strange how this and the variety can get overrated. I promise you," he continued, softly. "It will just be you and me."

The plane landed. The couple was driven down to the strip. And when they returned to the plane an hour later, it was Mr. and Mrs. Kelvin Petersen who entered.

23

Standing in the Need of Prayer

Tai sat at the island of her spacious kitchen, enjoying a cup of coffee flavored with Baileys Irish Cream. It was 10 a.m., and the house was quiet. King was up and out early, tying up last minute details at the church office before heading to Barbados, Michael hadn't come in last night, Tabitha had spent the night with Mama Max, and Tai imagined that Timothy—known for playing on Xbox or Wii until the wee hours of the morning—was probably still in bed with his head buried under the covers. Tai rubbed her shoulders, making a mental note to schedule a massage. It had been a hectic few weeks, a draining weekend, and she'd been up late last night as well, talking to King, thinking about Princess, and praying for Derrick.

As if on cue the phone rang. Tai knew that it was Vivian, without even looking at the caller ID. "Good morning, sis."

"Morning."

"How are you doing, Viv? Any news?"

"I'm on my way to the hospital now for a meeting with Dr. Black. They conducted some preliminary tests last night. I think I'll feel much better after talking to him."

"How are D2 and Elisia handling everything?"

"They're wearing stoic Stanford faces right now," Vivian answered, referring to their grandfather, who one never saw sweat. "But I can tell they're both shaken. Elisia asked if her father was going to die." Vivian's voice broke. "I barely held it together to give her an answer. Tai, I've prayed, I have faith, but I'm also frightened. If anything happened to Derrick..."

"Whatever happens, you're in God's hands. We just have to keep praying, believing, and speaking those things that are not, as though they are." Tai's conversation slid effortlessly into prayer. "God, by faith I'm thanking you that right now my friend Vivian's husband and your beloved son Derrick Montgomery is healed, healthy, and happy."

"Thank you, Lord."

"I thank you for blessing him with a strong body, a sound mind, and a long life."

"Yes, Father."

"We call upon you to be Jehovah Rafa right now, Lord, the God who heals. We call upon and thank you for the ministering angels even right now surrounding his bed."

"Thank you."

"We thank you for working through Dr. Keith Black, Father, to help diagnose, treat, and cure whatever is ailing our brother."

"Please, Jesus."

Tai's voice gained in intensity as she slid off the bar chair and began pacing the floor. "Father, we stretch our hands to Thee, no other help we know. If you withdraw yourself from me, oh wither would we go."

"We need you, Lord."

"You said we could ask you for anything, God, and that nothing would be impossible. You said that we could take a mustard seed of faith, Father, and move a mountain."

"Yes!"

"You said that before we called your name, God, you would answer. And that while we were yet speaking... you would hear. You said that if two or three gathered together in your name that you would be in the midst of us. We've gathered by way of this phone call, Father, and we're calling upon your name right now."

"Hear us, Lord!"

"The devil comes to steal and destroy but you come that we might have life, and have it more abundantly."

"Yes..."

"And so we thank you for the life of Derrick Montgomery, and that even now, by the stripes of Jesus Christ, he is healed!"

"Thank you, Jesus!"

Tai's voice softened. "Now, Father God, I pray your blessings upon my sister Vivian and her and Derrick's children, Elisia and Derrick Junior. Give them the strength to withstand the lies of the enemy, Father God, wisdom to navigate this treacherous journey, and peace in the middle of this storm. We stand on Your Word, believing that our prayer is already answered, and that it is so."

"It *is* so!"

"Thy will *is* done!"

"It's done right now!"

"In Jesus's name..."

"Thank you, Tai," Vivian whispered, after she wiped her eyes and blew her nose. "I didn't even know how much I needed that."

"God did," Tai answered, with a sniffle. "And like I told you yesterday, Viv, I and a bunch of other people are here for you. You can come out from behind that stoic Stanford face that you mentioned earlier. And let us help."

"Okay."

"I know you said otherwise, but I don't have to wait for the diagnosis. I can come now if you need me."

"Carla is a blessing. She came by last night. And the women of the church have rallied around me."

"Girl, we all know that Carla Chapman is one praying woman! I'm sure it's also helpful that Kelvin is there, especially for D2. Though you must have been shocked to see my daughter with him. I tried to phone and warn you, but couldn't get through. Did she stay there or get a hotel room? I haven't heard from her."

A brief hesitation and then, "They're staying at the Ritz, Tai, both Kelvin and Princess. He phoned late last night to say we'd see them in the morning."

One second passed. Two. Five. "Kelvin and Princess are at a hotel, instead of your house? Ah, hell."

"Now let's not jump to conclusions, sistah. They could be in separate rooms."

"Come on, Vivian. That's like saying that cows can fly and we both know better than that." Tai suddenly wished there was something stronger than coffee and Baileys in her cup. "I hope you have a few extra minutes before going to see Derrick...because now it's me standing in the need of prayer!"

24

Sex Ain't Better Than Love

Princess shifted and tried to rise. But Kelvin pulled her back against him. "I've got to use the bathroom," she said.

"Hurry back," he mumbled.

She did. And no sooner had her back hit the thousand-count sheet of the king-sized bed than Kelvin had his arms wrapped around her. It was almost as if he had to keep touching her to know that he wasn't dreaming—that the woman he wanted was not only by his side and his bed, but was also his wife.

"I love you," he said, lazily running his hand up her silky thigh and around to tweak her already hardening nipple. "I want you," he whispered, pulling down the sheet to kiss her shoulder.

"Again?"

"Ha!"

After landing in Los Angeles around 7 p.m., Kelvin's LA assistant met them at the airport and drove them directly to a boutique on Rodeo Drive. The owner was waiting in her custom Mercedes, along with her diamond-collared golden chow. An hour later, they left with everything that Princess would need, at least for the next few days: dresses, shoes, blouses, pants, underwear, jewelry ... and a few negligees. While Princess shopped, the assistant went around the corner and secured a complete set of MAC makeup, a curling iron, and a variety of toiletries. And while Princess and the assistant were busy, Kelvin set up an appointment that would make his wife's apparel complete.

They arrived at the hotel around nine, tired but giddy—a couple in love. As Mama Max would say, you couldn't hit Kelvin in the butt with a shiny red apple. He was the proudest man in the room. After making her decision to say yes, Princess got out of her head, let her heart take over, and truly felt like a brand new bride! Later, she'd compare how she felt now to how she felt the day before she was to marry Rafael, and she'd be stunned. She would wonder how she'd ever thought that she'd been truly happy. And be even more grateful for God and His timing.

The Ritz-Carlton suite was perfect, filled with marble, mahogany, and panoramic views from their twenty-fifth floor window. They spent little time looking at the fifty-inch TV or sitting in the formal dining room. But they made full use of the luxury bath with rain showerhead, mounted body jets, and soaking tub. Princess relaxed her no drinking rule for the occasion and shared a bottle of Krug Clos du Mesnil, which went perfectly with their elaborate room service choices: lobster-filled spring rolls, braised Kobe beef short ribs, and Alaskan king salmon. When the kitchen discovered who was in the suite and on what occasion, the executive chef appeared at their door. He explained that their meal and champagne were on the house, and offered them an elaborately decorated, absolutely decadent chocolate masterpiece that he'd whipped up just for them.

After that came the loving. And it looked as though Kelvin was nowhere near through.

"Baby, it's been so long," he murmured.

"We've been asleep for what—six, seven hours? It hasn't been long enough."

"I'm hungry."

"Order room service."

"What I want," Kelvin eased a hand between Princess's thighs, "is not on the menu."

Princess couldn't help but smile broadly as she turned to face her man. It had been almost four long, hard, sexless years where at times she thought she'd climb the walls with longing. She'd tried very hard to practice what she preached and was successful—for the most part. She hadn't had intercourse, hadn't fooled around. But God knew she'd be lying if there wasn't a time or two that she'd pleasured herself just to take off the edge. Unlike a virgin, she'd known exactly what she was missing. Sex between her and Kelvin had always been amazing; their connection during times of intimacy went deeper than the act. With them, getting back in the groove was just like riding a bicycle—everything came back as if no time had passed. Only it was even better than before.

"So . . . it's not on the menu, huh?" she asked, scooting closer and kissing Kelvin's thick, bow-shaped lips.

"Not at all." Kelvin deepened their kiss, even as he spread her legs with the hand that was between them, lazily and lightly running his middle finger between her slippery folds. She immediately got even wetter. He groaned, placing a finger inside her as he swirled his tongue around her mouth, reacquainting himself with every spot. Princess gasped, spreading her legs wider, running her hand up and down Kelvin's broad, muscled back. She felt his rock hard dick brush against her thigh as he shifted, and ran his hand from her shoulder to her knee, gently caressing spots in between.

"Umm." He left her mouth, kissed his way to her cheek and down to her neck, continuing on to her breasts, swirling his tongue around one nipple while using his fingers to rub the other one into a hardened pebble. Princess shivered from the assault, clutching the sheets when he continued lower still, swirling his tongue inside her navel, kissing the top of her bikini-waxed crotch, and each side of her thighs. Bypassing her paradise, he licked down the length of her thighs and back again, rubbing a sensitive area just behind her knee. He continued down to suckle a toe as his thumb sought and found her juicy button, flicking it and driving her into a frenzy; Kelvin was enjoying the mewling sounds coming from Princess, loving the feel of her flesh in his mouth. *I waited so long for this. You feel so good. . . .*

Princess couldn't think at all. Words pinged from one side of her brain to the other—random, spontaneous—a mental cacophony accompanying the physical aria that Kelvin so expertly played. Anticipation crawled up her leg along with Kelvin's tongue, from her ankle to her calf to her knee to her thigh, licks in and around her sweetness and then...boo yow! He literally hit her spot, his tongue licking her pussy as though it was a gourmet ice cream cone, his fingers stroking her breasts to spread out the joy. *Please. Kelvin. I can't wait much longer.*

Even as a relatively inexperienced teen, Kelvin had known how to rock her world. Brothah man had picked up some tips along the way and now had her universe tilting on its axis. It was as though her snatch was gold, Kelvin's tongue was a metal detector, and he was recreating the rush of 1848. He alternated between quick, tickling licks and long, purposeful swabs, causing Princess to scream so loud that she grabbed the pillow to stifle the intensity of her release. She shivered and shook and felt the power of Kelvin's lovemaking down to her core. But Kelvin Petersen wasn't finished. He was just getting started.

He kissed his way from her lower lips to her upper ones, barely giving her time to regain her senses before he joined them together in one, long, delicious plunge. Because of his size and the time she'd gone without sex, last night's reinitiation had been slow and methodic. The three or four times after that made Princess Kelvin's perfect fit. So this focused thrust was not only well-received, but Princess's inner walls clutched their welcome, her sticky wet kiss sang his copulatory praises. "Um," Kelvin moaned from a place deep in his soul, as he pulled out slowly, to the tip, and dove back in for a second helping of Princess's paradise. Languidly, methodically, he stroked her; soulfully, skillfully, he held her tight. "I'm so glad you married me," he whispered, letting his dick cosign on just how much. "I'm so glad you're my Princess. I'm so glad you're my wife."

After her third orgasm, a sweaty, sated Princess climbed on top and led the dance. She shifted so that Kelvin could fill her fully, laughed as he watched their connecting with glazed-over eyes. Placing her hands on his strong, broad shoulders, Princess recreated the glide of a merry-go-round, riding Kelvin like a cowgirl who would have done Bill Pickett proud. But Kelvin couldn't let her have all the fun. He once again switched positions, placing pillows under Princess's hips before placing himself behind her. The friction created from how his "Lord have mercy" met her "thank you, Jesus," caused them both to shout hallelujah in a lover's tongue. Princess blew an orgasmic gasket and Kelvin exploded inside her. They flopped down on the mattress, totally satiated, totally spent.

"I love you, Mrs. Petersen," Kelvin whispered as he wrapped a sheet around them.

"We have to go and see Uncle Derrick," Princess replied, taking deep breaths to steady her breathing. "We promised your mom."

"Okay, let me lie here for five, ten more minutes," he said, pulling Princess flush against him and resting his head on her shoulder.

The newlyweds fell into a deep sleep. They didn't wake up until noon. When they left the hotel a half hour later, their eyes were on each other. Which is why neither one of them saw that another pair of eyes was squarely on them.

25

Family Affairs

Vivian placed her hand behind her neck and moved her head from side to side. There was no doubt that she was stressed, and no doubt that she was literally carrying a world's worth of worry on her shoulders.

It had abated for a time. Following Tai's prayer and a brief conversation with her parents, who'd gotten up even earlier than her after arriving at the house last night, a peace that surpassed understanding had enveloped Vivian. It continued as she navigated LA traffic, arrived at Cedars-Sinai, and conversed with Dr. Black. Having had a feeling of what to expect from reading his life story, she was immediately put at ease with his obvious wealth of textbook knowledge combined with a refreshing and soothing down home charm. Dr. Black had been born in Tuskegee, Alabama, to educator parents, and had grown up in Ohio. He'd been fascinated by medicine his whole life, and this continued interest and dedication was immediately evident as he discussed plans for his latest patient. So why had veiled anguish returned to Vivian? Because she'd just left Dr. Black's office and learned that after performing initial tests on Derrick's senses, reflexes, mental status, and memory, the doctor had scheduled an MRI. He wouldn't reveal his thoughts before conclusive evidence was available, but Vivian knew enough to know why MRIs were mostly conducted—brain tumors. There was a very good chance that this was what caused her husband's symptoms, and an at least fifty percent chance that the tumor was malignant.

"Hey, sistah." When Carla Chapman had called as Vivian made her way to the hospital, she'd been assured that she didn't need to add to her already busy schedule by coming to the hospital. But her first lady friend had showed up nonetheless. She was in the hallway by the waiting room, talking on her cell phone when Vivian rounded the corner and thus, was the first person to see her following the meeting with Dr. Black. "What did you find out?"

Vivian took a deep breath and prayed away the unshed tears. "They're going to perform an MRI . . . tomorrow."

Carla hid her surprise. "That's probably best."

"Yes. The sooner they know what they're dealing with the faster they'll be able to treat it."

Carla enveloped her spiritual sister in a big bear hug, love oozing from every pore. "My dear, dear sister. I cannot imagine what you're going through. But it's going to be all right, Vivian. The outcome isn't up to Dr. Black. It's up to God."

"Thank you, Carla. I consider myself a person of faith, but in times like these . . . it's good to be reminded."

Carla ran her hand across her friend's tense back. She thought about how much she loved Lavon, and how devastated she'd be if he were suddenly snatched from her. Then she looked up. "Vivian, Derrick's son is here."

Vivian straightened up and turned around. Later, she'd congratulate herself on the blank face she delivered to the obvious lovebirds coming her way. Oh, they tried to play it off; their countenances properly subdued and concerned. But with one look at Princess, Vivian saw a young lady wearing an after-love glow—the relaxed, contented expression of one who'd been satisfied completely. Vivian was more than aware of that look. She'd worn it herself on countless occasions. The recent conversation with Tai flooded into her mind.

"Kelvin and Princess are at a hotel, instead of your house? Ah, hell."

"Now let's not jump to conclusions, sistah. They could be in separate rooms."

"Oh, come on, Vivian. That's like saying that cows could fly and we both know better than that."

The cows Vivian was looking at weren't becoming airborne anytime soon. "Hello, Kelvin . . . Princess." The greeting was about as dry as the Mojave Desert.

Kelvin leaned in for a hug. "Sorry we're late, Mom Vee. We overslept."

How telling, since I'm sure you overslept together. "I'm glad you're here." And she was.

Princess, meanwhile, had peeped Vivian's eyes as she and Kelvin had approached. She correctly guessed that Vivian's reader radar was as strong as ever and knew that she needed to call her mother . . . now! She stepped to Vivian and gave her a heartfelt hug. "Hey, Aunt Viv. How's Uncle Derrick?"

Vivian filled them in on the latest.

"Mom Vee, you look exhausted," Kelvin said when she'd finished. "Are you going to go home and get some rest?"

"Maybe later," was Vivian's answer. "Princess, have you talked to Tai?"

"I'm getting ready to call her right now." Princess gave a nod and then walked back toward the front door, pulling her phone out of her purse in the process. She swallowed fear along with her spit and took another calming breath as she waited for her mother to answer the phone.

"Princess, what the hell is going on up there?" Tai asked upon answering. Not "hi, how are you," or "how is Uncle Derrick?" but rather "what the *hell* was going on?"

This alerted Princess to the fact that Tai probably knew three things: that she'd arrived in LA the night before, that she hadn't seen Vivian last night, and that she and Kelvin had spent the night in the same hotel. *Damn, damn, damn!* After a few seconds of intense thinking that had followed hours and days of the same,

Princess decided that honesty was the best policy. "Mom, you may not like what I'm getting ready to tell you, but I'm very happy with what is happening right now."

Chagrin didn't begin to describe the sound of Tai's voice. "What's that, Princess, besides you laying up with Kelvin at his hotel?"

Princess took another deep breath, this time swallowing anger before she answered. "I was where I should be," she said slowly. "With my husband."

A train could have been driven through the silence that ensued.

"I'm trying to hold my temper," Tai finally said, talking like someone trying to explain the alphabet to a two-year-old. "If you're there with Rafael, then why didn't you say so straight out the gate?"

"I'm here with Kelvin," Princess clarified.

An explanation obviously clear as mud in Tai's mind. "I get that," Tai said, exasperation evident. "But Rafael is there, too?"

"Mom, Rafael is not here. Kelvin and I got married last night."

Later, Tai would have sworn that the earth stopped spinning in this moment. "You. What?"

"Mom, please, don't freak out. I love Kelvin, and God does, too. I believe I'm in His will."

Well, I'll be damned, is what Tai thought. "Uh-huh," is all she said. She was in such a state of shock that she didn't even realize that she'd hung up the phone without so much as a good-bye to her daughter.

For Tai, the next few hours went by in a haze. She talked to Vivian, who commiserated with her on the news that Princess had delivered, broke the news to a staunch Mama Max, and tried without success to reach Kelvin's mother, Janeé. By the time King called, whom she hadn't tried to reach only because she knew he was in the air, she was numb of all feeling, and had almost convinced herself that what she'd heard earlier was only a dream.

"Hey, baby. We just landed in Barbados. There's another plane in our gate right now so it will be about fifteen minutes before we actually get to deplane. I'm sorry about not calling you during the layover in Dallas, but Daddy left a pretty interesting message on my cell phone and I spent the entire layover talking to him. Tai, you're not going to believe what he told me."

"Yeah," Tai responded before he could go further. "You're not going to believe what I've got to tell you."

Pause. "Okay, I'm listening."

"Your daughter got married. To Kelvin . . . your ex-mistress's son."

"What?" King's loud reaction caused several heads to turn.

"My sentiments exactly. From the moment Derrick passed out during Princess's wedding, I've felt sick to my stomach . . . before that actually, but *anyway*. When she told me yesterday that she was flying to LA with Kelvin, because she was so concerned about her uncle, to hear her tell it, my anxiety increased. But what could I do? I felt a bit of comfort because there was no way she'd do something stupid with Kelvin since she and Rafael were still basically engaged. Well, I thought wrong. Your daughter left one man at the altar and married another."

"I'm stunned, baby. I mean, honestly, what was she thinking? Look, we're nearing the gate now. As soon as I get settled, I'll give her a call, talk to her and Kelvin. In the meantime, what's happening with Derrick?" After Tai gave him the update, he said, "Okay, baby, I'll call you back in an hour or two."

"Okay. I love you."

"Love you, too."

King and his team—which included his assistant, Joseph, the minister of music, and a scaled-down band and praise squad—prepared to exit the plane. King was in first class, the rest of them in coach. That is why he was the first one to hit the Jetway, and the first one to get his breath taken away by the stunning beauty standing next to a driver who held a placard bearing the words MOUNT

ZION. When she smiled, revealing a perfect set of straight, white teeth, his heart almost stopped. Fortunately his legs kept moving long enough for him to reach her side.

"Hello, Pastor Brook."

Her lyrical accent sounded like ambrosia to his ears. Could this possibly be the daughter of his dear friend, Pastor Wesley Freeman? The one whom he remembered wearing pigtails and bangs? "Charmaine?"

She chuckled, and King felt his dick smile. "I know it's been a while, Pastor, and, yes, I'm quite grown up. We have a limousine to transport your staff, but you, man of God, are to come with me. My father awaits you at our home."

Within a matter of minutes, a storm of tsunami proportions developed in the mind of prolific, successful, mega-pastor King Brook. On the one hand was his ongoing concern for the health of his best friend, Derrick Montgomery. On the other was the bomb his wife had just dropped—that his daughter had married his ex-mistress's son. And last but certainly not least was the myriad of undeniable fireworks going off between him and the daughter of a man whose church he'd fellowshipped with for more than a decade. As she draped a casual arm around his waist and expressed her excitement at his arrival, King too felt a growing excitement . . . one that would become a major game changer . . . for everyone.

26

Step By Step

Mama Max pulled a perfectly done rump roast out of the oven.
She raised the top on her cast iron casserole dish and spooned beef
juices over caramelized pieces of carrots, onions, celery, and potatoes. Satisfied that the perfect amount of tenderness existed
between vegetables and meat, she turned off the oven before re-
placing the dish inside it, removed the skillet of golden brown corn
bread and placed it on top of the stove, and stirred the pot of greens
that after two hours had been reduced to fork-tender goodness.
Wiping her hands on her apron, Mama Max then looked at her
watch and hummed a familiar tune as she left the kitchen and
headed toward her master bedroom to freshen up for dinner.

"Thank you, Jesus. Thank you, Jesus. Thank you, Jesus. Thank
you, Lord. Yes, you've brought me, from a mighty, a mighty long
way . . . a mighty long way! Thank you, Jesus." She climbed the
stairs and entered her bedroom, having removed her apron in the
kitchen downstairs and now crossing over to the walk-in closet to
change her blouse. The craziness of the past weekend involving her
granddaughter, and seeing Obadiah after an almost one-year absence, had Mama Max examining emotions she hadn't felt in
years. Memories long buried had risen to the surface and the need
to make sure and weighty decisions clamored for her thoughts.

Cooking what some would consider a Sunday dinner on a Monday night and inviting her trusty neighbor over to enjoy the meal and pass the time was a perfect way for Mama Max to insure that she kept her own mental normalcy intact. The doorbell rang just as she spritzed herself with Elizabeth Taylor's White Diamonds perfume. She continued to hum as she walked down the stairs, crossed the room, and unlocked the screen door.

"Evening, Henry."

"Evening, Maxie. Something in this house sure smells good."

"Rump roast and all the fixings," she threw over her shoulder.

"Your food is always delicious, Maxie. But I just got a whiff of some flowers or something like that."

"Oh, that's my perfume. Tabitha got it for my birthday. Every time she's over here she makes sure I'm wearing it."

"Your granddaughter gone already?" Henry had followed Mama Max into the kitchen and sat at the island, watching her work. Without asking if it were wanted, Mama Max placed a cold glass of water in front of him. "Thank you," he said, before downing almost half the glass.

"Yeah, one of her friends picked her up. They were going to the mall, I think. Or to the movies."

"Do you like going to the movies?"

"These days there's not much out there that I want to see." Mama Max cut the freshly baked corn bread into squares and placed some on a plate. "But I do love me some Tyler Perry."

Henry and Mama Max continued their small talk while she sliced a large heirloom tomato and a sweet white onion. After placing these on a smaller plate, she motioned to Henry. "If you'll put these on the table, I'll fix our plates."

Henry did as requested, then came back into the kitchen and poured himself more water from a pitcher in the fridge. "Do you want some water?"

"I believe I'll have some of that tea in there."

The two sat at the table, Maxine said grace, and they both dug into their food. After a few moments of eating in silence, Henry leaned back, wiped his mouth with a napkin, and took a long drink of water. "Maxie, I swear your cooking is about the best I've ever tasted."

"Go on, now, Henry. I've tasted Beatrice's food before. Your mama can cook!"

Henry finished chewing a piece of the fork-tender rump roast. "Not like this. No wonder they say that the way to a man's heart is through his stomach. Woman, you're going to make me fall for you!"

"You get on out of here, Henry Logan!" Mama Max admonished. "I'm probably old enough to be your mama!"

Henry chuckled. "I know you women don't like to tell your ages, so I won't ask, but I'm sixty-two."

"Hmph. Please, I'm not one of those women. I thank God for every one of these seventy-three years."

"Get outta here, Maxie. There's no way you're seventy-anything. You could pass for fifty, fifty-five years old."

"Boy, either your mouth is lying or your eyesight's bad...or both!"

"Ha!"

Mama Max laughed, enjoying her and Henry's exchange. Following Obadiah's leaving her for Dorothea, Mama Max's self-esteem had plummeted. She was a proud woman who kept her own counsel, so nobody really knew just how badly Obadiah's betrayal had affected her. In public, she was the strong, righteous woman people had come to know and love. But the nights were sometimes hard. True, it had been years since she and her husband had shared the same bed. But they'd shared the same house for more than half a century. Obadiah wasn't only her husband, but until last year, she'd considered him her closest friend. The fire of passion may have played out years ago, but Mama Max felt their lives had settled into a comfortable companionship. Each partner had their place and knew the rules. He preached the Word, she took care of him and home. She liked quilting and crocheting; he liked fishing and fiddling with golf. He watched sports, she preferred reruns of *Good Times* and *Sanford and Son*. Their conversation wasn't anything particularly special, centering mostly around church and family, but Mama Max had thought it was enough. Obviously, it wasn't.

"Forgive my being forward," Henry continued, "but you have to know that you are an attractive woman."

Mama Max thought back to the cherry red suit she'd worn yesterday, after having visited the hairdresser who'd fried, dyed, and laid her hair to the side. "I clean up all right, I reckon. But you best be careful, Henry Logan. If I recall correctly, Beatrice mentioned something to me about your having a wife."

A brief frown marred Henry's smooth brown countenance. "I was married," he acknowledged, finishing up the last bites from his plate. "But we got divorced after she had an affair."

Well, this certainly got Mama Max's attention. She was too near him not to hear him. "I'm sure sorry to hear that."

"I was, too, at the time. Remember my telling you about the problems I had after Vietnam?" Mama Max nodded. "Well, one of those problems involved my, uh, being able to perform my husbandly duties." Henry wiped his mouth, looking uncomfortable. "It's not easy for a man to talk about . . . these kinds of things. But you seem the type of woman who'd understand." He proceeded to tell Mama Max about the injury that at times caused him to be unable to perform, and the multiple affairs that his wife had had as a result of this problem. "What about you, Maxie? All this time I assumed that you and Obadiah were divorced, but after hearing the ladies at the church talk yesterday, it sounds like y'all are still married."

"That's the official version, that he's down in Texas helping out a ministry," Mama Max said without thinking. But somehow, strangely, she wasn't sorry that she'd been truthful. Aside from her son and daughter-in-law, King and Tai, and her dear friend, Nettie, who lived in Texas, Mama Max hadn't been able to share the burden of her marriage with anyone. Henry's obvious concern and compassion were palpable, creating a safe space for Mama Max to reveal her secrets. "But between you and me," she continued, cocking a brow and giving Henry a "don't spread my business" look, "me and Obadiah are still married only in name. He's actually down there helping out his mistress of the past forty years. He left me for her last year." Mama Max tried to deliver this last sentence with a strong, dispassionate voice, but her eyes misted over.

"I'm sorry, Maxie." Henry reached over and squeezed Mama Max's arm.

Mama Max covered the weak moment with a wry smile. "I'm still standing," she responded, getting up and gathering their empty dishes. "The Lord is my help. No, no, keep your seat. I can handle these few little dishes. We cleaned these plates real good, but I hope you left room for that peach cobbler I've got warming in the oven."

"C'mon now, Maxie. I've always got room for your sweets."

Mama Max had only been in the kitchen a few moments when she heard the screen door rattle. "Henry, can you go and unlock that front door? It's probably Tabitha coming back to get that Eye Pad she left here."

Henry walked to the door and, considering the recent conversation, was a bit surprised to see who was on the other side. "Yes?" he said by way of greeting, unlocking the door and opening it just a few inches. "May I help you?"

An immediately indignant Obadiah rose up to his full height of six feet. The man in front of him looked familiar, and he quickly placed him as the one who'd been seated next to Maxine in church yesterday. "You don't have to do nothing for me," Obadiah finally answered, taking a step forward. "I'm Maxine's husband and this is my house. Who are you?"

"I'm Henry Logan, the neighbor and friend who's going to make sure you don't hurt her no more."

A raised eyebrow was the only sign of Obadiah's surprise. That and his raised voice. "I suggest you move out the way before I have to move you out of it."

"Who is it, Henry?" Mama Max asked from the kitchen.

Henry stepped aside to let in Obadiah. "Your husband."

A surprised Mama Max came around the corner carrying two bowls filled with peach cobbler. "Obadiah? What are you doing here?" She continued to the dining room, where Henry quickly joined her. "I thought you'd be back in Dallas by now."

Obadiah's eyes narrowed as he took in the homey, cozy scene—Henry sitting at the dining room table that his preaching had bought, eating the cooking that for almost a year Obadiah had missed. His nose caught a whiff of one of his favorites, rump roast and potatoes, and that peach cobbler was smelling so good that Obadiah wanted to take the pie-filled fork that even now was on its way to Henry's mouth . . . and stab him with it.

After another awkward moment where Obadiah felt like a stranger in his own home, he straightened his back, swallowed a big dose of pride, and left the room. For the next several seconds, the only sounds heard were those of his heavy footsteps on the home's wooden stairs.

27

A Woman's Worth

"You want me to leave?" Henry had pushed back from the table and now sat—arms crossed, scowl on face.

"Not unless you want to." Mama Max calmly placed another bite of flaky-crusted cobbler into her mouth. It was the first time in her life that she'd seen Obadiah sweat behind another man giving her attention. It was an unexpected life development. Mama Max discovered that she quite liked it. But for all of the gloating that she felt, it was mixed with compassion. Before the mouthful of pride he had swallowed, Mama Max had detected sadness in Obadiah's eyes. Still, turnabout was fair play and Mama Max had no problem giving the good Reverend Doctor a taste of his own medicine. She turned to Henry and smiled sweetly. "You want some milk to go with your cobbler?"

Henry eyed Mama Max a long moment before a slight smile slid across his face and he picked up his fork. "I'd better let this water be enough, else I'll start to develop a paunch."

"Ha!" Mama Max patted her sizable stomach. "I guess you're right about that."

Mama Max settled back into a somewhat comfortable camaraderie that, considering the circumstances, was quite a feat. They'd almost gotten through the decadent cobbler dessert before the sound of Obadiah's returning footsteps echoed down the stairs.

"Maxine."

Obadiah had simply entered the living room and called her name, but Mama Max knew the plethora of conversation that lay beyond that one word: *I want to talk to you, alone. I'm hurt and angry for being ignored. I'm sorry for treating you so badly. There are some things we need to discuss. I'm not leaving here until we've settled a few things.* When two people had lived together for more than fifty years, this is the type of translation that could occur. And even though she had company and Obadiah had come over uninvited to what was still technically his house, well, Mama Max was too much of a Christian with a healthy dose of brought-upsy thrown in to not talk with the man who was still technically her husband.

Henry felt the shift in her demeanor. "I guess I'd better go." His voice was low, soothing.

"I think it would be best," Mama Max said, her voice equally low as she rose from the table. She walked Henry to the door, noting that Obadiah was standing with his back to them, looking at the large family portrait that hung over the fireplace. It was a picture taken at a family reunion five years ago and showed seventy-five smiling faces representing several family branches and four generations.

Seconds after he heard the screen door close and lock, Obadiah turned around and wasted no time in starting the interrogation. "What's going on here, Maxine?"

Maxine crossed her arms. "What's it to you, Obadiah?"

"I'd say having another man in the house I bought and paid for makes it my business." He knew the argument was flimsy and the words hypocritical, but he couldn't resist.

"And what does you committing adultery do, huh, Reverend? Whose business should that be?" Mama Max placed a hand on her hip, her chest heaving from the heavy breathing she did in an effort to keep some semblance of composure. "You've got a hell of a lot of nerve standing there and trying to tell me anything! You back-sliding hypocrite!"

"Don't you stand there acting all innocent and holy. If you'd performed your wifely duties, I wouldn't have gone sliding anywhere!"

"So that's still what you're telling yourself to help you sleep nights? That I'm the reason you're sinning? Is that what you're thinking sweating over that whore Dorothea? That it's *my* fault? If you believe that lie from the pit of hell, then not only are you a bigger fool than I thought you was, but you've gone and forgotten every scripture in the Bible from Genesis to Revelation!"

With eyes blazing and chests heaving, the two septuagenarians stared each other down. Finally, Obadiah heaved a sigh and ran a weary hand over his face. "Look, Maxine, I didn't come here to argue."

"Then why are you here?" Mama placed a firm hand on her ample hip.

"To get some more of my summer suits, and a few books from the study that I've been needing." Obadiah walked over to the couch and plopped down. "But honestly, I came over to get some of what that rascal had the nerve to be eating while sitting at my table. I've missed your good cooking, Maxine," he continued, his tone softer. The warmth in his eyes conveyed that he'd missed more than her food, but Mama Max was too angry to notice. Hers was still the stance of a warrior ready for battle. "Do you think you can find it in your heart to serve a hungry man a plate of food?"

Mama Max narrowed her eyes. "Well," she said after a pause, "I'd throw a bone to a dog walking on four legs, so I guess I can feed one walking on two." She left to fix his plate and upon returning, saw that Obadiah had moved to the dining room table, sitting at the head place Henry had recently vacated. "You want something to drink?"

"Some iced tea would be nice."

Lord, give me strength, Mama Max thought with a roll of the eyes. Still, she walked into the kitchen, poured his drink, and was quite proud of herself that the glass of tea actually ended up on the table instead of being thrown in his face!

Obadiah, who was already scarfing down the food as if it were his last meal, nodded when Mama Max set down the glass. "I 'preciate it." After taking a long swig, he belched, picked up the napkin that she'd also set down, and eyed Mama Max as he wiped his mouth. "That joker who was in here looks familiar. Who is he?"

"That's Henry," Mama Max said, sitting down with her own glass of tea. The move was natural, subconscious, honed from sitting down and chatting like this with Obadiah a thousand times. "Beatrice Logan's son."

"I thought he lived in Indianapolis."

"You didn't know that Beatrice had a stroke?"

"Sho'nuff?" Obadiah picked up the fork as he slowly shook his head. "No, I didn't know nothing about it."

"Well, she did, a few months back. They moved her to an assisted-living facility and he moved back to be closer to her. I thought either King or Tai would have mentioned it to you, or one of the deacons you stay in touch with.."

"I haven't been too in touch with anybody," Obadiah replied. "Folk forget about you when you're not around."

"We need to talk about that, Obadiah. About your not being around." Mama Max peered beyond him, stared at the large oak tree that dominated the front yard. "I won't go on like this, Obadiah. I won't continue to live a lie. So I guess it's about time to talk about splitting up everything and going our separate ways—for good."

Obadiah swirled the remaining piece of corn bread around the plate, soaking up the last juices from the roast and greens before placing the morsel into his mouth. He closed his eyes as he chewed, savoring the pleasure of this last bite. "So what you're telling me," he said, after swallowing the last of the tea, "is that you want us to go through with the divorce."

"This ain't about what I want, Negro! It's about what is. You're in Texas, I'm up here. We're already living separate lives. Might as well make it official."

"Does this have anything to do with that Logan fella sniffing 'round here?"

"That ain't none of your business, Obadiah. All you need to do is call that lawyer you said you filed the papers with and let's get this crying shame of a show on the road."

Obadiah left shortly thereafter, but not without half of Mama Max's peach cobbler. And not without a plan. What Mama Max didn't know was that Obadiah had never filed any papers with any lawyer. And he didn't plan to now. No, when Obadiah got on the plane the next morning headed for Texas, it was very clear what he needed to do: end the adulterous affair with Dorothea . . . and take back his rump roast.

28

Daydreaming

King walked out of the shower, naked and glistening, still marveling at the paradise in which he'd slept. As the financially secure pastor of a mega-church who'd traveled extensively, he regularly ate in five-star restaurants and experienced his share of luxurious resorts. But Minister Wesley Freeman's seventy-five-hundred square foot, oceanfront villa took opulence to a new level. Last night's lavish dinner had been superbly hosted by Wesley's daughter, Charmaine, and besides himself and Wesley, was enjoyed by seven of His Holy Word Cathedral's elite. After dessert, which was served on the expansive patio while lapping waves created a symphony of serenity mere feet from where they sat, Wesley informed King that for the next two weeks he'd be their personal guest, and that the two-thousand square foot guesthouse was to be used for his pleasure and convenience. Just after the other guests had left, King had pled exhaustion (the truth) and had been shown to his quarters by the lovely Charmaine, who'd made sure that he was aware of every amenity. And somehow, while exhibiting the utmost of propriety and decorum, she'd subtly yet unmistakably conveyed that she was one of them.

Keep your focus, brother. You're here for ministry, not messy affairs. And he had no doubt that any dabbling with Wesley Freeman's daughter would be messy. Following the untimely death of her mother several years ago, Charmaine had become the undisputed woman of the house while continuing to be the proverbial apple of her father's eye. *Yeah, Wesley's friendship is just the kind of buffer I need. Because if the coast were clear, I'd grab that smooth, round a*—King's ringing phone was a welcomed interruption.

"Hey, baby."

"King, please keep me from beating your child to within an inch of her life!"

King chuckled, placing the call on speaker and reaching for a container of lotion before sitting on the bed.

"Excuse me, but I fail to find any humor in this situation. I'm hoping there's some way we can get this marriage annulled before any damage is done. The Stevenses aren't talking to me, and I don't blame them. Rafael hasn't returned Princess's calls and that's without him even knowing about her shotgun wedding."

"Wait. I thought shotgun wedding referred to when the bride was pregnant."

"In this case it refers to when the mother-in-law wants to shoot the groom."

"Ha!"

Finally, a slight chuckle slipped from Tai's otherwise tight lips. "I'm still hoping to talk some sense into your stubborn daughter's head. She has agreed to meet with me, alone, when I fly out to LA."

The atmosphere changed as both thought of why Tai would be visiting the City of Angels. "How's he doing?"

"Vivian is really worried, King. They're conducting an MRI tomorrow and she's afraid of what they'll find."

A moment of silence and then, "I wonder if I should cut this trip short."

"I thought about that, too, baby. I know your heart is with your friend. At this point, however, I think it best for you to fulfill your obligation there in Barbados. This trip has been planned for almost two years. I'll keep you abreast of what's going on here and if the situation gets more critical . . . I'll definitely let you know."

After getting an update on his father's handling of yesterday's service and Mama Max's declaration that a divorce was imminent, King had to end the call. "Tai, I'm expected for brunch in less than an hour. I need to run."

"All right."

"Keep me posted on everything going on."

"I will."

Thirty minutes later, King walked the thirty or so yards from the guesthouse to the main residence. Between the two was a lush, tropical garden with strategically placed stone benches and a high-spewing water feature. He was greeted by the butler, and led down a path to the ocean's shore, where a canopied tent housed a white linen-covered table, a stainless steel buffet, and a dapperly dressed Wesley Freeman.

"Hey, Wes!" King shoulder-bumped the tall, lean man who was ten years his senior. In the light of a new morning, King recognized that Wesley gave Charmaine her tall, lean build and long, thick head of hair that most would assume was a weave. Her late mother, Charlotte, had blessed her daughter with the almond-shaped eyes and dark chocolate skin that made Charmaine's an exotic look that models would envy.

"My brother." Wesley took a seat and signaled the waiter to begin serving. "I trust our humble abode was to your liking?"

"Man, I've stayed in some fancy places, but I must say that this place truly is paradise."

Wesley nodded. "God is good."

"Indeed. Plants actually growing *in* the shower, half of which is outdoors? That was a first, something that we could never imagine in Kansas. Sleeping in that bed was like floating on a cloud. Seriously, man . . . I slept like a newborn babe."

The two men shared casual small talk while the waiter served a delectable combination of traditional American and Caribbean cuisine: fluffy scrambled eggs, fresh crab cakes, seasonal fruit, plantains, black and white pudding (without the soused pig head, much to King's relief), and freshly baked breads.

After a few moments of eating in silence, Wesley shifted the conversation to business matters. "We are indeed excited about taking our ministry to the next level. Incorporating the type of television ministry that we're envisioning will definitely place His Holy Word at the forefront of this latest global movement." Wesley leaned forward, looked King in the eye. "Tonight, you will meet a contingent of men from Africa, with their pulse on every single Christian ministry on that continent. King, I've always admired you, man, have always seen your star rise and not be limited to the states. It is now within your power to become a major player on the international front: in the Caribbean, African, and Asian communities as well. God is taking His Kingdom to another level. You and I are poised to lead this march into destiny!"

King nodded, taking in the excitement of Wesley's infectious words. He'd always liked this driven preacher's enthusiasm, ever since they'd met at a conference ten years ago. Now, all these years later, much of what he'd dreamed of then had come to pass. His Holy Word Cathedral was the largest church in the Caribbean, and Wesley wasn't even yet on TV.

The slight rustling of foliage and the scent of fresh jasmine announced Charmaine's arrival. King consciously steeled himself before looking up, but that didn't stop his heart from thumping and his dick from hardening at the vision that stood before him. Today, she wore a flowing, stark white dress with minimal jewelry and makeup. This only served to highlight her natural beauty. Her hair was piled atop her head, with a few tendrils framing her face and caressing her neck the way King longed to do.

"Hey, Daddy," she said, as she approached the table, her lyrical accent as soothing as a summer breeze. She kissed her father on the cheek before continuing around the table. "Good morning, Pastor," she crooned, before placing a kiss on his cheek as well.

"You headed to the church?" her father asked.

"Yes. I have to make sure that all of the host auxiliaries are in place and that this evening's dinner is going as planned. I won't see you until tonight so, gentlemen, you'll have to get through the day without me." She winked at King, placed a hand on her father's shoulder, and then breezed out as effortlessly as she'd walked in.

King watched her as she left. "The shy young girl I met ten years ago has matured into a stunning woman. You must be incredibly proud of her."

Wesley nodded. "Indeed."

"How old is she, twenty-six or -seven?"

"Charmaine turned twenty-eight a few months ago. But she's always been an old soul, with a grace, wisdom, and maturity far beyond her years."

"She's going to make some lucky man an awesome wife. If I was single and about twenty years younger..."

Wesley gave King a speculative look, rubbed the perfectly trimmed beard on his otherwise clean-shaven face before speaking. "King, my daughter has been in love with you since she was eighteen years old. She'd love to be your wife."

King hid the joy he felt at this revelation behind a casual smile. "That's flattering, Wesley. But she's a wife, four children, and a couple decades too late."

Wesley nodded. "Indeed." He looked at his watch. "We should leave here within the hour to meet the contingent from the Motherland."

"Thanks for the meal, Wes. As with everything else that you've provided, brothah, it just doesn't get any better."

"Oh, it can always get better," Wesley replied, giving King a brotherly slap on the back. "God can give us abundantly, exceedingly more than we ever dreamed."

Considering what King was dreaming about, he knew this wasn't true. How could God give him a wife when he already had one?

29

The Sideline Story

Rafael sat in his City Hall office, holding a report that he'd been trying to read for the past ten minutes. He hadn't been able to get past the first paragraph. Thoughts about Princess kept getting in the way. Was it just ten days ago that Derrick Montgomery had collapsed to the floor causing Rafael's world to crumble in the process? Yep, less than two weeks ago, Saturday before last, he was on his way to being the happiest man in Kansas City. There'd been a wedding ring in his pocket and tickets for a romantic getaway to Montego Bay in his hand. Less than two weeks ago, he was clear about his future, sure about his destiny. But today—Monday, June 25, Rafael wasn't sure about an em-effing thing.

"Mr. Stevens?" The voice of Rafael's assistant crackled through the office intercom. "You wanted to be reminded about your one o'clock meeting on the fourth floor?"

Rafael looked at his watch. It was 12:45. "Yes, thanks, Jennifer."

"You're welcome."

Reaching for his suit jacket, Rafael set his office voice mail and headed for the door. *Might as well go by the newsstand and grab a snack. . . . I'm not getting work done anyway.* In fact, he'd not been able to do much of anything—eat, sleep, focus—since Princess left him. His parents had suggested that he use one of the tickets and clear his head in Montego Bay, but Rafael knew that all he'd think about was the fact that Princess was supposed to be there with him. So he'd decided to cowboy up and face the music without taking time off. He'd endured the compassionate, inquisitive, and even smug stares of his coworkers as he'd showed up for work the Tuesday following his failed nuptials. He'd buried himself in work—the only woman who'd never left him and never done him wrong. And now he was getting ready to add to an already full schedule by becoming a consultant to a new nonprofit organization that paired successful African-American businessmen with at-risk male teens. It was just the type of cause Rafael needed to keep him from losing his mind, and help him heal his broken heart.

Rafael exited the elevator and walked into the small "newsstand," more like a small grocer really, on the City Hall's first floor. In addition to a plethora of newspapers from all over the country, tabloids, and magazines, the shop housed toiletries, over-the-counter medicines such as aspirin and cold tablets, a variety of sodas, juice, and water, and snacks like sandwiches, chips, and fruit. He waved at the woman behind the counter before walking back to the refrigerated section and grabbing an orange juice. On his way to the counter, he picked up a banana and a bag of chips. He'd probably lost five pounds since his broken engagement, but if and when his appetite returned, Rafael planned to be prepared.

The perky brunette behind the counter offered a warm smile. "Hello, Mr. Stevens."

"Hey, sweetie. How are you today?"

"Better now that Mr. Sunshine has walked into the building."

Rafael laughed, paid for his purchases, and headed out the door. As he walked by a row of newspapers and tabloids, a picture caught his eye. *Screech. Back up.* Rafael took two steps back, and bent down to peer at the tabloid cover. Even after his eyes confirmed it, he tried to convince himself that what he saw couldn't possibly actually be what was on this front page: SUPERSTAR BASKETBALL PLAYER SCORES BIG! Under the caption was a picture of

Kelvin and Princess, snuggled against each other with wide smiles on their faces. Rafael mindlessly pulled out a five-dollar bill, showed the cashier the tabloid while placing the money on the counter, and walked out.

He didn't stop walking until he was out of the building and about a half block from his workplace. Taking a seat on a park bench, Rafael worked hard to swallow past the lump in his throat as he shuffled through the pages until he found the story.

> *It seems that Kelvin Petersen, the superstar starting guard for the Phoenix Suns, has scored his biggest goal to date . . . a wife! Sources who spoke on condition of anonymity reported that Petersen and his on-again off-again girlfriend of several years, Princess Brook, slipped into Las Vegas and tied the knot at a chapel on the strip before holing up at LA's Ritz-Carlton hotel for a cozy honeymoon.*
>
> *Brook, known mostly for her costarring appearances on* Conversations with Carla, *was most recently engaged to her high school sweetheart, Rafael Stevens, an up-and-coming political player in Kansas City, Missouri. No word on what caused their breakup, but it looks as though Petersen, known to his fans as "the KP," has both "stolen the ball" and "scored a layup." Sounds like it's time for Stevens's concession speech!*

Rafael sat, stunned into immobility. He read the article once, twice, and yet a third time, and still the words failed to totally sink in. *Princess? Married? WTF?* He looked at the three pictures that accompanied the article in addition to the one that had been splashed across the front page. In one, Kelvin and Princess were by a valet podium, engaged in conversation. In another, Kelvin seemed to be showing Princess something on his cell phone, and in the third, he was reaching down to give her a hug. Upon closer examination, Rafael deduced that the pictures could have indeed been taken in front of a hotel, perhaps the Ritz as the article claimed. One thing was for certain. A picture was worth a thousand words. Princess Brook had dumped him and married Kelvin, the man who'd caused her so much pain. And Rafael had no words for that.

Rafael's phone buzzed. He looked down at it dispassionately. His rational mind tried to kick into action, and from somewhere came the vague reminder of something called a job and an obligation otherwise known as a meeting.

By rote, he pushed the talk button. "Hello?"

It was his assistant, Jennifer, on the line. Concern oozed in between her inquiring words. "Boss, are you all right?"

Silence.

"Rafael. The woman from the shop downstairs brought up the tabloid. I, uh, saw the picture. That was after Mitchell Sherman called to say that you hadn't arrived for your one o'clock meeting."

Rafael shook his head, trying to clear the fog. *Meeting. At one o'clock. Right. Regarding professional mentors and at-risk boys.* "I'm sorry, Jennifer," he responded, his raspy voice the evidence of his raw emotions. "What time is it?"

"It's one-fifteen, boss. Should I tell Mitchell that you'll have to reschedule?"

Rafael stood, began to walk, and continued to work his way out of the Twilight Zone. "No, Jennifer. Tell him I'm on my way. Offer up my apologies. I'll be there in five minutes."

Through prayer and sheer will, Rafael not only made it through the meeting, but through the rest of the day. Princess had taken away his confidence, his security, his self-esteem. He refused to let her rob him of his professional acumen and reputation. At promptly five o'clock, he put on his suit jacket, grabbed his briefcase, and left the building. He wasn't in his car a good ten minutes before his best friend, Greg, was blowing up his phone.

"El, dog, have you heard?"

No need to act as though he didn't know what Greg meant. "Saw it earlier today, a stack of bullshit hot off the press was at the newsstand."

"Wow, man, I can't believe it. I'm sorry, brothah. I don't know what else to say."

"Nothing more to be said."

A moment of silence and then, "What do you think happened? I mean, there's no way that this could have been planned—right?"

"Greg, I don't even know. I can't even think right now and truth be told, I don't want to. I don't want to speculate, ruminate, or try and imagine. I just want to try and forget I ever knew a woman named Princess Brook. That's real talk right there. Let alone when my parents find out about this. Moms is already ballistic, but after this news, even my calm, conservative father may be ready to kick some ass."

"I hear ya, man, but you're doing the right thing in putting her and this whole unfortunate experience behind you. And speaking of . . . I've got just the kind of night that will take your mind off Princess."

Rafael was almost as certain as a DNA paternity test that he didn't want to hear this, but he asked anyway. "What?"

"Just be ready to roll around nine o'clock. I'll swing by your place and then take you to a private party."

"On a Monday night?"

"Yeah, on a Monday. I'll tell you all about it on the way. Just be ready."

30

Lights, Camera, Attraction

By the time nine o'clock had rolled around, Rafael had changed his mind about going out. He knew that Greg was his boy and had his back, but really . . . was there anyone or anything that could take his mind off what had transpired in the last ten days? Rafael didn't think so, and he also didn't think he was up to schmoozing, networking, and being the mayoral-man-about-town, talking, laughing, and trying to wear a smile. That's why when Greg knocked on his door, Rafael was laid back on the couch sans shoes and shirt, watching C-SPAN and drinking a beer.

"Man, what are you doing?" Greg asked when Rafael opened the door. "It's nine o'clock. I told you to be ready."

"Yo, dog, I know you mean well and all, but a brothah isn't feeling the social scene right now."

Greg stood in the middle of Rafael's living room with a scowl on his face. He placed his hands on his hips and for a while, watched the boring discussion about global warming that seemed to have Rafael's rapt attention. "All right, man," he said at last, with a shake of his head. "It's clear that Princess has rendered you not only senseless, but immobile. I understand. After all, she was the last single woman on the planet." Ignoring Rafael's cutting glance, he continued. "The host was looking forward to having you, but I'll tell them that you're . . . not well." He headed toward the door.

"Yeah, well, forget you, man."

Greg sighed. "I know you're hurting, man. And I can't say that I feel your pain because I've never experienced what just happened to you."

"And I hope you never do."

"But what I do know is that the best way to get over a situation is to keep it moving, keep taking the next step." He opened the door. "I'll catch'cha later, dog. When you're ready to get back in the game of life . . . hollah at me."

Just before the door clicked shut, Rafael called out, "Greg." Greg turned around. "Give me ten minutes."

Thirty minutes later Greg had left downtown KC behind and was now on Paseo Avenue heading to the famed area of Eighteenth and Vine, which in its heyday served as a haven for premiere jazz talents such as Charlie Parker, Big Joe Turner, Count Basie, and the incomparable Jay McShann. The area also housed the Negro Leagues Baseball Museum, which among others honored the Kansas City Monarchs, led by Baseball Hall of Fame pitcher Satchel Paige. Thankfully, the area was experiencing a new birth due in part to Rafael's personally led promotion of the area, especially in terms of making it a premiere jazz and history aficionado's tourist destination.

Tonight, however, the streets were quiet. It was a Monday night in a worker's town; not too many people were hitting the scene. Rafael had been pretty quiet during the trip and it continued as his thoughts turned to where in the heck this party was. With as much improvement that had happened in the area, including the restored Gem Theater and the popular Kansas City Blues and Jazz Juke House, he was having a hard time fathoming where this "exclusive, upscale" party that Greg alluded to was taking place. When Greg took a left onto Eighteenth Street, a right on Highland, and pulled up in front of the Mutual Musicians Foundation, Rafael was further perplexed. The street was way more crowded than usual and he saw what looked like filming trucks and equipment lining the street. But before he could ask questions, Greg hopped out of the car.

Rafael caught up with Greg as they neared the building. "What's all this?"

Greg's look was unreadable. "You'll see."

They reached the Foundation. A security guard was at the door. Greg gave his name, the guard checked his clipboard, and after a curt nod, opened the door so that Greg and Rafael could pass through.

Inside was organized chaos. The small room that once served as home to the African-American Musician's Union Local 627, and for decades had continued as the after-hours jam spot for musicians, had been transformed into a 1930s speakeasy. Various film crew members scurried about. Some handled lighting. Others moved props. A makeup artist was set up in the far corner. Extras sat at the small round tables that were covered with white linen tablecloths and decorated with candles. Rafael noticed a couple of director chairs at the exact moment a young man got out of one and walked in their direction.

"Hey, Greg. Good to see you."

"Hey, Doug." Greg and Doug did the shake/shoulder bump.

Doug looked at Rafael. "Is this the actor?" He held out his hand. "Doug Thomas."

"Whoa, wait a minute." Rafael looked from Greg to Doug. "Trust me, you've got the wrong guy."

"I don't think so." The sultry, female voice came from just behind Rafael's ear.

He slowly turned around. "Kiki?"

"Last time I checked." She gave Rafael a hug and whispered in his ear. "I saw the story in the tabloid; figured you could use a distraction."

And just like that Rafael replaced one leading lady with another—at least until the director yelled "cut."

31

Tomorrow

"It's a tumor."

The words Vivian uttered hit Tai like a brick. She'd been dreading this phone call and praying for something other than this outcome ever since learning that the MRI results were in and the Montgomerys were headed to the hospital for a meeting with Dr. Black. "Viv, I'm so sorry."

Vivian didn't even try to keep the tears from flowing. "Me, too."

"Are they absolutely sure?"

Vivian filled Tai in on what had been discussed during the doctor visit. "We were so hoping that there was another less serious explanation for what happened that day, for why Derrick passed out. That he was seriously dehydrated, or even had pneumonia. This is the worst possible outcome."

"Wait. Have they already done the biopsy and know it's malignant?"

"No, the surgery is scheduled for Friday . . . three days from now."

"Then as bad as things look, Viv, we have to stay optimistic."

"Optimistic?" Vivian's voice was incredulous. "Just where am I supposed to find the optimism around the fact that they're getting ready to cut open my husband's head?"

Tai recognized the fear in her best friend's outburst. "I can only imagine how hard this must be for you, girl. It is only natural to be worried and upset. But these are the times when our anchor of faith must hold, and grip the solid Rock."

There was a long pause before Vivian spoke. "Of course you're right, Tai. But that's much easier said than done. Last night, I thought back to the countless counseling sessions I've had with members facing one type of challenge or the other, all the scriptures I'd quote and biblical examples I'd use. But when it's personal, when it's you facing the mountain . . ."

"Then you depend on friends who love you to quote those scriptures and cite those examples of when God came through. You can be still, and hear us say things like by His stripes, Derrick is healed, and that even though he walks through the valley of the shadow of death, we will fear no evil."

"Thank you, my dear sister," Vivian said, with a sniffle. "I really appreciate your words and your prayers. You know, I've never even considered life without Derrick and the mere thought is just about to drive me crazy. We often say that life is short, but when the reality of just how short it might be comes crashing in, the feeling is overwhelming."

"Let's stay focused on the positive, Vivian. Let's focus on what we want, not what we don't want."

"Girl, that sounds like something from one of Oprah's *Lifeclass* episodes."

Tai chuckled. "I think that's where I heard it."

Vivian's tone brightened. "I've been researching brain tumors on the Internet and have learned that benign tumors can almost always be successfully removed, and that patients can make a full recovery."

"Derrick is young, healthy; and I absolutely believe that that will be his outcome—a full and complete recovery."

"In Jesus's name."

The two women chatted a bit more with Tai confirming the

time of Derrick's surgery and assuring Vivian that she'd forward her flight information as soon as it was booked. After the call, Vivian continued to sit in her office, in silence, praying to God and composing herself before she rejoined Derrick, whom she'd left lounging in the great room. It had been a tough week, but the hardest part lay in front of them. Vivian knew she needed to be strong, not only for the kids but for Derrick. She meditated for a few moments, did an exercise in deep breathing, and then rose to join her husband in the other room.

"Hey, baby," she said, walking over to the couch and sitting so that his head rested in her lap "How are you doing?"

Derrick ignored her question. "Baby, I spoke with our attorney earlier. We need to handle a little business tomorrow."

Vivian stroked her husband's face. "What kind of business?"

"We need to make sure our wills are in order."

The stroking stopped. "No."

Derrick opened his eyes. "No? What do you mean *no*?"

"I'm not going down that road, Derrick. I don't even want to think like that."

He sat up. "Viv, nobody gets out of here alive, baby. This is something that we probably should have handled a long time ago. This situation that's going on with me has brought it to the forefront, that's all. . . . Look, baby, I don't plan on leaving you anytime soon. But we need to be prepared for whatever might happen."

Well, so much for Tai's words, the meditation, and the deep-breathing techniques. Vivian was once again wound as tight as a drum. "That may be," she said at last, "but I'm not going to talk about wills or death or anything like that until after your surgery, until this storm has passed. I'm not going to do anything that portends any outcome other than your having this operation and coming out in divine health on the other side."

"Baby—"

"I mean it, Derrick," Vivian snapped. "We need to update our wills. Fine. We can do it next month. But I am not going to do it tomorrow. So you might as well call your boy and give him the news." She stood. "And speaking of news, let's talk to the children tonight during dinner, okay?" She didn't wait for a response, but left and headed to the kitchen . . . where Derrick couldn't see her silent tears.

Later that evening, Derrick, Vivian, D2, and Elisia sat around the Montgomery dining room table. Vivian had fixed tacos, one of her children's favorite meals, rounding out the dinner with corn and rice. For a while, the room was filled with the kid's chatter: D2 wanting to spend time with Kelvin in Phoenix (we'll see) and Elisia wanting to dye her hair a Rihanna red (hell to the no).

"Mom, Dad, can I be excused to go play video games?" D2 asked, after finishing his fifth taco and effectively cleaning his plate.

"In a minute, son. There's something we need to discuss with you and Elisia." He looked at Vivian and gave an almost imperceptible nod.

"So, guys, we got back the results from your father's MRI." She looked at Elisia. "Do you remember what we told you an MRI is?"

Elisia nodded. "Where they look inside your body."

"Yes," Vivian replied.

"Magnetic resonance imaging," D2 added. Both Derrick and Vivian looked at him with raised brows. D2 shrugged. "I asked Kelvin and when he didn't know, we both looked it up online."

Derrick took over. "Well, they looked inside my head and it turns out there is a tumor growing there. I'm having surgery on Friday to have it removed."

Elisia gasped as she turned wide eyes on her father. "They're going to cut your head open?"

Vivian placed a comforting hand on Elisia's arm. "Yes, baby. A very skilled doctor who has performed this surgery hundreds of times is going to make an incision in his head, take out the tumor, and then sew it back up."

"That sounds scary, Daddy," Elisia said. "Don't do it."

Derrick glanced at Vivian before answering. "That's just it. I have to do it, baby, in order to get well."

"But if they cut you in the head, then you might die!" Elisia's eyes filled with tears.

"Oh, shut up, girl," Derrick Jr. said, his face fixed in a serious scowl. "Where's your faith?" He looked at his father. "Don't even sweat it, Daddy, for real. No weapon formed against you will prosper. Isn't that what you've always told me?" The questioning look in D2's eyes belied the bravado in his voice.

"Yes, son," Derrick answered, clearing the tears from his throat. "I believe that I'll be all right. This is simply a test of our faith and I will need all of you"—he looked lovingly at Elisia and gave her a wink—"to believe that God is able. In the meantime, Grandpa and Grandma have a trip planned for the four of you. . . . You're going to Disneyland!"

"Yes!" Elisia yelled.

D2 shot daggers at his sister. "I'm staying here." It didn't sound like a question.

"Derrick, I appreciate your wanting to be here for your father, but believe it or not, you'll be doing him a bigger favor by going away and having fun. It's all about lifting our prayers to God, and having a positive, happy attitude is a part of that." When D2's countenance continued to be doubtful, she continued. "Maybe after this is over, you can spend that time in Phoenix with your brother that you've wanted."

The family meeting continued for another hour. After that, they retired to the great room, played some board games, watched a movie, and then Derrick and Vivian tucked the children into bed.

The reverend and his wife retired soon afterward. They made love, slowly, soulfully. The words weren't spoken, but they were physically expressed: tomorrow is not promised. With each stroke, touch, kiss, thrust . . . they made the most of the moment they had tonight.

32

Yield Not To Temptation

King sat back in the cushiony leather chair that accommodated his bulky frame as he soared thirty-five-thousand feet above sea level. When Wesley Freeman offered the church's private jet as a means to hurry to his best friend's side, King did not hesitate in accepting the offer. Thinking about Derrick's health had kept his mind distracted all week. And any part of his thoughts that weren't on Derrick were dominated by Wesley's daughter, Charmaine. She had singularly and completely been the Barbados beauty for which he had not been prepared, had not even thought about prior to this visit. The last time he'd seen Charmaine, she'd been a lanky if somewhat attractive eighteen-year-old teenager. When he'd visited the ministry five years ago, she'd been studying abroad. Their interaction before this one had been while Charmaine was basically a kid. But King would be the first to tell anyone who'd listened that the little Barbados cutie was all grown up. After buckling his seat belt and accepting a sparkling water from the flight attendant, he reclined his seat and remembered the events of the past five days.

"Charmaine?"

"May I come in?"

It was two days after King had arrived in Barbados, and two

hours after he'd left the pulpit of His Holy Word's Prophetic Conference: sweaty, exhausted, exhilarated. Service was uplifting and the church had been packed. After a late-night dinner at the home of a high-ranking official, King was driven back to the Freeman villa. Once again, he enjoyed the indoor/outdoor shower and had just finished a call with Tai, who among other topics had given him an update on Derrick's condition, when he'd heard a knock on his guesthouse door.

"I'm surprised to see you here," he finally said.

"Are you really?" Charmaine's eyes were bright and searing, her tone as sultry as her silky pink dress. "Somehow, I believe my being at your doorstep is not totally unexpected. Besides," she continued, "I figured a nice cup of chamomile tea would be welcomed, perfect to ensure a peaceful night's sleep." She held up the tray. "So are we going to stand here chatting until the water gets cold, or are you going to be a gentleman and invite me inside?"

If you want me to be a gentleman, then inside this guesthouse is the very last place you need to be! Even as he thought this, King stepped back so that Charmaine could enter the abode. She smelled of flowers and moonlight, with her smile equaling the latter's light. He couldn't help eyeing how the silky dress fabric spilled over her luscious backside, and the thought of running his tongue along her long, creamy-looking legs happened before it could be censored.

Charmaine placed the tray on the dining room table and immediately went about the task of preparing two cups of tea. King walked over to the table and sat down, watching her work. A sex-filled tension filled the silence. After a moment, Charmaine gazed through narrowed eyes and long, thick lashes to ask King, "How sweet do you like your tea?"

Innocent question delivered in a way that was not so innocent.

"Fix it however you like yours."

"Okay."

She finished fixing the tea and, after placing the cup and saucer in front of where King sat, she sat down beside him. "My father told me that he spilled my secret—that I've been in love with you since I was a kid."

King took a sip of tea. It was delicious—perfectly doctored with honey and cream. "You're in love with an image. You don't even know me."

Charmaine boldly placed her small hand on top of his large one, running a nail down his thick, middle finger. "I'd like to."

Lord, have mercy. "You're a young, vivacious, intelligent woman who will someday make a wonderful wife. I'm sure you have your choice of men not only here on the island, but around the world. I'm flattered at the notion that you find me attractive, but I'm more than twenty years your senior, married, and have a son just a couple years younger than you. You deserve someone who can give all of themselves to you, instead of an unavailable man with whom the most you could have is a fling."

"Spoken like a wonderful husband and father," Charmaine said, her voice somewhere between a pout and a purr. "They are words I've heard before—what my father told me and what I've told myself. But like I told Dad, my love for you is very real. It goes beyond the mental reasoning of what I know or don't know about you. It goes beyond whether you're available or not. I'm not expecting you to leave your wife, or make any commitment to me. It's enough that you know that I love you . . . and always will."

The conversation moved from Charmaine's feelings to the evening's sermon, and how idyllic life was on the island. As he finished his cup of tea, King leaned back in his seat. "It's been a long day, Charmaine. Thank you for the tea, and the conversation. You truly are a special woman. Some guy is going to be a lucky man. And speaking of men, can I give you some unsolicited advice?" Charmaine nodded. "Don't settle for someone who is less than worthy of what you have to offer. Committing oneself to another for a lifetime should not be taken lightly."

"Thanks for that advice, King. May I call you King?" He nodded. "And now there's something I'd like to give you."

"What's that?"

"My virginity."

Your virginity? Good God, I haven't had a woman able to offer me that since . . . that's right, King—since the day more than a quarter of a century ago when you lay with YOUR WIFE. It was the reality check that he needed in this precarious moment. "Charmaine, I'm committed to my wife, Tai, and to my family."

"And I," Charmaine replied, nonplussed, "am committed to you."

The next night, the charming hostess once again brought a tray of tea. This time, however, the honey in the cup wasn't the only sweetness tasted. When the sun rose the next morning, King had yielded to temptation and Charmaine was no longer a virgin.

King welcomed the flight attendant who diverted his mind's meanderings by requesting whether he'd like beef, fish, or chicken for his dinner entrée. He also accepted a glass of red wine, a rarity in his list of drink choices but welcomed considering the circumstances. King was very much his father's son, and had experienced his share of pastoral dalliances. And as much as he'd been committed to upholding his vows and staying faithful to his wife, he'd not been able to withstand the wiles of the island temptress. He'd thoroughly enjoyed his night with Charmaine and prayed that his adulterous action wouldn't come back to bite him. Little did King know in this moment that the question wasn't *if* it would come back . . . but *when.*

33

Let's Stay Together

Vivian sat in the room with Derrick, marveling at how a shaved head could so change one's appearance. She'd often wondered how her husband would look bald. They'd even tossed the idea around a time or two—not only when Michael Jordan had made the look popular and acceptable, but also a few years ago when fellow LA pastor Stanley Lee had shaved his head. She'd give anything for the circumstances to be different, but if it were any consolation her husband looked just as handsome without his close-cropped, tight black curls as he did with them.

"I think you look better without hair," she said, offering her final decision on Derrick's new look.

Derrick continued to study his reflection in the handheld mirror. "You're just saying that to make me feel better."

"No, baby, I really mean it. The cut emphasizes your eyes and lips." Vivian kissed said lips to emphasize the point. "I've got my work cut out for me...to keep those holy hussies from trying to steal what's mine."

Her comment had the desired effect. Derrick blessed her with a smile, though his eyes were melancholy. "This isn't how I planned to spend my forty-eighth year...battling for my life."

Vivian left the chair where she'd been sitting and perched on the side of Derrick's hospital bed. "Life is what happens while we're busy making those plans," she whispered. She traced Derrick's prominent facial features with her fingers, remembering a lifetime of experiences with each soulful touch. "I remember the first time I saw you," she began, a wistful smile on her face. "The Kewana Valley District's Baptist Convention back in Kansas...remember? Tai had invited me to check out King and to tout her connection to a mini-star. Didn't matter that I was only on a local channel...I was on TV!" Vivian smiled at her own memory.

"Yeah, that was the early eighties," Derrick said, with a smile of his own. "No one had heard of Oprah."

"I thought of myself as the black Barbara Walters, ready to shake up journalistic television and put my name on the world-wide stage." She rubbed her hand over Derrick's still flat stomach, pausing it just above the manhood that had brought her so much pleasure. "You changed all of that, you know. One look at this brother in the perfectly fitting suit, the snakeskin boots, and the raspy voice and I was toast. I think I fell in love with you that first night, at first sight, before I'd even been formally introduced."

Derrick covered Vivian's hand with his own. "Dang, I wish I'd known that. I threw away every sistah's number in my wallet, just to make sure you didn't find it. If I'd known I already had you I might have been able to get a couple hits in before the wedding." Vivian swatted his hand. "Ha! Baby, I'm just messing with you. From the moment I saw your tight body sitting there in that navy blue suit—"

"You remember!"

"Of course. How could I forget? Girl, I could barely remember a scripture, especially since I had to cool down a hard-on while sitting in the pulpit of a crowded auditorium. I knew right then that I had to have you...and that it would be more than a simple affair."

"I knew you were special, too, even though I tried to convince myself that nothing could get in the way of my broadcasting career."

"Yeah, and nothing could get in the way of my ministry."

For a few moments, the couple was content to bask in the memories of those early days.

Vivian chuckled. "I remember the first time that I knew for sure that you weren't cool."

"Oh yeah? When was that?" Derrick looked at his wife with a skeptical expression, even though he had an idea exactly what she was going to say.

"When it was time to go to the hospital and deliver your first-born. . . ."

"And I took off in the car with everything but you inside it."

"Ha! You had the car seat and my overnight bag and the sack of groceries we'd bought for my stay. You were running around like a chicken with its head cut off, trying to look like you were calm and in control."

"No cell phones in those days. I got a block away from the house and didn't notice that I'd left you until my question of how you were doing was met with silence."

"And I'm standing there in the driveway still wet from my water breaking."

"God takes care of babies and fools. . . ."

"Derrick the second was a perfect child—short labor, sunny disposition."

"Yeah, he was giving us a break for when Elisia made her appearance."

"The first time I thought to whup a child less than thirty days old." She leaned over and kissed his cheek. "You were a perfect dad back then. Coming off the road from God only knows how many revivals, but you'd take the kids into the den and give me time to myself. Derrick, I've never told you how much I appreciate that but . . ." Vivian stopped as tears threatened.

"C'mon, now, baby. I need you to stay strong for both of us.

Remember what D2 said, that no weapon formed against his old man would prosper. . . ."

"Proof of your legacy . . . live and in living color."

"I know we don't want to talk about it but, baby, if for some reason I don't—"

"You're right. I don't want to talk about that, or think about that, or entertain any thought other than the fact that you will come out on the other side of this operation an even better and more godly man than you are right now." Vivian knew her voice was firm and harsh, but it was all that she could offer without totally coming undone. To change the focus of his thoughts, she leaned into him and whispered, "The way you licked my pussy last night? Can't nobody give it to me like that, baby. And nobody has that thick, curved dick that fits so perfectly inside me. You have no choice but to come back to me, love. We have some unfinished business in the bedroom. And I fully intend to see it done."

Derrick gazed at Vivian with a look that could only be described as love personified. When his First Lady talked nasty, it totally turned him on. Even now, even under these dire circumstances, he felt himself harden. "Have I told you lately that I love you?"

"Yes," Vivian said, her own eyes shining. "But you can tell me again."

"I love you, Vivian Stanford Montgomery. And I won't leave you. You have my promise."

"I'm going to remember these words," she said, gingerly caressing his face in her hands. "And if for some reason you die on me . . . I'll kill ya."

Shortly thereafter, the nurse came in to take Derrick's vitals, and to tell Vivian that visiting hours had been over for quite some time. Vivian dutifully nodded and allowed the woman to do her job. After the nurse had left, Vivian watched as her husband's eyes became droopy. "Stay with me," he whispered, "until I fall asleep."

As she watched her husband's peaceful slumber, Vivian's heart clenched. *I can't imagine life without him, God. Please let him be okay.*

She stood, but could not get her feet to walk away from his side. Instead, before even really thinking about it, she positioned herself in the only place she could imagine—beside him. She barely noticed the less than comfortable bed as she snuggled up against Derrick and placed her head on his chest. "Stay with me," she whispered as a lone tear fell from her eye. "For the rest of my life."

34

Let It Be

Tai sat in the Four Seasons lobby, rereading the article about her daughter's whirlwind marriage to Arizona's NBA darling. It was almost as if she were reading the story of a stranger. That's exactly how Princess felt to her right now. Even with the intuitive feelings she'd had regarding Kelvin, Tai never thought that her levelheaded (or so she'd thought) daughter would leave a smart, handsome man who was as steady as the second hand on London's Big Ben clock and marry a cocky, irreverent professional athlete who'd proven to be unfaithful. *How could that have happened?* Tai sighed, inwardly acknowledging that she knew exactly how this had happened. It was the same reason why she and King were still married, even after all he'd done and all they'd been through. Crazy love.

Princess entered the lobby, saw her mom, and immediately walked over to where she sat. About midway she saw what her mother was reading. For a second this revelation slowed her pace, but after a slight lifting of her chin, she decided to keep on going and face the music. Understandably, her mother was disappointed. There was never going to be a good time to have this conversation.

Tai looked up as her daughter approached. She closed the magazine, suddenly wishing that she were anywhere but here. As much as she loved Princess, she didn't have too much "like" for her right about now. Still, she put a smile on her face and vowed to try and be civil. Like her daughter, she knew that there would never be a good time for this conversation.

"Hello, Mom."

"Hi, Princess."

They hugged. Tai stepped back and examined her daughter's face. It was the first time seeing her since the quickie marriage almost a week ago. There was no denying the glow that was there. "You look happy."

"I am." Princess looked at her mother. "I wish you could be happy for me."

"You know how I feel about all of this, baby. But I'm going to try. Where is he?"

"At the hospital. He said to tell you hi."

Don't roll your eyes, Tai. "Are you hungry?"

"A little."

They walked to the sunny, breezy Cabana restaurant, the crowd of which was surprisingly sparse on this Friday afternoon. For a moment, conversation centered around the menu choices. Princess settled on mahimahi tacos. Tai chose the turkey club sandwich.

Once the waiter had placed down their drink orders and walked away, Tai spoke. "I talked with Phyllis."

Princess's regret was visible. "How is she?"

"Hurt, angry, embarrassed."

"I called, but she didn't want to talk to me. Neither does Rafael."

"Can you blame him?"

Princess shook her head. "I wrote him a letter, saying how sorry I am about what happened. Mom, Rafael and I have been friends since we were kids. I never wanted to hurt him. But when Uncle Derrick collapsed and I saw Kelvin at the hospital, I knew that I couldn't go through with the marriage, knew that my heart was still tied to him."

"But it had been a year since y'all even saw each other. If you still had these feelings, why would you say yes to Rafael's proposal? Why didn't you try and get back with Kelvin before now?"

"Because I was fighting these feelings, Mom. I didn't *want* to still be in love with him!" The waiter arrived, and sat down their plates. At the moment, neither woman had an appetite. The food went untouched. "The night before the wedding," Princess continued in a soft voice, "I prayed and asked God's blessing on our marriage. I asked for His guidance, and for assurance that I was doing the right thing. I believe that what happened to Uncle Derrick was God answering my prayer."

"Well, God definitely works in mysterious ways. And why you chose Kelvin over Rafael will always be a mystery to me."

Princess didn't even want to go down that convo road. "I told Mr. Stevens that I'd reimburse them for the honeymoon tickets, and any other monies they spent on the wedding."

"I guess Kelvin having money counts for something." Tai finally picked up her sandwich and took a bite.

"My being with Kelvin isn't about his money," Princess angrily retorted. "I'm going to use my money to pay them back!"

Tai took a calming breath. Knowing she had no power to change the situation, it was time to let it be. "I'm sorry for saying that, Princess. I really don't want to argue with you. What's done is done and you're the one who's going to have to live with your decision." And then, because she couldn't resist bringing up her nemesis: "Does Tootie know?"

Tai didn't miss the smile that scampered across Princess's face, before she replaced it with a blank expression. "Yes, she knows. She wants us to come over as soon as both of our schedules allow it, have a ceremony for his stepfather's side of the family."

Just like her to appreciate this messy situation. "Hopefully you'll save one of the holidays for your family. We don't really know Kelvin and"—Tai forced the words out of her mouth—"we'd like to." *Best to fake it till I make it. That's the only way to weather this storm.* Tai looked at her watch. "We probably should finish our lunch and head over to the hospital. King's plane should be landing any minute now, and Vivian hasn't called. I want to make sure she's all right."

Shortly afterward they left the restaurant. Tai rode with Princess to Cedars-Sinai, a mostly quiet ride. Tai's concern was not only for her best friend, but for her daughter. She wanted Princess to be okay. What Tai didn't know then, was that in time, she would be wishing this for herself as well.

35

Ring My Bell

Mama Max hadn't been on a date in, well, ever. And that's what she'd told Henry when he came up with the cockamamie idea for them to go to dinner and then on to the movies.

"It's not a date," Henry had argued.

"Well, what is it?" Mama Max had asked, hand on hip, brow raised.

"Two good friends enjoying each other."

She did enjoy Henry Logan's company. This, Mama Max could not deny. And that's why she'd said yes and even now was putting on one of her signature oversized tops and a pair of wide-legged jeans. She'd balked when her granddaughter, Tabitha, had brought the jeans over, saying she'd seen them on a sale rack and thought they'd go perfectly with Mama Max's big tops. Mama Max had told her that jeans were something that you donned to go fishing or hunting or maybe picking greens. But then she'd put them on and the soft, stretchy denim was not only surprisingly comfortable but stylish as well.

"Thank you, Jesus, thank you, Lord. Yes, you've brought me from a mighty, a mighty long way. A mighty long way!" Mama Max interrupted her own song as she remembered her friend Nettie's earlier phone call. "Oh, shoot. I plumb forgot about calling

Nettie back." She looked at the clock on the wall, figured she had a good twenty or so minutes before Henry came over, and went into the kitchen to use the phone there. "Hey, Nettie Johnson."

"Hey there, Maxine Brook!"

"Sorry I'm just now getting back to you. I got busy cleaning up the house and am on my way to dinner in a little bit."

"Oh, yeah? You going over to your son and daughter-in-law's house?"

"No, we're going to the Golden Corral. It's a buffet-style restaurant."

"They have one of those in Dallas."

"Good to eat out for a change."

"Pastor Montgomery must be doing a lot better with King and Tai already back home."

"They're not here. They're still in LA."

"Oh, when you said 'we,' I just assumed . . ."

"Watch out there now, Nettie Johnson. You know what they say about that word. Making a you-know-what out of you and me!"

Nettie chuckled. "Hush your mouth, now, Mama Max. 'Cause I've sure gotten into trouble for that very reason, more than a time or two. So who are you going to dinner with? One of the sisters from the church?"

"No." Mama Max felt girlish all of a sudden and chided herself for feeling so. She'd battled this feeling off and on for about a week now, ever since Henry had talked about her looking young and cooking good and falling in love and other such nonsense. "It's Beatrice Logan's son, Henry. Remember I told you about him moving back home to care for her after the stroke?"

"I sure do. Bless his soul for taking care of his mama." Silence, and then, "How old is Henry?"

Again, that giddy feeling. Mama Max chided herself for entertaining notionss best left to young girls. "Sixty-two." She cleared her throat.

"And you say he's staying next door, in Beatrice's house?"

"Yes. He's holding out hope that she'll come back home, I

know he is. He's keeping up the place while she's in that assisted-living complex."

"With God all things are possible."

"Yes, and it will take the hand of the Almighty for that woman to come back home. The stroke was a bad one, bless her human heart. I just keep praying."

"I'll add her to the prayer list at Gospel Truth." And then, "Obadiah was supposed to be here this coming Sunday. I understand that something came up, and he's sending an old retired preacher friend from Dallas instead."

"Oh." This was said with all of the excitement of watching a bird fly.

"I know y'all are still...unsettled."

Mama Max snorted.

"But it's not good for a man to be alone, Mama Max."

"He's ain't alone! He's with that hussy!"

"From what I hear, he's in his apartment more than not."

"And just who are you hearing this from?"

"Somebody who'd be better served minding their own business. But people talk."

"Ain't no business of mine what he does. When King and Tai get back from tending to Derrick, I'm going to have them help me find a lawyer."

"Lord, Jesus, Mama Max. You sure?"

"I've been living a lie long enough, Nettie," Mama Max responded behind a sigh. "Never thought anything but death would separate me and the reverend, but it looks as though I thought wrong."

"But I thought that your kids wanted you to wait this out. Obadiah has to come to his senses before long. It don't matter that your children are long gone and grown, Mama," Nettie softly continued. "No child wants to see their parents divorced."

"We don't always get what we want, Nettie. You know that better than anybody!"

Silence, as both women remembered just how well Nettie

Johnson knew this fact. Officially, she'd lost her husband, Daniel Thicke, to a tragic car accident. But in reality, she'd lost him years before...to Dorothea Jenkins's sister, Katherine Noble. Her late husband and Katherine had an affair that lasted for years and some believe had he not died, he would have divorced Nettie to be with her. "Old man Jenkins is in the hospital," she said at last.

"Sho'nuff?"

"Yes."

"Man ought to have somebody he loves around him in his time of need."

"Dorothea's been around. Word has it that she's staying at the Fairfield Inn, though I haven't seen her as yet."

"Where'd she get that bone?"

"Excuse me?"

"The one needed to visit the sick and shut-in. Lord knows if she got one it's nigh unto brand new."

"Mama Max, you're a mess."

"Just telling the truth and shaming the devil."

"Folks say he hasn't been the same since she divorced him. Thank God for his faithful church members. They're rallying around him, along with the rest of the community."

"I'll keep him in my prayers." Mama Max's doorbell rang. "I need to run, Nettie. Henry's at the door." After hasty good-byes, Mama Max left the kitchen, humming a verse of "Search Me, Lord" on the way. She opened the door, unlocked the screen, and asked in righteous indignation...

"Obadiah, what are you doing here?"

36

They Say He's Just a Friend

Obadiah took in Mama Max's youthful appearance. Yes, a youthful seventy-three. Her hair was perfectly coiffed as always, done up in a chignon, the gray-sprinkled coloring a complement to her sienna-toned skin. The oversized top was no surprise either. It was a wardrobe staple, a safe bet for anyone wanting to get her a gift. But he didn't think he'd seen this one before. *When did she exchange her cotton numbers for this silky looking thing? And are those jeans she's wearing? For the love of God!*

"Maxine." The unspoken words behind this one word utterance would have filled the Library of Congress.

Mama Max hid her surprise behind genuine perplexity. "What are you doing here, Obadiah?"

"My name's on this here deed, last time I checked."

Mama Max's eyes narrowed. "Are you sure that's the limb you want to climb out on?"

Not unless I want to break my neck. Obadiah sighed. "Maxine, after all the driving I've been doing, all I want is a good hot meal and a place to lay my head."

Remembering that King and Tai were out of town and that the twins were vacationing in Florida with Tai's parents, Mama Max opened the door and stepped aside for Obadiah to enter. "You drove here?"

"Figured that I'd need my vehicle since I plan to be here awhile."

This tidbit of information stopped Mama Max in her tracks. "What's going on, Obadiah?"

Too much for Obadiah to explain on an empty stomach. He'd never liked fast food, and the chicken an associate minister's wife had brought over for his journey had been eaten long ago. "What's for supper?"

"Hey, Maxie!" Henry followed his usual route through the side door into the kitchen.

The shock of seeing Obadiah on her doorstep had made Mama Max forget all about Henry. She went to cut him off in the kitchen, but hadn't moved fast enough.

"I sure hope you're hungry, girl, because I've—" He saw Obadiah and stopped short. "I, uh, didn't notice that you had company."

Both Obadiah and Mama Max noted the beautiful bouquet of flowers Henry clutched in his hand. Obadiah took a step closer to Mama Max.

Mama Max walked over to where Henry stood. "Why, Henry, these flowers are lovely!"

A surprised Henry followed her into the kitchen. A scowling Obadiah trailed them both. "I saw them in the store and remembered how much you like lilies. They had a buy one, get one free sale so . . . I bought you two."

"You shouldn't have bought her any," Obadiah growled from just inside the kitchen. "Maxine's a married woman—just in case you didn't know."

"Don't look like her husband's been too keen on that fact," Henry drawled, as he slowly turned around. "She was living here by herself, last time I checked."

Obadiah took a step forward. "Boy, you'd better watch who you're messing with."

"If you see a boy, you kick his ass." Henry took a step as well.

Mama Max stepped between them. "I'm going to take a rolling pin to both you rascals if you don't calm down!" She looked from Henry to Obadiah and back again. "Last time I checked we were all grown folk. Now, can we act like it or do I need to put both of y'all out of my house?"

A still glowering Obadiah walked over to the table located in the kitchen and sat down in a huff. Henry leaned against the refrigerator and crossed his arms. Mama Max took the flowers that he still clutched. "Let me put these in some water."

"We should be going, Maxie," Henry said, looking at his watch and then at Obadiah. "I don't want us to have to rush through dinner before the movie starts."

Dinner? Movie? A bulldog couldn't have scowled any deeper than Obadiah did right then.

"I guess you're right," Mama Max said, walking past the two men to set the vase of flowers on the dining room table.

Obadiah was hot on her heels. "Do you mean to tell me that you're going out with this man, and that you are going to do it right under my nose?"

"Yes, Obadiah. My neighbor, Henry, and I are going out to eat and then to see Tyler Perry." Mama Max was cucumber-calm. "And when I made these plans, I had no idea your nose would be in my house."

"It's my house, too, Maxine."

"Maxie, let's go."

"Let me get my purse."

"Her name ain't Maxie, you ignorant heathen! My *wife's* name is *Maxine!*"

Ignoring him, Henry crossed into the living room to the front door. "I'll be waiting for you outside, *Maxie,*" he countered. He left without looking back.

Obadiah watched as Mama Max descended the stairs with purse in hand. "I never thought you'd step out on me, Maxine," he said somberly. "But you are."

"I never thought you'd forsake your wedding vows to live in sin. But you did." She walked out the door with her head held high, humming "What a Friend We Have in Jesus."

When she returned more than four hours later, she assumed that Obadiah would be long gone. But he wasn't.

37

Losing My Religion

"Your mama done lost her religion . . . and her mind." After several hours of stewing in his own juices, Obadiah had reached out to his son, King.

"What's going on now, Daddy?"

"I walked in on your mama fixing to go out on a *date*." He spat out the word as though it were poison.

"You're in Kansas City?" King's question was laced with surprise.

"Yeah, thought it was about time I came back home. And looks like it wasn't a moment too soon."

Even more incredulity wafted around King's words. "Wait, Dad, back up. You've *moved* back to Kansas City, and you're trying to get back with Mama?"

"My things are still down in Dallas but, yes, son. I want to come back home."

"And you came back without asking?" King's mind was reeling. Of all of the conversations he might have expected to have with his dad, this was not one of them. And considering everything else on his mental plate, the timing wasn't necessarily the best either. *Daddy back home? Mama on a date? WTH???*

"Son, I'm a grown-ass man. I don't need nobody's permission to come back to my own house."

When he got the call, King had stepped out of the room where members of the Montgomery clan, the Brooks, and various church members waited. Now he felt even more distance was needed, lest any part of this conversation be overheard. He stepped outside. "Dad, need I remind you that you've spent the better part of a year in an affair?"

"Boy, you don't need to remind me of nothing!"

"Evidently somebody does, Dad. You've been hanging out with another woman for way too long, come home unannounced, and are surprised to see that Mama has gone on with her life. What was she supposed to do?"

Obadiah didn't have an answer for that one.

"Who was she, uh, going out with?" Being the first time in his life that he'd spoken them, King found it hard to get these words out of his mouth.

"Henry Logan." Spoken through a countenance as one who smelled dookey.

"He any kin to her neighbor, Mrs. Logan?"

"He's Beatrice's son."

King was floored. He'd been so busy with the ministry lately that conversation with his mother had been regular but brief. They'd talked about the usual—kids, church, politics—before he'd either get another call or hand over the phone to Tai. He wondered if Tai knew about his mother's . . . his mother's what? Friend? Love interest? Brothah man on the side? King didn't even know if he wanted to find out.

"Daddy, if he's Mrs. Logan's son, then there's a good chance that this is less about something between Mama and Henry and more about Miss Beatrice. You know what good friends she and Mama are, and that Mama has been visiting her regularly since the stroke." This was an explanation that King could live with. He gained confidence in its probable truth with each word he spoke. "As a matter of fact, I now remember Mama saying something about Miss Beatrice's son moving back home to take care of his mom. He was probably over at Mama's giving her an update."

"He was at your mama's house with a bouquet of flowers, and they were on their way to have dinner and go to a movie. Does that sound like them talking about Miss Beatrice to you?"

This time it was King without an answer. Because if what his father said was to be believed (and there was no reason not to believe him), it looked as though his conservative, church-going mama was channeling Stella . . . and trying to get back her groove!

King saw Tai walking down the hall. He assumed she was looking for him. "Look, Dad, I've got to run. We're expecting Derrick out of surgery any minute and then we'll know whether the tumor they removed was malignant or benign."

"I'll pray for Derrick, son." A pause and then, "You pray for me."

38

A Healer In The Sickroom

All eyes were on Vivian as she walked into one of Cedars-Sinai's private rooms. She took a deep breath, before saying two words. "It's benign."

Instant celebration. Spontaneous praise.

"Thank you, Jesus!" Derrick's mother cried, while his father simply hung his head to hide the tears.

"Praise the Lord," Victor Stanford whispered. It was a rare time that Vivian's father was subdued or at a loss for words. His reaction showed just how much he loved his son-in-law and just how frightened for him he had been.

Other exclamations echoed around the room, a multiplicity of "glories" and "hallelujahs" among them. Tai walked over and embraced her friend. "I'm so happy for you, sis," she whispered in her ear. "God answers prayers."

Vivian looked into Tai's tear-filled eyes. They mirrored her own. "That He does."

Kelvin and Princess walked up to where Vivian and Tai were standing. He hugged Vivian. She hugged Tai.

After he stepped back from Vivian, Kelvin addressed Princess's mother. "Hello, Miss Tai."

Not wanting to place a sour note in such a celebratory moment, Tai responded simply, "Kelvin."

King walked over. Like Tai, he hadn't had a chance for a real tête-à-tête with his daughter, and his former lover's son. And on top of this unresolved drama was the recent phone call with Obadiah, not to mention what had happened in Barbados. For the moment, at least, King felt he could be thankful. For the moment his best friend who was like a brother was out of the proverbial woods.

He hugged Vivian. "God heard our prayers, sistah." Vivian nodded. He hugged Tai.

"I'm glad you're here," she said. She leaned back to look into his eyes and was bothered by the troubled orbs that stared back at her. But of course he'd be showing signs of concern. His best friend had been given a reprieve from death's sure door, and he was standing next to the young man he'd almost beat down just three years before. "You look tired," she whispered.

King pulled back. "I am." His cell phone rang. It was an unknown number. "King Brook."

"Hello, handsome."

His heart skipped a beat. He shot a quick glance at Tai before stepping away from the tense atmosphere surrounding his wife, Princess, and their new son-in-law. "Hello," he said, once he'd stepped outside the room.

"How are you, lover?"

"I thought we already had this conversation and agreed that what happened on the island was going to have to stay there." King had tried to forget what took place just before he left Barbados, when his mind was distracted and his flesh was weak. He'd all but pushed aside the exhilarating feeling of that incredibly delicious night: her baby soft skin underneath him, his muscular body hovering above, her gasps, his pants, her tears, his comforting, her pledges of undying love, his heartfelt joy tempered by plaguing guilt. With all the events he'd dealt with since returning home, blocking out that night of indiscretion hadn't been too difficult. But now, "indiscretion" was on the line.

"I am still here. I just want you with me."

King heard the door to the private room open. He looked over and saw a couple Kingdom Citizens church members exit the room. "Why are you calling me?" he asked through clenched teeth.

"I miss you. I want to know how you are." A pause, and then, "I want to feel you inside of me again."

King closed his eyes in frustration, cursing his weakness for the umpteenth time, and vowing yet again that what had happened in Barbados had occurred for the absolute last time.

"Charmaine, what we shared will always be special. I'll never forget the time that I spent with you, and will always wish you well. Someday, you're going to meet an awesome man and he'll be very blessed to call you his wife. As I told you before I left there . . . I am *not* that man."

Her voice was barely above a whisper, filled with truth and longing. "I wish you were."

"If wishes came true, many things would be different." King looked up to see Tai walking toward him. "Look, I've got to go." He hung up without a good-bye.

"Who was that?"

"Joseph," King said, the lie rolling smoothly and convincingly off his tongue. "He wanted to know whether I'd be staying here or returning to Barbados to finish our work there."

"What'd you tell him?"

"I don't know." A memory of Charmaine's long, silky legs wrapped itself around King's mind. Just that quickly, his resolve weakened. "I'm thinking to go back . . . especially since we've received Derrick's good news."

Tai nodded, and placed her head on King's shoulder. "I'm so glad his tumor was benign. I truly don't know how Vivian would have handled any other outcome."

"Thankfully, we don't have to find out." King placed his arm around Tai. "Guess it's now time to deal with this other situation."

Tai raised her head. "Your daughter?"

King chuckled. "So now she's all mine, huh?"

"You know it. There's no part of me that would be so stupid as to make the decision that she did. Kelvin over Rafael? No, let's go back even farther. Marriage at all at the age of twenty-two? Ridiculous."

"Let's hope you didn't share these positive feelings with her and her new hubby."

"Not in so many words," Tai sarcastically replied. "Princess and I had lunch before we came here. I'm trying to be civil about it, King, but you can surely understand my difficulty in accepting this."

Considering that King's affair with Kelvin's mother spanned a decade, he surely could. "Why don't we invite them out for a late dinner; try and make a new start with the man Princess married."

"That sounds like a plan, but let's go someplace where I can order soup. Because if I have something sharper than a spoon, like a knife or fork at my disposal . . . things might get ugly."

39

More Family Affairs

Later that night, King, Tai, Kelvin, and Princess walked into Cut, Wolfgang Puck's restaurant located in Beverly Hills. They were immediately led to a corner table, given water and menus, and left to make choices. After deciding on a diverse selection that included Kobe steak sashimi, maple-glazed pork belly, salads, Porterhouse steak, filet mignon, and seasonal vegetables, King started out the conversation.

"I think it's important for us to speak our minds here, even as we are respectful of each other. At the end of the day, both Tai and I just want our daughter to be happy and if you're the one to bring her that happiness, then and only then, Kelvin, will I welcome you into our family."

Kelvin leaned back in his chair. "I believe your daughter is very happy." Tai fought to keep from frowning...and lost. "Listen, Mr. and Mrs. Brook, when it comes to who Princess married, I know that I wasn't y'all's first choice. Heck, I probably wasn't even on the list. But the truth of the matter is, from the moment I laid eyes on her I knew that Princess was the one for me. Yes, I'm young and have done my share of sowing wild oats and whatnot," (okay, Tai should really be forgiven for the frown here), "but those women didn't mean anything. They never did."

Tai looked at her daughter, who'd said very little since they'd sat down. "You're awfully quiet, Princess. What are you thinking?"

Princess glanced at her mother and father. "I think that we should address the elephant that is crowding us at this table—Kelvin's mom."

"Princess..." Tai's tone was full of warning.

"Mom, we're all grown-ups here. And until we have this conversation, the topic of Janeé will always stand between us. Why not just put it out on the table and get it over with?"

Tai kept her hands folded in her lap, far away from the knives and forks. "I understand your reasoning, Princess. Really, I do. And I know that in your"—*immature, sex-whipped, crazy-ass*—"mind, you feel that this is something that we can talk about. If you two ever have your own children you'll understand what I'm about to tell you. There are some conversations that will never take place between you and your child. No matter what. No matter how old the child gets, his or her parents will always have forgotten more than they will ever remember, and be in tune with things the child will never understand. Any conversation about Janeé will happen with Janeé, not you." Tai looked from Princess to Kelvin. "Understand?"

Kelvin crossed his arms. "Look, I understand the problems you may have with my moms, but she's my mother. As long as you respect that fact... we'll be fine."

Tai met Kelvin's unflinching stare. *Lord, please help me not to hate, or kill, this child.* Just behind this thought was the one acknowledging that anger and animosity would not get any of them anywhere. If there was any chance of this union working, they were going to have to clear Kelvin's slate and give him a fair chance. Tai took a deep breath and continued. "It is no secret how we feel about what Princess has done. Rafael practically grew up in our church. We're friends with his parents and know his values. Plus, he has never given our daughter one minute of heartbreak. So it isn't personal, Kelvin, it really isn't.

"No matter what has happened between your parents, this marriage is between the two of you. You've made your choice and I will respect your decision. Kelvin"—Tai forced love into her eyes as she looked at her new son-in-law—"on behalf of King and myself, welcome to our family."

King shifted in his seat.

"Are you on board with this, Dad?" Princess asked. "Do you accept my husband?"

"I meant what I said earlier. Time will tell whether I accept him or not."

"You said that you'd see if he made me happy. Dad, I couldn't be happier, and more importantly, I remember your counsel in honoring my husband, cleaving to him, and the two of us becoming one. So if you don't want Kelvin in the family, that means you don't want me either."

King and Tai looked at each other, both experiencing déjà vu at the last time their daughter had sided with this man. Then, as now, they knew it futile to try and change her mind. Then, as now, they silently agreed to go along to get along. Later, they'd also agree that Princess would now have to sleep in the bed she made.

"You've made your decision," King said, even though tension could still be cut with a knife. "And we'll abide by it."

The waiter began delivering food and the conversation shifted to lighter, less volatile topics.

"How was Barbados, Daddy?" Princess asked, glad that she and Kelvin were no longer the topic of discussion. "Kelvin and I plan to take a honeymoon at some point, and we're thinking about the islands."

"It's beautiful," King answered, "Crystal blue water. Miles of white sand." *Chocolate-covered cuties with toned, lush bods.* It was a topic he needed to get off of, lest a physical reaction put him in a bind. "How do you feel about the season, Kelvin? Do you think y'all have a chance at taking the crown?"

That question, and the delivery of their drinks, set the tone for the rest of the evening. The men chatted somewhat amicably about basketball and sports in general while Tai and Princess caught up on her participation in *Conversations with Carla*. "She feels it best for me to come on the show and talk about everything," Princess finished. "Especially since the tabloid story, she feels it will help me retake control."

"She knows from whence she speaks," Tai replied.

The others nodded. Everyone sitting there knew about Carla Lee Chapman's own brush with tabloid fame, how an overzealous church member sold pictures of her and a film producer to *LA Gospel*, the number-one church weekly. Later, it would be proven that Carla and the film producer were indeed having an affair. It caused the divorce between her and her then mega-preacher husband, Stan Lee, the subsequent marriage between her and the producer, Lavon Chapman, and the eventual marriage of Stan and the overzealous church member who'd exposed the affair, Passion Perkins Lee.

"Are you going to do it?" King asked Princess. "Are you going to do a tell-all on national TV? And are you ready for what comes with that?"

"We haven't talked about it yet," Princess replied, glancing over at Kelvin. He squeezed her hand. "There's been so much going on that there hasn't been time. But considering that Kel is in the NBA and I'm a regular cohost—"

"And a best-selling author," Kelvin interjected.

"It might be the best way to go."

The foursome continued to talk and get to know each other. Tai developed a cautious respect for the well-mannered humorous man who was the love of her daughter's life, and King admitted that under different circumstances, he might actually like the young man who reminded him of himself at that age.

By the end of the evening, some decisions had been made. King and Tai would respect Kelvin as long as he respected their daughter. Princess confirmed that she would go on TV and tell her failed wedding/quickie marriage story. And King vowed that he would not sleep with Charmaine Freeman again.

40

Like Father, Like Son

It was Friday, a week since Derrick's surgery. He was home. The crowd had left. His parents had left on Thursday morning; Vivian's parents, the Stanfords, had left earlier today. Vivian had shooed the members of Kingdom Citizens Christian Center out of her house an hour ago and now here she sat with just the immediate Montgomery clan: Derrick, D2, and Elisia.

After placing the relatively simple meal that the church mothers had prepared on the table—lasagna, salad, and Texas toast—Vivian asked, "Who would like to lead us in prayer?"

"I will," Derrick Jr. replied. Vivian hid her smile. She'd expected no less than little preacher man to step up to the plate, especially when it involved a prayer of thanksgiving for his dad.

The family joined hands. "Heavenly Father, I want to thank you for healing my dad. Thank you, God, for saving his life ... and for holding the doctor's hands through his surgery. Thank you, Father God, for bringing him back to our family, so that he can see us grow up and..."—Derrick's voice broke—"stay in our lives. Please stay with him while he recovers, God, until he is well, one-hundred percent. In Jesus's name we pray...."

In unison, the family said, "Amen."

"Thank you, son," Derrick added, his voice hoarse with emotion.

"I want to say thank you, too, Daddy." Without waiting for an answer, Elisia bowed her head and held her small palms together in the prayer position. "God, thank you for saving my daddy and blessing our family. Amen."

"Amen."

Following her children's lead, Vivian continued. "Father God, thank you for saving the life of my husband, my children's father, the senior pastor of Kingdom Citizens, and one of the most prolific men of God that you've ever created. I pray that you bless other families, Lord, who have loved ones in need of healing, and families wanting to be restored. Keep me humbled in this gratitude, Father God... amen."

"Amen."

The room was quiet as expectant eyes turned toward Derrick, man of God, biblical scholar, preacher's preacher, and speaker extraordinaire. And for the first (and perhaps only) time in his life... there were no words. "Father God, thank you," he said, clearing his throat and wiping a tear away from his eye. He bowed his head, unable to continue.

Vivian reached across the table and squeezed her husband's hand. "Amen."

"Amen."

"It's so quiet, Mommy," Elisia said, after she'd asked for a large helping of salad and a modest portion of the lasagna.

"We've had a full household," Vivian replied. "Are you already missing your grandparents?"

Elisia nodded.

"I'm missing my brother," D2 said. He'd spent a considerable amount of time with Kelvin and Princess. Kelvin, especially, had been a calming influence in the life of a very fearful fourteen-year-old boy. "Can I go and stay with him this summer?"

Derrick and Vivian exchanged a look. "He just got married," Vivian answered. "Let's give him a few months to enjoy married life before we invade his space. Okay?"

D2 looked at his father. "How you doing, Daddy?"

"I'm feeling good, son."

"Daddy, how long is it going to take for your hair to grow back?"

"Elisia, are you telling me that you don't like my bald head?"

"I like it," D2 said. "Mom, can I shave my head, too?"

Vivian knew that this was less about the hairstyle and more about D2 trying to look just like his father...in every way. He could do worse for an example. "If you want to, son," she answered.

Father and son high-fived.

The questions continued to flow, rapidly and continuously. During Derrick's first few days home, Vivian had allowed the children little access. She'd wanted his sole concentration to be on healing. But yesterday's checkup with Dr. Black had left Vivian feeling more confident in Derrick's recovery and more relaxed overall. His stitches had been removed and the doctor had been pleased with how the incision was healing.

"Mom, can we stay up late tonight?" Elisia lived for the weekends, when she could stay up past 9 p.m.

"Yes, you can," Vivian said, smiling at the precocious twelve-year-old who seemed to be growing up way too fast. "In fact, your dad and I have a bit of a treat for you two. Anastacia is taking you to Universal Studios!"

Elisia clapped her hands in delight. D2's reaction was subdued.

"What's up, champ?" Derrick said, eyeing his son. "You too old for the amusement park?"

"We just went to Disneyland. I want to stay here."

Derrick's eyes clouded with emotion. "I appreciate that, son. Come here, let me talk to you man to man for a minute." He looked at Vivian. "Excuse us."

He led D2 into his study and closed the door. For a moment, he simply looked at his son. "Son, I want to thank you for stepping up to the plate while I was in the hospital, taking care of your sister and your mom for me."

D2 shifted from one foot to the other. A wisp of a smile crossed his face. "Thank you."

"In a few more weeks, we'll be able to get back on the basketball court. I hope you've been practicing, because you needed to step up your game."

"Kelvin showed me a couple new moves. I'll be ready for you."

Derrick laughed. "No doubt." Again, his eyes clouded. Since finding himself lying on Mount Progressive's carpet having a chat with Mr. Death, his emotions had been up close and raw. Thanking God daily for his life was something he'd always done, but now, in the wake of possibly losing it, gratitude took on new meaning. He looked at his teenage son, his once round body becoming tall and lanky, the baby face being replaced by handsome juts and angles. *Looks like it's about time to take "the talk" to another level.* Which reminded Derrick why he'd pulled his son aside.

"Son, about tonight. It's been crazy these past two weeks and while I can't wait to spend more time with you, right now, I need some quiet, quality time with my wife." Derrick crossed his arms and spread his legs in a streetlike pose. "Know what I'm sayin'?"

D2 laughed. "Dad!"

"This is man to man real talk, son. Women are like flowers. They need to be tended to, nourished, cherished. One day, I pray that you have a classy woman like your mother, one who you can shower with love and affection. But for right now, I need you to go with Anastacia, take care of your sister, and let me and your mama have some alone time. Can you do that for me?"

D2 nodded. They bumped fists.

"I love you, son."

"I love you, Dad. Hey, Dad."

"Yes?"

"Can y'all not call me D2 no more? I want to be called by my real name."

"Sure, Derrick," Derrick Sr. said. "Although it might get a little confusing around here."

"Then call me Derrick Jr., but not D2. I want people to say my name."

"All right, Derrick Jr. Will do."

In that moment, the father-son relationship shifted. Derrick's life wasn't the only one that had changed because of his brain tumor. His son's life had been transformed, too. Both were older, wiser, and filled with more love than they ever knew existed.

41

I'll Make Love To You

"Finally." Derrick wrapped his arms around Vivian's soft, lush body. They were sitting against the headboard of their king-sized bed, the home's master suite. It was the first time they'd been truly alone in two weeks.

"This feels good," Vivian purred, nestling her head against Derrick's shoulder. She ran her hand down from his chest to his groin and was immediately rewarded with hardening interest. "Um, this feels good, too."

Derrick kissed Vivian's temple. "I've missed you, baby."

"Likewise. Thought I was going to go stone crazy sometimes." She shifted, raised her head, and kissed Derrick on the lips. She pulled back, but Derrick caught her chin, pulled her back to him, and instigated a deeper, wetter kiss. "Baby, are you sure this is okay? I want you badly but—"

"Vivian. My head was bandaged but trust me, my dick is fine."

Vivian chuckled, reaching back down to stroke the love wand that had brought her pleasure for almost twenty years. "It sure is." She continued to kiss Derrick—lovingly, languidly—enjoying the feel of his tongue as it swirled against hers and his large, firm fingers as they caressed her bare skin. They lay down and continued reintroducing themselves to each other. Derrick twirled Vivian's

nipple between his thumb and forefinger until it pebbled into a familiar hardness. Vivian ran her hand up and down Derrick's shaft
until prelove juices spilled from its tip. She smiled, while placing
kisses on Derrick's lips, cheek, temple, and bald head. She carefully
kissed his incision, running her tongue along its length. The act reminded her of the sacredness of this event, and how she'd come
close to not ever having this experience again.

The acknowledgment spurred her on.

She scooted away from him, just enough so that she could
continue raining kisses all over the dark caramel-covered body that
she loved. She kissed his neck, shoulders, and chest. Still massaging
his manhood, she licked his nipples, and was rewarded by their
pebbled response. She followed the light hair trail that ran down
the middle of Derrick's defined abdomen. It wasn't quite a six-
pack, but that he'd worked out three days a week for the past
decade or more was evident. She bent down to his navel, and
swirled her tongue into his inward belly button. Derrick shifted,
grabbed her head and pushed it farther south. Vivian's chuckle was
deep and husky as she followed his lead. She ran her tongue across
his abdomen, heard his intake of breath as she gently massaged his
balls and kissed his dick. She swirled her tongue around the tip before taking him in as much as she could, treating his long, swollen
member like a large lollipop, giving it loving licks from base to
head, outlining the perfectly mushroomed tip before taking him in
again. Derrick moaned and tilted back his upper head, giving Vivian total access. She shifted, too, until her juicy backside swayed
invitingly in Derrick's face even as her mouth continued to play an
award-winning melody on Derrick's rod. Derrick made the love
solo a duet, flicking his tongue along Vivian's folds, finding her
nub and giving it pleasure. He placed his hands on her hips and
deepened the assault.

Now, it was Vivian's turn to moan, and Derrick's turn to smile.

He tickled one opening while licking another, all while Vivian
showed skills that, had she been bobbing for apples, would have

garnered her first place. They were fully engaged in the dance of love, totally lost in their desire to please each other. Licking, sucking, teasing, moaning, groaning, laughing, and then doing all of it all over again.

"Baby," Derrick said at last, "I can't take any more. I need you now."

"Let me do it," Vivian whispered as she turned around to face him. "You stay relaxed, don't strain yourself. Okay? Just lay back and enjoy the ride." She repositioned herself yet again and slowly, oh...so...slowly...lowered herself onto Derrick's willing, waiting love sword. They both exhaled at being joined together for the first time in two weeks. Aside from after she'd had the children, it was the longest they'd ever gone without making love. She sheathed him inside her inner walls, welcoming his presence with her muscles, squeezing him tightly with her love. There were tears in both of their eyes as she rose up and eased down, slowly, reverently, and then once more. Derrick's eyes looked deeply into hers as he grabbed her hips and lifted her up, over and again. They ground against each other, letting nature take its course and spirit take its pleasure. With one hand still guiding her hips, he reached the other up to her berry-colored nipple, flicking it with his thumbnail and increasing the delicious pain and pleasure of it all. Vivian continued to move her hips in a circular motion, her head thrown back, jaws slack, entire body fully engaged in the feeling, the blessing, of her husband inside her. *Thank you, God. Thank you for sparing his life.*

"Ah!" Vivian's eyes opened as Derrick shifted their positions. "Wait, baby. You need to take it easy, remember?"

"I've got this," Derrick whispered. He placed Vivian's legs over his shoulders and sank in deeply, fully, all the way to the hilt. He set up a leisurely pace, licking Vivian's toes before sucking the big toe into his mouth. A hiss from Vivian was his reward. He knew every way to please her, and this pleased him immensely. They continued in this way for untold moments, before he eased her legs off his shoulders and led her to her knees. He got behind her and readied himself for one of their favorite positions, using his tongue to tease and tantalize forbidden places before he continued the dance. He ran his hand along her crease and then increased momentum until both he and Vivian were hurdling over the edge, voluntarily free-falling into mind-blowing ecstasy. Afterward, he slumped down on top of her. Vivian welcomed his body weight, wrapped her arms around his sweaty back and kissed him everywhere.

"Thank you, baby. I love you." His whispered voice was raspy with emotion.

"I love you more, Derrick Montgomery. Welcome home."

42

Friends and Lovers

Still in Los Angeles, Kelvin and Princess sat in the comfortable, cozy MTM offices that housed Carla Chapman's Emmy-award-winning television show: *Conversations with Carla*. Where they sat was more than twice the size of the office Carla had occupied three years ago, when the show had debuted. Now there were three distinct areas: a sitting area for cozy conversations, the office area that housed desks, file cabinets, and an eight-seater conference table, and a state-of-the-art kitchen.

"Well, I tell you what. Y'all sure know how to make a head-line!" Carla poured glasses of orange juice to go with the vegetable and sausage quiche she'd whipped up for their meeting.

"It's crazy, Miss Carla," Kelvin replied. "Whoever said that any publicity is good publicity obviously never went through it."

"You're probably right, Kelvin. And while I appreciate your display of brought-upsy, please, call me Carla. I have a feeling we'll be seeing a lot of each other in these next few months so might as well get on a first-name basis right now."

"Okay, Carla. I appreciate that." He took a bite of the quiche. "Wow, this is bangin'."

"Ha! I'm glad you like it." Carla noticed that Princess's appetite didn't seem to be nearly as hearty as that of her husband. "What about you, Princess? Is the food to your liking?"

Princess nodded. "It's delicious, really. It's just that with all that's been happening these past few weeks...I don't have much of an appetite." The story of her and Kelvin's quickie wedding had spread from one tabloid to another, with hints that she was pregnant, lies about a fight between Kelvin and Rafael, and an even bigger lie added to the mix that she'd been cheating on Rafael with Kelvin the whole time. Suing a tabloid was a huge headache, but she still hadn't counted out the idea.

"I know what you're going through, darlin'." Carla's usually boisterous voice was soft, and filled with compassion. "I've been down the road you're going; people all up in my business, making judgments on that which they really knew nothing about. It's a world of crazy, Princess, but I can tell you this. Nobody can tell your story like you can. I don't want to pressure you into doing anything you don't want to do. I'm here for you as your friend, and your mother's friend, way before I'm here as a talk show host. We can shelve this story and go on with another topic. Lord knows there's enough to keep talk show tongues wagging from now until Jesus comes. But I suggest that you consider turning what's perceived as a negative situation into a positive one. Doing so, and here's where the talk show host comes in, will surely benefit your new book due out in the fall."

"I've thought about everything you're saying, Carla. But right now"—Princess stole a quick glance at her husband—"I'm not so concerned about myself as I am about my ex-fiancé. He never asked for any of this and I can only imagine what he's going through right now."

"You haven't talked to him since...all of this happened?"

Princess shook her head. "I've tried but"—another glance at Kelvin—"he won't talk to me. I've left several messages, but he won't return my calls."

Carla was silent as she digested this information. "I'm sorry to hear that, Princess. But all you can do is your part—making sure that he knows about any show we have where he's involved, however indirectly. Perhaps Tai can act as our liaison, at the very least speaking with his parents if he chooses not to talk with you directly. I wouldn't want to be responsible for his being blindsided by some media piece involving a sensitive part of his past. Let's definitely make sure that gets handled before we move forward."

The three conversationalists looked up as the door opened. It was Carla's husband, Lavon, who along with being the love of her life was the executive producer of the show that made hers a household name.

"Hey, baby," he said, walking over to Carla and leaning down for a kiss. "Hello, Kelvin, Princess." He gave Kelvin a fist bump and Princess a hug.

"We're discussing how to handle the announcement of their marriage," Carla said to Lavon. "And how we should handle Rafael's name, and respect his privacy."

"That's easy," Lavon said with a shrug. "He doesn't need to be mentioned at all." Three pairs of eyes stared with a look that said *huh.* "We make the focus of not only this but all subsequent shows on this issue all about you, Kelvin, and you, Princess. We talk about the aspect of your journey that was previously anonymously mentioned in your novel, if you're comfortable with that, and with the whole notion of destiny . . . and soul mate love." He looked at Carla with such love that the temperature in the room seemed to rise a notch or two. Leaning forward, with his elbows resting on his knees, he continued. "But I want whatever we do on Carla's show to be just the beginning. I've got a meeting scheduled with the brass later this afternoon and I'd like to propose to them our first reality show starring"—Lavon looked from Kelvin to Princess—"the two of you."

Princess's eyes widened as images of shows like *The Real Housewives of Atlanta, Basketball Wives,* and *Love & Hip Hop* flashed into her mind. She slowly began shaking her head from side to side, not trusting herself to speak lest a slew of expletives roll out. She was not trying to be that neck-rolling, finger-pointing sistah with an attitude, blowing up on national TV. Even more, Princess knew that the waters she was wading into with her professional basketball player husband were very likely to present some situations where neck-rolling, finger-pointing... even ass-kicking would be in order.

"I don't know about that, man," Kelvin drawled, crossing his arms as he stretched out his long legs in front of him. "I'm not down with putting my business on blast like that."

"I understand," Lavon calmly replied. "That's because you're thinking about the reality shows that are on now. I'm wanting to take the genre to a new level, mix Kendra with Oprah and get you and Princess, know what I'm saying?"

"Who's Kendra?" Princess asked.

Lavon explained that she was a reality TV star who started out on a show involving Playboy's Hugh Hefner and more recently had a show with her football-playing husband, Hank. "I'd like to see our reality show be more... real... if you know what I'm saying. Instead of the extravagant lifestyles that are routinely highlighted, I want to show that people with money can have a grounded, spiritual, beautiful lifestyle as they work through their problems and challenges together... with God at the center. This is a type of reality we haven't seen on these shows and one that I think you two could beautifully convey."

Princess was still not convinced. "I don't know, Lavon. We just got married. I don't know if I want the first days and years of my life caught on tape."

"But you have said that you wanted your life to be a light, and your tests to be a testimony. This can take the manifestation of that desire to a whole new level. Just sleep on it a week or two," Lavon finished, looking at his watch and standing. "A successful show of this sort can do wonders for your career. Make you lots of money, expand your fan base, and establish a brand that will ensure every book that you ever write a spot on the *NYT* best-seller list. And then there's life after the NBA to think about. This type of show can serve as a foundation for the rest of your lives."

Princess agreed to think about it and Lavon's words stayed with her the rest of the evening, long after she and Kelvin had left Carla's office and headed to Derrick and Vivian's for dinner. She decided that taking everything one step at a time was the best way to move forward, starting with their appearance on Carla's show. And for that, she needed to talk to Rafael or at least get a message to him through his parents. She quieted, thinking about the man she'd called friend for most of her life. *I wonder where he is . . . how he's doing.* It wasn't going to be long before she found out.

43

It's A Small World

"Ooh, baby, you look good." Kiki gazed appreciatively at the man standing before her, looking suave and stylish in a casual black suit.

"Yeah, if you say so." Rafael's response was subdued, but he too liked what he saw when he looked in the mirror. They were at a high-end boutique on Sunset Boulevard, outfitting Rafael for what Kiki described as a Fourth of July kickoff party. She had assured him that everybody who was anybody would be there. "But I don't know about this shirt you picked out. I think I'd rather wear a button down, a few buttons open, and no tie."

"But that is such a common look, El. If you're going to be the new Mr. Hollywood, you've got to stand out, make a statement."

"Ain't nobody trying to be Mr. Hollywood, girl," he threw over his shoulder as he walked back into the dressing room.

His tone was serious, but Kiki didn't miss the smile that followed. She was still trying to wrap her mind around what had happened in these past three weeks. That she'd been set to film in Kansas City a week after the wedding was a coincidence that had been scheduled before she'd asked to participate in Rafael's wedding. But there was no way that she could know that 1) the wedding would start but would not finish; 2) that she'd be able to get Rafael a walk-on part in her movie; 3) that because of Rafael's natural talent for acting, his walk-on role would expand to a small but significant character in the independent film; and 4) that she'd fall in love with him. Before now, she would have scoffed at the thought of love at first sight. Like many twenty-somethings, she'd seen her share of heartbreak, had kissed a slew of frogs. But from the first night that she spent with Rafael, she'd detected a prince. And while his ex-fiancée had been too dumb or naive or misguided to realize this fact, Kiki intended to be his new and only princess.

"We don't have to stay long, baby. But I told my boys that we'd show up." Kelvin reached over for Princess's hand. She didn't pull away, but turned her attention out the window. "Bran and Joni are going to be there. And my boy X-Factor is rocking the mike. We'll just do a walk around, pose for a couple pics, and bounce. I'm just as tired as you are, baby. I'm ready to head back to Arizona myself."

Princess took a deep breath, and thought of the very valid reasons why she didn't want to step back into the LA party scene. Some of Kelvin's adoring public was bound to be here. She'd have to get used to women ogling him, ignoring her, and basically being thoughtless witches. She finally surmised that now was as good a time as any to develop the backbone she'd need as a professional athlete's wife.

"When is the last time you partied here?" she asked him.

"A couple weeks ago."

"Any particular woman we may run into that I should know about?"

Kelvin looked at Princess and tried to read the message behind her words. Her face was placid; she seemed to simply want an answer to the question, not the names, dates and phone numbers of the women he'd screwed since they'd broken up; a list that he'd be hard-pressed to put together if asked. A list that was too long, even by professional athlete's standards. He'd bedded these women to try and get over Princess. To say that hadn't worked would be an understatement. "I've only had one other steady girlfriend besides you and that situation ended some time ago."

"Do you think she'll be here?" Kelvin shook his head. "What about Fawn?"

"You know me and her never got down like that."

"Please. You lived together."

"The only reason she was with me as long as she was is because she lied about Kelvin, Junior's paternity. Since finding out the truth about his real father, I haven't had two words to say to her."

"What about her? Is she still trying to be in your life?"

"I can't help what women try and do, Princess. I can only be responsible for my actions. I've said it before and I'll say it again—as many times as need be until you believe me. I want to be faithful to you. I'm going to be faithful to you. Okay?"

Princess turned, looked out the window. "Okay."

After a moment of silence, he continued. "The rev looks good."

Princess welcomed the change in subject. "It's hard to believe that he just had brain surgery."

The conversation continued to meander from one subject to the next until their driver turned onto a street lined with luxury vehicles: Mercedes, Maybachs, Jags, BMWs, various pimped out SUVs, and a couple Bentleys. They pulled into a circular driveway behind several limos. The driver got out and opened Princess's door.

Kelvin looked at her. "You ready?"

"As ready as I'll ever be."

She prepared to exit. He squeezed her hand. "I'm glad you're with me."

Princess looked at Kelvin, the love of her life. "I'm glad to be here."

The pre-Fourth of July party was being held at a home in the Holmby Hills, far above the lives of normal folk. The house was forty-two-hundred square feet of beautiful, plush, and don't-ask-the-price furnishings. A couple hundred people milled about: in the home, on the patio, by the pool, and in the garden. When Kelvin and Princess arrived, the holiday celebration was in full swing. They weren't five minutes into the house before Kelvin ran into another NBA baller, Princess saw a producer who worked at MTM, and then they ran into Brandon and Joni.

"What's up, dude?" Brandon and Kelvin bumped shoulders.

"You got it," Kelvin replied, looking around and noticing all of the fine and fly honeys sending rhythm his way. He remembered his promise to Princess, shifted his eyes away from the women and focused on talking to one of his best friends. "How long y'all been here?"

"About half an hour. It's crazy, man. X-Factor is holding it down in the great room. That's where the dance floor is—downstairs. The food is just down that hall, in the dining room. Don't go upstairs unless you want to engage in something pornographic or illegal. It's grown folks business up there all day long."

"Good looking out," Kelvin replied, a part of him wanting to head toward the stairs even as the God in him protested. He continued talking to Brandon, noticing that Princess and Joni had stepped a couple feet away.

"A reality show? No way!" Joni had asked Princess about the meeting with Carla. Her reaction mirrored Princess's first thoughts.

"I felt the same way, at first. But the more I think about it, the more I think this may be God's way of expanding my horizons."

Joni nodded, deep in thought. "At least by having Carla in charge of the programming you know that they aren't going to exploit you, that they are going to place you and Kelvin in the best possible light."

"Exactly."

"So you're thinking about doing it?"

Princess nodded.

Joni looked past Princess to the hallway behind her. "Whoa, it's a small world."

Princess looked back, but didn't see anyone she recognized. "Why do you say that?"

"I just saw Kiki Minor."

"Really? That's great! I need to talk to her." Princess felt badly about all of the people she'd left hanging following her ruined nuptials. She'd had letters sent out to her bridesmaids and made sure that the musicians and others on the program got paid. But her newly acquired friend, Kiki Minor, had traveled to Kansas City at her own expense, and performed at her wedding ceremony as a gift to her and Rafael. Things hadn't worked out as anyone planned, but Princess wanted to let Kiki know how much she'd appreciated having her there, and how much she'd enjoyed her original spoken word piece. "I think I'll try and find—

"I'll. Be. Damned." *Think of the devil and she will appear.*

Joni's eyes widened. It was a rare moment that a curse word escaped Princess's lips. She turned around and closed her eyes against the sight that greeted her. Of all the people. Of all the parties. *Damn, damn, damn!* "What the hell is *she* doing here?"

Princess shrugged. "I don't know, but since she's making a beeline for my husband I guess it's about time that I find out." She made quick work of the ten or so feet that separated her and Kelvin. She reached her husband and immediately linked her arm through his.

The woman in front of Kelvin slid her eyes in Princess's direction before refocusing on him. She wore a short, pixie-style haircut that highlighted perfect bone structure, big doe eyes, and kiss-me lips. "I hear congratulations are in order."

Princess rose to the full five-foot-eight height she was rocking, thanks to four-inch Louboutin heels. "You heard correctly."

The vixen pointedly ignored Princess and boldly took a step closer to Kelvin, who placed his arm around Princess and spoke to the woman who he at one time thought was his baby's mama. "What's up, Fawn? A bit out of the neighborhood, wouldn't you say?"

44

Hey Ya

Fawn took the verbal punch with no outward sign of discomfort. "I'm not chained to Phoenix. When it comes to the happenings, I get around."

"I see. Where's your son?"

"You're not the biological so what do you care?"

Kelvin's eyes narrowed. "You know that I don't hold the lies you told against the boy. He was the innocent player in your sordid game."

Princess couldn't agree with her husband more. She positioned herself tall and proud beside him, remembering that in her role as Mrs. Kelvin Petersen standing up against women like the beautiful be-yatch who stood before her was test number one. From the moment she and Kelvin became UCLA's campus darlings, Fawn had made it her business to tear them apart. She'd hounded him relentlessly and unashamedly, had screwed him in the laundry room right under Princess's nose, and when all else had failed, had falsely accused him of being the father of her now three-year-old son. A chance illness that felled the child had brought about the truth of his rare blood type, which was not shared by either Kelvin or Fawn. A DNA test had proved beyond a shadow of a doubt that when it came to Kelvin Petersen and the child known as his junior... he was *not* the father. Kelvin had kicked Fawn out of his home, but still supported the boy financially. Kelvin Jr.'s real father, a former student who'd also gone to UCLA, was now serving a five-year prison term for drug trafficking and was due out in a couple years.

Princess decided to try and take the high road, if she could find it. "How is little Kelvin, Fawn? I've continued to pray for his health."

Fawn eyed Princess in surprise. "He's doing as fine as Kelvin is looking." Showing that old habits died hard, she placed a hand on his arm. "We missed you at the White Party in Malibu last month."

Kelvin scowled slightly as he deftly removed his arm from Fawn's grasp and clung to Princess more tightly. "I was busy."

"There's another party happening on the fourth. Call me and I'll give you the details."

"We won't be attending," Princess stated. "Technically, we're still on our honeymoon and will be spending a lot of time *alone*."

Fawn eyed Princess with disdain. "I gotta hand it to both you *and* Rafael," she began, her tone smug and haughty. "Nobody seeing you two now would guess that just a few short weeks ago you and he were set to marry each other. Now you're here with a man many of us have had and will have again while that steady-looking dude has moved on and up from your stupid ass."

Kelvin took a step forward. "Watch how you talk to my wife."

With that cryptic message, and after pointedly ignoring Kelvin's defense of Princess's intelligence level, Fawn slithered over to an interested-looking NFL rookie, her next prey.

Princess appeared cool, calm, and collected on the outside, but inwardly she reeled from this confrontation. She needed some time alone, in silence, to regroup. She touched Kelvin's arm. "I'll be back."

Her journey to the nearest restroom was interrupted several times: by a few people she'd gone to school with at UCLA; Tori, Lavon's right-hand woman at MTM; and by the couple who also lived in Phoenix—NFL player Tony Johnson and his wife, Stacy. She didn't know them well, but knew that R & B singer Darius Crenshaw, the controversial gay minister of music at her uncle's church, was Stacy's son's biological father, and that she'd made peace with the fact that Bo Jenkins, Darius's life partner, would be a significant part of her young son's life.

"Hello, Stacy."

"Hello, Princess." The women hugged. "Girl, I'm sorry about all the stuff about you going down in the press. I got just a small taste of the spotlight while with Darius and know how hot those glaring lights can be."

"It's pretty crazy."

"Tony and I are praying for y'all."

"Thanks. I appreciate that."

"Here." Stacy reached into her bag. "Here's my card. I sure could have used a friend close by when I moved to Phoenix. So please, if you ever need anything—conversation, suggestions on the best shopping spots, a cup of sugar, whatever—then give me a call."

They chatted a bit more and by the time Princess reached the luxuriously appointed bathroom, she was truly worn out. She went into the separate stall area where the commode was housed, placed down the lid and sat down. In this moment she realized just what a whirlwind she'd been on, how drained she was emotionally, and how an upscale cut-throat Hollywood party was the last place she needed to be right now. *Then why are you here, Princess?* "Exactly. We need to get out of here, right now."

After using the facilities, Princess and her determined attitude went in search of her husband. Reaching an intersection of halls, she noticed gold and platinum albums lining the walls. The need to flee temporarily forgotten, she moseyed over to where they hung just above eye level, spaced equally apart. The producer in whose home they partied was evidently enjoying a very successful career. The albums numbered more than a dozen and most were platinum. As she neared the last album, she heard tinkling laughter coming from the room just beyond it. The sound was vaguely familiar, though Princess doubted that it was anyone she knew. She'd already seen or spoken to those at the party with whom she was familiar, and had left them all either poolside or on the lower level. A low murmuring ensued, and Princess realized what may have brought a smile to the face of the woman situated in the room beyond her. She'd attended her share of parties and knew that getting one's groove on in a strange place could bring on the type of titillation contained within the female chuckle. And then another memory came to mind, another woman's voice at another party, the one where Princess had walked in on Kelvin and Fawn. She turned away from the room and the sound and then . . . the woman said the man's name.

"You feel good, Rafael."

Princess stopped. My *Rafael? No, couldn't be.*

"You do, too, Kiki."

WTH? Her mind told her to walk in the opposite direction, but her feet had other plans. Before she'd even had time to think about consequences, she was in the room, standing in front of an oversized reclining chair and ottoman that easily accommodated Rafael—even with Kiki on his lap.

Princess crossed her arms, thinking that she might be looking at why her phone calls had gone unreturned. "Well, well, well."

45

From One Lover To Another

Kiki removed her arms from around Rafael's neck and sat up. "Hello, Princess."

"Hello." Princess's words were for Kiki, but her eyes were on Rafael. "I know you're angry with me, Rafael. But we need to talk."

"Conversation between me and you—really? Let me get this straight. You leave me hanging on the courthouse steps," he began, using his fingers to count off the indictments. "Leave town with your ex not long after that, marry his ass before the icing can melt on our wedding cake, have me find out about it from a tabloid at a newsstand . . . and now you stand there with an attitude demanding we talk." Rafael straightened in the seat while keeping Kiki close by his side. "I have nothing to say to you, Princess. And I don't owe you a damn thing."

Princess didn't know why she felt like crying. All of what Rafael said was true. *So why am I feeling betrayed?* Kiki's hand on Rafael's thigh was her answer. "Looks like you delivered more than a poem in Kansas City," she said, more sarcastically than she intended.

"Not until you left," Kiki calmly replied. "This wasn't planned, Princess. It—"

"Hasn't a damn thing to do with you," Rafael interrupted.

"Whatever goes on in my life is my business, *Mrs.* Petersen," he spat. "So if you have any sense left in that fucked-up head of yours, you'll get the hell out now. Before I get really angry."

Princess left, more like ran out of the room and away from the madness she'd just helped create. *What the hell is wrong with me?* If there was anybody who had a right to be angry it was Rafael, and if there was anybody who had absolutely no right to ask him any questions about anything . . . it was her. *And what's with these jealous feelings?* Princess couldn't even begin to process what that was about. She was married to her soul mate, her first love, and the man of her dreams. What did she care that Rafael was with Kiki? Good question. Because she did care and she shouldn't, and couldn't. She was married to Kelvin. Rafael was right. That was fucked up.

If she'd followed her first instinct she wouldn't even have seen Rafael, wouldn't have found out that he was seeing Kiki, wouldn't be thinking about the protective stance he took with Kiki, holding her close and defending her against Princess, wouldn't be remembering what an outstanding man he was.

I've got to get out of here. Princess walked through the mansion with the sole intent of finding Kelvin and doing what she should have done fifteen minutes ago. She found him out by the swimming pool, and the tableau surrounding him stopped her in her tracks. Suddenly, she was eighteen again—the recently deflowered virgin with her nose wide open, and he was the hot jock on campus. Surrounding him were his adoring fans as he held court with the ease and finesse of a man well used to the royal throne. The fact that Fawn was nowhere to be seen was Princess's somber reminder that aside from her nemesis there was still a throng of women who'd always be vying for her man, throwing their pussies at his dick and their lies in his face. She took a step forward and at the same moment, a gorgeous brunette appeared at Kelvin's side. He turned to her in acknowledgment and when she opened her arms as invitation for a hug . . . he obliged. She whispered something in his ear. He laughed.

Oh. My. God. Princess was frozen in place, thoughts spinning around her head like a Tilt-A-Whirl. *What in the hell was I thinking? How could I ever have given up a man like Rafael for one like Kelvin? How could I have given up the steady and predictable for the wild and spontaneous? How could I ever have thought that this could be my life?* The woman leaned in for a kiss and Princess saw red. She pushed aside the waiter who'd come up with a tray of drinks and stormed toward Kelvin. And then, with his next action, she stopped yet again. The smile fled from his face as he gently yet firmly grabbed the woman's arm and set her away from him. He lifted his left hand, pointed to his wedding ring, and delivered what looked like a short, stern message. Princess watched in awe as Kelvin nodded at the throng of ladies and began walking away. Obviously on a mission. Obviously looking for somebody . . . his wife.

"Kelvin!" So furiously was he walking that she had to hurry to catch up. "I'm right here."

He reached for her hand. "We're out of here."

She'd felt exactly the same way! Princess's heart soared. "I saw what happened." Kelvin didn't respond, simply walked them over to the valet, gave up his coupon, and stood with his arms crossed and a face that could have been made of stone. "Are you all right?"

"Not really," he said.

Princess placed a hand on his arm. It was tight with muscle, sinew, and tension. "I saw what happened," she repeated, her voice as soft as the thumb that stroked his forearm. "I saw that woman come on to you, and I saw you stand behind your ring . . . and your wedding vows. I'm so proud you, Kelvin. I love you." She raised up on her tiptoes to kiss his still clenched cheek.

"I love you, too, baby." He said it, but he was still distracted.

"I love you more," she whispered, leaning over to kiss him again. "And when we get back to the room, I'm going to show you just how much more."

His jaw unclenched, and a slight smile accompanied his glance in her direction.

And in this moment, all of Princess's earlier questions were answered. Seeing Rafael's unquestionable dedication to Kiki had made her question her decision, made her doubt Kelvin being capable of the same type of loyalty. And now, less than ten minutes later, she had her answer. There was a reason she'd followed her heart. And she was standing right next to it.

Later, after hours of both strenuous and languid lovemaking, Kelvin and Princess spooned against each other. Princess's eyelids were heavy and after the workout she'd just had, compliments of her husband, she welcomed the sleep. Kelvin continued to run a strong, forefinger up her thigh, before caressing her hip and stomach. Periodically, he'd lean over and kiss her temple, or shoulder, or neck.

After kissing her shoulder yet again, Kelvin spoke. "I think we should do that show."

"Hmm?"

"I think we should do that reality show that Lavon spoke about."

"I don't know, baby," Princess murmured, nestling her head into a more comfortable position for the sleep that now felt only seconds away. "People will be all up in our business."

"They're already in it, baby. So why not take control of the reins and work this to our advantage? We've got to be a team, baby, present a united front. I've got bitches coming at me all day long. I'ma need you with me, for real."

Princess turned to face Kelvin. "I don't like that word being used to describe women."

"It doesn't describe all women," Kelvin said, now sitting up against the backboard. "Just the ones coming at me even though they know I'm married. Why y'all do that?" he asked, looking down at Princess and twirling a piece of her hair in his fingers. "Why y'all make it so hard on a brother to stay faithful?"

"That's not all women," Princess said, using the words that he'd just spoken. She rolled to her side, repositioned the sheet and yawned as she added, "Just those itches with needs they're trying to scratch."

"Ha! So *bitches* is a bad word, but *itches* is allowed?"

"Of course. Bitches are curses, but itches are simply inconveniences."

Kelvin scooted back down next to Princess. "Damn, my baby's smart!"

"Whatever, Kelvin! I want to go to sleep!"

"Okay, baby." He leaned over and whispered in her ear, "But are you with me?"

A sigh and then, "Yes, I'm with you."

"We'll do the show?"

Princess reached over and placed his arm around her waist. "I'll tell you in the morning."

46

Home Is Where The Heart Is

"You can't keep doing this, Obadiah." Mama Max shook her head as she placed a steaming hot plate of grits, fried eggs, link sausage, freshly baked biscuits, and homemade strawberry jam in front of her estranged-yet-not-so-estranged husband. "Coming here at all hours of the morning and night, expecting to eat meals like it's your due."

"I'm your husband," Obadiah replied around a forkful of grits and eggs. "It is my due."

"Negro? Is you crazy or is you just lost your mind? What you did a year ago cancels out anything I ever owed you and fifty years of putting up with your mess marks my balance paid in full. You made your choice when you left this here house to sleep with Dorothea. You can't have your . . . biscuit . . . and eat it, too!"

For a few moments, Obadiah ate in silence. Then he leaned back, picked up his cup of coffee (doctored with the preferred half and half and brown sugar combo that Maxine had perfected over half a century ago), and took a thoughtful sip. Finally, staring over the rim of his cup at his wife, he offered, "How many times do you want me to say it, Maxine? I was wrong."

"Hmph. Is that all you have to say? That you were wrong? Hell, anybody looking at the situation can see that you're wrong.

Blind Bartimaeus can see that you're wrong. A dead man peering through empty sockets can see that you're wrong. That don't change nothing about what's happened—that you left your wife for a whore, and your pulpit for pussy that's past its prime."

"Maxine..."

"Tell the truth, shame the devil."

Better past its prime than not present at all! Wisely, Obadiah chose not to voice this thought. If he'd learned anything over the past several months it was that no amount of poontang could stack up to what the woman sitting across from him had added to his life. Pleasure pokes were a dime a dozen, but women like Maxine Fredonia Brook were like rare coins. Less than a month after leaving Mama Max for Dorothea, Obadiah was aware of the mistake he'd made. But his stubbornness mixed with the way Dorothea blew his pole convinced him that everything would get better with time. It hadn't. It had gotten worse. Before coming back to Kansas City a week ago, Obadiah had spent a lot of time thinking about how he could rectify his life. And since the day after he'd arrived, when after being kicked out of his own house he'd set up residence at an extended stay hotel, he'd been devising the plan to get back into her good graces, into the Lord's favor, and return to where he belonged.

"A man has needs, Maxine," he said instead, placing the focus of the conversation on the matter that had aided in his leaving almost a year ago and that in one way or another had dominated their conversation for the past week. "We have't shared the bedroom in ten, fifteen years. I tried to use... other means to answer nature's call, but you had a problem with that way, too!"

"That plastic vagina? The full-sized, real-life blow-up doll?" Maxine was getting so worked up that she couldn't sit still. She stood from the table, reached for her empty plate, and after placing it into the sink, began to fix herself a second cup of coffee. "You datgum right I had a problem with it, and any woman who wouldn't have a problem with it needs to get smacked upside the head with that very doll!"

Had it been left up to Mama Max, that's exactly what would have happened. A year ago, while Obadiah had been pastoring Gospel Truth Church in Palestine, Texas, and just before he left to be with Dorothea, Maxine had made what to her was a gruesome discovery: an amazingly authentic life-size sex doll in a private room off from Obadiah's study. Also found in the room was a comfy chair, flat-screen TV, porno tapes, and bottles of Viagra. After calming from the shock, Mama Max had loaded "plastic pussy" into her car, planning to take "her" to the church and leaving Obadiah as exposed as the doll's almost-real vagina. Had it not been for Nettie Thicke Johnson talking sense, restoring order, and convincing Mama Max to handle "PP" in private, Lord only knows what would have taken place.

"We been round and round with this here issue," Obadiah said into the silence. "We can't really talk about it... we've tried not talking about it... I've tried going without it."

Mama Max snorted.

"I've tried," Obadiah continued. "But it ain't natural not to do what comes naturally. I know you don't understand it, and you don't agree, honey, but that's the God's truth right there. It ain't natural!"

Mama Max returned to the table and took a seat. She looked beyond Obadiah, out into the living room—a cozy combination of earth-tone colors and blended styles of country, contemporary, and antique. Mama Max's love was draped throughout the room: doilies, needlepoint, and a knitted throw that, even if it was summer and eighty degrees, adorned the couch year round. She didn't see any of this though. She looked beyond the furniture and out the window, back through more than sixty years of history and one of the moments that changed her life.

"I told you that I didn't like it when we were courtin'.... You just didn't believe me."

"But you've never told me why. I figured with your being so fire and brimstone religious and all that, you were just making sure

I kept my boundaries, but that after we got married you'd . . . you know . . . loosen up."

"Mama did teach that sex was a sin, and that the only reason a man did his business with you was to make babies. I believed that." *Still do.*

Obadiah took another sip of coffee, seeing past the septuagenarian who sat before him and into the eyes of the girl he'd fallen in love with and swore he'd marry when he was only sixteen. "It's funny how in all of these years I never thought to ask you. But . . . did something happen, Maxine? Something else that makes you dislike being with a man?"

After a long moment, Maxine turned water-filled eyes on her husband and nodded. "I never told nobody. I only wanted to forget what I—"

"Mornin', Maxie!"

Maxine hurried from the table, hollering as she went. "Mornin', Henry. Come on in here and get some breakfast."

"He's going back to her. He's going back to Maxine." Dorothea paced the length of her one-bedroom apartment as she talked to her sister, still in her robe even though it was noon.

"Did he tell you that?" Dorothea's sister, Katherine Noble, sat in her luxuriously appointed condominium in New Orleans, watching two birds flit between the branches just beyond her patio. She'd listened to her sister's pain for the four-plus decades that Dorothea had pined after this married man, so even though she wasn't in the mood for lamentations and would rather be shopping, she lent her support. "All you have is a note that says he's going to Kansas City and doesn't know when he'll be back."

"But why, Kat? Why would he just up and go to Kansas City without telling me? If there was something happening in his family, why wouldn't he just tell me that? No, this is different," Dorothea continued, her voice dripping with sadness. "I can feel it. I'm getting ready to lose my man . . . again."

47

Every Goodbye Ain't Gone

Obadiah sat stewing in the living room, holding a newspaper that he wasn't reading and looking out the window without seeing a thing. It didn't matter that Maxine insisted she and Henry were just friends, the fact that she wouldn't stop her daily walks with him, even after Obadiah had asked her to (quite kindly, he would have added had anyone asked), was a serious stick in his craw. Not to mention the cakes and pies that she routinely took over, along with helpings of whatever dinner she'd prepared. Nor did he appreciate the smirk he swore happened every time Henry looked his way. It didn't matter how Maxine felt about Henry. Obadiah hadn't missed how Henry looked at Maxine; he was convinced that joining her for prayer service was not the type of meeting that her neighbor had in mind.

"I'm getting ready to put an end to these shenanigans," Obadiah mumbled, tossing the newspaper aside as he rose from the couch. He walked over to the window, looked up and down the street, and tried to spot his wife and her neighbor.

Don't you think you need to end something else first?

Obadiah scowled. He knew the voice of God almost as well as he knew his own. "Yes, Lord, I need to end things with her. I need to do right by Dorothea and send her on her way."

Then what are you waiting on?

"She's not going to like it. I'm not ready to face her drama."

Are you ready to face your own?

A host of memories assailed Obadiah as he stood looking out the window. He'd loved Dorothea since they both were in their twenties, having met her shortly after his second child, Queen, was born.

The year was 1961. Obadiah was twenty-three years old and already a preaching sensation. His deep baritone, tall stature, and wealthy knowledge of scripture were known throughout Texas and beyond, as was his suave dressing and conked, Jackie Wilson-inspired hair. He'd always had a way with the ladies and the fact that he was married didn't stop them from flocking to his anointed side like moths to a flame.

The night he first saw Dorothea, she took his breath away. She was easily the classiest, most beautiful woman he'd ever seen, could have given Lena Horne a run for her money any day of the week. During the service, he put her out of his mind, but after church—when he found himself seated next to her at the hosting pastor's dinner table—he knew that he had to have her. She'd felt the same way, and let him know it.

"I can love you hard, but I can't love you long." That's what he'd told her that night, before several rounds of lovemaking. But he did end up loving her long—for more than forty years.

"I love Maxine more," Obadiah said, as if the statement was a revelation to his own ears. And in a way, it was. He'd taken many parts of Maxine for granted: her love, wisdom, faithfulness, and her God-fearing ways. He'd lessened the importance of what she'd been in his life, not only as a loyal companion but as the mother of his children and a faithful friend. *She's always been a good mother.*

And a good wife—don't leave that out. A wife who deserves better than how you're treating her.

"You're right, Lord," Obadiah said. He turned away from the

window and passed a hand over weary eyes as he made his way to the phone in his study. *There's never going to be a good time for this conversation.* And even though he knew that it was probably one best handled in person, he couldn't wait the ten hours it would take to drive to Dallas or even the ninety minutes it would take to fly.

"Obadiah! Where are you?" Dorothea had picked up on the first ring.

"I'm still in Kansas City, but I'll be back this weekend."

"Thank God. I was about to go crazy down here without my joy stick."

Obadiah cleared his throat. "I've got to end things with us, Dorothea. I love you, but I'm married to Maxine and I can't leave her. I know this will hurt you and I'm sorry. But I'm a man of God who's been living in sin. I've got to get back in His will."

A pause and then, "What happened? Did somebody find out about our arrangement here?"

"This ain't about nobody finding out. It's about me doing the right thing."

"What, did Maxine finally get to you? According to you, she was fine with our being together, and even threatened to take over the divorce matter herself to speed things along. Right?"

"That was just hurt talking."

"I don't get it!" Panic raised the volume of Dorothea's voice. "We've been basically living together for almost a year. She let you go. We're supposed to be getting married. I've waited forty years!"

"I know, sugar. I'm sorry."

When Dorothea spoke, Obadiah could hear her tears. "Don't do this, Obadiah. Don't let go of our love. If you have to go back home, fine. I understand you're a man with a reputation to uphold. But don't end us. I'll do whatever it takes, whatever you want."

"I'll always love you, Dorothea. But I've made up my mind. I need to stay with Maxine if I want to make heaven my home."

"She doesn't love you like I do."

"I know."

"She won't even sleep with you!"

"You're right."

When Dorothea spoke her voice had changed, hardened to a tone that Obadiah had never heard. "Come back to me, you selfish motherfucker! Come back or I'll tell everybody about us!"

Obadiah sighed. "Do what you need to do, Dorothea. I'll have a couple deacons from Gospel Truth come over and get the rest of my things out of the apartment before the end of the month." Dorothea was openly crying now. "There're some good men down there in Dallas, Dorothea. Some who'd give their eyeteeth for the pleasure of your company. It's not too late for you to meet one and enjoy these last years of your life. And even though it will be hard knowing that I'll never see you again—and believe me, it will— this is how it has to be."

"All these years," she whispered, her tone returning to one more familiar even though it was filled with torment and pain. "I gave you all these years of my life, bided my time, accepted your crumbs. And this is how you thank me?"

"I'll continue to pay the rent on your condo—"

"This isn't about money, Obadiah! I love you. I want *you!*"

Obadiah placed a hand to his cheek, surprised to find that it was wet with tears. "I hope that someday you'll find it in your heart to forgive me, Dorothea. I feel bad, girl, but there was no way that somebody wouldn't get hurt in all this. I've hurt everybody, made a mess of things. Now it's time to make amends. Good-bye, Dorothea." He waited for a response and, hearing none, slowly placed the phone on its receiver.

In Texas, Dorothea stood clinging to her cell phone, long after she'd heard the call disconnect. "No," she whispered, sinking to the floor. "No!" She landed in a heap, cried her heart out, cursed Oba- diah, God, and the day that Mama Max had been born. *It's over, he said. Just like that. And having someone else come get his things? He didn't even have the decency to come in person to break my heart.*

Dorothea wasn't sure how long she lay on the floor. But the longer she did so, the madder she got. So angry that by the time she sat up she was filled with malice—and a plan.

"I might go away, Obadiah," she spat, angrily swatting away the remaining tears as she stood. "But I will not go quietly."

48

Falling

King was texting someone he shouldn't, but looked up as his assistant, Joseph, came away from the carousel at baggage claim with his luggage. He hurriedly typed the last line:

You deserve better than me. Stay beautiful.

"Car's waiting for you, Doc," Joseph said, once he reached King's side. "Barbados is paradise, but I bet you're glad to be home."

King didn't know how he felt about being home, or anything else right about now. But he provided an answer that sounded nice. "You know what they say. There's no place like it." The two men headed toward the door. "Thanks again for all your hard work," King continued. "Especially the three days while I was away, visiting Derrick in LA. Hadn't been for all you and Benjamin did, they would have wanted me to stay another week."

"I never thought we'd find someone to replace Lavon when he left. But Ben's one heck of a media director. And he loved Barbados. Don't be surprised if we're looking for someone to replace him soon."

King gave Joseph a sideways look. "You know something I don't?"

Joseph shrugged. "I know brothah man was feeling that sistah with the golden voice. The one who looks like Rihanna and sounds like Yolanda?"

"Yeah, I bet a bunch of brothahs are feeling her."

"He was eyeing the pastor's daughter, too, with her fine self."

King congratulated himself on appearing nonchalant. "I'm not surprised. But he may have to get in line." They reached the car. "All right, then," King finished, giving Joseph a soul brother's handshake. "Take off the next couple days. Get some rest. I'll see you after that."

"Thanks, boss. Call me if you need me."

King got into the luxury Town Car and settled back against its soft leather seat. It had only been two weeks, but felt more like a lifetime since he'd been home. He knew why. Everything had changed. King looked at the passing scenery as the car merged from the I-29 onto the I-635. He took in the flat landscape dotted with hotels, restaurants, and office buildings. That's what was in front of him. But in his mind's eye he was seeing turquoise blue waters, powdery white sand . . . and Charmaine.

Ah, man! How'd you get back here, huh? You said you weren't going to do this again. Ever! You promised Tai, promised God. And for almost three years now, he'd kept that promise. With the way women threw themselves at him it hadn't always been easy. But he'd turned into the dick dominator and forced himself to say no to the offers he'd gotten. Right before the trip to Barbados, he'd had a wealthy Kansas City realtor offer him carte blanche to her millions to be a chick on the side. And he'd said no. Before that it had been a well-known gospel singer and before that it had been the new, attractive, thirty-something member who tithed into the thousands, attended church every Sunday, sat in the third row, and ate him up with her eyes. And those were just the serious offers. There was something about this six-foot dark chocolate brother with the hulky build and husky voice that drew the women better than a magnet did steel. Until two weeks ago, his resolve to remain faithful had been as strong as steel. And then came a game changer with long, thick hair, velvety skin, and a sultry voice that spoke what was on her keen mind. King had been blindsided, and even though he'd said no the first time she'd offered her virginity, had told her to find a man who could love her in the way she deserved, it had not been enough. She'd kept coming, Derrick had insisted that he finish his work on the island, and her father had—gasp, sputter, and gasp again—given somewhat of a blessing on seeing his daughter. "I've always respected and admired you," her father, Wesley Freeman, had said. "And since even before becoming an adult, my daughter has always loved you." He'd then pierced him with an unreadable look. "God's will be done." King didn't know whose will it was; all that he knew was that he was lost and turned out like a mutha—*Bzzz*. The vibrating phone interrupted the quiet. King felt a myriad of emotions as he looked at the ID.

"Hello, Tai."

"Hey, King. You're back?"

"Just landed not too long ago."

"Are you on your way home?" In the past, it hadn't been unusual for King to arrive from out of town and head straight to the church. The staff was plentiful and capable, but King had been hands on from day one. "I'm asking so that I can know when to serve dinner."

"I'm on my way; should be there in about thirty minutes."

A pause and then, "How are you, King? You sound distracted."

"Just tired, Tai. From Barbados to LA back to Barbados again, and all of the work that happened while there—it was a grueling two weeks."

"I can only imagine. Did you guys get done what you set out to accomplish?"

King nodded. "Pretty much. I was able to meet with ministers from more than a dozen Caribbean and African nations and the evening services were standing room only."

"The one and only King Brook was in town. What did you expect?"

The smile in Tai's voice made King's heart clench. *Damn!* In this moment, he hated himself for being weak, for having given in to his flesh and the lure of a woman's lusciousness. There was more to it, King knew, but he refused to think about that now. He refused to give in to any flights of fancy about what could happen and who it could happen with, refused to entertain the carrot that Wesley and his contingent of ministers had dangled in his face: heading up a new organization of ministers and church leaders representing African, Asian, and Caribbean nations, an organization with millions of dollars and a blank slate. And most of all, he refused to give in to his strong feelings for Charmaine Freeman. Another day, another time, and who knows what might have happened. But King didn't live in "another." He lived in now: as the married father of four children, the senior pastor of a thriving ministry, and a core member of an American ministerial organization called Total Truth. And he intended for things to stay that way.

"King? Did you hear me?"

"I'm sorry, baby. What did you say?"

"Never mind. I'll let you go."

"Sorry, baby. I've got a lot on my mind. When I get home, I'll tell you all about it."

"Okay, bye."

King had barely disconnected that call before his phone rang again. "Hey, Dad."

"Son," Obadiah said.

"Tai said that you'd driven back to Kansas City. Are you still here?"

"Yes, and I plan to stay here. I plan to reconcile with your mother . . . if she'll have me."

King closed his eyes in relief. "That's great, Dad!"

"Well, now. Don't put the cart before the horse. She hasn't taken me back yet."

"Hey now, you think I don't know who I'm talking to? It's just a matter of time." Until now, King hadn't realized how badly his parents being separated had made him feel. But now he had something to compare it to: a heart bursting with joy. King leaned forward and pushed the button to close the partition. "So how's that going—you being at the house but not yet back in Mama's good graces?"

Obadiah cleared his throat before responding. "Would you believe that woman won't let me back in my own house?"

"What!" King sat up straight. "Are you at my house?"

"No, son. You know how I like my own space; I didn't feel comfortable staying there this long."

This long? "How long have you been here?"

"About a week."

"Where are you staying?"

"One of those extended stay places."

"Daddy, that's a shame."

"Naw, it's all right, son. Really, it is. Come to find out, I've needed this time to myself, time to think and reflect. Time to get my priorities straight and my house in order."

"What about . . . the other woman?" King knew Dorothea's name, but he rarely said it. "She all right with this?"

"Ain't none of us all right. Son, I know I haven't always been the best example and for that, I sincerely apologize. But if you ever hear anything that I say to you, hear this: love your wife. Honor your marriage vows. Because outside of them is just a bunch of pain and heartache. You hear me?"

"I hear you, Dad."

The two men talked for a while longer, until King was just five minutes away from his home. He'd come close to disclosing his own recent discretion, but figured if anybody ought to hear about it first, it should be his wife.

King Brook, son of the Reverend Doctor Pastor Bishop Overseer Mister Stanley Obadiah Meshach Brook Jr., was the epitome of an apple who hadn't fallen far from the tree. But unless his wife showed him grace and mercy, King would fall some more.

49

This Is My Confession

King opened the door to a quiet home. He was still getting used to the sound of it. Tai had been six months pregnant when they married over a quarter century ago. Their last kids, twins Timothy and Tabitha, were six years younger than their oldest, Michael. Princess was in between them. So, basically, they'd had children in their house their whole marriage. Until now. For the twins, their best friends had long ago replaced Mama and Daddy as who they'd rather hang out with, and when home, they stayed holed up in their rooms. In three short months, Tabitha would be moving to Los Angeles to attend UCLA and Timothy would follow Michael's footsteps to Northwestern University in Chicago to study law. King and Tai had often talked about how they'd celebrate their empty nest. King could only hope that after the conversation he had with Tai . . . there'd still be reason to party.

After allowing the driver to place his luggage in the foyer, offering a generous tip and sending the man on his way, King walked down the hallway into the living room. "Tai!"

"I'm upstairs. I'll be down in a minute!"

King followed the delicious smells into the kitchen. He peaked through the oven glass and smiled. Braised short ribs was one of his favorites. He lifted the lids to one of the pots on the stove. *Umm.*

Garlic mashed potatoes. He lifted a final lid. Fresh green beans with corn on the cob filled the pan. *Dang, woman, you threw down!*

"Like what you see?"

King turned around. As he took in the vision before him, the quick retort he'd prepared died on his lips. Tai was leaning against the doorjamb in a saucy pose, her full hips and generous breasts on full display beneath a thigh-high caftan. Its silky fabric, emblazoned with bold, geometric shapes in primary colors, was very forgiving of the extra pounds Tai carried, and the inch-high, satin mules that covered her feet emphasized her strong, shapely calves.

King's eyes traveled from the tip of her toes to the top of her curls before he looked in her eyes and warmly responded, "I like what I see...very much."

Tai pushed away from the door and entered the kitchen. King took two steps and was enveloped in her open arms. "I very much like what I see...*very* much." *How could I ever have jeopardized this? We've worked so hard....*

"You're a pretty nice sight for sore eyes, too." She hugged him, snuggled into him, loving the feel of his hard shoulder beneath her cheek, and the scent of his cologne.

King pulled back, once again looking into Tai's eyes as he traced her face with his finger. "I like your hair short like this. It emphasizes your cheekbones, those beautiful brown eyes...and these." He leaned over and placed a whisper of a kiss on Tai's lips. She moaned, placed her arms around King's neck and deepened the exchange. Opening her mouth, she molded her body against that of the only man she'd ever known intimately, the only man she'd ever truly loved. He responded by sliding his hands down to her backside, giving each cheek a generous squeeze as he ground a quickly hardening erection against her willing flesh.

"Umm..." Tai's head fell back against the wall, leaving a perfect opening for King's tongue to slide across her cheek, down her neck, and into her bosom. "The food's ready," she managed to whisper, as her nipple hardened into a perfect peak.

"You've awakened a different kind of appetite." King's tongue formed a trail from one nipple to the other. "Where are the twins?"

"Won't be back until late," Tai managed, her breath coming heavier, her body on fire.

King lifted Tai into his arms and walked them over to the breakfast nook.

"The food," Tai whispered, as he gingerly set her down. "Turn off the burners . . . and the oven."

King walked over to the stove and made quick work of her request. When he turned back to look at his wife his eyes were black with desire, his dick ready to burst out of its trouser confines. He unbuckled his belt, unzipped his slacks, and let them fall right there on the kitchen floor. Still staring at Tai, he stepped out of them, his shoes and his boxers. Mr. Happy was delighted and Miss Kitty purred her appreciation. Tai was glad that she'd not bothered to put on underwear. It was one less piece of clothing she'd have to take off. "Come here, baby," she said, her voice as slick as her nana with wanting. "Come get this."

"Your wish is my command."

He sat down, and guided Tai onto his fully engorged shaft. A satisfied hiss escaped her mouth as she aligned her body with his, and they began a lover's dance. She ground herself against him, and he raised himself for deeper thrusts. No words were spoken. But none were needed. Their bodies were communicating messages that no language ever could. They reacquainted themselves with each other's anatomy: breasts, chest, arms, thighs, lips and tongues that swirled in the same motion as their lower bodies. Ecstasy came quickly, full and complete.

"Oh, baby!" Tai exclaimed, as her body shattered into a thousand pieces.

King grunted, increased his speed, and soon he too was spiraling over the edge . . . into an erotic paradise, an Eden of their own.

Some time later, King and Tai sat at the dining room table, enjoying the meal that Tai had earlier prepared. Tai watched King put a short end bone into his mouth and pull it out clean. She laughed, dotting his mouth with a napkin and removing sauce from his lips. "I'm glad you're enjoying it," she playfully said.

"I must admit . . . I'm enjoying this meat almost as much as I did that earlier course."

The smile on Tai's face slipped away, replaced by a look of subtle remorse. "I enjoyed it, too, baby. And I need to apologize for how rare that dish has been lately."

King frowned. "What do you mean?" True, he and Tai hadn't shared many intimacies as of late, but with the wedding, Derrick's illness, and the state of his parents' affairs . . . a lot had been going on and he told her so.

"I'm glad that you feel that way, but I know you're a man with a voracious appetite and I plan to focus more on that in the future." She leaned over and kissed him on the mouth. "I love you, King Brook."

"I love you, too."

After a rare occurrence of King helping Tai clean up the kitchen, the two lovers retired to their master suite. They showered together, both anticipating another round of lovemaking before the night was through. Tai asked about what had transpired in Barbados and King gave her the short version. "They want me to head up this new organization," he finished.

"But you're already so involved with Total Truth."

"I know. I'd definitely have to reorganize my priorities."

"So you're thinking about doing it?"

"I probably shouldn't." He tried, but couldn't look Tai in the eye.

Her antennae went up immediately, even as she scooted closer to his side. "Baby, what is it?"

"Nothing."

He said this, but Tai noted the sudden tenseness of his body, and how the hands that not long ago had played a beautiful melody on her body were now removing her arm from around him. *What is going on?*

King sat up in the bed as another heavy breath escaped him. He blinked his eyes rapidly.

Tai became worried. *Wait, are those tears he's trying to hold back?* She couldn't imagine what could have changed the mood so quickly, what it was about his possibly working closely with Wesley Freeman and other international ministers that would cause her husband such angst. "Baby, you always weigh everything out and make the right decision. This time will be no different."

It already is, is what he thought. "You're probably right," is what he said. When Tai tried once again to comfort him, he moved away from her and got out of bed.

"King, what's going on?"

He stood with his back to her before turning around. Once he did, his chocolate brown eyes bore into hers for a long moment. "I love you so much, Tai. All that you are, all that you've been to me and this family. I never would have become who I am without you."

"Oh, baby, don't worry about me. I'll do whatever I can to support you, even if—"

"Wait." King stopped Tai before she could continue and before the tears that threatened began to fall. "Earlier you apologized for not being more attentive. Baby"—King dropped his head briefly, before standing straighter with his shoulders erect—"you've attended to me better than any woman ever could. Which is why this need to apologize to you hurts so much."

Tai's brow creased in confusion. "Why would you have to apologize to me?"

King sat on the bed and placed Tai's hand between both of his. He worked to force the words past the lump in his throat, but determined that the only way for him to handle his mistake was by being truthful with his wife. His mind did a quick calculation of all the times he'd cheated, and all the times he'd lied. But no more.

She deserved his faithfulness, and once again he'd failed her. But he never again wanted to keep secrets from Tai...even something as hard as this. "I slipped up again, baby."

Tai's heart dropped. "What do you mean?" She pulled her hand out of his grasp, believing she knew what he meant all too well.

"While in Barbados, I made a mistake."

Tai's entire body stilled as she absorbed his words. She didn't have to ask for a more definitive explanation, didn't need to ask for a better understanding. This wasn't Tai Brook's first time at this particular rodeo, and whatever the basis of this forthcoming apology...she knew that a filly was involved. Her eyes went from love and warmth to suspicion and coldness in an instant. But she did not say a word.

"It meant nothing," King explained. "I was weak, she was there and—"

Whack! The sound of Tai's hand connecting with King's jaw reverberated throughout the bedroom. She jumped out of bed, backing away from him as though he were a stranger.

"You fuck me, and *then* tell me this? You put yourself in me and *then* you find the courage to tell me that you've been with someone else?"

King stood, too. "Baby, I—"

"Don't you dare 'baby' me." Tears seemed to push against the back of Tai's eyes, but anger prevented them from coming out. She turned away from him. "King, just get out." Her voice was weary but otherwise devoid of emotion.

"Tai, just let me explain—"

With anger rising, she pushed through clenched teeth, "Get. Out. Now."

King looked at Tai a long moment, feeling totally defeated. She was acting exactly as she should, had a right to be even angrier, matter of fact. Her point about the sex was well taken. This confession probably should have come out before they'd made love.

But he'd been caught up in the moment where once again, his lower head overruled his higher one.

"Okay, Tai. I'll leave. But you need to understand something. This conversation isn't over. I won't let this be over until you hear me out. I'll fight tooth and nail against anything you throw at me, any argument you bring to me, no matter how valid. Understand?"

Tai crossed her arms. "Here's what I understand, King. You promised me that you would never have another affair. You broke that promise. I promised that if you ever cheated on me again that I'd get a divorce. I don't intend to break mine."

King watched Tai leave the room before turning and walking into their large, custom-designed closet. He pulled on a pair of sweats, made a phone call, and fifteen minutes later was back in the same car that had dropped him off just hours before. The same bags that had been delivered to the foyer were now in the trunk, moving with King toward his ironic destination, the first place of refuge that came to mind. He tipped the driver and waved off the offer to have his bags carried up. Instead King gripped the handles of both rolling suitcases and after walking a short distance, knocked on the door. Silence. King waited, and then knocked again.

Finally, a gravelly voice sounded from the other side of the door. "Who is it?"

"It's me, Dad," King said with a heavy sigh. "Let me in."

50

Father and Son (The Remix)

"Okay, Carla, are you here?" Vivian asked.

"Yes."

"Tai, I still have you on the line?"

"I'm here."

"Good. Sorry about dropping you earlier, Carla. I'm still trying to get used to how to conference on this phone. Well, ladies," Vivian continued, shifting the chair in her home office so that she could cross her legs and peer out the window. "I don't even know where to begin for today's call. So much has happened in this last month and, needless to say, neither SOS nor Ladies First has entered my mind."

All three of these women were members of LF, a group exclusive to pastors' wives, and were the backbone of the Sanctity of Sisterhood organization, a group Vivian founded to address the specific needs of women. For the past two years, Vivian, Tai, and Carla had enjoyed bimonthly conference calls, conversations that had initially begun as discussions about upcoming conferences and now extended to whatever was going on in each woman's life.

"Carla, could you start us off with a prayer?" Vivian asked.

"Sure. Dear Heavenly Father, we thank you for this opportunity to gather together once again by way of this phone call. You said that where two or three of us are joined together, that you would be in the midst of us. So I thank you now, Lord, that you are here, joining us in our endeavors, guiding our thoughts and leading our actions. Thank you once again for healing our brother, Derrick. Thank you for your ministering angels, and the angels of protection that brought back King safely from his travels. Thank you for continuing to bless us, our families, and our ministries. Be with us now, Father God, as we move forward in your name. Amen."

"Amen," Vivian added.

Tai remained silent.

"How is Derrick?" Carla asked.

"Well, as Mother Moseley would say—may her soul rest in peace—Jesus is still in the healing business! Dr. Black says that Derrick's recovery is nothing short of amazing. His motor skills are normal, the headaches have totally ceased, and there is no sign of any brain damage as a result of the tumor. Of course, he'll have to continue to be closely monitored, but everyone is optimistic that Derrick will make a full and complete recovery and that this tumor will not grow back."

"Thank God!" Carla said enthusiastically before her voice lowered as she continued. "Does that mean that brothah man is back in business . . . if you know what I mean?"

"Ha! I absolutely know what you mean and, trust and believe, my husband is back in stride again!"

"Well, thank God again!" Vivian and Carla laughed. "What about King?" Carla continued. "How was his time in Barbados?"

Silence.

"Tai?" Vivian asked, her voice suddenly laced with unease. She'd noticed that Tai had been silent, but considering that King had just arrived home last night, thought that her friend may have been still recuperating from their reunion. "You're awfully quiet. Are you all right?"

More silence.

"Tai," Vivian said softly. "What is it, sistah?"

Another long pause and then, "King cheated on me."

"Jesus," Carla hissed under her breath.

"Oh, no, Tai," Vivian said, immediately feeling an intense wave of compassion and sadness for her friend.

"Oh, yes," Tai replied calmly, a little bit too calmly for her friends. "He dropped this bomb on me last night when he came home, not long after we'd made love." Now it was Vivian and Carla who had nothing to say. "He told me that this would never happen again," Tai continued, almost as though she were talking to herself. "He promised me that I'd never have to feel this type of pain again. And after his being faithful for the longest time period since we've been married, at least that I'm aware of, I actually believed he meant it. Now look who's the fool."

"Certainly not you," Carla retorted. "The woman who slept with your husband is foolish and King is crazy for letting it happen...but you didn't have any part in it, Tai. Please don't blame yourself or beat yourself up. You've done nothing wrong."

"Who was it?" Vivian's voice was soft, caring.

"I don't know and it doesn't matter. But while away, his ass cheated again and that's all the information I need."

Again, no words. What was there to be said?

"I understand if you don't want to talk about this, sistah," Carla began. "But I'm curious as to why King said anything in the first place. If he hadn't told you what happened on the island, then his slipping and dipping may have stayed on the island."

Tai told them about her and King's conversation, and how after they'd enjoyed making love that she'd apologized for not being more intimately available. "He then confessed that he had an apology, too."

"Wow," Vivian said, slowly shaking her head and trying to wrap her brain around this unexpected conversation. "I'm just shocked, Tai. After everything you two have been through, I am surprised that he cheated. But I'm even more surprised that he told you."

"Most men wouldn't have come clean like that," Carla added.

"Yeah, well, I guess his conscience was killing him and he felt the need to confess his sin."

"That's not an easy thing to do," Carla said. "Believe me, I know." And she did. Even though it was nearly five years ago that Carla had survived her own cheating scandal, the pain of it was something she'd never forget. "I know you're angry, Tai. Hurt, disappointed, disillusioned . . . all of that. But the fact that he told you, especially since he didn't have to, says a lot."

"How are you feeling, Tai?" Vivian asked.

"Honestly? I don't even know. Numb, I guess. I'm beyond anger; I'm just done. Through with King, and with this whole situation."

"I'm so sorry this is happening," Vivian said, still feeling Tai's hurt in her own heart. "Where's King now?"

"I don't know. I kicked him out after he told me. He's at a hotel, I guess."

"What are you going to do?" Carla asked.

"Divorce him. Hold on a minute," Tai said, rising from the couch as she did so. "There's someone at the door." She walked down the hallway and looked through the paned glass. "It's King, with his father."

"Reverend Doctor O?" Vivian's voice reflected the surprise she felt. She was one of only a handful of people who knew the real deal between him and Mama Max. "He's back in Kansas?"

"Back in Kansas and now on my doorstep. Let me get off here and handle this. Y'all pray for me."

51

Fistful of Tears

Tai opened the door but kept her mouth closed. Rather than look at King, she looked just beyond his right shoulder, and tried to see a future without him. The image was hazy at best.

"I don't deserve your forgiveness," King said by way of greeting, jumping right into the heart of the matter. "I don't deserve your love. I've messed up, and gone back on the promise I made years ago. I didn't mean to, didn't want to, but that doesn't change the fact that I did it. All I ask is that you hear me out and maybe then you'll at least understand how it happened."

"Daughter," Obadiah intoned in his firm, rich voice, "I have no right or desire to meddle in your and my son's affairs. People living in glass houses shouldn't throw stones. But if there's one thing I know for sure it's this: King loves you with every fiber of his being and from the depths of his soul. If he could change what happened to set y'all apart, he'd do it in a heartbeat."

"Please, baby. Just let me in and hear me out."

It was the tears in King's voice that caused Tai to finally shift her eyes and look at him. That it hadn't been a good night was written all over his face. Dark circles surrounded his bloodshot eyes and there was an ashen tone to his usually velvety chocolate skin. His eyes bore into hers—pleading, searching, wanting. She turned away before her heart could turn back to flesh from stone and, leaving the door open, walked into the living room. Once her resolve was firmly back in place, she again turned around.

"It's Saturday, King. Why aren't you at the church?"

"I had more important places where I needed to be."

Tai looked behind King and, when she didn't see Obadiah, asked, "Where's your father?"

"He's going to run over to Mama's house, and then come back and pick me up."

"Why'd you bring him here?"

"He asked to come, believes that in a way he's partly to blame for what's happening with us. I never thought I'd hear him admit that in some areas of life he hadn't been the best example . . . but he did."

Tai said nothing as she walked over to one of two chairs that framed the large picture window. She sat, back rigid, eyes looking outside.

"He's determined to win back Mama . . . no matter how long it takes." King looked at his forlorn wife, could actually feel the pain emanating from her body. It tore his soul. He'd been heartless and selfish to envision a life without Tai in it, a life with someone new. "I am *so* sorry."

"You said that already."

"I know, but I can't think of any better words to use." King took a step and saw Tai's straight back get even straighter. He stopped, placed his hands in his pockets. For King, being unsure, unsteady, and not in control was unfamiliar territory. "I got caught up in a fantasy, one that had been orchestrated to snare me and reel me in. I hate that I took the bait."

Tai gave King a sideways look, her brow raised in mock incredulity. "Oh, so this is somebody else's fault?"

"Not at all. I blame nobody else for what happened but me. I was seduced, but I should have been strong enough to resist the temptation."

"Who was it?" Tai asked, crossing her arms as she again looked out the window.

A deep breath and then, "Charmaine Freeman."

Tai's head whipped around. "Bishop Freeman's daughter?" King nodded. "My God, King. She's got to be young enough to be your daughter."

"She's twenty-eight."

"Just when I thought you couldn't sink any lower," Tai murmured, sadly shaking her head. "And you expect me to believe that *she* seduced *you?*"

King met Tai's stare without blinking. "Yes. I'm sure you don't want to hear the details—"

"No, I don't."

"But trust me, it was a seduction. Her father was even in on it."

"The bishop was okay with you sexing his child?"

"Yes." King wanted to tell Tai everything: about their switching him from the hotel to their private beachfront villa, the planned encounters involving Charmaine, her late night visits to his guesthouse, her naked sunbathing just outside his bedroom window, the offer from Wesley and, yes, even the fact that Charmaine had offered up her virginity on a thousand-thread count Egyptian cotton platter. But he dared not say more.

The air fairly crackled between them. Finally Tai spoke into the silence. "Why did you tell me?"

King walked over to the chair opposite where Tai was sitting. This time, he noted, she did not flinch. "I had to, Tai. As much as I knew it would hurt you and maybe even cause you to leave me, I didn't want to do like I have in the past and lie to you. I didn't want there to be any secrets between us, didn't want to carry the guilt around in my heart. I got caught up in a moment, in a highly charged, horribly wrong block of time. But even as it happened I knew that it meant nothing. That I'd leave the island and that it would never happen again."

Tai banged the chair arm with her fist. "And that made it okay?"

King's voice was just above a whisper. "No."

Tai was silent a long moment. When she turned to face him her demeanor was calm, her eyes bright and clear. "I have loved you since I was fifteen years old. You are the only man I've ever known, and the only one I've ever given my whole heart."

"I know and—"

"No, King. Let me finish." King sat back heavily in the chair, his eyes boring into Tai's as she continued. "My whole world has been you, our children, and the ministry. I gave up everything to help you live your dream, and I did it gladly, willingly, never doubting that by your side was where I wanted to be. Like I said last night, after your last affair you promised me that it would never happen again. And I promised you that if it did, I would end the marriage." Tai turned from the window and looked him straight in the eye. "I meant it."

With that, Tai walked out of the room and up the stairs to their bedroom, head high, back straight, countenance one of strong determination. It wasn't until she reached the master suite and had turned and locked the door that she wept for all of what had been . . . and all of what now would never be.

52

My Princess and Me

Kelvin and Princess sat out on Lavon and Carla's spacious patio, enjoying the nighttime view and summer breeze. Since last week and the Fourth of July party fiasco starring Fawn, Kiki, Rafael, and the nameless brunette, the Petersen's had visited with the Chapman's almost nightly, not only getting marital counseling but also working on Lavon's idea of a reality show starring Kelvin and Princess. Carla had been especially excited when Kelvin and Princess shared their vision for the show's direction—showing a young, married couple determined to remain faithful to each other and to make commitment not only look attractive, but look like something to be envied if not achieved.

"Okay, so check this out." Kelvin lifted his six-foot-five-inch frame off the chaise lounge and came to a sitting position. His eyes twinkled with excitement, and the barely there dimple on his right cheek deepened with his smile. "I've been thinking of an idea for the show intro. Like a theme song or whatever."

"Who's going to sing it?" Carla's question was accompanied by a devilish grin. "Because as much as I love Princess, she can't carry a tune in a bucket and, Kelvin, I doubt your crooning skills equal those displayed on the basketball court."

"I got skills, Carla. You didn't know?"

Carla's look clearly showed that not only did she not know, she didn't believe it.

"I thought maybe Princess and I could do something," Kelvin said, not at all shaken by Carla's lack of confidence. He shared a couple of the ideas he'd run by Princess over the past weekend.

"I like this!" Lavon said, once Kelvin had finished. Production was his passion and the creative process was his favorite part. "Maybe we could get Darius to write something. Either him or I know a couple hip-hop artists who might work for what we want."

"Well, uh, actually I came up with a little sumpin', sumpin'." Having both Lavon and Carla's attention, Kelvin reached into his jeans pocket and pulled out a piece of paper. "Y'all want to hear it?"

"Are you sure you want to sing it?" Carla retorted with a smile.

"Show us what you've got, man," Lavon said.

Kelvin winked at Princess, who was smiling broadly, and made a big show of clearing his throat. "Okay, now understand that I'm not a rapper and this is a work in progress, so it might be a little rough around the edges right now. I mean it's not like we—"

"Baby!" Princess cried. "Just do it!"

Kelvin actually looked a little uncomfortable as he shifted from one foot to the other. "Okay, here we go. Unh, unh ... here we go, here we go, yeah. Bob your head." Princess was already grooving and snapping her fingers to Kelvin's beat. Lavon and Carla joined in.

"You're 'bout to see a story about me and my girl,
About the prince who found his princess when she rocked his world.
She flipped the script and sent the digits when I asked to call her,
Said she was down and would stick around with an NBA baller."

To Lavon and Carla's surprise and delight, Princess stood and took over the rap without missing a beat.

"Hang with me and the man who is my one and only,
And watch us navigate this thing called matrimony.
Share the ins and outs and ups and downs with me and
KP...."

Kelvin put his arm around Princess as he finished. "And spend a day in the life of my princess and me."

"Uh-huh, me and KP."

"My princess and me."

"It's just me and KP."

"It's just my princess and me."

"Yeah, baby!" Princess gave Kelvin a high five before molding herself to his broad chest. They'd worked on this ditty all weekend and had rehearsed it over and over. It sounded even better than they'd hoped it would, and regardless of what Lavon and Carla thought about it, would call it a success.

"That was great!" Lavon exclaimed. Too excited to stay seated, he stood and walked over to where Kelvin and Princess embraced. "Did y'all write that?"

Kelvin released Princess and turned to Lavon. "Yeah, me and baby girl wrote it together."

Lavon and Kelvin shared a brother-man handshake. "I love that, man; can see doing some cross-marketing with that joint, maybe even releasing it as a single with a companion video."

As Kelvin and Lavon continued putting their business heads together, Princess walked over to the custom-made bamboo bar where Carla sat perched on a bar chair. "What did you think, Carla?" She pulled out a chair and sat next to her, then reached for the pitcher of fresh-squeezed orange juice on the bar and poured a glass.

"You and Kelvin are so cute," Carla admitted, "and work so well together."

Princess looked up, the glass from which she was about to take a drink suspended between her mouth and the table. "Why do I feel that there's a *but* coming?"

"But . . ." Carla began with a laugh, "I want y'all to be careful."

"What do you mean?"

"This business is hard, Princess, and marriage is harder. Viewers like nothing better than to build you up, way up, just so that they can see you come crashing down. Remember Jessica Simpson and, oh, what was her husband's name?"

"Nick Lachey."

"Right. Remember what a nice couple they made, and what a fairy-tale life they seemed to live? I don't think their reality show lasted two seasons before the rumors started, the tabloids did their thing, and the next place we saw them was divorce court. And then there was that family whose daughter's highly hyped on-screen marriage lasted less than three months."

Princess's facial expression showed her concern. "Maybe we shouldn't do this," she finally said. All excitement had left her now subdued voice as she thought about a high-profile breakup.

"No, baby, I'm not saying don't do it. I'm just saying be careful. Go into this with your heads on tight and your eyes wide open. Stay humble, stay grateful . . . and stay in counseling."

"What do you two ladies have your heads together about?" Lavon asked as he walked to where Carla and Princess sat, and then noticed the serious countenance on both of their faces. "What's wrong?"

Kelvin walked up behind Princess and placed a hand on her shoulder.

Carla smiled at Lavon. "We were just discussing the pros and cons of life in the spotlight. I love this whole concept of their show revolving around their marriage, with the added components of Kelvin's basketball career and Princess's work on my show. But you know how we like to build people up and then tear them down. I was just telling Princess to be careful."

"Ah, don't sweat it, Miss C," Kelvin said, kissing Princess on the temple. "I ain't going nowhere and Princess can't leave me so—"

"Oh, really?" Princess said, turning to see Kelvin's face.

"You know that without me you can't breathe, girl. Don't play."

"Whatever," Princess said, with a laugh. Though she'd be damned if what he'd said hadn't sounded true.

"Look, most people go into marriage head over heels in love with each other and believing it will last a lifetime. But things change." Carla looked at Princess and in that instant realized that she didn't know yet—that this beautiful young woman so sure of her marriage had no idea that her own mother and father were headed for divorce. As she continued, Carla wasn't thinking about what was happening in Tai's marriage. She was focused on what had happened in her own. "People grow in different directions, desires and affections can change . . . affairs can happen."

"No, Carla," Princess said with a vehemence that surprised even herself. "I've already told Kelvin that when it comes to cheating, I have a zero tolerance rule in full effect."

So did your mother, is what Carla thought. "And I'm sure you mean it," is what she said. "Listen, guys, I'm not telling you what I've heard. I'm telling you what I know. When I married Stanley I swore that I would never, ever, cheat on him, that I would be a loving, dutiful, and faithful wife. I said those words and I meant them with every fiber of my being. But fifteen years later, the situation looked very different, had changed in ways that I could not have imagined. And now, here I sit. Happier than I ever could have dreamed, granted, but having gone through the fire and been dragged through the mud. I'm just trying to help y'all not get dirty."

"So, Kelvin," Lavon asked, "given how women throw themselves at you, what safeguards or measures do you have in place to protect yourself from yourself, and from the temptations that are sure to come?"

Kelvin came from in back of Princess and joined Lavon on the other side of the bar. His brow furrowed in thought as he took a seat. "One day not long ago," he began, "I asked my dad how he did it. How he and Mom Vee maintained a successful marriage, and how he'd been able to stay faithful to her all these years. I'll never forget his answer—that any type of man can have all kinds of women, but the man who chooses to be with just one woman is one of a kind. He said that there were levels of love, and the deepest one was the exclusive bond between two people. He talked of the bond that happens when your wife is also your confidant, your lover, your counselor and best friend." He looked at Princess with love in his eyes. "I want to experience the type of love that he and Mom Vee have, that forever kind."

Carla walked over to Kelvin and gave him a big hug. "If you want it you can have it, darlin'." She reached over to include Princess in the embrace. "Both of you. And Lavon and I will be cheering you on, every step of the way."

"Speak for yourself, baby," Lavon said. Three sets of eyes looked at him. "Let's face it. Drama sells. Your lovey-dovey is good and all, but this is about ratings! I say we let y'all have a honeymoon for, oh, two-three months or so, and then we'll hit 'em with a little bit of scandal and . . ."

Carla's eyes narrowed to dangerous slits. She adopted a strong stance with legs apart and placed her hands on her ample hips.

"What?"

"You keep talking like that," she warned, "and we'll have some drama all right. . . . And no one to yell 'cut' either!"

"I'm just kidding, baby."

"I know."

"I love you, Carla Chapman."

Carla sidled up to the love of her life. "I know that, too."

They talked well into the evening and by the time Princess and Kelvin said their good-byes, the four friends were excited and more than ready to rock and roll with television's next hot reality show: *KP and His Princess*.

53

Fire and Desire

A week had passed since Obadiah's phone call ended Dorothea's life as she knew it. Since then she existed as if in a daze, her mind filled with memories of her and Obadiah's times together, and wondering how she could possibly go on, knowing that they'd never share such times again. Dorothea was not a drinker, but after her ex-lover's devastating news she had gone to a nearby liquor store and on the cashier's recommendation had purchased a fruity tasting wine called Moscato. The worker had chosen a brand he felt sure she'd like, even though she wasn't necessarily fond of the taste of alcohol. He'd been right. Dorothea had taken home the bottle and once the wine was thoroughly chilled, took a tentative sip. It was surprisingly delicious, reminding her of the sparkling juices she so enjoyed. Before she knew it, she'd drunk the whole bottle and the next time she left the liquor store, it was with a case.

Dorothea eased open the screen door to her balcony and took a deep breath as she stepped outside. Though it was only 10:30 a.m., there was a glass of Moscato in her hand. It wasn't her first, which may have been why she swayed a bit as she walked over to the patio table and clumsily sat down. "Why aren't you calling me, baby?" she asked the open air. "Why you trying to act like we're over?" Her words were slurred slightly, and the unkempt appearance that she'd adopted over the past seventy-two hours was not a good look. "We're never going to be over!" A crow, perched on the next building's roof, cosigned. *Caw! Caw!*

"That's what I'm saying," Dorothea said to the bird. "That son of a bitch needs to call! Call!" She reacted to her own joke, but the sound that started as a chuckle ended as a sob. *Why can't he just do the right thing? And why can't I get over him?* It wasn't as though she'd never loved anyone else. She'd not only been married twice before but she'd had her share of paramours and sugar daddies. The first one had come calling in the midfifties, when she was sweet sixteen and one of the finest beauties in New Orleans. She and Thomas Rutherford were deeply in love, and when he proposed marriage she was over the moon. His status-conscious mother was underwhelmed. Dorothea had the looks but not the pedigree, while the Rutherfords' wealth and success was legendary, dating back to the early 1800s. Thomas gave her a ring and took her virginity. But when he took back his proposal as well, she was crushed.

The following year Dorothea fled New Orleans and landed in Dallas, where a friend secured her a job at a black-owned dress shop. Trading matrimony for money, Dorothea quickly caught the eye of an older, wealthy, and well-established doctor whose wife was infirmed. All of her living expenses were paid and she was given every luxury. The affair lasted until her benefactor died. It was during this time that at her sister Ruthanne's insistence, Dorothea had attended a church meeting to hear a "hot new preacher" who was all the rave. After the service, she and her sister were invited to dine at the host pastor's house. She found herself seated next to the man who'd held her enthralled from the moment he spoke, and the rest, as they say, was history. Like her doctor, Obadiah was married, but that didn't stop Dorothea from giving him her heart. While his wife, Maxine, stayed home with the babies, Dorothea traveled from state to state, meeting him at conferences and revivals, and warming his bed. It was during one such conference, the National Baptist Convention in 1963, where their relationship shifted. His wife found out about them and, even though the affair continued, things were never the same after that June in Dallas.

Eventually Dorothea fled Dallas for the bright lights and big city. Fed up with being somebody's seconds, she vowed to become a smashing success, and then rub that triumph in the faces of the men who'd not valued her worth. In Harlem, she became a moderately known name, but even more important, she became a wife. George Bates was a hardworking, loving man whose brain aneurysm at age fifty-three caused him to leave the world way too soon. Between him and her last husband, Reverend Reginald Jenkins of Palestine, Texas, she'd seen many men come and go. But none of them had ever held a candle to the Reverend Doctor Pastor Bishop Overseer Mister Stanley Obadiah Meshach Brook Jr. And now, it seemed, no one ever would.

Dorothea looked at her glass and was surprised to find it empty. Even more surprising was the fact that no matter how much alcohol she consumed, it wasn't enough to fill the emptiness that was in her heart. She still loved Obadiah. She still missed him. And she was still alone.

"Damn you!" She flung the wineglass across the expanse and watched it shatter against the patio's stucco wall. "I'm not going to let you just walk away from me. If I have to suffer, you're going to suffer, too."

She left the patio and re-entered her condo, looking around as if the answer to how to hurt him was in the room. She walked from the living room into the kitchen, retrieved another glass, filled it with wine, and then returned to the living room. While downing the drink as though it was Kool-Aid or water instead of alcohol, her eyes fell on the fireplace. She slowly lowered the glass from her lips as a thought took hold. She laughed, its sound sinister and hollow as she imagined the fallout from her actions.

"Obadiah would be furious!" she told the empty room. She knew how much he loved his tailored suits and how meticulous and fastidious he was with not only their care but that of his alligator shoes, his gold jewelry, his spun cotton shirts, and Italian silk ties. Oh, and don't leave out his beloved books. He'd purchased a bookcase that covered the back wall of his bedroom and it was filled with Bibles and teaching aids and other religious works. More than once, he'd shared with Dorothea how much these books of knowledge meant to him. "Yeah, well, at one time," Dorothea slurred, "I meant something to you, too."

Mind made up, Dorothea plunked down the wineglass and picked up her purse. She was well aware of her state of inebriation but she wasn't worried. She wouldn't drive far. Just to the neighborhood gas station less than five minutes away. She left the house with the lights blazing and TV blaring. It didn't matter to Dorothea. She wouldn't be gone long.

Ten minutes later, Dorothea used the spare key Obadiah had given her to enter his apartment. Immediately, she was assailed with the spirit of him, the scent of him. She barely looked at the sparsely furnished living room as she walked toward her destination—the bedroom. That's where she and Obadiah had spent much of their time together and where all of Obadiah's most precious possessions lay. A feeling of melancholy came over Dorothea, and she almost changed her mind about what she was going to do. But hell—she'd already bought the gas, right?

Placing three of the four filled plastic gas cans she'd purchased on the bed, she walked with the other one into Obadiah's closet. She uncapped it and quickly doused suits, shirts, slacks, shoes, and everything else within the enclosed space. The smell of gas almost gagged her as she emptied the can of its contents and threw it on the closet floor. Then she emptied the other three containers: one for the bookcase and its contents, one for the dresser, table, walls, and floor, and the fourth and final one for the bed. She virtually soaked the spread and sheets with the flammable liquid, crying openly now as, like her love affair, this room was about to go up in flames.

"Ah, hell, forgot the matches." Dorothea walked from the bedroom to the kitchen and was delighted to find a box of wooden matches in one of the drawers next to the stove. She smiled through her tears, an evil smirk really, as she walked to the closet, struck the first match, and tossed it against the clothes soaked with gas. It fell to the carpet and promptly went out.

"Dammit!" She placed the matches down and in a mad rampage pulled the clothes from their neatly arranged position on the rods down to the floor. Then, to make sure a fire would catch, she rushed into the living room for the stack of newspapers she'd glimpsed while passing through. She tore them with her bare hands before piling them on top of the clothes. Satisfied that she had the makings of a proper fire, she scraped a second match against the box's rough side and was rewarded with a blaze. "Burn, Obadiah," she hissed before throwing another match onto the heap. "Burn!"

She tossed the match and was instantly rewarded as a second burst of flames shot up from the gas-soaked clothing. Knowing that she needed to work quickly, she walked over to the bookcase, lit another match, and placed it on top of a row of paperback books. A slow burn began, but grew quickly as the flames lapped at and began to consume the paint-covered plywood from which the bookcase was made. Finally she turned toward the bed, lit a final match, and after throwing the box of matches onto the bed, tossed the match on the navy blue silk comforter she'd purchased for Obadiah. "Now it's really over."

Whoosh! A huge ball of fire shot up instantly, actually making a sound with its intensity. Belatedly, Dorothea realized it probably would have been a better idea had she been standing next to the bedroom door when she struck that final match.

I've got to get out of here!

Dorothea turned to run but as she did so, a portion of the burning bookcase fell to the floor. Dorothea tripped on it, lost her balance, and went flying through the air. On her way down, her right temple made its acquaintance with the left edge of Obadiah's heavy oak nightstand. And then her world went black.

54

Oh My God

Nettie absentmindedly rubbed her stomach as she lay on the couch. It was the second day of her not feeling well and if she wasn't better by the morning, she'd have to visit the doctor. Reaching for the phone, she called her husband, Gordon, and asked him to bring home some over-the-counter medicine for what she hoped was just a bad case of indigestion. She was just about to place the phone back on its receiver when it rang in her hand. "Hello?"

"Hey there, Nettie. What you know good?"

"How do, Mama Max. I guess I can't complain."

"You sound a bit tired. You all right?"

"A bit under the weather; stomach been bothering me the last few days."

"Gordon ain't cooking is he? Ha!"

"Lord, child, if that were the case, I'd be dead by now!"

The women laughed. "What about you?" Nettie asked. "How are things in your neck of the woods?"

"Heart still keeping the proper time," Mama Max responded. "And Obadiah still acting a fool."

Nettie sat up and frowned as her stomach roiled. "How so?"

"He came over here yesterday with a mess of dandelions and a prime piece of smoked pork. Said he'd gotten it from a friend who works at the city market. The day before that it was fresh green beans and tomatoes and the day before that it was fillet mignon."

"Hmm. Sounds like somebody's gone a'courtin'."

"Hmph. It'll take more than prime beef to undo what he did to me, that's for sure."

"But he is trying, Mama Max. You said it yourself that it took a lot for him to return to Kansas with his tail basically between his legs."

"That's where dogs usually hang 'em."

"And he's staying at that hotel, ready to wait it out until you invite him back in. For a proud man like Obadiah, that's quite a lot."

"No more than it should be."

A pause and then, "I thought you said that you forgave him?"

"I did. That don't mean I'm going to let him waltz back in here without sweating a little . . . or a lot."

"But you *are* going to let him back in."

"I don't know," Mama Max said with a sigh. "Sometimes I wake up and forget he don't live here and other times I kinda like having the house to myself."

"That Henry still sniffing around there?"

"Henry ain't sniffing nowhere. He's my neighbor's son, a good man who's become a good friend."

"All right, Mama. If you say so."

"I say so."

"Lord have mercy!"

"What? You think I should just let him treat me any kind of way and then take him back just because that's what he wants?"

"No, no, not you, Mama. I'm watching the news and they're showing a breaking story about a huge fire that broke out over in Dallas. They just flashed pictures of the damage on the screen and the place looked like a bomb hit it. Hold on." Nettie reached for her remote and turned up the volume.

"... the time the firefighters arrived at the Meadowbrook condominiums, the entire unit was engulfed in flames."

Nettie sat up and peered at the screen. "Meadowbrook ... isn't that where Obadiah was staying?'

"I think so," Mama Max answered. "Is that where the fire broke out?"

"Hold on."

Nettie turned up the volume as the story continued. "Police say that so far the body of one victim has been recovered. Fire and police personnel continue to search for more possible casualties, as well as for the cause of the blaze."

Nettie muted the television. "So far they've only confirmed that one person died," she explained to Mama Max. "They're looking to see if there were others."

"Lord have mercy on that person's soul," Mama Max replied. "I sure hope they were saved and their soul went to heaven. It would be every kind of bad luck to burn up twice."

"Mama, you're a mess."

"Just telling the truth and shaming the devil."

The women conversed for another fifteen minutes before Gordon walked through the door and Nettie ended the call.

Later that night, Gordon and Nettie sat up in bed reading the newspaper and the Bible, respectively, and waiting for the ten o'-clock news.

"You feeling better?" he asked.

Nettie nodded her head. "That medicine helped and so did the soup."

"Could have been something you ate."

"I'm just glad that whatever it was seems to have subsided." Nettie glanced up at the television. "Turn up the volume, Gordon. Here's that fire story I told you about." They both listened as the somber-toned reporter spoke from the scene.

"Residents of the Meadowbrook Condominium Complex are breathing a sigh of relief tonight following today's tragic fire that claimed one victim. Firefighters responded to a call in the fourteen-hundred block of Kensington Avenue early this afternoon, after a nine-one-one call claimed that a fire was burning out of control. Firefighters arriving on the scene found unit one-twenty-seven engulfed in extremely hot flames, the interior of the unit totally destroyed. Fire chief William Sutton says the fire seems to have been intentionally set as several burned gas containers were found at the scene. The victim who died in the fire has been identified as seventy-three-year old Dorothea Jenkins, a—"

Nettie gasped.

Gordon looked at her, his brow creased in confusion and concern. "What is it, Nettie?"

"Oh my Lord!" She turned to her husband. "We know her, Gordon. That's the woman who was married to Reverend Jenkins, the one who came over for dinner shortly after they married. Remember?"

"The one what brought those pecan pralines?"

Nettie nodded. "Oh my God." She reached for the phone and quickly dialed a number. "Mama Max, you're not going to believe this."

"Believe what?"

"What me and Gordon just saw on the news." Nettie hesitated before delivering the unthinkably unbelievable news. "I think Dorothea is dead."

55

Back In Stride Again

Mama Max sat straight up in her bed. "What?"

"That fire I saw when we were talking earlier, the one at Meadowbrook?"

"Uh-huh."

"They released the name of the victim just now, on the news. Said it was seventy-three-year-old Dorothea Jenkins. I can't imagine that there would be two at the same age with the same name, can you?"

"Sounds highly unlikely." Mama Max got out of bed, slipping on her robe and house shoes before turning up the dimmer. "Lord Jesus, if this is true, Obadiah is going to be devastated. That man is going to be beside himself."

"They gave the apartment number. I think it was one-twenty-seven."

"Okay. Nettie, let me get off from here and call Obadiah. Let me know if you hear anything more."

"Will do."

Mama Max ended the call to Nettie and immediately called Obadiah. Upon hearing his voice heavy with sleep, she admonished, "Obadiah, wake up!"

"What in the world, Maxine?"

"I know it's late but this might be important. Have you talked to Dorothea lately?"

Obadiah, who'd indeed been sound asleep, now tried to clear his brain enough to think of why his wife was asking about his mistress. "What?"

"Dor-o-the-a, Obadiah. Stop acting like you're deaf and dumb. Have you talked to her?"

"Not since a week ago, when I ended things between us and told her good-bye. Why?"

Mama Max took a breath. "Because I just got off the phone with Nettie. She heard something disturbing on the news."

"Nettie? What'd she hear?" Mama Max told him. A long pause and then, "Maxine, I've got to go." And then he hung up the phone.

"Jesus," Mama Max said while dialing King's cell phone. "Just like I figured. . . . King," she shifted her thoughts once again when her son answered, "where are you?"

"At the hotel."

"Go next door and see about your daddy. I just gave him some bad news."

"What happened?"

"We think that Dorothea is dead. I just told Obadiah and he hung up on me. I need you to go and make sure he's okay."

King got off the phone, slipped back into the warm-ups he'd discarded for his preferred sleeping attire, nudity, and went next door. "Dad!" he yelled, as he knocked. No answer. "Dad!" He knocked several more times, waited a few minutes, then went back into his room and retrieved his phone. Standing outside his father's hotel room, he dialed his dad's cell phone number. King could hear it ringing from the other side of the door, but his father didn't answer. King looked over the railing into the parking lot. Yes, his father's Cadillac was parked in the same spot it had been in for the past two weeks. Panic set in as King pounded on the door. He rushed down the steps and over to the office.

A studious-looking twenty-something stood behind the counter. "Hi, may I h—"

"It's my dad," King said, breathless from excitement and his run to the office. "I think something has happened to him."

"And your dad is . . ."

"Obadiah Brook. Room four-twenty-five. I'm his son, King, staying next door. I need you to open the door."

"I'm sorry, Mr.—"

King didn't realize he was going for the young man's collar until the material was twisted around his fist. "If you don't open that door and my daddy dies I swear I will—"

"Okay, okay," the clerk croaked through a cotton choke hold. King released him. The clerk coughed as he walked over to a case filled with keys. "It's against policy," he said as he came around the counter and followed a fast-walking King out the door. "But we'll"—King turned around and glared—"make an exception."

They reached the room. The clerk opened the door. King went inside and found his father sprawled out on the floor. Whether or not he was breathing was anyone's guess.

Mama Max stood at the front door, watching as her tall, strapping son helped his old, feeble-looking father exit King's Lincoln SUV. It looked as though Obadiah had aged ten years in as many days. He'd lost weight, which caused him to have sunken jaws and slack skin. His usually bright, astute eyes were filmy and his hair had turned even grayer than it had been. Using a cane, Obadiah stood to his full height, batted away King's assisting arm, and looked toward his destination, the front door of the house he'd shared with Maxine Brook for more than thirty years. There, he saw her, looking fine and formidable, her expression unreadable. He faltered just a bit, but straightening his spine once again, made the slow journey up the sidewalk, up the steps, and into the living room.

"How you feeling?" Mama Max asked, as Obadiah reached the couch and sat down heavily. "You hungry?"

Obadiah shook his head.

Hmm, not a good sign. Obadiah never turned down Mama Max's food. Ever. "Thirsty?"

"I'll take some water," Obadiah replied. His hoarse voice mirrored his tired soul.

"What about you, son? Have you eaten dinner?"

"No, Mama, but I have a meeting at the church. I need to run." He kissed his mother and shook hands with his dad. "I'll have Tabitha call y'all later to see if you need anything."

"We'll be fine, son," Obadiah assured him. "Go and take care of your ministry."

Mama Max went into the kitchen and busied herself by warming up the dinner she'd prepared: smothered chicken and gravy, rice, peas, fried corn, and freshly baked biscuits. As she did so, she tried to get a hold of her emotions. Obadiah's reaction a week ago, when he found out about Dorothea's death, hadn't been lost on her. The man had almost gone into cardiac arrest and, had the hospital been farther away than the five minutes it took for the ambulance to arrive and get him stabilized, the Brooks may have been attending a funeral, too. The doctors had performed a surgery to relieve pressure on his arteries and help the blood flow to his heart. And when she'd delivered the news confirming Dorothea's demise, he'd collapsed in her arms and cried like a baby.

"I did this, I killed her," he'd lamented.

And while Mama Max had shushed him and demanded he stop talking foolishness, a part of her thought that he might have been right.

Twenty minutes later, Mama Max walked into the living room carrying a tray of piping hot food. "I know you said you weren't hungry," she said as she positioned the tray on his lap and secured a large, cloth napkin over his shirt. "But you need to eat something to get your strength back."

Obadiah looked at Mama Max a long moment. He picked up the fork, speared a good chunk of the succulent chicken, and brought it to his mouth. He chewed slowly, thoughtfully, closing his eyes as he did so. "I guess you right," he said at last, placing the fork down on the plate. "Especially since I'm going to be leaving here soon."

Mama Max straightened to her full five foot four and fixed Obadiah with a look that while not lethal, could do major damage. "What are you talking 'bout, leaving? You going back to Dallas?"

"No, woman! But you've made it clear I can't stay here. Seems like I'm in the way of you and that Henry fella dallying around. My grandchild is going to help me find an apartment around here, or something, until you come to your senses."

"Oh, now it's me who's got to come to my senses? Well, at least I've got some sense. I'm not a crippled-ass old man at a woman's mercy, trying to argue with her while he eats her food!" She spoke with vehemence, but there was a twinkle in her eye. "Your old room is ready for you, Obadiah. You don't have to go nowhere."

Obadiah looked up. "For how long?"

A moment passed between them, nearly magical in its arrival. It was almost like Obadiah was sixteen again, Mama Max was fourteen, and they were meeting at the fork in the road that separated the two family's farms...the place where Obadiah had confidently declared that Maxine Brook would be his wife.

"I guess you can stay here as long as your heart's beating," Mama Max finally replied, batting away unexpected tears. "Now eat your food," she continued brusquely to cover the moment's emotion. "Before it gets cold."

"Woman don't know how to welcome a man home," Obadiah mumbled under his breath.

"Man don't know how to appreciate being here," Mama Max stuck her head out of the kitchen to retort. Obviously, Obadiah's mumble hadn't been low enough.

And just like that the marriage was back...fifty-four years and counting.

56

Something Inside So Strong

Vivian navigated her Mercedes along Wilshire Boulevard before turning onto I-405 and heading south, toward Redondo Beach. She was thankful for whoever invented hands-free devices, otherwise Tai's news may have caused an accident. "Don't get me wrong," she said, continuing their conversation. "I'm always happy to see a marriage stay together, to hear of couples who are able to work things out. But honestly? After Reverend Doctor O left her to be with Dorothea down in Dallas, I never thought she'd take him back."

"I didn't either." Tai was driving also, leaving Gates Bar-B-Q, where she'd stopped after her hair and nail appointment, even now trying to stop her mouth from watering caused by the ribs she smelled. "But I think his heart attack, or whatever it was, caused her to rethink her position. Mama Max wouldn't be able to live with herself if Daddy O died in some remote hotel room, all alone."

"I feel so sorry for Mrs. Jenkins's family," Vivian said.

"Why?" Tai asked.

"Tai! Whatever your family feels about that woman, she had her own relatives who I'm sure loved her very much."

"Don't we all," Tai said with chagrin.

Vivian paused. "Why do I get the feeling that we're no longer talking about Dorothea Jenkins? Look, don't even answer that question. What's going on with you and King?"

"Oh, girl, everything is so messed up. I told our children that King and I were divorcing."

"You told me that you were going to tell them. What happened?"

"They pretty much went ballistic. Out of all of them, Michael really surprised me. I mean he's the oldest, and has been away from home the longest. I thought his would be the calmest reaction. But that award goes to Princess."

"Really?"

"I'm just as shocked as you are, but yes, when I called and told her that her Daddy and I were divorcing, she asked a few questions, and then said that she would be praying for us."

"Wow."

"Tell me about it."

"How are the twins?"

Tai sighed. "Everybody is better now."

"Because . . ."

"Because King has talked me into delaying my filing a divorce petition until after the holidays. It will give our family time to adjust to this new situation, give Daddy O time to get better, and give King and I time to slowly break this to the church family. I don't want to hate King, Vivian. Really, I don't. I don't want to see the ministry suffer. Heck, my blood, sweat, and tears went into its success just as much as his did. We want to formulate a strategy whereby I can make my exit as smoothly and seamlessly as possible. I want to let our members know that my divorcing King in no way reflects on my feelings about the ministry. King is a great pastor. He's just a lousy husband."

"I don't know, Tai. Members have a tendency to react strongly to divorce. What happened at Logos Word following Stan and Carla's separation comes to mind. I don't think there's any way that you and King will avoid some type of fallout from what's getting ready to happen."

"I know. But if I can help minimize it, then I will."

"So does that mean that King is back home? I've always worried that some church member would see him coming out of his hotel room."

"Me, too. Even though they were staying in Olathe, which is about fifteen miles from the church, I still believed in the possibility of somebody seeing either him or his father, and wondering why in the heck they weren't home with their wives."

"Tai, don't get mad at me for what I'm about to ask you, but—"

"I know what you're thinking, Viv. You're wondering if there is any chance that I won't go through with my plans to divorce King."

"It's totally your choice, sistah, and I support you in whatever you decide. But you know how I feel—that at least he came straight to you, confessed his sins, and since that day has made you privy to everything including his e-mails and cell phone records. I agree that for a married man, one time in somebody else's bed is one time too many, but it just seems like a couple days of island foolishness versus twenty-five years of marriage is something to seriously weigh before throwing in the towel."

"If this decision was purely based on a couple days of island foolishness, then we might not be having this conversation. But it's not. It's based on a long string of infidelities throughout our twenty-five-year marriage. At the end of the day I need to be able to look my daughters, church members, and myself in the eye and know that as much as I love King, I love myself more." For a moment both Tai and Vivian were silent, as Tai watched the buildings pass on I-35 and Vivian observed the boats bobbing in the marina as she neared her destination. "I have thought about it," Tai continued at last. "Staying with him. I remember a *Lifeclass* show on OWN where they talked about the ego, and I realize a lot of my hurt, anger, indignation, and sadness comes from that place. When viewing life from my higher self, it's easy to think of staying with King. But when I think with my brain, and feel with my heart, leaving is the only answer."

"I'm praying for you, sis," Vivian said as she turned into the parking lot of a popular restaurant. She reached the valet station and exited the car. "I'll have to call you later, Tai. I'm here. Guess who I'm about to meet for lunch."

"Who?"

"Passion."

"Really?"

"Yes. She called the church and has some ideas about Ladies First that she'd like to share. She'd also like to become active in the SOS conferences."

"Interesting."

"Isn't it? You know I have a loyalty to Carla, but I've determined to put aside my personal feelings and listen to her with my heart. She is Stan's wife, a first lady, and a California resident, which means that by right there's no reason she shouldn't be a part of either organization."

"I wonder what Carla will say about having the woman who had a part to play in her divorce now joining her at the planning table."

"If I know Carla, it will be plenty."

"Ha! No doubt. There's Passion," Vivian said, with a wave to the first lady of Logos Word. "I've got to run . . . but, Tai?"

"Yes?"

"When it comes to your marriage, whatever decision you make is the right one. Stay strong."

57

All The King's Horses

It was quiet at the dining room table, and not because it was just the three of them—Tabitha, Tai, and King. It was because while Tai had agreed to let King back into the house, she was determined not to let him back into her heart. Easier said than done, she'd discovered in the past tumultuous and trying week. Since returning to the home they'd shared for more than a decade, King had been on his best behavior. That in itself was no surprise; this was neither his nor Tai's first time at this dance. But what struck Tai was the true feeling of remorse that she felt from him. It wasn't just the fact that he'd brought her flowers every day, flowers she knew that instead of sending the secretary he'd picked up himself. It wasn't the gift boxes she'd found sprinkled throughout the house, making her entire abode resemble a treasure hunt. Just this morning, she'd gotten into her car and once on the road heading east, had pulled down her visor to block out the sun...and into her lap had fallen front row tickets to an old school show happening Labor Day weekend: Cameo, Gap Band, Rose Royce, the Time, Evelyn "Champagne" King.... And that was just on Friday night. Saturday included the Whispers, Kool and the Gang, and one of Tai's favorite male vocal groups, Boyz II Men. Just thinking of them brought back memories of a trip she and King had taken to Hawaii. Their hit song, "I'll Make Love to You," had just come out. She and King had laid out a blanket on a private section of beach, enjoyed a candlelight dinner, and then made love almost all night to that song.

"Mom, you're not listening to me!"

Tai shook herself out of her reverie. "I'm sorry, baby. What did you say?"

"I asked if you and Daddy were going to come with me to LA next month. Freshmen orientation begins in August and I'll want to show y'all around the campus and show you where I'll be hanging out."

King and Tai exchanged a look and a slight smile. Each knew what the other was thinking. "We've already seen the campus," Tai said. "Your sister went there, remember?"

"Of course I remember," Tabitha said with a roll of her eyes. "But that was her experience. I want you guys to be a part of mine. You guys can get a hotel room near the campus, or stay with Uncle Derrick and Aunt Viv. Okay?"

"We'll see, baby girl," King said, with another glance in Tai's direction. "We'll see."

After dinner, Tai followed her usual pattern and went into the den. This was her quiet time, when she'd read, reflect, or watch TV. Tonight, she didn't feel like thinking over much and so reached for the remote. After flipping through a couple dozen channels, she settled on HGTV, and a show where ordinary rooms were transformed into masterpieces.

"Thinking of redecorating?" *Or moving?* King stepped farther into the room.

"Maybe," was Tai's noncommittal answer. King joining her in the den was also new. Normally after dinner he'd retire to his office. Sometimes he'd go back to the church, or if it had been an extremely long day, he'd lounge in the master suite. But every night this week, he'd found wherever Tai was and joined her.

King sat, and for several moments there was silence between

them. "Crazy how different the girls are," he finally said. "Can you even imagine Princess asking us to join her anywhere?"

"No. If you'll remember, our visit to the UCLA campus was most unexpected, and most unwelcomed."

"That's for sure."

Both were silent again, remembering what had happened when they discovered that Princess had lied to them about sharing a condo with her best friend. They'd made a surprise visit and discovered the truth: that Princess and her best friend, Joni, were living together all right, but they were cohabitating with their boyfriends, Kelvin and Brandon.

"I'll have to check the schedule, but I'm almost sure there will be time during the conference that I can get away to visit where she'll be staying on campus. It will be nice to see her home away from home for the next four years."

"I told Derrick that I'd try and get out to see him whenever I got a break in my schedule. It might be around that time."

More silence. More thoughts and words that were left unsaid. Tai sat there thinking about all of the times she and King had spent casual evenings talking about a bunch of nothing, taking for granted the fact that they shared a life. King sat there feeling hopeful that what he was experiencing at this moment, he'd continue enjoying for years to come.

"Thanks for the tickets."

King turned to Tai with a smile. "Oh, you found those, huh?" He crossed his right ankle over his left knee and rested his arm across the couch... precariously close to Tai's shoulder.

"More like they found me. They fell in my lap when I pulled down the visor."

"There's a limo ride that goes with those front row tickets. And dinner at Crown Center."

"King, I—"

"I don't have to go," he interrupted. "I thought you might invite down Viv or Carla or even look up your old girl from Sprint, the one you used to work with. What's her name?"

"Sandy."

"Right, Sandy. I just know that those are some of your favorite groups and I wanted to make it a night you'd remember. I want you and whoever you take to have a great time." Silence, and then, "I wouldn't mind seeing the Gap Band though, or Cameo. Man, hearing those songs would take me back." He looked at Tai and began to sing. " 'When I first saw you, you had sparkle in your eye . . .' "

"King, don't."

"I'm not trying to start anything. I'm just remembering what we grooved to in seventy-nine. What about this." He jumped off the couch and started dancing around the room. " 'All pretty ladies, around the world.' "

Tai burst out laughing. She hadn't seen this carefree King in a long time, but his antics reminded her of the good years, the years in between his affairs. *Affairs, remember? The reason you can't enjoy him now. The reason you're leaving.* "I think I'm going to go read a bit and make it an early night. Thanks again for the tickets. I just might call Sandy." She got up from the couch and left the room before he could answer.

King slowly made his way to his home office and once there, sat down in the chair. Discussing those old songs with Tai had put him in a contemplative mood. He'd jacked up royally, and it would take a Herculean effort to win her back. "And a miracle, buddy," he mumbled to himself. "Don't forget that." Then he remembered the glint in her eyes as he sang Cameo, and the wide smile that graced her face before she remembered she wasn't happy. The concert was over a month away. King clung to the belief that they'd attend it together.

His phone rang, and when King looked at the caller ID his good mood fled. After not calling for almost a month, following his assurance to her that their sexual rendezvous was over, Charmaine had been blowing up his phone for two days straight. He reached over and picked up the phone. *I might as well end this once and for all.*

"Hello."

"Hello, King." In spite of his resolve, he warmed at the sultry sound of her voice.

"You've been calling nonstop for two days. What is it?"

"I miss you, among other things."

He looked toward the stairs and, convinced that Tai was not within hearing range continued, his voice low and filled with chagrin. "Look, Charmaine. We've already been down this road. Let's not do it again. What we shared was beautiful, but it is over. You only make this harder by continuing to call."

"But that's just it, King. What we had is far from over. It will never be over."

A foreboding feeling climbed from King's core and spread over his chest. "Why not?" he asked, sitting up as he did so.

A short pause and then, "I'm pregnant."

And just like that, the world that King Wesley Brook had known for more than twenty-five years began to unravel as he foresaw his fall. And all the king's horses, and all the king's men, would not be able to put his life back together again.

58

End Of The Road

Tai frowned at the knock that interrupted her reading. She glanced at the clock on the nightstand—just after midnight. More than four hours since she, King, and Tabitha had parted ways after dinner, and a little less than eight hours when she'd need to be up again. For a quick second, she thought that this was the beginning of a seduction of the King kind. She looked down at her nondescript cotton nightgown and again, for a split second, thought of the negligees in her closet, gathering way too much dust and too little use. *What am I thinking? The last thing I want is that adulterer in my bed.* She thought this, but her va-jay-jay tingled anyway.

"Yes?"

A slight hesitation and then the door opened. King's head peeked in. "You asleep?"

Tai closed her book. "What does it look like?"

King stepped inside the bedroom and closed the door. Only then did Tai notice the tightness of his lips and the sadness in his eyes. Her heart dropped. "What's wrong?"

He leaned back against the door and sighed. Tai waited. He gazed at her with a look that she couldn't read. And then he looked away.

"King. What is it?" More silence. Tai's heart constricted before its beating increased. "Baby, I'm becoming concerned. What is going on?"

King pushed away from the door, crossed over to the bed, and sat down on the bench at its base. "I got some disturbing news tonight."

"About what? Derrick? Did you talk to him?" King shook his head. "Doctor O and Mama?" Again, a negative head shake. "Well, what then?" Tai huffed, before picking up her book. "You know what? Never mind. I'm not even going to try and pry info out of you. If you weren't going to say what's on your mind, why even knock on my door?"

"She says she's pregnant."

Tai's mind went to the only other female besides herself that she'd recently encountered. "Who?" She threw the book down on the bed and sat straight up. "Please don't say Tabitha. I don't think I can handle my youngest daughter being pregnant right now."

"No, not her." King's voice was barely above a whisper and Tai could have sworn she saw water in his eyes.

"Then who?"

Silence.

And then, reality dawned. "Not the chick you screwed on the island." In this moment Tai realized she'd almost take the news that it was Tabitha instead of the young woman with whom her husband had sexed. "Please, King. Tell me it's anybody but her."

"She's lying."

Tai snorted. "Oh, really?" *Is that why you're sitting there with troubled eyes and ashen skin?* "Granted, someone who would screw a married man obviously scores low in the morals department. But the very fact that you couldn't keep your dick to yourself puts your hat in the could-be-baby-daddy ring, huh?" When King continued to be silent, Tai's sarcasm turned to something else. Dread. *He really thinks this chick is pregnant with his child!*

In an instant, Tai's mind rolled back to another day, and another time, when she thought another woman had birthed King's child. She'd enlisted help in tracking down the young man who was just months younger than her oldest daughter, Princess. In a wicked twist of fate, that young man was now her son-in-law, Kelvin, whose father turned out to be the husband of her best friend. The incredulity of these events was the only reason Tai wasn't off the bed with her hands wrapped around King's throat right about now, and the only reason she spoke calmly instead of calling the man who sat in front of her every name but a child of God. "Do you think she's lying about being pregnant or lying that the baby is yours?"

Honestly, King feared that every word Charmaine had spoken was true. But he wasn't ready to admit that. So he used the non-committal phrase that men picked up around the age of four and often used until they'd breathed their last. "I don't know."

"Well, you need to be finding out!" Anger began to replace the numbness that had been Tai's initial feeling and suddenly the room was too small for them both. She stood and looked down on the man she'd loved since she was fourteen years old, the only man she'd ever known in an intimate way. "There's one thing I can say for sure," she said after taking a deep breath. "I did everything I could to stay in this marriage—put up with your intense focus on the ministry that led to absences in the home, your lack of attention, and countless affairs. These last couple years have been good ones, and I actually thought that finally we'd gotten past . . . all our problems. But I guess not."

"We'll get through this," King said. "I love you, Tai. After what happened with Ap—" Tai's eyes narrowed. "Well, uh, the last time, and you took me back? I fell in love with you all over again. I didn't mean for what happened in Barbados to ever take place. It was a moment's weakness and I'm so sor—"

Tai put up her hand to stop King's apology. "If I had a dollar for every *sorry* you've given me, I'd be rich." Slowly shaking her head from side to side, she continued. "*Sorry* isn't going to fix it this time. I'm going to go downstairs and when I come back, I don't want you to be in the room."

Is this really it? Is this really how it all ends? An eerie calm came over Tai as she reached for her purse sitting on the kitchen counter, retrieved the cell phone inside it, and scrolled down to a number she hadn't dialed in a while.

"Hey, Tai!" came the cheerful voice on the other end.

"Hello, Sandy." At another time, Tai would have smiled and been happy for her longtime friend. Since working together at Sprint back in the day, she and Sandy had formed an unlikely but long-standing friendship. Theirs wasn't the "call each other every week" friendship, yet whenever they talked, it was as if no time had passed. When Sandy divorced several years ago, she'd leaned on Tai for counseling and support. And when Sandy and the man she'd met online fled to Cabo San Lucas for an impromptu wedding after knowing each other only six short weeks, Tai was one of the first women she'd called. *And now the tables have turned,* Tai thought with a grimace that she tried to pass for a smile. *Funny how life works out that way.*

"Uh-oh. What's wrong?"

"I called to ask you something."

"I'm listening."

"You know the attorney you raved about who helped you in your divorce proceedings?"

A sigh could be heard on the other end. "Tai, no. Are you and King—"

"Yes, Sandy. King and I are over. Now, can you give me your attorney's number? I need to give him a call."

One week later, King exited his car at the Plaza, Kansas City's tony shopping and eatery district that had been fashioned after its sister city, Seville, Spain. He was there to meet with a young man who'd come highly recommended, a bright, innovative Web designer who'd created an interactive model for ministries to connect more fully and directly with supporters in other countries. During his visit with Wesley Freeman in Barbados, and during subsequent conversations with him and other international ministers, he'd grown increasingly excited about taking his ministry and message to a truly worldwide stage. King had the clout and Wesley had the connections. Together, King figured, he could increase his reach into the hundreds of millions in less than two years.

As he approached the restaurant, a young man walked toward him. King took in the look—bushy red hair, bright blue eyes framed with horn-rimmed glasses, high-water khakis, and a button down blue shirt—and knew immediately that this was the computer nerd who would join the team taking King and Mount Zion to new heights.

"King Brook," he said, once he'd reached the young man. He held out his hand for a shake.

Instead of a handshake, King was given a manila envelope. Before his mind could form a question, the stranger before him provided an answer in three simple words:

"You've been served."

59

Praise God from Whom All Blessings Flow

It was the second Sunday in August and in sunny Southern California, the day was fabulous. The weather was picture perfect and in the Montgomery household, all was well. Derrick Jr. played a handheld video in the formal living room. As usual, the fourteen-year-old was the first one ready for church. His staid, formal attire was in stark contrast to the kiddie activity of video playing, but suit, tie, starched shirt, and buffed shoes was just how this young blood rolled. Upstairs the housekeeper, Anastacia, helped Elisia by piling her long curls atop her head before securing it with a satiny ribbon. The girly tendrils framed a face quickly losing its baby fat to reveal high cheekbones, a soft jawline, and to highlight big doe-brown eyes. Frilly yellow and pink chiffon dresses and patent leathers had been replaced by a stylish designer outfit and high-heeled shoes. She picked out matching earrings and a bulky bracelet with the precision of a well-trained fashionista and finished her look with a spritz of Someday. Elisia looked in the mirror and loved what she saw. But her approval of self had nothing on the heights of adoration happening in the master suite.

Derrick eyed himself critically as he looked in the massive dressing room mirror. "You sure this looks okay?"

"You look amazing," Vivian answered, walking up behind her

husband and wrapping her arms around his waist. Derrick continued to eye himself in the mirror. "So good, in fact, that I suggest we skip the morning service, send the kids away, and spend the day in bed."

Derrick was a handsome man who'd always felt confident about his appearance. Yet a rare glimmer of doubt flitted across his face. He raised his hands and further secured the off-white and tan knitted skull cap that covered his still baldness and more importantly, the neat yet noticeable three-inch scar from the incision that had been made in the back of his head. "I look like a Muslim," he concluded, with a sigh. "Makes me feel like I should address the congregation with an *assalamu alaikum.*"

"Baby, God has spared your life and made it possible for you to walk back into Kingdom Citizens clothed and in your right mind, as Mother Moseley would say, and with your heart keeping the proper time. The members have waited six long weeks for this moment. It's not important how you address them. It's important that you still can."

Derrick's eyes twinkled with lifelong love as he stared into Vivian's sincere eyes. "When did you get to be so smart?" he asked, wrapping his arms around her.

"I've always been this smart," she retorted with a smile, stepping fully into his embrace. "I thought that's why you married me."

"No," Derrick replied. He placed his hands on her booty and gave a firm squeeze. "This is why I married you." He kissed her gently, tenderly. "And this." He slid his mouth from her cheek to her neck, giving it a quick swipe with his tongue before he began to nibble. "And this . . ."

Vivian moaned. "Man, if you keep this up you won't be *ad*dressing anybody because I'll be *un*dressing you!" She wiggled out of his strong arms and walked over to where the jacket to his off-white, perfectly tailored designer suit was hung. Derrick's eyes followed her as she did so, taking in the dangerous yet delectable curves showcased in her ivory Dior, the strong calves above her jeweled Louboutin pumps, and the soft, just-turned-under jet black hair that swung just below her shoulders. His mouth watered as her cheeks winked at him with each step she took. She looked good enough to eat, he decided. And the next time they were in private, he planned to do just that.

Thirty minutes later Kingdom Citizens Christian Center's first family pulled into the packed church parking lot. Derrick eased his brand new pearl white Jaguar into the reserved spot just steps from the pastor's private entrance. His assistant, Lionel, had perfectly timed their arrival and stepped out onto the concrete before Derrick could turn off the engine. The family exited the car looking as if they should be on the cover of *Ebony,* or a greeting card. Elisia held on to her father's hand while Derrick Jr. gripped his Bible and fell into step just behind his dad. Their countenance and build were eerily similar, especially since Derrick had lost weight following surgery and Derrick Jr. seemed to grow an inch every day. It also didn't hurt that as a sign of solidarity the son was sporting an ivory and tan skull cap . . . just like his dad.

"Good to see you, man," Lionel said, foregoing a handshake to engulf his pastor, mentor, and friend in a hug. After a couple back pats, he stepped back and took in Derrick's appearance. Neither Vivian nor Derrick missed the mistiness of his eyes. "Sporting a new look, I see," he continued, clearing the raspiness from his voice. Using humor to cover his emotion, he added, "What are you getting ready to do, sell bean pies?"

Derrick cut his eyes at Vivian as he stepped past the door that Lionel held open. "I told you."

Vivian cut her eyes at Lionel as she hurried to catch up with Derrick. "You two are way too intelligent to be giving in to stereotypes. Not all Muslim men wear skull caps and not all men who wear these caps are Muslim men or religious at all. So give it a rest, will you?"

"Ah, Lady Vee, I was just messing with Pastor. Nobody could mistake his faith with that big platinum cross he's rockin'!"

Derrick turned around as he heard the vibrating doorbell. Lionel quickly crossed over and, after identifying who was on the other side of the door, opened it and ushered Kelvin and Princess inside.

"Hey Rev," Kelvin said, his long strides quickly eating up the distance between him and his dad. "Look at you sporting a new look and whatnot."

"Yeah, well..." Derrick answered, bringing a self-conscious hand to his cap-covered head.

"Naw, man. I likes that. It's cool." He noticed Derrick Jr.'s replica and asked, "What? Y'all didn't buy me one?" When Derrick Jr.'s eyes widened, Kelvin continued. "Oh, I see how it is."

"Sorry, brother," Derrick Jr. said, hanging his head.

Kelvin gave him a playful punch. "It's a'ight, dog. We'll go get one after church."

Princess hugged her aunt and uncle and the family continued down the hall. As soon as Derrick turned the corner and staff members noted his arrival, he was engulfed in hugs and love and "welcome backs" and tears of joy. Derrick took it all in, and wasn't at all ashamed of the tears he also shed. Their hearty welcome reminded him yet again of how blessed he was to be alive. When he saw his number-one associate minister and good friend Cy Taylor and Cy's wife, Hope, standing just beyond the group of well-wishers, he politely extracted himself and walked over to greet them.

"My man!" Cy exclaimed, adding a shoulder bump to his handshake. He stepped back. "Are you sure you just had brain surgery a month ago? Because it sure doesn't look like it."

Smiling, Derrick turned to Hope for the hug that awaited. "It's good to see you, Pastor," she managed past a choked up throat.

"God is faithful, Mrs. Taylor," Derrick said with a wink. While Vivian and Hope greeted each other with hugs, he looked back and noted the hallways filling with people who could access the executive offices. The word was out. Pastor Derrick was back. "Go handle that, will you, Lionel?"

Lionel nodded and turned on his heel with military precision, ready to politely yet firmly usher everyone to their seats with the promise that Pastor was well aware of their concern and love, and would soon be thanking all of them from the pulpit. Derrick then turned to Cy and Hope. "Y'all come into the office."

A short time later, Derrick, Vivian, Cy, Hope, other associate ministers and some executive staff headed to the side door leading to the pulpit. As Derrick neared the door, he paused, drinking in the sounds of Darius Crenshaw and the Kingdom Citizens Choir. They were doing a jazzed up version of a timeless gospel classic.

All hail the power of Jesus' Name, let angels prostrate fall;
Bring forth the royal diadem, and crown Him Lord of all!

Ye chosen seed of Israel's race, ye ransomed from the fall,
Hail Him Who saves you by His grace, and crown Him Lord of all!

Let every kindred, every tribe, on this terrestrial ball,
To Him all majesty ascribe, and crown Him Lord of all!

Oh, that with yonder sacred throng, we at His feet may fall!
We'll join the everlasting song, and crown Him Lord of all!

Derrick closed his eyes and clenched his jaw, forcing himself to keep it together when he really wanted to fall to his knees and bawl like a baby.

"You ready, Pastor?" Lionel asked, his hand on the doorknob as he looked back.

Derrick felt Vivian's reassuring touch on his back, and after taking a deep breath, he nodded. Lionel opened the door and the stately procession into the sanctuary began. At the first glimpse of their Pastor Derrick, the congregation rose as one to their feet: clapping, shouting, and praising God. As the others took their seats, Derrick continued to the podium where he stood and silently acknowledged the crowd. Tears freely flowed down his face as he looked into the eyes of members he'd known for decades and others he'd recently baptized. He nodded an acknowledgment to Lavon and Carla, and those from other ministries who'd come to show their support of this—his triumphant return. After a couple minutes, Derrick held up his hands to quiet the crowd. But they only cheered louder, their joy at seeing God's grace and mercy lasting almost five full minutes, lasting until KCCC's minister of music, Darius Crenshaw, began striking melodious chords on the keyboard, joined by a hauntingly beautiful saxophonist and an alto whose voice sounded straight from heaven's gate:

> *"Praise God from whom all blessings flow.*
> *Praise Him all creatures here below.*
> *Praise Him above, ye heavenly hosts.*
> *Praise Father, Son, and Holy Ghost!"*

Derrick reached for the microphone. The crowd quieted. Gripping the podium, he closed his eyes and summoned the strength to speak to his flock. If only he could stop the tears of gratitude and joy.

"Take your time, Pastor!" a congregant shouted.

"Hallelujah!" someone yelled.

Not to be outdone, someone from the Mother Board stood and exclaimed, "Thank you, Jesus!"

Derrick turned to the woman who, along with the late Mother Moseley, was a founding member, and one of his oldest. "I do thank Him, Mother Gertrude," he said with a smile. "I can't thank Him enough." He turned to the congregation. "And I can't thank you enough. Your thoughts, prayers, cards, gifts . . . your love . . . sustained me and my family during this trying time. But I'm here to tell you something. God is able."

Darius cosigned Derrick's statement with a keyboard riff. This evoked words of praise from various members, most of whom were still on their feet.

"See, when I was looking for a miracle..."

"Yes!" a member shouted. Darius struck a chord.

"And when I was expecting the impossible..."

"Bless his name!" And from Darius, a chord one-half note up from the last one.

Derrick took the microphone from its holder. "I began to feel the intangible."

"My Lord!" Another chord, another half-note up.

"And I began to see the invisible. Oh, y'all don't hear me now."

"We hear you, Pastor!"

Derrick crossed his arms, and looked over the congregants, who were beginning to sit down. When almost all had taken their seats, he continued, his voice low, his tone intense. "See, when I heard the diagnosis, that there was a tumor growing in my brain... I've got to be honest with you, family. There were some dark moments that followed. I felt fear, distress, uncertainty. And when Dr. Black"—Derrick paused to acknowledge the miracle-working doctor who, along with his wife, occupied seats in the front row—"told me that he wanted to cut open my head and take something out..." Derrick shook his head and said as an aside, "My wife might tell you that I didn't have much in there to begin with." The audience chuckled while Vivian shook her head in disagreement. "But when the doctors explained *to* me what was going on *with* me, and all of the possible outcomes... I saw the lightning flashing, church."

Yet again, Darius cosigned with a B-flat minor while the drummer ran his fingers along his silver chimes. And yet again, members rose to their feet.

"And I heard the thunder roar."

An associate minister took a step forward, as if to swipe Derrick with a large, white handkerchief. "Preach, Preacher!"

"I felt the breakers dashing, trying to conquer my soul. But—" Derrick held up his hand. "How many of y'all know that where the enemy puts a 'block,' God will put a 'but'?" Church members waved their hands and shouted their agreement. "But I heard the voice of Jesus telling me still to fight on. And he told me something else."

"What'd he tell you, Pastor?" the oldest associate minister queried.

Derrick turned to him and answered. "Reverend McKinley, he promised never to leave me. That he would never leave me alone." And then back to the crowd, "No, never alone! Praise His Holy name today. God said I might go through a test, but I stand here today with a testimony!"

That did it. The crowd went wild, not only praising God for the trial Derrick and his family had experienced, but for the storms that He'd brought them through. Derrick's short speech was about all of the preaching that happened that day. The rest of the service was pretty much a praise party. And for Derrick Montgomery—a man who'd looked death in the face and lived to tell about it—he wouldn't have had his first day back in the house of the Lord go any other way.

60

Love Me Down

It was just after 9 p.m. and Kelvin and Princess were headed to the airport. They'd enjoyed every moment of the time they'd spent with the Montgomerys—from the spirited church service to the boisterous dinner after church where no less than thirty people gathered in the upscale Beverly Hills home, to the intimate gathering of people who afterward remained to bask in the glory of Derrick's recovery. Even as they'd left, a remnant remained: Lavon and Carla, Hope and Cy, and fellow LA mega-minister Stan Lee, who'd passed along his evening service duties to his assistant minister so that he and his wife, Passion, could come and share the day. That's why the Petersens hadn't felt bad in leaving; they knew that the Montgomery household would be a busy one for days and weeks to come. But as for these newlyweds, they were more than ready to go back to Phoenix for some quiet time . . . and each other.

"That was good, baby," Kelvin said, placing his arm around Princess's shoulder as he stretched his long legs out in the limousine.

Princess nestled her head against his shoulder. "Uh-huh. Uncle Derrick looked so good. And Aunt Viv was so happy."

"Everyone was."

"Uh-huh." After a pause, Princess continued. "I'm glad about you and your dad's relationship . . . that you two are so close." There was a time when Princess doubted that would happen, especially after Kelvin's refusal to attend church got him kicked out of the Montgomery abode.

"Yeah, me, too. When I was growing up, I couldn't imagine a life with my real father and now, well, I can't imagine one without him. And speaking of . . . have you talked to your father?"

Princess sighed and turned so that her body was leaned against Kelvin's as she looked out the window. "No, and I'm not sure I want to." Even though well aware of their problems through the years, including her father's infidelities, the news of her parents divorcing had been devastating. But Princess didn't know the half of it. It would be another two months before she found out why her parents split up, and that another Brook sibling was on the way.

"It's going to be all right," Kelvin assured her, with a kiss to the top of her head. "Divorce isn't as taboo as it used to be."

Princess sat up and swatted his arm. "That doesn't make it right!"

"I didn't say it did. I'm just saying that it happens, and that people are able to pick up the pieces and go on with their lives."

"Can we change the subject? This one is depressing and after such a wonderful day, it's bringing down my high."

"Yeah, I can change the subject," Kelvin drawled, running a lazy finger down Princess's arms and leaving goose bumps along the way. "In fact, I need to let you know what's going to happen once we get on the plane."

Princess's brow creased in confusion. "What?"

"We're going to become members of the Mile High Club."

"What's that?"

"An exclusive group of couples who've made love in planes."

Princess nestled back against Kelvin. "Oh, really?"

"Yeah, really."

"And what if I don't want to become a member?"

Kelvin's chuckle was low and cocky. "Just wait until we get on the plane and close the privacy door. I'll make you want to be a member. Trust me."

They reached the hangar for private planes and were quickly ushered inside the jet. While Kelvin requested a meat, cheese, and fruit platter along with a bottle of pricey bubbly from the flight attendant, Princess made her way to the back of the plane, a tastefully decorated room that rivaled a five-star hotel suite. There was a living, dining, bath, and office area, and the wine-colored leather couch converted to a queen-size bed. She placed her purse on the dining room table, sat on the couch, idly picked up a magazine—and her jaw hit the floor. She blinked, sure that she'd misread the heading that virtually blared from the cover page of a tabloid magazine:

KIKI MINOR PREGNANT AND READY TO WED!

Princess's eyes shifted from the heading to the picture below it—a happy and smiling Kiki clinging to a handsome and satisfied-looking Rafael. *Wow, he's getting married.* Princess was surprised at the longing she felt at the sight of her former best friend. Not for a love affair—she truly loved Kelvin. But before she and Rafael were engaged to be married, they were dear friends. She missed their camaraderie honed through shared interests. She missed their playful teasing. In short, she missed Rafael.

She'd turned to the story and was reading it as Kelvin entered. "Put that down," he said, snatching the magazine from her and tossing it on the table before he plopped down beside her and took her in his arms. "We've got better things than reading to do."

"Rafael's getting married," was Princess's response.

"For real? Him and Kiki?"

Princess nodded. "She's pregnant."

Kelvin looked closely at his wife. "What, you sad or something? Why the hell you care about any of that?"

"I don't care," Princess insisted. "Not in the way you mean. But Rafael and I have been friends since we were like nine years old. We used to share everything. . . ."

"Damn, Princess!" Kelvin pushed away from Princess and turned to observe her. "It sounds like you miss him and shit."

"I miss someone who used to be a friend."

"Oh, so I'm supposed to be cool with that? What if I told you that I missed Fawn? Would you be understanding about that?"

Princess whispered, "It's not the same."

"So what's different?"

Princess looked at Kelvin in a huff. "Rafael and I were platonic friends. You and Fawn were fucking. *That's* the difference." Princess hadn't even realized that her halo had slipped a notch or two and her inner sistah-girl was on full display.

Their repartee was interrupted as the pilot knocked, came into their quarters, and after a moment of small talk informed them that they'd be airborne in five minutes. It was enough time for both parties to calm down: for Princess to look at the situation from Kelvin's point of view, and for Kelvin to do vice versa.

"I'm sorry, baby," he said as soon as the pilot closed the door behind him. "I understand you still having feelings for your boy. I just don't like to know about it, that's all."

Princess turned to look at Kelvin, her eyes clear and sincere. "Rafael is a good human being, a kind, decent, and intelligent man. While I don't regret it, I feel bad for how our... relationship ended. I regret that even now, Rafael still refuses to speak to me, that I don't know whether or not I have his forgiveness. Please don't misunderstand where I'm coming from, Kel. I'm happy for Rafael and Kiki, glad that he's found someone to love and someone who obviously loves him back in the way he deserves. While I didn't know Kiki all that well, I always liked her. I think that they're a good match, and I'm happy they're having a baby. I just... I just pray that someday Rafael and I can put aside our differences and who knows? Maybe God will grant another miracle like the one he gave Uncle Derrick where the four of us can actually become friends."

The flight attendant arrived with their tray and the champagne. Kelvin walked behind her as she left and locked the door. He walked back to where Princess sat, taking off his shirt in the process. His eyes were black with desire, his countenance one of quiet determination. He reached for her leg and without words, proceeded to take off her heels.

"What are you doing?" Princess breathlessly asked.

"What does it look like? I'm getting ready to help us work up an appetite before we cool down with nice glasses of bubbly. I'm getting ready to sex you straight into the Mile High Club."

An hour later, they landed in Phoenix. And one would have sworn there was something in the water because a membership to the Mile High Club wasn't the only thing this couple experienced. A month later, Princess would discover that she was about to have more in common with Kiki than she realized.

61

I'll Always Love You

A few months later...

Mama Max shooed people from her overly crowded kitchen to the living room. She didn't mind a little help every once in a while, but nobody was going to mess up her carefully prepared chicken and dumplings, and if somebody stomped and made her cranberry-apple-pecan bundt cake fall, well, it was going to be a problem.

One woman remained behind, a very grateful member of Mount Zion Progressive named Celeste Adams. She was the single mother of two grown children, a godly daughter of Zion who'd prayed that the Lord would send her a good man. When Mama Max had told her that she had somebody that she wanted her to meet, Celeste had cringed inside. But she had deep respect for her pastor and loved Mama Max. So against her better judgment, the fifty-one-year-old size-eight sistah, with big dimples, a ready laugh, and a memorable badonkadonk, had walked into a coffee shop near where she worked and locked eyes with her future. She and Henry had talked every day since they'd met.

"So how's it going?" Mama Max asked, looking at Celeste with a twinkle in her eye. She didn't miss the blush that crept up along her church member's cheek.

Celeste nodded. "Really good, Mama Max. He wants to take it slow, but I believe he's worth the wait. Henry is an amazing man. He's no nonsense, you know? No games, no BS . . . With him, what you see is what you get."

Mama Max nodded her satisfaction. "Told you he was a good man. All he needed was a woman to remind him of that fact."

The two ladies continued to converse on general topics as they finished what Mama Max referred to as "a little holiday meal" that included roasted duck, glazed ham, candied yams, mashed potatoes, corn on the cob, a green bean casserole, a sautéed collard and mustard green medley, beets, dressing . . . and then there was dessert: besides the cranberry-apple-pecan bundt cake, there were sweet potato pies, an apple cobbler, and homemade ice cream.

"Where's the good Reverend Doctor?" Celeste asked as they placed the last of the dishes on the table and announced that dinner would be served soon.

"He went to visit the sick and shut-in," Mama Max replied. "He'll probably make a stop and see Beatrice, Henry's mama, over at that there assisted-living facility."

"We're two blessed women," Celeste said in a whispery voice.

Mama Max didn't respond to that. She'd agreed to let Obadiah back in the house, but the jury was still out on how blessed she was. And while she'd finally told him the story that along with her mother's whispered admonishments had shaped her views on intimacy—how she'd gone over to visit a childhood friend, walked in on the preteen being sexually assaulted in brutal fashion by a relative, and then been threatened with the same fate if she ever told a soul—their road back to marital happiness was nowhere near assured. "I'll think about having you back in the bedroom," is how she'd left the conversation that had taken place a few days before. She still didn't know if that would happen and even if they shared a room, had no idea if they'd share a bed, especially in the way Obadiah wanted. What she knew for sure was that this holiday was by far the most unusual she'd witnessed in quite some time. King and Tai's breakup had sent their family to various parts of the country for the holiday, but his siblings—Queen, Daniel, Ester, and their families—had all come to Kansas to support their recently reunited mother and dad.

Obadiah returned and entered the house through the kitchen door, just as Celeste had gone in there to retrieve the freshly baked yeast rolls that would round out the meal. They looked up simultaneously, their eyes locked, their breath held. Obadiah's hand clutched the doorknob as he quickly scanned the church member who'd caught his eye some years ago. The air was thick with tension as their silence screamed in protest.

Obadiah recovered first. He released the knob and walked into the room. "Afternoon, Sister Adams." He walked over with hand outstretched.

"Reverend Doctor," Celeste acknowledged, filling her hands with the platter of rolls, thereby thwarting the need to touch this particular man of God.

"I didn't know that you and my wife were friendly, but I'm glad to welcome you into our home."

"My friendship with Mama Max is just beginning," Celeste responded. "But on behalf of myself and my date, Henry Logan, we are delighted to accept your welcome."

With that, Celeste turned and sashayed out of the kitchen. And in that instant both Reverend Doctor O and the woman who several years ago he'd screwed seven ways from Sunday knew they'd take this little one-night stand secret that they shared all the way to their graves.

Dinner was served and a cacophony of conversation commenced. Even though both King and Tai were noticeably absent, it almost felt like old times. After dinner, the festivities continued throughout the house. There was a moment where Reverend Doctor O and Mama Max found themselves seated next to each other in the living room. They watched as some grandchildren haggled over video games, while others trash-talked around a game of Uno. Mama Max looked up to find Obadiah's eyes on her, soft and reminiscent. "I haven't always been the perfect husband," he said, placing his hand on Mama Max's arm. "But I always loved you, Maxine. At the end of the day, you're the only one I *always* loved."

Mama Max placed her hand on top of Obadiah's, with over fifty years of marriage upholding a bond not easily broken. "I know," she said softly, patting his hand as she gazed fondly at their legacy around the room. She looked at Obadiah and smiled. "I know."

As King sat at the massive table set up in the Freeman's elaborately landscaped backyard, it was ironic that one of Tai's favorite songs flitted through his head. His smile was bittersweet as he heard Sugarfoot declare that heaven must be like this. He sat back and looked around, still disbelieving at how quickly his life had turned. After being served the papers, Tai had further surprised him by announcing that she was moving out of the home they'd shared for over a decade and was staying at a hotel, alone, so that she could clear her head and plot her next move. The children, extended family and close friends had already been told, and while each person took the news differently, all were slowly adjusting to the idea of visiting their parents in two different households.

The reaction from Mount Zion Progressive members? Equally diverse but much more heartfelt. Even though he and Tai had stood together as they'd announced their impending separation, and even though Tai had encouraged the members to forgive her straying husband as she'd already done, there'd still been an obvious split among members—those standing staunchly behind their man of God versus those who demanded that he exit stage left. Two members who fled along with the others were Elsie Wanthers and Margie Stokes, Sistah Alrighty and Sistah Almighty, respectively. Sistah Almighty had called him a disgrace to the pulpit while Sistah Alrighty had declared that she wasn't going to worship in the devil's playground. After a one-month leave of absence (during which time he and Tai had hammered out the divorce arrangements, division of assets, properties, etc.) he'd returned to a noticeably smaller congregation and, after asking the remaining members their forgiveness, vowed to spend the rest of his life regaining their respect and rebuilding his ministry. The first step to that would be in bringing honor to the expectant mother of his fifth child. On New Year's Eve, Charmaine Freeman would become the new Mrs. King Brook and arrive in Kansas as Mount Zion Progressive's new first lady.

"Where are you, darling?" Charmaine's voice caressed King's body and calmed his nerves the way it always did. "You were a million miles away."

"A lot on my mind," King replied, giving Wesley a wink and Charmaine's hand a squeeze. "Plus I'm trying to decide how I'm going to move given this feast of a meal you've just served me."

The others at the table nodded their agreement, and gave their own accolades on the meal that had been prepared by Wesley's more-than-capable cooks. Besides, King, Wesley, and his daughter, the table of twelve was filled with two associate ministers and their wives, the prime minister of Barbados and his guest, an international singing sensation, a world-renowned author, and a stunning international model who was Wesley Freeman's "special guest."

Charmaine cleared her throat and stood. "Your company has been delightful, but if you'll excuse me, I think the little one and I"—she placed a hand on her gently rounding stomach—"could use a walk." She reached a hand out to King, her skin glowing, her smile brilliant. "Darling, will you join me?"

King didn't hesitate. "If you'll excuse us," he said to the table, taking Charmaine's hand in his and leading her down the short walkway to the pristine white sand and the turquoise blue waters just beyond. He'd tried to fight it, had tried to deny it, and while living with Tai had desperately tried to hide it, but the truth of the matter was that he was head over heels in love with Charmaine Freeman, this island vixen who'd reeled him in hook, line, and sinker, and had stolen his heart in the process. The pain he'd caused his soon-to-be ex-wife and family would never be forgotten, but the sheer joy and unexplainable peace he felt at being exactly where he thought he needed to be could not be overlooked.

He and Charmaine walked in silence a long while before she stopped and turned to him. Her large, light brown eyes were filled with tears.

"What is it, baby?" King caressed her chin tenderly before reaching up to brush an errant tear away from her face.

"I want to be everything to you, King. The best wife, the best mother, the best first lady, the best lover. I'm so afraid that I will fail you in some way. It is my deepest fear." Her full bottom lip quivered as she worked to remain calm. "I love you so much. I want to make you proud, and happier than you've ever been."

King looked at the sincerity mixed with vulnerability in her eyes and his heart flip-flopped. "Come here," he whispered, crushing this woman-child against his chest. "I'm already proud of you," he whispered, kissing her temple, and again on her cheek. "And I'm very, very happy."

Six days later, King and Charmaine became husband and wife. Five days after that, the newlyweds moved into a lavishly appointed home in one of Overland Park's most upscale communities. And two weeks after that . . . Charmaine lost the baby.

62

Love On Top

"Hey, girl." Tai closed the door to the guest bedroom in her parents' home and plopped on the bed. It had been a long day and while she'd been happy to spend it with her parents in Ohio, putting on a happy face had worn her out.

"Hey, sis," Vivian replied. "How'd it go?"

"Could have been worse," Tai replied. "You know that Daddy doesn't pry much, and I gave Mama the rundown before she could start the grill. She was trying to talk reconciliation, but telling her about King's love child shut that talk right up. It was good for the kids to be here, though. They're much closer to King's parents than they are to mine and if anything good comes of this sordid mess it will be that they get to know their maternal grands."

"Where are the kids now?"

"Mama and Daddy took the twins to a movie. Michael said he was taking Sonya on a tour of Cleveland."

"Who's Sonya?"

"His flavor of the month. She seems like a good girl. Graduated a year behind Michael with a degree in English, is thinking about joining the Peace Corps, and eventually wants to teach on Chicago's South Side."

"Sounds noble."

"Very."

"Not sure how that gels with your mover-shaker son on the fast track to becoming a high-powered attorney."

"She's got other things gelling, like big breasts, a big butt, a pretty face, and a thick head of natural hair."

"Ha!"

"I have a feeling that this 'tour' will be less about the sites of Cleveland and more about the sites around Sonya's hotel suite or more specifically . . . around her body."

"Tai, please. I've known Michael since he was in diapers and can do without the visual."

"I'm his mother! How do you think I feel? But he is King's son and his grandfather's kin. Brook men will screw anything, even if it's just a lightbulb into the socket."

"Oh, Lord . . ."

"I might have been born at night, but it wasn't last night."

"Ha!" The two best friends chatted a little longer, confirming Tai's plans to visit LA the following month. With an empty nest and newfound freedom, Tai had decided on a totally fresh start in a brand new location. She was moving to California! While the hustle and bustle of LA was too much for her laid-back style, she'd liked the vibe in Palm Springs, where she'd attended a conference, and was also interested in checking out the smaller communities near San Diego.

"I'll forward my flight info as soon as it's confirmed," Tai concluded. Hearing murmuring in the background, she added, "Sounds like we're being interrupted."

Vivian laughed and murmured something before speaking into the phone. "It's Derrick, acting like a spoiled brat clamoring for attention. It's been a long day and we finally have the house to ourselves so . . . he's feeling neglected." He was also feeling underneath Vivian's top in search of her breasts, but Vivian figured some facts were best left unsaid.

"Say no more," Tai said, as she tamped down a twinge of lone-liness at the thought that no one was clamoring for her attention. "Give Derrick my love. You two have a good night."

"Can't wait to see you, sis." Vivian put down the receiver and turned to her husband, who was gently squeezing one nipple as he reached for the band of her lounging pants. "What are you doing?"

"Isn't it obvious, woman? I'm trying to get you naked!"

"Here? In the kitchen?"

Derrick shrugged. "We've got the house to ourselves. I figured this is about as good a place as any."

He pulled the string that held up Vivian's pants and gave a tug. They slid down to her hips and he didn't hesitate to take advantage. Pulling her against him, he reached inside to palm the luscious behind that had attracted him in the first place...over twenty years ago. Vivian moaned and offered up her mouth for a kiss. Derrick took the cue and licked her thick lips before pressing his mouth against hers and using his tongue to force an opening. She quickly complied, lazily placing one arm around his neck while the other moved across his back, down his arm, and settled dangerously close to the family jewels. He broke the kiss long enough to push Vivian's pants down to her ankles. She stepped out of them, relieving herself of her top as she did so. Her nipples were hard and at full attention, something that Derrick immediately acknowledged with his tongue. He sucked the nub into his mouth before circling her areola with agonizing precision. Not wanting the other nipple to feel ignored, he lightly ran his thumb back and forth, over and again, while he plundered Vivian's mouth like a ravenous carnivore in a gourmet meat shop. And once again....he broke the kiss. This time it was to lay Vivian's soft, hot body on top of the cool, hard granite of the kitchen island. She hardly felt the rock, so caught up was she in the fact that Derrick had placed her legs over his shoulders and had lowered his head to "acknowledge" another set of lips. Their moans mingled as his sure, stiff tongue parted her folds and lapped her nectar. Slow and easy. Fast and light. He parted her legs wider still and went deeper, licking, nibbling, sucking, driving her crazy. The light fuzz from his rapidly growing hair tickled the inside of Vivian's thighs and added to the sensation of feelings. She grabbed his head and pressed him into her, even as her own head was thrown back in ecstasy, all thoughts gone except for those of the man she loved and what he was doing to her. Right. Now.

"Oh! Baby I'm..." Vivian's words faded as a frenetic energy spiraled within her core, causing her legs to shake and her toes to curl. "Ahhhhhhh!" The orgasm was prolonged and intense, so much so that she didn't even realize Derrick had stepped away and shed his clothes until he came back, lifted her off the island and marched them to the dining room that had been filled to capacity just hours ago.

"Stay on your knees," he whispered, as he gingerly sat Vivian down on a large corner chair. Before she could protest or question he was inside her, nine inches of thick dickalicious slamming into her core. Vivian grabbed the chair and tossed back her hair, giving as good as she got, grinding herself against him, trying to love the man she'd almost lost with every fiber of her being. He reached around and slid a finger along her wet folds, massaging her nub as he pounded her insides. "So good," he whispered, kissing the back of her neck, now sweaty from their feverish ride. "So. Good." He slowed down, pulled out, and then slid back in one inch at a time.

"Um..."

He did it again.

"Derrick, please."

He chuckled, pulling all the way out yet again. "What?"

"You know what?!" Vivian hissed, reaching back to find and then force him back inside her.

He ran his dick across her cheeks and along her crease. "Is this what you're looking for?"

"Yes," Vivian replied, pushing herself against him. "Give it to me, baby. I want it hard. I want it all."

Derrick lifted her off the chair and sat down. "Then come and get it." He spread his strong legs, and what Vivian wanted between said strong legs waved a strong and hearty greeting. Wasting no time, she straddled Derrick and the chair and eased herself down on the blessing that God had created and then called good. *It sure is.* She looked deep into Derrick's eyes as she rode him, slowly . . . methodically . . . as if they had all the time in the world. Derrick let her take the lead. For a while. Until he too wanted it hard, and wanted it all. Then he grabbed her hips and led the dance as Vivian jumped and Derrick pumped with the kind of sexual healing that Marvin spoke about. As Derrick increased the rhythm, Vivian felt another explosion building, this one seeming to start at the balls of her feet and shooting through the roots of her hair. They came together, Derrick pushing in as deep as he could and Vivian holding him just as tight with her inner walls as the arms that were around his neck. It was an amazing moment, as if they saw stars and heard trumpets. In the midst of their sex-induced haze, both knew they'd heard something. Was it their own heartbeats? The scraping of the chair against the floor? Or was it . . .

"Derrick? Vivian?"

No! Vivian's eyes widened.

Crap! Derrick's eyes closed.

She jumped off his lap and Derrick was hot on her tail. They ran into the kitchen and scooped up their scattered clothing as the footsteps of Vivian's parents, Mrs. and Mrs. Victor Stanford, came closer. With time running out and options limited, preacher extraordinaire Derrick Montgomery and Sanctity of Sisterhood founder and flawless first lady Vivian Montgomery did what any upstanding, fearless couple would do when faced with the prospect of parents finding them naked. They ducked into the pantry!

"I thought you said they were going to the movies," Derrick hissed.

"That's what they told me," Vivian retorted, trying without much success to put on thongs in the dark. Her foot got caught in the string, causing her to hop on one leg. She stumbled into Derrick, who in throwing up his arm to catch her, knocked a slew of canned goods off the shelf.

"Vivian! Derrick! Is that you?" Vivian's mother's voice was closer. Too close. It sounded like she was in the kitchen.

"Shh, don't answer," Derrick whispered against her ear.

"You think?" was Vivian's sarcastic retort.

Then, into the silence a snicker. Followed by another.

"Stop laughing," Vivian warned her husband, even as her own lips curled into a grin. "I mean it, you'll make me laugh out loud."

"Okay," Derrick said, though his whole body was now shaking with the force of his mirth.

"Stop it," Vivian admonished, but soon she was holding her hand over her mouth to keep from busting out laughing and blowing their cover while Derrick's amusement sent him to his knees.

"Where are they?" Vivian heard her father ask.

"I thought they were in here," her mother replied. "I heard a noise, some type of rumbling or something."

"You're always hearing something," her father said. "You're one of the scariest women I know. They're probably upstairs, in bed. Where we should be. Come on, let's go."

"All right, dear."

Derrick and Vivian held their breath and waited as the sound of voices and footsteps receded into the distance. After about five minutes, Derrick peeked his head out of the pantry. When it seemed the coast was clear, he reached back for Vivian's hand and, like errant teenagers on a forbidden date, they sneaked into their own bedroom in their own house where they proceeded to laugh and make love and laugh again...until the wee hours of the morning.

★ ★ ★

"Why are you trippin'? Just go in there and pee on that thing. How hard can that be?!" An exasperated Kelvin plopped down on the bed.

"But what if it comes back positive?" Princess asked, her voiced filled with trepidation.

"Then you're pregnant," Kelvin deadpanned.

"But what if it comes back negative?"

"And this from a *NYT* best-selling author who graduated from UCLA. Are you serious?"

"I'm scared, Kelvin."

"What's there to be scared of?"

"I don't know."

But in reality, Princess knew exactly why this situation had her so freaked out. Ever since she'd missed her period, she'd thought that she was pregnant. When she'd almost cursed Joni out for a simple, innocuous comment made in jest, she was almost sure of it. And while Princess would be happy and proud to carry Kelvin's child, the very thought of doing so conjured up memories of another time. Another pregnancy test. And another child.

"I do know," Princess acknowledged, walking over to join Kelvin on the bed. "I'm remembering the last time I did this, that Christmas we spent with your family in Germany. Remember?" Kelvin slowly nodded, avoiding her eyes. "I was so afraid then, just like now, and your mother helped me through it. She could relate, you know, and calmed me down. It helped having her there."

Kelvin sat up and took Princess's small hand in his much larger one. "I'm sorry I wasn't there for you then, Princess. Not like I should have been. We were both young, didn't know nothing. The scouts were hounding me." *Chicks were trippin' and everywhere I turned.* "So much was going on. I wish I hadn't talked you into having an abortion."

"I didn't think I wanted it either, Kelvin. I had no idea how much you could miss something that you never really had."

"So it's cool then, a'ight? If you're pregnant, then we'll celebrate. If you're not, then we'll keep practicing. Every day." Princess smiled. "All day."

"Shut up . . ."

"I'm serious. I'm about ready for a mini-me."

"Or mini-me!"

"Naw, I'm not ready to fight off the young bloods. Give me a hardhead so I can show him the ropes."

Princess scooted off the bed. "Whatever." She walked to the en suite master bath and turned before she entered. "Come with me?"

Kelvin rose from the bed and met her at the door. "Come on, girl. I should know by now that you can't do nothing without me." He dodged the hit aimed at his shoulder and leaned back on the vanity. "Go ahead and do it."

Princess sat down. "I can't pee!"

"Girl, come on now."

"Really," Princess said, with a laugh. "I just used the bathroom. Nothing will come out."

"Hold on, let me go get you some water. I'm going to pour it down your throat until you pee."

This made Princess laugh so hard that a small trickle finally eased itself onto the wand. "The directions say to wait two minutes," she said, holding the long white stick in her hand.

"Then how do you know?"

"If it has . . ." Her voice faded as she looked at the small circle showing the results. "Two pink stripes—that means I'm pregnant."

Kelvin looked over her shoulder and came face to face with two bold pink stripes.

"You're pregnant?"

Princess nodded, as her eyes filled with tears.

Kelvin picked her up, kissing her all over as he walked them back into the bedroom. He laid her down on the bed and then joined her. "My baby's pregnant with my baby," he murmured, before kissing her deeply, thoroughly and again. "I'm getting ready to have a son."

"Or daughter."

"It will be ours," Kelvin replied, snuggling her body against his. "That's all that matters."

During her first ultrasound, Princess and Kelvin found out that they were both right. They were pregnant with twins: a boy and a girl. It was yet another masterful intervention. Of the divine kind.

DIVINE INTERVENTION

Lutishia Lovely

ABOUT THIS GUIDE

The suggested questions that follow
are included to enhance your group's
reading of this book.

Discussion Questions

1. Regarding the tug-of-war for Princess Brook, who were you rooting for, Rafael or Kelvin? Why?

2. Kelvin seems to be making a genuine effort to stop being a womanizer. Do you think it's possible for a professional athlete to be monogamous and remain faithful to their significant other?

3. Rafael develops an unexpected friendship with Kiki Minor, someone who befriended Princess and then invited herself to be a part of Princess's wedding. Thoughts?

4. It's ironic that both Princess and Kiki end up in the same situation at the same time. Princess alluded to the four of them—her, Kelvin, Kiki, and Rafael—being friends. Do you think this is possible?

5. Tai knew that her daughter still held deep feelings for Kelvin. Should she have done more to talk Princess out of marrying Rafael?

6. Regarding the tug-of-war for Princess's grandmother, Mama Max, who were you rooting for, Obadiah or Henry? Why?

7. We finally learned what caused Mama Max's aversion to sex. Did her nonparticipation in this marital act justify Obadiah's affair? Why or why not?

8. In most of this book's romantic entanglements, sex plays a major role. How important do you think sex is to a relationship? What other qualities are equally important?

9. In some instances, drastic measures were taken to show love and loyalty. Have you ever done something drastic to get the attention of a love interest? To prove your love? To get revenge?

10. After discovering Derrick's illness, the Montgomerys' faith was sorely tested. What challenges in your life have tested your belief in what God can do?

11. For King Brook, Charmaine Freeman was an instant temptation. Have you ever been tempted? If so, by what, and what did you do about it?

12. Were you surprised with Tai's reaction to what occurred on the island? Do you think this action was justified? Can you ever think of an instance where her actions wouldn't be okay?

13. How did you feel about what eventually happened to Charmaine? Was that divine intervention, an extremely unfortunately incident, or both?

14. Charmaine's father, Minister Freeman, seemed to not only approve of her relationship with a married man, King, but endorse it. What are your thoughts on this?

15. It's interesting that King and his father found themselves in the same place, at the same time. Has there ever been an instance in your life where you've told your child or someone else to "do as I say, not as I do"? What happened?

16. Despite all that had happened, Mama Max forgave Obadiah. Is there someone in your life who you need to forgive? Is there someone from whom you need to ask forgiveness?

17. Despite appearing completely healthy, Derrick faced a serious issue. When is the last time you've had a complete, head-to-toe checkup? If it's been more than a year, make that appointment now! Please and thank you!

18. In the front of this book, I shared with you my first conscious experience with divine intervention. Share one (or more) times in your life when a miracle occurred.

Up next in the Hallelujah Love series....

The members of Kingdom Citizens Christian Center believe in sharing the spirit of love and generosity to others. Even so, they can't seem to follow the ten commandments, a fact that suggests it just might be time to add another rule....

The Eleventh Commandment

Coming in March 2013 from Dafina Books

Here's an excerpt from *The Eleventh Commandment*....

1

Friendships and Fatherhood

"Ooh, yeah, just like that, just like that!" Frieda Moore-Livingston cooed as expert hands moved up and down her bare back, across her shoulders and back down... kneading, rubbing, before coming to that sensitive dimpled spot just above her juicy assets. "That... feels... so... good." Oohs and aahs surrounded each word that oozed from her lips. Strong, lean fingers continued down her thighs, paying special attention to the calves and feet before coming back the way they'd come, lingering at the small of her back, switching to feather-light strokes as they splayed across her shoulders and along the nape of her neck. Frieda felt as though she'd have an orgasm right on the spot. It had taken her awhile to understand the hype. But now she was a true believer: there was nothing better than an afternoon massage.

"We're done, pretty lady." Tyson, the masseur to the stars and to those with star quality (translated, plenty of cash), tapped Frieda lightly on the shoulder to signal the end of their session. "See you next week?"

"Of course, baby," Frieda said, turning over and getting off the table, shamelessly letting the towel fall on the floor. More than once Tyson had suggested she wait until he leave to begin dressing but Frieda had other plans. Often, she'd wondered how it would be to have other body parts massaged during these sessions, but so far her not-too-subtle hints had only been met with a patient smile. The first assumption had been that he was gay. After all, who would turn down what Frieda called "pussy on a platter?" But her friend Stacy's baby daddy, Darius, had told her that Tyson didn't get down in that club and since the platinum selling R&B singing sensation was patently homosexual and very much a part of that world, Frieda thought that he would know. If not for the fact that she was now headed to a thick link of sausage not far from her old stomping grounds, she might have been insulted. As it was, she simply laughed as Tyson quickly averted his eyes and left the room.

Moments later, Frieda clicked the locks on her shiny new Lexus LX and slid inside. Ever since she'd purchased the pearl wonder with light tan seats, she'd given to wearing outfits and/or accessories in the same color, often finished off with Louboutin pumps and pearl-colored Gucci shades. Frieda's picture could have appeared next to the word materialistic, but she didn't mind. She'd learned that in L.A. image was everything. She had faked it until she made it and snagged a doctor in the process. Thinking of Gabriel, the hard-working husband and sponsor of the designer duds she wore, caused a tiny tinge of guilt as she turned down Martin Luther King Boulevard and headed toward where she used to live. Passing row after row of modest apartments much like the one she'd rented upon arrival from Kansas City, she reflected on her journey from then till now, and how far she'd come in less than five years. When she'd left the Midwest and a drug-slinging boyfriend to join her cousin and best friend, Hope Taylor, in the City of Angels, all she'd hoped for was a good time. And now here she was a wife and mother, living in a tony Westside neighborhood amid five-thousand square feet of luxury, a bank account courtesy of her husband that never boasted less than five figures, credit cards with no limits, a chef, a maid, and a nanny/housekeeper. Sometimes she had to pinch herself to make sure she wasn't dreaming. And sometimes she had to do what she was doing now...go slumming for something that money couldn't buy. A thick piece of sausage.

"Get in here girl," a tall brothah said as he opened his apartment door. His island accent was as sexy as his long thick locks, his ebony skin, his straight white teeth and his washboard abs. "You know me don't like to wait for ya."

Frieda was nonplussed as she threw her purse on the couch. She kept silent as she unzipped the front zipper on her pearl-colored mini and let it fall to the floor. Her cell phone vibrated, but she ignored it as she reached behind her and unclasped her bra. The youngblood's eyes narrowed, and he licked his lips. *That's right. This caramel goodness is worth the wait, isn't it?* Her nanny/housekeeper 's son, Clark, could say whatever he wanted to just as long as he did what she told him to. And he did. Long and hard. Every single time. "Stop sulking and get over here," she said, looking fierce while wearing nothing but a wispy thong, five-inch pumps and a smile. "And show *mami* how much you've missed me since I've been gone."

Two hours later a totally satiated and satisfied Frieda left the hood and headed back toward the Westside, and her appointment at the spa. The man was a beast, and she needed professional help to wipe the just-been-sexed-to-within-an-inch-of-my-life look off her face and body. It would be the last appointment of the day before heading home to a quiet evening, probably alone. Even though it was likely that Gabriel would work well into the night, Frieda always scheduled a spa visit after her romps with Clark. She never wanted to make her husband suspicious and had learned early on that the astute doctor didn't miss much. No, tonight she was not in the mood for a lecture on what he sometimes called "behavior inappropriate for a doctor's wife." There was already enough on her mind. Like Gabriel, and how she was going to continue to have her cake and eat it too.

Her phone rang and as she looked at the dash, she again felt a twinge of guilt. The last thing in the world she ever thought would happen is that she'd go soft. The old Frieda wouldn't have given two hoots about what anybody else thought or felt. Undoubtedly her cousin would attribute it to the Holy Spirit that Hope swore never left Frieda's side. *I hope that brothah took a break just now. Otherwise He got an eyeful!* Frieda thought it was less likely divine intervention and more probably motherhood that had unearthed the heart she'd buried during her teenage years, fending for herself on Prospect Avenue, perhaps dug up by the two-year-old who had both his parents wrapped around his finger. *Or maybe it's you,* she thought, reaching to connect the call. She could honestly say she loved the somewhat stodgy, somewhat geeky doctor whose work was his passion. Even though he bored her to tears.

"Hey, Gabe." Frieda turned down the sounds blasting from her speakers as she spoke.

"Where are you?" Gabriel Livingston's voice was just short of curt. "I've called you three times."

Just then Frieda remembered that her phone had vibrated earlier, when she'd been so focused on...well...various types of massages and she'd forgotten to turn it back on. "I've been out running errands," she said, the beginning of an attitude creeping into her voice. Having basically been on her own since she was fifteen years old, she wasn't too used to having to report her whereabouts.

"Evelyn said you've been gone for hours."

That nosey housekeeper needs to mind her own business! Frieda made a mental note to speak to her housekeeper at the next opportunity. Sistah-girl wouldn't get fired as long as her tenderoni son was handling that pipe like he did, but his mama was definitely going to have to put her mouth on lock. "After my workout I went to get my weekly massage, then went shopping"—*screwing but hey, they both have eight letters and start with an S*—"so yeah, I guess I've been gone for awhile."

"You can't keep doing this, Frieda; spending your afternoons gallivanting while Evelyn watches our child. In the two years that she's worked for us, I'm beginning to think Junior considers the nanny his mom."

"Did you call to make me feel bad about taking care of myself?"

Gabriel's exasperated huff came through the phone. "I called to tell you about a dinner engagement tonight with a prominent couple from D.C. An unexpected change of plans has them here for the evening; time enough to make an impression that will hopefully result in a large donation for the new oncology ward." He told her the name of the restaurant. "Reservations are at eight."

"Looks like it's a good thing I'm on my way to the salon," Frieda purred. "So I can look good and help impress your guests."

By the time the call ended, Frieda knew that she'd flipped the frown that had undoubtedly marked Gabriel's face when the call began. She turned back up the music as she thought about how opposite she was from Gabriel in so many ways, and how her vibrant personality is what had drawn him to her like a hummingbird to sugar water. He was often exasperated with her, but a witty quip, flirty phrase, or naughty innuendo could usually brighten his mood. *He's so easy to manipulate.* And when it came to fathers, there was none better. That heart that Frieda liked to ignore constricted a bit. She really did love Gabriel. He'd do anything for her, and even more for his namesake, the namesake that every day was looking less and less like the good doctor and more and more like one of the men that Frieda used to know.

2

The Ex Factor

It was a picture-perfect evening in La Jolla, California, an upscale suburb of San Diego. Cy and Hope Taylor sat on their ocean-front patio, sipping wine and enjoying a sunset that was painted by God. The chilled wine they sipped was a rare vintage that Cy had procured on a recent trip to Italy, vino that Hope had unashamedly poured into sensibly-priced crystal wine glasses purchased at a discount chain. God had blessed her with the good life, a life beyond her wildest dreams. But she wasn't bougie. A no-nonsense mother, matter-of-fact father and growing up in the tight-knit Baptist church community in Tulsa, Oklahoma, had grounded her designer-clad feet firmly on the ground. "Don't get so high that you can't see low," her mother would tell her on more than one occasion, like after the church when mothers fawned over a song she'd sung or a dance she'd choreographed. Or when the teachers commented on the well-mannered pretty girl with big brown eyes, thick braids and good grades, Pat would remind Hope that God had given her the ability to have those things, that they'd not been achieved simply through actions of her own. Even now, this down-to-earth mother was in La Jolla, passing down that same wisdom to Cy and Hope's three-year old twins, Camon and Acacia. Hope and Cy relished the quiet time, and each other.

"It's been awhile since we've done this, huh?" Cy reached over and took his wife's hand in his, held it up to kiss the back of it.

"The world is so quiet when they are gone; I almost can't remember what life was like without them." Having refused Cy's offer to hire a nanny, Hope's life had turned from that of a 9-5 working girl to a full-time doting mom. She'd have it no other way. "For years, I thought I'd never have children. I'm thankful for them every day." She leaned over and kissed her husband on the cheek, still reveling in his star good looks after almost six years of marriage. His tall stature, dark caramel skin, soft curly hair and cocoa eyes framed by ridiculously long lashes never ceased to make her heart skip a beat and her panties grow wet. Cy Taylor had been one heck of a catch, another blessing that was above and beyond what she ever dared dream.

Cy turned, and took the chaste kiss Hope had intended to another level, brushing his lips across hers before running his tongue across the opening of her mouth and when she complied, slipping it inside. The headiness of their love matched the potency of the wine and within seconds, the lovebirds were caught up in a dance they'd perfected over time: lips touching, tongues twirling, hearts beating as one. He looked up through desire-darkened eyes and gazed upon the woman he loved: her chocolate skin, big doe-eyes, and thick lips parted with wanting.

"Let's go inside." The insistency in Cy's voice hinted of a desire to take her here, now, on the smooth slate stones of the patio.

"Mama will be back with the kids anytime," Hope replied. At Cy's sigh, she smiled. Their love-making schedule was forever changed when the kids came, and getting in where fitting in had taken on a whole new meaning. "I know, me too," she finished, with a final peck on his lips before sitting up, reaching for her wineglass, and a taking a cooling swallow. "Don't worry. I'll take care of all of that," Hope gestured at his obvious erection, "later tonight."

"All right." Cy stretched his long legs in front of him to offer a bit of relief to the long leg in the middle. "Best to change the subject then. Otherwise, Mom Pat will walk into a situation best not seen by mother-in-laws."

"Not to mention our children."

"Remember that time—"

"Ha! The twins coming in the room..."

"Standing at the end of the bed—"

"Eyes wide, wondering..."

"And then little Camon pipes up, 'what y'all doin'?' "

Cy is really laughing now. "I look down and all I see are two sets of eyes barely able to peer over the mattress."

"And my response to their question, 'we're just playing.' "

"Good thing I was riding it low and slow, instead of punching you like a time clock with your legs thrown over my shoulders."

"Ha! Not exactly our idea of a teachable moment, huh?"

"No, baby. Not especially." They were silent a moment, both reflecting on what had been one of the funniest incidents of their parenthood. "You know what, baby? I had no idea how much having children would change our household, or being a father would change my life."

Headlights coming up their quarter-mile long entrance signaled the end of the couple's alone time and Pat's return with the twins from their outing. As they left the patio, Hope looked at Cy, noted the look of contentment on his face. It mirrored her own. For years, more than a decade, she'd prayed (cried, begged, bargained) for a husband and children. It had been her singular goal for most of her adulthood. And here she was, living out the answer to that prayer. *Thank you, God. Thank you for everything that I have, and all that I am. Thank you for my family, my parents, my friends. Bless those whose prayers you have yet to answer, Lord. Bless them with the desires of their heart, the same way you've done for me. Amen.*

On the other side of the country, in a beautifully restored brownstone in the Edgecomb area of Harlem, New York, side, another woman had just finished a prayer. She was still reeling from news received a month before, news that had caused her to take stock of her life. Highlight accomplishments, acknowledge regrets. The latter is why she'd just typed an email to a man she'd not recently seen but had never forgotten, the first and only man she'd ever truly loved. Reading the letter one more time, hoping that it contained the right mix of casualness and desire, her finger hovered uncertainly over the button before she finally pushed send.

Okay, God. I've done what I can do. What happens at this point is up to You . . . and Cy Taylor.

3

Sistah-Girls, Sistah-Chats

The next morning, Hope bounded out of bed at seven a.m., wanting to be ready when her personal trainer, Yvette, arrived at seven-thirty. The popular L.A. trainer, who came at a hefty one-fifty an hour, had proved herself well worth the payment: Hope was smaller than she'd been before getting pregnant, actually in the best shape of her life. Yvette combined several popular training modules—pilates, aerobics, Zumba—along with her own brand of stretch and cardio. She achieved in forty minutes the same results that usually required sixty to ninety minutes of working out. The routine was grueling, fast-paced, relentless and, aside from time spent with her husband and/or children, the absolute best time of Hope's day. She donned workout gear and picked up the children's monitor before walking over to the other side of the second floor to check on the twins. Satisfied that they slept soundly, she kissed first Camon and then Acacia's forehead and then made sure that the room monitor was turned up so that any noise coming from the room could be heard over Yvette's barked orders in the down-stairs gym. Going into the kitchen for a bottle of water, she smiled as she spotted a note on the fridge:

Baby: I hope your workout this morning is half as good as the one we gave each other last night. Have I told you lately that you're amazing? Hope these meetings go quickly. I already miss you. Cy.

"I miss you, too, baby," Hope murmured, as she ran her hand over the note. It was a habit they'd started in the early days of their marriage, leaving each other notes in various parts of the house, but most often on the kitchen fridge. Even with the popularity of texting, emails and the old school phone call, there was nothing quite like seeing pen having been put to paper, hearts hastily drawn or an 'I love you' scrawled in Cy's bold handwriting. *Bold. Strong. Yes, that's my baby.* She remembered how well he'd sexed her last night and then again this morning before leaving on his New York business trip. During the downturn in the nation's economy and the subsequent falling real estate prices, Cy had greatly expanded his company's portfolio, picking up several prime pieces of land and property from the eastern seaboard all the way down to the Florida Keys. He and one of his newest business partners, Jack Kirtz, had also secured property outside of the United States, including ocean-front property in Dakkar on which they'd built a sanctuary for children orphaned as a result of war and disease. The simple yet sturdy housing complex was comprised of one-thousand units and included a school, gym, playground, general store and medical facility. It was one of Cy's proudest achievements and since she and Jack's wife had been a part of the planning process, it was Hope's pride and joy as well.

"Perfect timing!" Hope opened the side door that led directly to the area of the mansion that housed the gym, game room, laundry room, and maid's quarters.

"The traffic cooperated this morning," Yvette replied. "A good thing since your neighbor hates it when I'm late." The ladies continued chatting as they walked the short distance to the gym, and Yvette replaced sandals with athletic shoes. "I still don't get why you and Millicent don't work out together."

"It's a long story," Hope replied, placing her water on a nearby bench before stretching her hands high above her head. "Besides, I like our one-on-one routine."

"That's just it. The routines I've designed for both of you are very similar; it would be less work for me and more fun for you. I'd even give you a discount. So what's the story?" Yvette asked when Hope continued stretching in silence.

"You don't want to know and probably wouldn't believe it if I told you. Millicent and I have known each other for a long time and while we've learned to co-exist quite nicely, we'll never be BFFs, okay?"

"Okay." Yvette knew when she was coming close to a line she dared not cross. She walked over and placed her iPod on the dock. Soon, Adam Levine and Maroon Five were talking about moving like Jagger. "Let's get to work."

An hour later Hope had finished her workout, showered, helped the housekeeper and part-time nanny dress the kids and had made sure they were settled in for their Spanish lesson followed by lunch and their daily "wear them out so they'll take a nap" romp in a nearby park. Ironically enough, her housekeeper Teresa was a member of Open Arms, the church pastured by Cy's business partner, Jack Kirtz. He was also her former nemesis Millicent's husband and she had been the one who, after Hope had mentioned her desire to have someone help her with her growing and increasingly rambunctious children, suggested Teresa as a perfect fit for the job. She'd been right. The forty-five year old mother of four grown children had melded into the Taylor household right away and quickly become invaluable to Hope's running of it. In addition to housekeeping and baby-sitting, she taught the children her native language. These days in California, and increasingly in other parts of the country as well, knowing Spanish was not an option, but a necessity.

Hope was in the kitchen and had just downed a bagel with her daily superfood smoothie when her cell phone rang. "Hey, cuz! How's the doctor's wife?"

"Bored as hell," Frieda grumbled. "Gabriel has me at this vanilla-ass breakfast with some snooty-ass women flaunting their husbands' millions. I had to come out for some air before my face fell into the eggs Benedict."

"It's probably a very nice breakfast." Even as Hope said this, she could barely keep from laughing. Her ride-or-die former hoodrat cousin wasn't much for high-class hobnobbing.

"Please," Frieda responded, proving Hope's point. "There's enough silicone and bleach in this room to open up a business on the black market. Wish I'd known what kind of paper would be in here. I could have had one of my former neighbors stick this joint and walk away with diamonds worth at least five mil!"

"Frieda, you don't mean that."

"Hell, if I hadn't stopped carrying my piece like you told me, I could have stuck up these bitches myself!"

"Ha!" Hope knew her cousin was playing, mostly.

"The best part of the whole morning was the mimosas. I know my man Dom when I taste him."

Hope could hear that Frieda had bought "her man" out with her and was now taking a healthy gulp. "We're not drinking and driving are we?"

"We're not. I am. But don't worry. I'm not driving far; heading back to the house as soon as this is over so I can get my groo... never mind."

"Since when have you been coy about love-making? You'se married now," Hope continued in her best Suge Avery voice. "Sex is allowed."

"What are you doing?"

Hope didn't miss that Frieda was changing the subject, a red flag since it was one of her cousin's favorites. "Wait. Why do I feel there is something you're not telling me?"

"Nothing, girl."

"Frieda..." She heard her cousin taking another drink.

"Aw, hell. I might as well tell you since I might need you to cover for me one of these days." A pause and then, "I've got a new boo."

"What?"

"A tenderoni girl, with a big, thick black dick that he knows how to use!"

"Frieda!" Hope jumped off the bar chair where she'd been lounging. "Tell me you're not serious."

"As serious as a blod clot on its way to the brain."

"Frieda, Gabriel is a good guy, a wonderful man. He's the man supporting your lavish lifestyle, the father of your child!"

"Maybe . . ."

"What?" Hope's voice went from a low G to a high C in no time flat. "Okay, I know you're joking but girl, that's not funny." Silence. "You are joking, right?" Before Frieda answered, Hope's phone beeped, indicating an incoming call. "Don't hang up," she warned Frieda before switching over. "Hello?"

"Hey, girl."

"Stacy! Hold on a minute, Frieda's on the other line talking crazy. Let me do a three-way."

"Okay."

Hope clicked back to the other call. "Frieda, you there? It's Stacy. I'm going to click her into the mix. Frieda? Cuz, you there?"

Cuz wasn't there. Cuz had dropped two bombs and then left the building.